ELLE M KEATING

POISON SUMMER

A Greek island. A second honeymoon. A handsome stranger...

First published by Amberwell Books 2024

Warning: This novel includes profanities, explores sensitive themes and includes references to coercive control and assault which may be triggering or upsetting for some readers.

First edition

ISBN: 978-1-3999-7673-2

Cover art by Eloise Keating

This book was professionally typeset on Reedsy.
Find out more at reedsy.com

Dedicated to my lovely husband who gave me wings to fly, and my beautiful daughter who has always been the wind beneath them.

Also to John Derek Keating. You were like a father to me, and treated me like a daughter. I really hope you knew how much it meant.

Thank you to everyone who has supported, encouraged and believed in me, particularly Mike Keating, Jessica Boston, Sean Baker-Hunter, and Kay Hopwood who said I should write this story. Grateful thanks to Eloise for the cover formatting.

'The sand, the sea, the sky above.
Love? How am I to know?'

CHRISTIANA FIELD

Contents

Foreword

This book was inspired by a myriad stories, whispers, recollections, anecdotes and observations garnered during my extensive travels over many years throughout Greece, a country I love and whose people I hold a deep affection for.

All it takes is a drift of wild herbs on the mountainside, the tinkling of a goat's bell, a ripple across the Aegean, an unexpected shadow crossing the sun, and my imagination is sparked alight.

Preface

As a writer, I enjoy painting pictures with words. I'm filled with curiosity. I like to use my imagination. I like to wonder 'what if', to daydream, siting quietly listening to ideas, characters and plots forming. I prefer a dark twist over a 'happy ever after'.

The story was only half devised by me. The other half involved my cast of fictional characters doing their own thing and going off at a tangent. It was a complete surprise to me at the time but I allowed them free rein to do what they liked. I hope you think I made the right decision.

As a result, Poison Summer is a hybrid of fact and fiction, love and hate, truth and lies; little snippets from here, little anecdotes from there, bruised hearts, memories, optimism, flawed relationships, all thrown into a blender and blitzed. The resulting Frappé is frothy and delicious, perfect for a summer's day ...yet despite its sweetness there's a lingering and decidedly bitter aftertaste.

I hope you will enjoy it.

1

A New Flame

1988

There was something in the air that summer. It was almost palpable, throbbing with the underlying heaviness that precedes an electrical storm. The whole city seemed pressurised, volatile, on edge, with a tight knot of tension in everything, including me. Like an overwound guitar string, I was ready to snap.

I must have wanted change so badly I'd somehow manifested it into being, because when I'd stepped off the plane that night, I'd just known it was out there, waiting for me in the blackness. Resentful, dissatisfied, desperate for something exciting to happen, I was dancing on the edge, ready to throw life as I knew it onto a bonfire. Just one careless spark and it would all go up, yet there I was, Melanie Cassidy, twenty-seven years old, unhappily married and playing with matches.

I'd watched Rob, my husband of six years, dragging his suitcase, his new holiday haircut instilling so much murderous intent within me I'd had to catch my breath for a moment. The terrifyingly brutal Grade I made his already large ears appear massive and his scalp resemble a cornfield savaged by teenage joyriders who'd nicked a combine harvester. Any last feelings for him had been swept away with those clippings on the barber's floor.

Rob's response when I'd mentioned divorce had been to suggest a holiday. 'Everything will be different after a fortnight in the sun,' he'd said.

He'd come home the next day armed with brochures from Thomas Cook so we'd selected a self-catering fortnight on the Greek Island of Thassos at a resort called Skala Potamia. I'd only agreed because I felt I owed him one last try. A second honeymoon, Rob had called it. We hadn't even had a first.

The night before our flight, I'd run a deep bath and, pulling the shower curtain all the way around, had held my nose and completely submerged myself for a moment.

'Is this it?' I'd thought, as I'd surfaced again. 'Is this really all there is?'

I sometimes wonder how different things might have been if we'd gone to Skala Potamia, but a week later, the embarrassed travel agent phoned, explaining there'd been a booking mix up and they'd have to offer us an alternative holiday on a different island for the same fortnight. Instead, we were going to a quiet, under-developed island called Aftonisi, to stay at the Beehive Apartments in the 'charmingly Greek' resort of Lathos.

Rob had paused to light up yet another Rothmans. Staring miserably at the back of his head, my heart plummeted at the thought of spending a whole fortnight alone with him. There'd be no one else to talk to, no means of avoiding enforced coupledom. How ironic, only a few years earlier, he'd been my escape route.

In the sepia evening light, he looked punily British, his wiry arms with tea-cup sized muscles resembling pieces of knotted rope, his white flesh an open invitation to the local insect populace. He'd ignored my suggestion of insect repellent, so when we arrived, he was peppered with livid mosquito bites, whinging like a toddler, and scratching frantically like a mangy dog. I don't get bitten. Mosquitoes find me repulsive, however, Rob was clearly a delicious banquet to them, and they'd wasted no time in calling in the troops.

This isn't going to be all about me and Rob. I would rather pretend my unwise marriage to a manipulative liar had never happened. He'd brought little to our relationship apart from a Fidelity record player, an impressive collection of New Wave albums and an ever-growing raft of debts. It had only been my youth, naivety and insecurities keeping me with him. That, and an attempt to win Dad's respect by demonstrating staying power. Dad always despised a quitter.

Rob may have once been my husband, but I can barely remember being married to him, apart from the bad times... and there'd been quite a few of those. It's almost like I have a form of post-traumatic amnesia, but in reverse. There must have been good times, but if there were, I can't remember. It was many years ago. That life happened to a completely different me. Our bodies regenerate roughly every seven years, something I've always found fascinating. It's like regularly having a chance to reinvent yourself, to change and grow, to step out of an outgrown suit. The body that Rob once knew has long gone, shed like a lizard's scales; nothing of her now remains. The imprint of his fingers is no longer on my skin.

Our room was basic at best. Twin wooden beds on a tiled floor, a wardrobe, a shower, and a small ledge masquerading as a balcony. I remember being relieved the beds were twins, not a double, but also being acutely aware I wasn't supposed to feel like that. In the dark there was little to see outside, but the next morning, I'd pulled the shutters apart to discover a massive mountain dominating the view, its vastness unexpected. True to the accommodation's name, there was an actual Beehive in the garden, pushed against a low concrete wall on which perched old catering-sized marmalade cans planted with geraniums. There was also a banana tree.

I've since seen magnificent banana trees laden with fruit in the Caribbean, swaying under a canopy of dark, glossy leaves, but this one was nothing like those. It was more like a spindly, neglected and somewhat stunted relative, pushing up determinedly through the parched earth with more defiance than vigour. I felt a kind of empathy with that banana tree. It probably didn't want to be there any more than I did.

We hadn't intended to go to Dimitri's Place at first. Rob would have been quite happy to remain at the bar, necking Amstel and eating crisps, but we hadn't eaten since the flight, so I made it clear if I didn't eat proper food, and soon, I was likely to die. I'm a breakfast person and I'd felt hugely deprived. I didn't want a beer. I wanted to go to a taverna I'd spotted, right on the edge of the beach, inches from the sea.

A woman smiled up at us from the coffee machine as we sat to examine the menu. With her very pale complexion and blonde hair, she didn't look particularly Greek, so when she came to take our orders, I wasn't wholly surprised by her Mancunian accent. She introduced herself as Jenny as we chose Greek salads, toasted cheese sandwiches and coffees, with a sparkling water for me and a beer for Rob.

I remember asking her what she was doing there, a girl from Manchester on a Greek island, as she set down a water carafe and two glasses.

'Came out with friends, met Dimitris and never went back,' she said, tucking an escaped strand of blonde hair back behind her ear as she poured us each a glass of water. She smiled back toward the servery at a tall Greek man frying something on a hot plate, his mouth contracting in concentration as he poked around with a spatula. 'It's the kind of place that gets under your skin.'

I watched her sashay back to the kitchen, calling out a stream of rapid Greek as she ripped our order from her notepad. For someone living in such a hot climate, I'd been surprised at her white skin which had an almost bluish translucency, no hint of a tan.

Squinting into the sun, watching its light glinting off impossibly blue waves, I scanned the wide stretch of creamy sand. A small wooden pier jutted into the water, a few sunbeds were dotted here and there, occupied by reclining sunbathers. In the sea, girls in bikinis were tossing giggling babies into the air while women hitched up sarongs to paddle, and men in swimming trunks strode back through the shallows towards their towels.

The heads of swimmers bobbed and ducked under the barely perceptible ripples as lilting Greek folk music drifted from the bar. It seemed simple, emotional, and raw, with repetitive chords and lyrics. Music which invaded your soul and stirred the senses. The fact I couldn't understand a single word made it all the better, somehow. They could have been singing a shopping list for all I cared.

I moved my leg into the shade as a beam of persistent sunlight lasered my skin, and lifted the iced water to my lips. The hotplate in the bar was sizzling audibly now, an enticing aroma of chargrilled food, fresh coffee and wild herbs drifting on the breeze. Voices tinkled on the air like wind chimes. In a language I didn't know, their rise and fall, carried and dissipated by the wind and waves, was melodic and intriguing rather than intrusive. A deep sense of relaxation and acceptance washed over me as though someone was massaging my shoulders, soothing the knots and tension from my spine with expert fingertips. Cicadas were burring in the trees. I could almost forget Rob was there at all. It was heaven.

Slipping off my Foster Grants, I'd barely glanced up as a waiter brought us a small basket of bread and our Horiatiki Salata, better known as Greek Salad. The peeled, chopped cucumber, slices of sweet red onion and quartered ruby-red Greek tomatoes were topped with a big slab of sharp, salty feta drizzled with dark green, peppery olive oil and dusted with oregano. I had no idea the portions would be so huge, so when the waiter then returned with our 'toasts' - massive, griddled bread slices, freshly branded on the hotplate and oozing mozzarella - he seemed amused.

'You are hungry,' he teased with a lopsided grin, opening Rob's Amstel with a deft flick of his bottle opener, laughing good-naturedly with us both at our sizeable feast.

'We haven't eaten for ages,' I explained, embarrassed at our apparent greed, wiping my sunglasses on a paper napkin before replacing them. I glanced sideways at him as he twisted a cap and my sparkling water hissed into life. He was young, mid-twenties maybe, and tall, with a tumble of collar-length black curls, thick-set arms with a deep tan, a wrist full of leather and silver thongs, and a plastic Swatch watch. He was wearing a faded denim shirt over sand-dusted swim shorts as though he'd been lying on the beach before waiting at our table. I didn't have time to register much more than his dark eyes with deep copper flecks which mirrored the sunlight and waves.

'English?' he said, setting down my coffee. It was more a statement than a question.

'Yep.' Rob replied, already tucking in, masticating with great determination as he chomped his way through a thick slice of bread, his response practically incoherent. I felt I needed to clarify, explaining we were from Southampton as I helped myself to a smaller, daintier slice from the basket he offered. I felt my face glowing in the heat.

'South…amp…ton?' It sounded different, more exotic when he rolled the word over, repeating it hesitantly. 'Is it near to London?'

'Not really, its on the south coast.' Rob inhaled yet another Rothmans, smoke pluming upwards past his eyebrows. He necked his Amstel directly from the bottle, his eyes flickering over a curvaceous blonde walking past.

'You speak good English.' I smiled up at the waiter, unwrapping my cutlery from its paper napkin.

'Thank you, we learn at school.'

His voice was deep and melodic, rippling with a Greek accent yet laced with something altogether more cosmopolitan as he smiled right into my sunglasses. Held my gaze. I remember thinking little more than how confident and friendly he was.

'I speak French, German and a little Italian too,' he added with clear pride. I'd been impressed. It had occurred to me how much we English arrogantly assume everyone speaks our language, as though we are the master race. I could barely string a few sentences of school French together, yet here was our waiter, speaking four languages. I must admit, I'd felt more than a little inadequate and had made a mental note to make more effort with the Greek phrase book I'd bought at the airport.

Rob was enthusiastically stabbing his feta as the waiter loitered. I just picked at mine, wishing he'd go away. I was starving but I'd always hated eating in front of anyone I didn't know, particularly when they were now, somewhat unnervingly, just staring at me. I'd wondered why and had assumed he'd been hoping for a tip, but Rob had hung onto the Drachma, so nothing had been forthcoming.

Finally, with a courteous nod and saying 'kali orexi,' enjoy your meals, he'd sauntered languidly back towards the bar as if he had all the time in the world.

That's virtually all I remember of when I first saw you.

2

Owner Of A Lonely Heart

I saw you again a few days later as we sat on sunbeds at the water's edge in front of Dimitri's Place, playing cards before lunch. You were chatting to a dark-haired girl in a white *broderie anglaise* sundress. Perched on a barstool, her hair was caught up in a topknot, flip-flops on her narrow brown feet. I watched you lean over, smooth her hair, whispering something into her ear which made her smile, before you ambled like a cat around the tables, taking orders, chatting to customers, clearing plates.

I watched the two of you, feeling a stab of regret and longing. I still believed in love. But not just any old love. I wanted something special, something hopelessly romantic like you and that girl shared. I wanted a *grande passion.* I glanced at Rob, hunched over his fan of cards, jaw slack, a fag stuck to his bottom lip, and was overwhelmed by a sudden wave of sadness. This was an idyllic holiday paradise. We should be really enjoying it, and each other, yet I felt dreadfully alone. I admit I'd felt sorry for myself.

Bored with the cards, I'd closed my eyes for a while but when I opened them again, you were running towards the water, hand in hand with her. I propped myself onto one elbow watching you both run past, your heels scattering a cascade of sand onto our sunbeds. You were laughing, and she was shrieking helplessly as you whirled her effortlessly off her feet before threatening to throw her into the waves. Struggling free, she ran after you into the shallows, pretending to hit you, splashing through a rainbow arc of sunlit water.

The image of you grabbing and kissing her, pulling her by the hand towards two sunbeds at the water's edge, and the way you both hurled yourselves onto them, still hand in hand, was indelibly burned into my mind. In that one, crystalline, sun-warmed, carefree moment, I could see exactly what was wrong with my life. In that sun-splashed second on those white plastic sunbeds, everything changed.

Interestingly, rather than giving up, it strengthened my resolve to try to make something of my sham of a marriage. I felt I owed Rob and was feeling guilty at being the architect of our downfall. After all, I was the unhappy one, not him, and he could be good company when he wanted. Maybe I'd catch a glimpse of the old Rob, the one I'd first known, the one who was fun, the one who wasn't always drunk.

The first days passed quickly. We'd eaten melon slices in the shade of the old shipwreck at Agia Maria, swum through startlingly turquoise water at Zenomeros, and had watched the sky catch fire with a spectacular sunset at Pervasi under the shadow of the cross of martyrs.

If we'd just been two people with nothing more than friendship invested in the relationship, it could have been the perfect holiday, which gave me hope we might at least be civil in future. But, at nightfall, when cicadas were tuning up their crazy orchestra, and fairy lights glittered like necklaces on the throats of ancient olive trees, alcohol completely changed Rob's personality. It turned him into a predator, leering at other women while criticising me, pointing out my shortcomings.

The night after I'd seen you with the girl on the sunbeds, Rob and I made love. Okay, that's not actually true. We just had sex. Isn't consent a funny thing? Just because you agree to something, it doesn't mean you want to do it. It was perfunctory, formulaic, over quickly, and emotionless. It was only sex. We didn't kiss. To me, kissing is way more personal. Just plain sex didn't mean a thing, but it did help to assuage my guilty conscience, because, unlike Rob, I already knew it was over. I was simply marking time.

Later, while we lay together in the relentless heat of the small, airless room, I could feel his hot breath against my neck as he spoke.

'Sometimes…it's like I really want to hurt you.'

I knew then I was done.

On one of our last days, as the sea curled around the legs of our sunbeds outside Dimitri's, you'd padded down the beach with a tray and a cold drink I hadn't ordered. Rob was snorkelling by the pier, and I'd been drifting through a confusing dream, rising, and falling through the heat of the sun, fighting to stay awake but needing to surrender to the sleep pulling me back under, when you appeared at my side. It took me a moment to register your broad arm offering the tray, the curve of your neck, the glint of a gold chain, those dark curls grazing your open collar.

'You look hot,' you said, squatting at my side, putting down the tray on the sand with a grin and handing me an iced Sprite I hadn't ordered. I didn't like to say I wasn't keen on Sprite so I smiled and took it politely, feeling horribly exposed as your gaze scanned my bikini, my legs and back into my eyes. Flushing at the inference of your words, I turned onto my side, sucking my tummy in and smiling up at you as you glanced across the bay. I think it was then I fully registered how attractive you were.

'Where's your man?' you asked.

'Snorkelling.'

'What?' You said it in a slightly impatient, irritated tone, a way which would sound bad mannered if delivered by an Englishman. I put it down to a language thing.

'In the sea, over there.'

I pointed to Rob treading water in his red Speedos, fiddling with his snorkel tube, banging it against the pier and blowing water out before slipping back below the surface.

You gave this little upwards jerk of your chin before fixing me with those dark, coppery eyes.

'Why you with him?'

I was fully awake now.

'What, I mean, pardon?' My eyes narrowed as I glared at you. My British reserve boundaries had been invaded.

'He disrespects you. I've watched him looking at women. He is *ena ilithios*, an idiot, but I think you know this.'

The smile slid from my face as my stomach contracted. It was like you were seeing directly into my soul. Everything tightened inside. I felt a spark of indignance, although I knew you were right.

Rob had been the warehouse supervisor at a factory in Park Royal where I was temping as the sales director's secretary, blagging my way into the post by claiming a working knowledge of German and saying I could speak French. Neither were *exactly* true, but I did have a German dictionary and a French 'O' Level. That summed me up perfectly: act first, think later.

Several years older than me, he was not a looker, in fact he was borderline ugly, with sticky-out ears, too-wide a mouth and a shock of peroxided, spiky hair. Despite this, there'd been something magnetic about Rob, an arrogance I'd found strangely attractive. With a cocky attitude, a battered leather jacket and nicotine-stained fingers, there was something of the punk rebel about him, but I'd quickly learned he was more Billy No-Mates than Billy Idol. A grown man with no friends or family. This should have been a warning sign, but it only served to pique my interest. He was also a heavy drinker, so he didn't have much to recommend him, however there had been one, big attraction. At twenty-one, I'd been desperate to get away from home, and he had a rented attic flat in Kilburn. Within weeks of us meeting, I'd impulsively agreed to marry him. I was jumping ship, clutching at what I thought was a life belt. Turns out, it was one with a massive puncture in it.

I changed the direction of the conversation.

'So, where's your girlfriend today?'

'What?'

Again, a clipped interrogative. I ignored its sting of rudeness, my bristling of British correctness, and continued.

'The dark-haired girl, from the other day. You were sunbathing together.'

I'd searched your face as you'd looked confused for a moment, then realisation seemed to flood you.

'Ah, you mean Jane.' I couldn't read your expression. A small twist of a smile played on your lips, your rich accent making such a plain name sound beautiful, exotic. 'She's not my girlfriend, it's nothing.'

It hadn't looked like nothing to me. I'd watched you kiss her, stroke her hair. I'd even felt a little jealous of what you'd both had. I remember feeling surprised at your indifference, in the romance I'd assumed and the matter-of-fact way you'd brushed it off. Appearances can be deceptive.

'I'm sorry, I just assumed—'

'She goes home today,' you'd affirmed carelessly, with a nonchalant shrug and a lazy smile.

I was still reeling from the boldness of your earlier unsolicited statement, your frank analyses of my marriage, the fact a comparative stranger could be so clear sighted, to decide whether your statement about her was unfeeling and callous, or just objectively honest. I couldn't help wondering if she'd agree, or whether she was now sitting heartbroken at the airport. I was also embarrassed it must now be clear I'd been watching you both, and with enough interest to assume Jane was your girlfriend. I wondered if you could tell, in that moment, I was surprisingly relieved she meant nothing to you. I felt as though I'd been outed, exposed, caught snooping. I was glad the sun was burning my cheeks already.

'Sorry, how much please?' I nodded at the drink to change the subject and summoned up my latest phrase book learning. 'Um...*poso kani?*'

'You speak Greek?' Your smile split open like sunlight breaking onto the mountains and you began speaking rapidly, animatedly, in your native tongue.

'No,' I interrupted, alarmed. I was worried you'd expect so much more of me, and I didn't want to be embarrassed. 'Just learning a few phrases.'

'This is good,' you said. 'One day, I will teach you more.'

We'd smiled at each other, a genuine smile, an understanding, a zing of connection zipped down the wire tightly strung between us.

I fumbled for a few Drachmas in my beach bag and offered them to you.

'No.' You emphatically shook your head as I held my hand out. 'A present, from me.'

Then you'd given me a brilliant smile, and, with the tray under your arm, had strolled back into the bar.

I'd seen you again the next morning when we'd had breakfast.

'How long you here for?' you'd asked with the same matter-of-fact bluntness of the previous day as you set down our menus and cutlery.

'Going Sunday.' Rob barely looked up, flicking his lighter and drawing smoke deep into his lungs before narrowing his eyes. I looked across the water to the boats bobbing. A fisherman was unloading his catch onto the beach, wriggling Red Mullet were slapped onto the hot sand, flapping and flailing.

'Sun...day,' you repeated, dragging the word out as though doing so might extend it. Did I imagine you'd looked straight-faced for a moment? A bit disappointed, even? Or was I projecting something unfathomable, indistinct, and wishful onto it. But I felt it. It was *there*, all the same. I glanced guiltily at Rob. Could he feel it too?

'Yeah,' I said, softly, regretfully, examining my manicure closely. 'I don't want to go home.'

'Well, don't,' you said. 'Tear up your tickets and stay. There are worse places.'

And you'd laughed, throwing back your head. Life was so simple to you, but you were right. There were certainly worse places. Southampton, for one.

'Not a bad idea.' Rob had said.

We'd all continued making small talk. I remember enjoying the banter, the harmless chit-chat as you loitered, asking questions, gently teasing us, but then our conversation was pierced by a shrill voice shrieking 'Mario!'

You'd turned, shocked, then a grin had slid across your face as you'd said, 'excuse me' and headed over to a short girl in a tight, white dress. Wearing a particularly large, brown sun hat, she resembled a mushroom. She was clearly delighted to see you.

'Karen, *agapē mou*,' I heard you shout as you bounded towards her. 'You came back, my love.'

13

I tried not to stare as you embraced her, even though I wanted to. Was your name Mario? I tried not to look at her and concentrated hard on my coffee cup until curiosity got the better of me. I looked up again.

I can't explain, but I'd felt a sickening jolt deep inside my stomach. *My love. Agapē mou.* I'd looked at her sideways. *Really?* She was unremarkably ordinary. Jane had been far prettier, you weren't physically well matched at all.

'Is that your name, Mario?' I'd tentatively asked when you came back, hoping I wasn't showing more interest than any other tourist might. I'd felt strangely self-conscious using your name.

'Yes, I am Mario.'

You'd said it with such immense pride in delivery I wasn't sure if you were joking so I nearly laughed until I saw how earnest your face was.

'I am referred to as Marios, but when you speak to me, you say Mario, without the S. Greek language, confusing, eh?'

'Well, I am Robert, referred to as Rob,' said Rob, putting on a stupid accent, deliberately imitating your pride. This made you laugh but it irritated me. I felt he was mocking you. 'And this is my wife, referred to as Melanie.'

'Mel...a...nie,' you made my name sound so pretty, with a lift, an inflection at the end. 'Now this is a Greek name, a goddess name.'

'Everyone calls me Mel.' I was annoyed Rob had called me his wife, affirming his possession, his property, when we both knew the circumstances. I wanted out. This was our last stand.

'Goddess of what?' Rob enquired, his smile not quite reaching his eyes. 'And what am I the god of then?'

I squirmed uncomfortably for a moment. You said nothing but your eyes had fastened onto mine.

'Come on, there must be a god called Robert.'

I knew that tone in Rob's voice. He used it when baiting me into an argument. Quickly, I checked my watch for no other reason than it broke the intensity of your gaze. You paused for a moment, still looking at me, before answering.

'Your name, it means...dark, blackness...*Melaina*, the bringer of nightmares.'

How apt,' Rob said, as I rolled my eyes, but you continued.

'*Melaina*, her beauty drives men to madness, and for Robert we say *Roverto*, but it means nothing, it's only a name, not a god.'

'What does your name mean then?' I interrupted, desperate to stop Rob responding, aware of a sudden change in temperature around us.

'It is from Mars, god of war.'

'It's not Greek then, is it?' Rob was leaning on his elbow now, lighting his Rothmans, clearly enjoying this debate, relishing his own cleverness. 'Mars is Roman.'

I detected the briefest suspicion of a smile about your lips as your eyes met mine again before they flickered back to Rob's.

'It is also Greek.'

Rob considered your dismissive response for a moment.

'God of war, eh. Like fighting, do you?'

No one spoke for a moment. I shuffled in my raffia seat, examining the menu closely, trying to ignore Rob as he leaned back in his chair. His confrontational tone was something I was hardwired to listen for, the regular barbs, the comments passing as humour yet with something darker lurking beneath.

'So, you're both gods together but I'm a lowly peasant.' He regarded us both with challenging gaze, waving his cigarette for emphasis. 'Should I bow, or something?'

I picked at the varnish on my thumbnail, wishing he'd just shut up, but, unperturbed, you laughed.

I took another sideways glance at Karen as you took our orders: coffee, toast, scrambled eggs and mushrooms for me, a full English for Rob. I couldn't understand the attraction. You were beautiful, she was a potato. I concentrated on the navy-blue horizon and the glitter dancing on the sea.

'Ah, when I say *my love*, I mean, she's only a friend,' you'd unexpectedly added, looking straight at me. 'Not a girlfriend.' Then, tucking your pencil behind your ear, you'd loped off with your notepad.

Why did you bother saying that?

We didn't see you again for a couple of days because we'd been on our day trips. Rob had been drinking during our tour of the monastery and became argumentative later. Back in the room, he'd shouted at me so much the couple next door had threatened to call the manager, so he'd craned over the railings, calling them 'nosey morons.' Luckily, he'd passed out shortly afterwards.

I'd grabbed a bottle of water and stomped downhill to the track leading directly onto the beach. It was in-between afternoon and evening, siesta time. I'd found a deserted spot where I'd sat with my back against the wall of an ugly apartment building, having a good, long think about how I could get divorced in the quickest, easiest, and least expensive way. I'd never felt so determined before. I didn't want to be Melanie Cassidy any more. I wanted to be Melanie Wright again.

We had a mortgage, a cat, a few sticks of furniture, but little else of value and thankfully no children. With the security of a good job in estate agency, I could probably afford to rent somewhere on my own, or maybe get a flat share. I could even get a transfer back to London and live with my parents, if I could get past it feeling like failure.

I'd felt a jab of regret over the gorgeous Victorian terraced house we were renovating, with its wide bay windows and intricate plaster cornices. We'd have to sell it but even though the mortgage was high, there'd still be something left over. Or maybe we could share it if I kept the front bedroom, and Rob had the back one, but I'd also wondered how we'd manage, trapped in close proximity while trying to escape into separate lives.

A little brown lizard had darted up from a crack in the wall, freezing under my gaze before disappearing in a flick of the tail. For a moment, my vision distorted. I'd be back home soon, and all this beauty would only be a memory. Swiping my cheek with the back of a hand, I stared across the waves. Eventually, as the sun had dipped lower over the Ionian, I'd reluctantly torn my gaze from the sea to begin the slow, arduous trudge back uphill. It had felt like a metaphor for life.

On our last evening, I'd felt sorry for myself. I was so reluctant to leave, so conflicted, so emotionally wounded. I'd felt as though blindsided by something I hadn't seen coming at all, something I didn't fully understand.

We'd had a meal at a restaurant, The Grill House, on the main road, then we'd wandered back uphill before calling into one last bar, the nearest one to our apartments. I'd only had a little wine earlier, drinking mainly water as I knew I'd have to face a flight the next morning. Rob, however, had clearly decided it was his last chance to go on a bender, so he'd enthusiastically embraced everything available to him: Retsina, Vodka, and, towards the end of the evening, a woman from Northampton. More of that later.

The sun had slipped behind the hills of Stavouna, and a magical, deep lapis blue was bleeding through the sky like ink, infusing everything with an unreal, stained-glass quality. With darkness edging in, all the ugly concrete buildings became primary school artwork, black sugar-paper houses layered over jewel-bright tissue. The light had changed everything. Nothing seemed real any more.

Tropic Bar was tucked behind a row of white-painted olive trees. I wanted to have time to sit there, to decompress and wind down. Rob, however, thanks to his pre-loading and continual refuelling, was overly animated, his eyes glazed, gait unsteady. He heaved himself straight over to the bar without even asking what I wanted as I resigned myself to his lack of imagination, knowing he'd order me a white wine.

When he didn't return straight away, I sat staring over the balcony at the now barely perceptible ridge of mountains and a cloud of bats doing a loop-the-loop around the floodlit garden. The sky was stippled with tiny stars, diamonds glinting on some celestial jeweller's black velvet tray. Their cold, twinkling imperiousness took my breath away. This holiday had left me restless, on edge and wholly dissatisfied with everything waiting for me back in England.

Each time I'd tentatively tried to discuss our situation, Rob had dismissed it, promising everything would be different at home, but that's exactly what I was afraid of: being at home. I looked over at him. He appeared to be in deep conversation with a woman, while my chilled white wine warmed up on the bar beside him. Suddenly, I couldn't have wanted that drink more, or him less.

Elbowing my way through, I stood there for a moment, listening to the over-made-up blonde telling him she was from Kettering, waiting for him introduce me, he didn't. I watched his hand smoothing her bare shoulder as he leaned in close, her tanned breasts jiggling inches from his face as she threw her head back, laughing. There was lipstick on her teeth. I took my drink. My husband was pawing some stranger, but I couldn't have cared less. Instead, I went back to my seat and continued stargazing, draining my glass in a few gulps. I was going to regret this tomorrow. *Carpe Diem*.

By then, with the heat closing in around me, it had occurred to me I might be a tiny little bit pissed. Well, maybe more than a tiny bit. Not enough to be unaware, but enough to not really care. That sweet spot. The sensible thing would have been to get a bottle of water. An even more sensible thing would have been to go back to the room and sleep, but the driving beat of the music, the warmth of the honeyed air and gazing up at the peppering of stars had disoriented me, skewing my judgement. The devil at my shoulder told me to get another glass of dry white.

As I stood up, my head spun and I stumbled a little, grabbing the balcony rail for support. Rob was nowhere to be seen, which wasn't a total surprise. He often went missing when we were out. Now he appeared to be missing with some woman from Northampton.

The air was misted with humidity and scented with the wild thyme from the mountainside as I pushed my way through the crowd to lean my elbows on the wooden bar, waiting, holding my drachma aloft. The barman finally took my order, as someone pushed in next to me. Someone with a strong wrist, a black Swatch watch, leather and silver thong bracelets.

3

Sign Your Name

I'd never been so close to you before. I could feel the heat radiating from your white cotton shirt and smell the salty sweetness of your skin, an undefinable and intoxicating perfume of the sea, the sand, the herbs on the mountainside. My breath caught as your eyes lasered mine for an instant. Dark as blackened sea glass, warm as mountain honey, flecked with copper, reflecting the lights above the bar. It was as though something passed between us then, something I still can't explain, but it zipped through me like an electric current, so strong, so visceral, I almost expected the halo of moths circling the bulkhead to ignite and fall charred to the polished wood.

'Yassou, moré,' you said, with your lopsided smile. 'I thought you were going home?'

'I was, I mean, I am...' I replied, aware of how dumbstruck I appeared. You watched me intently as I spoke and, for one, inexplicable moment, I wanted to wrap myself in your warmth, slip safely into your pocket, fold into you. God, that wine must have been strong.

I remember you indicating to the barman with little more than a flick of the chin and he put a bottle of beer down in front of you straight away. I'd been waiting ages for the glass he'd finally plonked in front of me earlier.

'How did you do that?' I said, in awe.

'He's my friend,' you replied. A pause. You were looking at me, taking in every detail of my face. Your eyes drinking me in. 'When you go home?'

'In the morning.' I felt deflated, sad, overcome.

My face must have fallen. Did I imagine yours did too? Tomorrow, I would be in Southampton. Tomorrow I would still be married to Rob. They say tomorrow never comes. Well, this particular tomorrow was coming in less than twelve hours.

'Where is he now, your…man?'

'I don't know. With some woman, I think.' I remember adding *from Northampton,* as if it made a difference. I didn't care all that much. I was more worried he'd end up somewhere other than our room and I wouldn't get him to the airport in time.

We said nothing else for what seemed like ages, standing within each other's aura, the heat from our bodies forming a layer around us. The cicadas' humming reached a crescendo.

'Come,' you eventually said. '*Ela.*'

As if it were the most natural, normal thing in the word, you reached over and took my hand in yours, pulling me behind you to a table. Such a small gesture, but such a seismic reaction. Even the brief touch of your hand made me feel I was cheating. Electricity zapping through my fingers, the current running up my arm, the air around us crackling, charged, everything dangerously and gloriously alive. I knew then nothing would ever be the same again.

Something occurred to me later, when I replayed the events of the evening over and over in my mind, watching it flicker like technicolour video footage on my memory screen. Rob and I never held hands. It wasn't like that. Whatever 'it' was.

You chose a small table on the edge of the balcony, far away from the main throng of people, where we sat together, my bare legs pressed up against your jeans.

'Can I ask you something?' you said, 'Why are you with him, *moré?*'

I watched your thumb circling the wet rim of your beer bottle as you waited for my response. I had no answer. I hardly understood it then myself, so it was going to be hard to explain to a stranger. Instead, I changed the subject.

'Tell me about you.'

'There's not much to tell. I live in Stavouna, with my family.'

'Family?' I returned your smile as I sipped my wine.

'My mother, father, sisters and grandfather. I am building a bar for when I return from the army, so I work now to save money. Not much more to say.'

'You're a soldier?' I was a little confused. I'd thought you'd worked at Dimitri's Place.

'No, but we all do our conscription. From age nineteen, we wait to be called. I am still waiting.'

I was intrigued.

'So, when will you know?'

'I don't know, soon maybe.' I felt your smile connect with something deep inside me. 'I have friends who are also twenty but have already gone to the army.'

Your age stung me like a slap. How could you be only twenty? You looked so much older, you were so self-assured, confident, with such mature, intelligent observations. I was shocked. I was seven years older than you. Seven. It wasn't so much a gap as a gulf.

'You're twenty!' I couldn't help blurting it out. I felt myself stiffen and something contract within me.

You softly inclined your head slightly sideways and down, a gesture I quickly learned was the Greek affirmative and a slow smile spread over your face. 'I'm twenty-one soon.'

I didn't want to break the intoxicating web I was caught in. But there was no option. So, I took a deep breath, fixing you with my eyes. If this was to be the last time we spoke, the last connection, I wanted to remember you. I wanted to sear your image onto my brain before I said something I knew was going to make you realise this was futile, going nowhere.

'Well, I'm twenty-seven,' I said. 'Twenty-eight soon.'

It was done.

21

The end.

Telos.

You continued to hold my gaze, unperturbed, and you shrugged.

'Age is only a number. My friend, Sakis, for three years had a Swedish girl who came here for him. She was ten years older.'

I quickly did the maths. Assuming this Sakis was your age, had he begun a relationship aged seventeen with a twenty-seven-year-old? It seemed quite shocking to me, conveniently overlooking the fact our age gap wasn't all that different. But, then again, we weren't having a relationship. We were simply having a conversation, a flirtation maybe, but innocent enough.

You must have read my mind.

'Sakis was not a boy. He was nineteen and had graduated Lyceum.'

Well, that was a relief. The girl in question at least hadn't started a fling with a schoolboy.

'It's still quite an age gap, though,' I said, putting my glass down.

'And do you think we have the age gaps?' As you gazed at me intently, I noticed your English wasn't always perfect at times. 'You see, I don't think so. I thought you were maybe two, three years older, but you were beautiful and it didn't matter to me how old you were.'

You smiled at me, draining your beer. Here it comes, I thought. You will get up now and make an excuse to leave. And half of me wanted you to. This was turning out to be quite a complicated evening so it might be for the best. But part of me wanted to stay there, in that bar, with you. For the first time in ages, I'd felt valued, appreciated, free. You weren't a drunk. You'd called me beautiful. I couldn't remember anyone doing that before. You weren't rambling on in an alcohol-fuelled stupor or spitting across the table at me with glazed eyes and a red face. You weren't talking bollocks, you were asking me intelligent questions. You were listening to me. You weren't Rob.

'I get you another drink,' you said. Not a question, a statement.

As you headed to the bar, I sat there, fishing in my bag for my pocket mirror and lip-gloss. My age hadn't appeared to have bothered you in the least. Checking my face, I slicked on more gloss and fluffed up my hair, but then I quickly shoved the mirror away, looking around furtively. What the hell was I doing? Would anyone sitting nearby see a daft tourist woman fawning over a handsome local? A handsome *young* local. Would they see a married woman doing something reprehensible, or simply a couple having a drink? I knew in many ways it was nothing to be ashamed of, but I felt I was radiating guilt, the words 'cheat' and 'she's married' pulsing above me in imaginary neon letters with a gigantic, fluorescent arrow pointing down accusingly at my head.

I glanced at a group of tourists nearby, wondering what their opinion of us might be. But when I saw you weaving your way back with a beer and another glass of wine for me; saw your broad shoulders, the curve of your jawline, your generous, open smile, I realised I didn't give a fuck about anyone else's opinion.

We continued talking, sharing, laughing. I was so struck with how mature you were, how interesting to be with and how much intelligent conversation you had to offer. You decided to begin my Greek lessons straight away, so you taught me various phrases and words. If I asked what something was in Greek, you told me. I already knew yes and no, please and thank you, but you taught me how to count to ten, how to tell someone what my name was, how to ask for a table in a taverna, and, somewhat bizarrely, 'let's go to our house', *pame sto spiti mas,* a kind of colloquial way to say, 'let's go home'.

'*Bravo.* I love it when you speak Greek,' you said, leaning across, cupping my chin with your hand. I knew you were going to kiss me, but then Rob lurched blindly past, and I pulled back. You dropped your hand as we both watched him wandering towards the road. I could see he was drunk. What was I doing? I was going home in the morning. I suddenly felt very sober indeed as guilt began to kick in as well as a long-suffering sense of duty. Anything could happen to Rob in that state. I knew I had to move quickly.

'Don't go.' You pulled my arm as I stood up. 'Please.'

'Can't you see he's really drunk?' I shook you off.

'But I don't want to lose you now.'

You'd said it perfectly seriously, although it sounded like a line from a romantic novel; quite ridiculous. You were standing up now, blocking my way but I sidestepped you.

'Thank you for the drink.' I said, politely, remembering my very English manners, before quickly running out to catch up with Rob.

'Constanoon Afterble,' he gibbered as he staggered uphill. 'Here she comes, the Fun Police.'

'I beg your pardon?'

'Pardon, garden,' he guffawed, clearly delighted with his hilarity.

'Keep going.' Fury surged up so strongly within me I could have so easily punched him. 'Walk.'

'You don't have to worry, I can walk all by myself you know.' He executed a few silly dance steps.

'Well fucking *walk* then.' I pushed him hard, my palm damp from his sweaty shirt.

'Okay, okay.' Rob shook me off, staring glassily through me. 'I'm going, I'm going.'

I was right up beside him now. He smelled like a distillery, his breathing laboured and heavy.

Then he began to sing in an irritating voice.

'Saw you…with that… bar…man.'

I froze for a moment as he clomped ahead.

'Well, I saw you too, with that woman.' I pushed him harder than necessary as he lurched backwards again, thinking my response had been under my breath, but he spun around.

'She's only a friend.'

Beads of spittle flew into my face. A snapshot developed of Rob, glistening with sweat, leaning right into her deep slice of cleavage. I remembered the warmth of your strong, capable hand grasping mine. Two wrongs don't make a right. Two wrongs can only ever make two wrongs. But nothing had felt wrong tonight, in fact everything had felt so right.

'So's he. You left me on my own in case you'd forgotten. He looked after me.'

He regarded his shoes quizzically for a moment then stumbled onwards. We were right outside the Beehive Apartments now where a few guests were on their balconies, having drinks, citronella candles burning. I surveyed Rob's waxy face, recoiling at his tainted breath. What a way to end my last ever night in Lathos. An extreme high and a crashing low.

I looked regretfully back down the road. The night air was heavy with heat, sweet like wild mastic honey, yet spiked with citrus, herbs, and pine. I could see you standing in the clearing outside the bar, the vast sky above you studded with thousands of tiny, blinking stars. Within a second, I'd decided.

'Here.' I shoved the room key, somewhat unwisely under the circumstances, into Rob's hand. 'I know you won't understand this, but I've got to go back. Down there. I won't be long.'

He seemed more interested in trying to focus on the key dangling limply from his finger, than the prospect his wife might be going to another man.

'I didn't say thank-you for the drinks,' I lied.

'Yeah, yeah, whatever.' Rob slumped down heavily on the wall next to the geraniums. I stood there for a moment, then quickly snatched the key back. He might lose it.

'Stay there. I won't be a minute.'

'Ask him to get us a Mythos while you're there. After all, he's a barman.'

He began to sing. Loudly.

'There's a bar man, waiting in the sky...'

Fuck's Sake. People were watching now. I knew I should stay and shut him up because he was drawing attention. I should tuck him up in bed with a pint of water. In fact, I should stay up all night, watching him. What if he threw up and choked in his own vomit? I should do the correct thing and be a good wife.

Only, I wasn't a good wife, was I?

I ran back down the hill and straight into your arms.

I don't know how long we stood there, my face pressed against your neck, your arms wrapped tightly around me, warm fragrant air dancing against my hair. It felt like forever; like time had stood still, but it probably wasn't very long at all. I wanted to melt into you, to liquefy like ice in the sun. We hadn't even kissed, which is part of what made it all so unbelievable. I tried to pull away.

'I've got to go.'

I edged back but you held me softly by the shoulders, leaned in and kissed me.

My head was spinning out of control, I was somewhere else entirely, like a comet in space. What the hell was I doing? I was a married woman. My inebriated husband was perched on a wall a few hundred yards uphill like a life-size garden gnome and I was kissing a Greek waiter. Or barman. Take your pick, he was both. And he was seven years younger than me.

Okay, listen,' you said when we eventually stopped. 'You tear up your ticket and you stay, okay?'

'I can't.'

'Why, moré?'

'Because I can't.' I must have sounded exasperated. Of course, I couldn't, I had to go home. There was no question about it. Whether I wanted to go, though? Now, that was quite a different matter.

'Then you must come back.' You'd sounded deadly serious, grabbing my arm, your eyes probing mine. 'You come back, endaxi?'

I remember you kissing me again, your stubble grazing my cheek, the scent of the sea in your hair. I was kissing someone else. Did it constitute cheating when I knew I was going home, I wasn't ever going to see you again and my husband had already disappeared earlier with another woman anyway?

'This is ridiculous.' I said, when we pulled apart.

'What?'

'Me, you, this. It's all wrong.'

But it felt so right. I knew I was going to feel dreadful in the morning; confused, tangled, horribly conflicted however I had to summon up the strength to see this for what it really was. A glitch, an interval, a moment out of time.

I pulled sharply away, angry with myself for letting everything go this far, angrier for knowing in a different setting I'd have let it go much further.

I glanced furtively back uphill towards the Beehive Apartments knowing Rob was lurking somewhere as I peeled your fingers from my arm.

'Look, I've got to go. Right now. It's getting late, and I've got a flight tomorrow.'

I turned away.

'Wait,' you said. 'You have a pen?'

I shook my head.

'Okay, you wait.'

You waved at a group of girls walking past.

'Hey, you have a pen?' They hesitated at first. Then you mimed writing something with an imaginary pen in your hand and one of them came over offering a biro.

'*Efkharisto.*' You'd treated her to a blinding smile as I watched her twirling a strand of her hair. Then you took a piece of what turned out to be a crumpled bar tariff from your jeans pocket, tore it in half and scribbled quickly on the back of it. You were left-handed. You handed the pen to me with the other half of the tariff. You'd written down your name, address, and a phone number.

'Now you?' you said, nodding in encouragement as I hesitated. Unbelievably I found myself writing down my name and address, balancing the small slip of torn paper against my bare leg. I stalled at the phone number, though. I could imagine how Rob would react if he answered, not that I truly believed even for one infinitesimal moment you would call. You were a Greek waiter and sometime barman on a holiday island after all, and I was a tourist. This type of thing happened all the time. It was called a holiday romance, but it wasn't even that, really. It was little more than two people with a connection, a brief encounter in the wrong place, at the wrong time. It was little more than a trick of the light, an illusion, a lovely dream. One I was going to wake up from tomorrow.

'I don't have a phone,' I lied, as I handed the paper to you. I was getting good at lying these days, something I must have learned from Rob. You patted it straight into the breast pocket of your shirt before giving the biro back to the girl who fluffed her hair up, looking at you rather too long in my opinion. You didn't seem to notice.

'The phone number is for the Athenian Kiosk,' you explained as I read your stylised, angular scrawl. It was the sort which clearly struggled with cursive as opposed to Greek writing. 'You can call there and ask for me. If I am not there, they will find me, and I will call you back.'

I smiled somewhat sadly at this. I knew in my heart you'd forget all about me when the next coachload of Janes or Karens arrived, so I certainly wasn't going to call and ask for you at the local kiosk. How desperate and tragic would that look? The whole thing was quite mad.

'But you will call me, yes?' you said, your eyes searching my face anxiously. I didn't answer.

I nodded, even though I knew I wouldn't. I couldn't. There would be no point. You probably did this sort of thing all the time, I reasoned. I certainly wasn't going to ring you, whatever you thought. That way lay complete madness. Then, with a last look back to imprint your image onto my mind, I ran quickly back up the hill again. Two weeks earlier, Rob and I had arrived, ready to see whether we had anything at all left to salvage of our relationship, but now everything had changed. I had completely changed. There was nothing of that me left any more.

Despite the sinking feeling of desolation settling in my stomach as I reached the Beehive Apartments, I convinced myself the events of the night were nothing. You'd have gone back into the bar by then, and the girl you'd borrowed the biro from would have been there. Within minutes you'd have probably been teaching her Greek too. I'd only needed to know for a moment what it was like to be wanted, to be the object of someone's undivided attention, just for a while.

It had been nice while it lasted but I knew nothing more could come of it. How could it? After all, I was married. I had a job, a mortgage, commitments, a whole life in England. I had responsibilities. No-one sane gives everything up for a crazy fantasy, for someone they've only just met. No-one.

4

It's My Life

On the flight home I'd written in my journal. I often wrote stories and poems as well as kept a diary, nurturing a dream of being a writer, but Dad had convinced me I wasn't good enough.

'That's no way to make money,' he'd said. 'Even those with real talent don't make money doing that. What you need to do is take a secretarial course.'

It had crushed me at the time. Dad was a draughtsman but wrote short stories for the village magazine so I'd hoped he might have been proud of me, maybe even encouraged me to follow in his footsteps, but for as long as I could remember, he'd smothered every effort with cold indifference or a calculated one-upmanship. I could never measure up to his own greatness.

I'd kept furtively reading the piece of paper you'd given me, tracing your handwriting with a fingertip as I replayed the previous night's events in my head, shivering at the memory of your arms around me. I shouldered Rob towards the window with a shudder of distaste as he sagged towards me, snoring through his hangover, his mouth flaccid. Last night he'd slept like a baby through the oppressive heat in our room but I'd remained awake, staring up into the blackness, trying to make sense of everything, wondering if Rob would even remember the woman from earlier, the one who'd scribbled Angela, a kiss, and phone number, on the book of matches I'd found on the floor.

I don't think he truly believed I'd leave him for one minute because I'd threatened it so many times yet never followed it though but this time, when we'd discussed it while waiting for our flight announcement, it was different. He didn't ask me to reconsider. He didn't once ask about the previous night either, although I was bracing myself for it, ready to deal with any ensuing fallout, a fallout I deserved. He wasn't prepared to fight for me. He never even queried why his wife had run back downhill to a man she barely knew, which I took as either complete disinterest or the result of a drunken blackout at the time. Either wasn't great.

After being used to sunlight striping through the shutters and the rhythmic drag of the sea, the greyness of early morning Southampton, and the continual scream of traffic on the wet road, was a contrasting hell. An uninspiring summer drizzle had begun a steady descent, it was brutally early, and the street light outside our house wasn't working, shrouding everything in gloom. Yanking my suitcase over the threshold, I kicked a pile of Rob's trainers to one side to scoop up the post as he collapsed onto the sofa with a grunt.

Our relationship had been on its knees when we'd moved to the south coast. Rob had got into financial difficulties, so it made sense to clear his debts and get something bigger for less. Our tiny two-bedroom flat on the fringe of Ealing was then worth twice what we'd paid for it but in complete contrast, houses on the south coast were ridiculously cheap. I'd initially been reluctant, but Rob had been unwaveringly persuasive and, as I now realise, manipulative too. He was skilfully separating me from my friends and family, ensuring my continued dependency on him. I was selling my soul for a double bay and forecourt.

I stared blankly at the crimson damask sofa, the patterned rugs on the stripped wood floor, the pine dresser I'd spent hours waxing, the large Goodman's stereo system, the ornately tiled Victorian fireplace. All this had felt so harmonious two weeks earlier, but now it jarred and grated, each shape and texture strange and unwanted. I missed the sun, I missed the sea, I missed the hot sand squeaking under my feet, but most of all I missed you. Thinking about you gave me a nasty little jolt inside which physically hurt.

Returning to the hallway I'd painstakingly rag-rolled with help from my Jocasta Innes book, I glanced towards the open living room door. I could still see the back of Rob's head, the severe shearing now giving way to an uneven crop of spikes, his huge ears red with sunburn. I shuddered. A totally uninspiring comedown doesn't even begin to cover it. That night, I slept so far over my side of our King Size bed I nearly fell out. The next morning, Rob moved into the back bedroom.

The quickest way to get divorced without lots of unpleasantness was by citing *two year's separation with consent*. The easier, but longer, alternative was *five years separation without consent*. Five years seemed unthinkable. I'd be thirty-two by then, so, four days after we'd arrived home, and after a mutually tearful soul-searching which left us both under no illusion we could stay married, I arranged a fixed fee interview with a local solicitor. Rob had agreed to meet me there on his lunch break, but as he strolled towards me, his hands weighing his pockets down, I felt something was wrong. His eyes were unusually bright, his cheeks flushed. My nostrils flared, detecting alcohol.

'What the hell are you doing?'

'What d'you mean?'

He looked theatrically affronted.

'I mean, you've had a drink. We're due in there in a minute.' I jabbed a finger towards the porticoed doorway of Grantley and Symes. 'What are you playing at?'

An infuriating grin began to twist the edges of Rob's mouth. His eyes danced as he tapped the side of his nose conspiratorially before producing a breath spray from his pocket.

'Please just tell me you didn't drive.' I shot him a look which he acknowledged with a barely perceptible shrug.

'You selfish prick, what if you'd hit someone?' I folded my arms and glared

31

at him.

'Just take a chill pill, Melons. Turned up, didn't I?'

Just the close proximity of him, his creased shirt, the halo of staleness surrounding him, his tainted breath, made a violent shudder of distaste flood me. I was so furious I couldn't even look at him, so, instead, I stared hard at the greengrocers stall across the road, where a woman was selecting glossy Granny Smiths, until a bus obstructed my view. The tight silence between us was relieved only by the constant whirr of midday traffic and the shrieks of college students pushing and shoving each other along the pavement. I checked my watch. Time to end this charade. Staring resolutely ahead, I pushed the brass bell on the black gloss door.

The meeting was supposed to be for half an hour, but it only lasted minutes because Rob had unexpectedly stood up, mumbled something vaguely incoherent about divorce not being his idea, and had walked out, leaving me sat rigid and wholly embarrassed, on my own.

'If you want my advice, Mrs Cassidy,' the solicitor had said, 'There's little point in us taking on a case of this nature unless you want to cite Mr Cassidy's unreasonable behaviour, which I understand you don't.'

I shook my head. I didn't want it getting horribly messy and expensive. The onus would have been on me to have kept records and to have had witnesses to prove everything. I hadn't. I looked down at my hands twisting in my lap, for a moment, feeling strangely ashamed. Was this all largely my fault? Somehow, I'd always known Rob and I wouldn't last. I'd never been equipped to deal with his complex web of problems and should have run a mile when he first asked me out. I'd always known he had more baggage than lost luggage at Waterloo Station. Did that make me the selfish one instead?

The solicitor continued.

'As you have no children and nothing to contest except for a jointly owned property in which I understand there's little equity, save yourself the expense, and get a DIY divorce.'

Walking home with ten minutes to spare of my lunch break, everything weighed down so heavily on me. I opened our front door. On the mat, a blue airmail envelope.

I don't know whether you remember, but you sent me several letters, one after the other. Letters full of longing for me to return. Letters telling me how you'd never met anyone like me before and how you wanted me to come back. Each complained how dull life was without me, how no one compared to me and how you couldn't stop thinking about us and what we could be. After Rob's indifference, my ego was pirouetting on a cloud.

You asked me to send photographs to you, sending one to me you'd taken in a photo machine. I frowned. I'd nurtured a vision of you in my mind, a pencil sketch from memory coloured with imagination, a collage of light and shade which somehow didn't completely match the picture I now held. Staring into your eyes, I searched for familiarity, taking in the dark curls and the lopsided smile which had made my stomach lurch deliciously.

Somehow, your chin seemed stronger, your brows heavier, your expression more intense and determined. There was also something in your eyes, something I couldn't quite fathom. For a moment I was just looking at a handsome stranger in a photograph. I felt a bite of apprehension, but, remembering the intensity of your kiss, I knew I'd have to follow this journey as far as it led me. I was in the grip of madness. Nothing was going to stop me.

You'd said to come as soon as I could, and you'd get me a room, imploring me to come on a one-way ticket and stay, but I explained it wasn't that simple. I had a job and a life, one which was already complicated and getting more so by the day. I wanted to be with you, but the idea of going alone was a terrifying prospect, something I mentioned that afternoon when I bumped into Lisa.

Lisa wasn't a proper friend, she was a former client who'd once gone out with my colleague Darren, and we'd bonded over a shared love of David Bowie and Roxy Music. She'd insisted on a quick catch up in the bakery near work and had listened intently before saying she'd always fancied a trip to Aftonisi herself. I didn't know her all that well, but in the time it took us to each demolish a coffee and a jam donut, she'd somehow invited herself along. Thankfully I was still owed some time, so my boss, Alan, signed me off once more. The following day, we booked flights for mid-September.

I could hardly believe what I'd done. Although apprehensive about Rob's potential reaction, I took a deep breath and told him I was going back to Aftonisi with Lisa Wilson, but if he'd shown any less interest, I'd have been forgiven for thinking he was dead. It was in strong contrast to the emotions of the night we'd finally agreed to part. I'd wept, flooded with so much remorse and anguish for hurting him but also in indescribable pain for myself, for letting it all get this far, for marrying him in the first place. I'd been so young, so stupid, so headstrong and impulsive. He deserved better than me. I deserved better than him. We were two people who should never have been together.

I'd watched his face closely, chewing the inside of my lip as I scanned his features for a reaction. Somewhere, deep inside, I think I was expecting - maybe, if I'm honest with myself, even hoping - there'd be a monumental fallout, a seismic apology, anything to show he cared. I even half wondered if it might have made a difference, but it felt like he couldn't have cared less. He made no attempt to stop me. When caught between a man who was desperate to see me and another who appeared completely blind to my existence, there was no contest.

5

Faith

On the Britannia flight over, I became gripped with absolute dread at what had seemed a good idea at the time. Nerves were making my stomach flip like a World War One Biplane but there was no turning back. Whatever happened, that evening I would be landing at Aftonisi airport and getting in a Thomson coach bound for Lathos to be with someone who was little more than a chemical attraction, without the faintest idea of where we were supposed to be staying. I also hadn't thought too hard about having a holiday with Lisa, someone I didn't know all that well. Somewhat selfishly, I'd just been relieved to have someone to go with.

I must have bored her witless, jabbering on about you, but she was a patient listener and good at asking probing questions, probably helped by her professional role as a fraud investigator for an insurance firm. I talked and talked.

'So,' Lisa probed, eyes dancing with anticipation. 'What's he like then...you know?' She nudged me suggestively. 'Are Greek men as passionate as they say?'

I felt myself redden.

'Well...we haven't exactly, you know...yet.'

'Seriously?' She stared in disbelief at me, lowering her voice as she leaned in. 'What, you mean you've left Rob for him, but you haven't even—'

The fasten seatbelts sign flashed on.

'It's not like that.' I caught the tone of defensiveness in my voice. Had the plane suddenly got much hotter? I was grateful the man in the aisle seat was still plugged into his Sony Walkman, nodding as he tapped out a tune on the in-flight magazine. 'We have a... a connection. It's special. Anyway, I didn't leave Rob for him, I left Rob because things haven't been right for ages.'

I wasn't sure they ever had been.

I cringed inwardly. Lisa now knew I'd dropped a bomb on my marriage for little more than a kiss. She'd think I was insane.

'Okay,' she continued. 'I'll rephrase. Are Greek men as... *romantic* as they say?'

Laughing, I gave her a playful punch on the arm as the plane began its decent into Aftonisi, but in that moment, it occurred to me, this wasn't all because of you because I'd always known I'd cheat on Rob one day. It was inevitable. I just hadn't known when until then.

When I'd told you I was bringing Lisa, you'd said you had a friend, Nikos, who wanted to meet a nice English girl and Lisa had been up for a spot of Inter-European blind dating, so she was excited to land. In contrast, I was terrified.

Making our way out from the tiny arrivals hall, we'd walked into the embrace of an evening heavy with heat and droning with cicadas, the welcoming warmth I'd missed so much wrapping around me like a blanket. For a moment, the sights and sounds of the island proved such a sensory overload, I couldn't trust myself to speak.

Lisa grinned at me, eyes wide with excitement. She clearly couldn't wait to meet Nikos. I was far more reserved. The enormity of what I had done began to hit home. I could be impulsive, that much was true, but this was a huge risk of a magnitude I'd never taken before. In a game of probability, the odds weren't exactly stacked in my favour either. You were younger than me, I hardly knew you and I was married, yet I'd merrily tossed a grenade into the centre of everything for you. I'd travelled over two thousand miles purely on the aftermath of a romantic evening when the stars had shone brighter than any I'd seen before, the velvety blackness of the sky providing the perfect contrasting milieu. It was also an evening when I'd had quite a lot to drink…

On the coach, I took your photo from my purse and stared at you again, trying hard to remember the person I'd committed to memory, instead of the photographic evidence in front of me. Would we still like each other? What the hell was I doing? I slicked on more lip-gloss as the coach lurched along mountainous roads, passing petrol stations standing incongruously in the middle of nowhere and small parades of tourist shops strung with racks of flip flops and snorkel masks.

Half-finished buildings with ironwork projecting from the roofs flew past as did dirt tracks studded with abandoned farm machinery. Battered cars, grit lorries and trucks full of livestock trundled by and, on one occasion, an old lady riding side saddle on a donkey caused us to slow down as she swayed along with all the time in the world at her disposal. Sometimes we'd pass Greek families lounging outside their homes in the stifling heat on furniture you'd relegate to the tip in England. It was a completely different life to the one I knew. I nibbled my cuticles as we drew closer to Lathos. Glancing at other tourists, it dawned on me I was wearing something far more suited to an English nightclub than a quiet island backwater, especially with the contrast of Lisa in shorts, a vest top, and sensible sandals. My skirt had ridden up, so I tugged it back down my thighs, glancing regretfully at my vertiginous white stiletto courts. These weren't suitable shoes for Greece.

Horribly aware of how incongruous I must have looked, I climbed down from the coach in my too short skirt, revealing vest top and the embroidered denim jacket I'd blown a week's wages on at Chic Boutique. Lisa looked at me for guidance as I stood hesitantly where you'd kissed me six weeks earlier, wondering what on earth to do. The next thing I knew, you were striding through the small crowd outside Tropic Bar and wrapping me in the tightest embrace ever, kissing me, lifting me off my feet, nearly breaking my back with your crush and spinning me around. I could hardly believe I was with you. It seemed so surreal.

'Baby *mou*,' you breathed into my hair. 'My baby, you came back.'

Instantly, I knew I'd done the right thing. All my fears and reservations drained away. Nothing else mattered.

Then I noticed someone waiting to be introduced; someone short and stocky with a round, shiny face, wearing long camouflage shorts, flip flops and a yellow Tweety Pie T-shirt. His scalp shone through sparse hair, which he more than made up for with gorilla-like arms and legs. This, I assumed, must be Nikos. Judging by the very wide grin he was extremely pleased to see us. Cringing inwardly, I felt embarrassed for dragging poor Lisa all the way to Aftonisi for what was most unlikely to be the Greek Adonis of her dreams. Holding my breath, I hardly dared look at her, but astonishingly, when I did, she was glancing coyly at him, her head tilted to one side. Clearly Lisa didn't have particularly high standards, but come to think of it, Darren hadn't exactly been Mel Gibson.

Exhaling with relief, I moved further into your warmth. The scent of your skin, the powerful grip of your arms, the sound of your voice all made me realise there was nothing left for me with Rob. Nothing. The intensity between us was overpowering, intoxicating, terrifying. Whether I was making a carefully considered choice or a chaotic, hormonal mistake made no difference now because, when you looked into my eyes, I became helpless, lost, pulled into your orbit like iron filings to a magnet. Rob who?

Together, the four of us walked up the hill, with you and Nikos pulling our cases, until we turned into a familiar driveway where, like old friends, the riot of luminous pink geraniums in their marmalade tins greeted us on the whitewashed wall where I'd propped Rob up weeks before. Nikos's family owned the apartments and he ran the taverna next door.

You both expertly hauled our cases up the stairs while we waited nervously in the lobby, then you returned, throwing yourself onto a wicker sofa, your feet up on a glass coffee table, while Nikos leaned over the reception desk to get our key.

'Be quick, and then we will go to eat,' you said with a new authority in your voice I hadn't expected, yet it wasn't altogether unwelcome after years of Rob's nebulous lack of direction. For once, I didn't need to be the one in charge.

It wasn't the same room I'd shared with Rob. It was a lot bigger, with a separate bathroom, two double beds and a small, tiled balcony overlooking the road.

'Are you okay?' I turned to Lisa, as she squirted herself with a cloud of insect repellent, ready to brave the mosquito laden air. I felt so responsible for her and making sure she'd have a good time, even though she'd technically invited herself along and hadn't taken much persuading about having a Greek blind date either.

'More than okay.' She inched her neckline down low as she smiled back at herself in the wardrobe mirror, patting her hair. 'Did you see those muscles?'

I hadn't. I'd found it hard to get past Tweety Pie.

Okay, well only if you're sure...' I felt a little doubtful but reassured myself that people, thankfully, have different tastes. Throwing the contents of my flight holdall onto my bed, I dug out my hairbrush and a can of Silvikrin to tame my long mane of dark hair then, as an afterthought, I changed into flat espadrilles. The road outside was lethal in the dark, little more than a dirt track and even though the white heels were perfect for an English night out, we were in Greece now. Full of excitement, we skipped back down the marble stairs, and walked out into the humid, fragrant darkness.

You draped your arm territorially around my neck and kept turning to kiss my face as we walked, which slowed us down considerably. I couldn't stop smiling. All the time you and Nikos chattered loudly and rapidly in Greek. I had no idea what you were saying but I enjoyed the melody and rhythm of the words. They were richly beautiful, rising with a bright sharpness before falling with depth, a percussive quality which marked a beat with our footsteps. Whitewashed walls and sparse foliage lined the road before it gave way to creaking olive trees and the occasional chain-link fence behind which a tethered donkey stooped. Nikos's heavily thatched arm was now around Lisa, his palm grazing her bum, but she didn't seem to object.

Soon we reached the main road, intersected by what was little more than a track winding onto the quietest part of the beach. Nikos and Lisa were heading towards a scattering of bars and tavernas ahead, but you took my hand and pulled me towards the sea instead.

'*Ela*,' you said, 'Come.'

We stood in silence for a moment. All that could be heard was the gentle waves crawling up the sand and receding again. Although my eyes became gradually accustomed to the darkness, it was still hard to make out where the sand stopped, and the sea began. You held my hand and pointed upwards. I gasped. The sky had become an artist's palette stippled with stars, smeared with the cloudy whiteness of the milky way. I caught my breath as a shooting star darted like an arrow high above. Any misgivings I'd had about coming back had all disappeared, vanished, gone.

'It's so beautiful,' I breathed, winding my fingers in yours while gazing up in awe.

'*You* are so beautiful.' You kissed me again.

We caught up with Nikos and Lisa at a pretty, candlelit bar where they'd already ordered *meze*: fat slabs of oil-drenched feta, creamy hummus and sharp, garlicky tzatziki all surrounded by fat, salty olives, cured meats, and rich, ripe tomatoes.

'Eat,' you instructed, unselfconsciously mopping up a lake of tzatziki with a large chunk of bread as Greek folk music drifted through the air. I reservedly picked at a tomato. Afterwards, you ordered flaming Sambucas. That would have been quite enough for me, but you insisted I also tried ouzo, made milky with a dash of water. Knocking back the vaguely medicinal, aniseed shot, I was finally given a thick, gritty Greek coffee in a tiny cup, *sketo* – without sugar.

You detected my stifled yawn.

'You are tired, *moro mou?*'

Leaning in, you kissed my forehead as I inhaled the scent of your neck. I loved you calling me 'my baby' in Greek. Rob never used any endearments whatsoever, usually calling me just Mel or Melons, with the added prefix of *oi* when he wanted my attention.

'Yes, a bit,' I admitted, fully yawning now. I didn't want the evening to end, but after too little sleep and too much alcohol, I had to admit defeat. You pulled me in and kissed me again, the vague taste of garlic and ouzo on your breath, your cheek rasping my face. I didn't want to leave but I was nearly asleep on your shoulder.

As Lisa and Nikos were now wound around each other, her leg across his knee, his hand snaking under her top, I wondered if she'd object to me calling an abrupt end to our first night. After all, it was her holiday too. I didn't want to upset her, but she confirmed she probably felt the same by way of a large, wide-open yawn.

'Well, then, you must both sleep.'

You planted a firm kiss on my head.

After buying large bottles of water for us both, you threw a handful of drachmae onto the table, took my hand and we all walked back up the starlit hill.

6

Infidelity

The next morning, you were working at Dimitri's, but although I wanted to see you, I wasn't sure whether it was a good idea to turn up there uninvited as you'd promised to meet me after your shift.

I couldn't help feeling jealous of all the pretty girls you'd be serving but I thought back to all the wonderful letters you'd sent me, full of how much you missed me and how much you were desperate to see me. Letters full of hunger and longing. They were always so detailed, so personal, so unselfconsciously romantic. I'd replied to each one, scenting them all liberally with my perfume. Sometimes, after sealing my letter, I'd remember something else I wanted to say, so I'd write all over the back of the envelope too.

Encouraged by your outpouring, I'd allowed myself to be less guarded and more vulnerable, copying the same initials within hearts you'd drawn, checking I wasn't short-changing you with the number of kisses I signed off in comparison to yours. It was like being back at school, in many ways so innocent, yet so loaded, so intoxicating.

As the blue, airmail envelopes had flown backwards and forwards over the miles, it had become nothing short of passion by post. I lived for those letters, and I know you did too because you told me so. You tried to write so perfectly in English, in your distinctive scrawl, beginning each one with 'my baby', and signing off with 'always yours, forever'. You'd become a drug I craved. It was crazy, a kind of delicious, temporary insanity I didn't want to end.

Thinking of those letters helped to appease any natural insecurity still I felt. You must have had the pick of the tourists so I couldn't see why you'd have made all that effort unless there had been at least a modicum of truth in them. I remembered how you'd treated me on the previous night. No, as George Michael said, I'd got to have faith.

Later, glowing from our day on the beach and from the full beam of your undivided attention earlier, I waited with Lisa outside the Beehive Apartments for you and Nikos to walk downhill to meet us. I knew you liked my black cotton dress, with its low-cut hook and eye bodice and swirling, calf-length skirt, because your eyes widened when you saw me, lingering over the curves of my body and appraising my appearance, clearly impressed.

'This dress is my favourite,' you announced, whirling me up off my feet, spinning me round, smothering me in kisses before draping an arm proprietorially around my neck. You were talking animatedly to Nikos who was walking ahead with Lisa, his fingers now purposefully digging into her bum cheek. I giggled incredulously to myself. I just couldn't see the attraction but at least she seemed happy.

Nikos and Lisa then wandered off together, leaving us alone. I can't remember what we talked about, I was far too busy immersing myself in every second of the time we spent together, enjoying the attention. I'd honestly never felt so beautiful, so valued, or so precious before.

My mind drifted momentarily to Rob. I hoped he'd be okay. Our good friend and neighbour, Dan, had promised to keep an eye on him. I think he'd been quite shocked when he'd learned I was leaving, but he'd tried to be positive and supportive. I was always mindful he was Rob's friend too. His loyalty must have felt divided. Dan was the closest thing I had to a brother. I knew Rob's behaviour exasperated him but he still cared about him. Despite everything, I still cared about Rob too. I didn't want him getting into any trouble and I felt a degree of guilt, but not as much as perhaps I should. My head and heart were filled with little else but you.

We'd drained another vodka when a slow, lazy smile had melted across your face, and you'd held out your hand.

'*Ela*,' you'd said. 'Come.'

Together we'd walked down a dusty road which curved past the pier onto an unmade track. Here the ground gave way to beach, and the night air was sharp with salt. It was hard to walk in my sandals, so I took them off and went barefoot, luxuriating in the sensation of cashmere-soft sand between my toes. All the while, you were caressing my fingers, entwining my hand tightly with yours.

I had no idea where we were walking to or any idea where Lisa was either. I wasn't even the slighted bit worried she had our room key. I had no way of getting back in, but I didn't care any more. The bars we'd passed along the shore seemed further and further away now. Disappearing, distant, gone, like any thoughts of Rob, thoughts of what the hell was I doing, thoughts of tomorrow.

Soon, we came to a narrow track, bordered with wire fences behind which a bleating goat was tethered to a whitewashed tree. You pulled me to you in front of an unfinished, two-storey building, crowned with iron armature rods which pointed into the sky.

'This is mine,' You declared with great reverence, both arms wide. 'My bar.' A cloud of moths danced around the single bulkhead lighting a breeze block doorway and a warm and darkly intoxicating breeze, whining with mosquitos and laden with the scent of herbs, drifted across the Ionian as you kissed me. Softly, tentatively at first, then more urgently, exploring, before devouring my mouth. It made my head spin, standing there in the blackness of the night, wrapped in your warmth, your lips against mine. Your hand, at first just exploring my bodice, was now pushing my cotton dress up my thigh, your breath heavy in my ear, your fingers edging under the lace of my panties.

'Not here,' I gasped, light-headed with desire.

Wordlessly, you led me through an open doorway, past buckets of dried cement, lidless paint cans and a coiled snake of cables. Clutching your hand, I followed up the flight of concrete steps, into a wide room with openings where windows would one day be. A balcony yawned out over an olive grove which shivered below the star-sprinkled black velvet gown of sky. On the bare concrete floor was an inflatable mattress, a torch, and a few empty beer bottles. There was also a portable radio.

'You want music?' You tried in vain to tune it. Eventually, a not particularly melodic Greek song echoed through the concrete shell. I wondered for a moment if this was a regular haunt. Had the girl in the white dress been here? This whole setup seemed too convenient, too practised, but of course, you'd bought others there. For someone like you, living like most young Greeks, in extended families with parents, siblings and grandparents, you couldn't exactly bring a girl home. You had to have somewhere to go, and I could hardly complain. I was a married woman.

I knew my next decision would change everything. I remember thinking, *'I'm cheating on Rob. I'm actually cheating on Rob'*, as I unhooked my dress, freeing the swell of my breasts, before slipping it over the curve of my hips and letting it fall like a wave at my feet. Sliding a whisper of lace panties down my thighs, I held your gaze. There was no turning back.

Afterwards, we lay entwined, laughing at the scurrying geckos clinging to the ceiling, staring at millions of stars which looked as though they'd been flung carelessly across the sky by the hands of gods. Your skin smelled of the sea, the pine on the mountainsides, of heat and dust as you turned to me, propped onto one elbow, and stroked my face.

'You belong to me now,' you said emphatically, seriously, unclasping the gold chain hung with a cornucopia charm you wore around your neck. You fastened it around mine.

During our second week, I spent every minute I could with you and not with Lisa. I was so caught up in you, in us, I didn't even bother to check how she was. I'd assumed she was okay with Nikos. You'd told me she was sleeping with him, and I was a little surprised she hadn't told me herself, after all, we were friends and I'd told her all about us, however, I assumed she had her reasons. She'd tell me when she wanted to.

Lisa and I usually had breakfast together each morning then we'd sit quietly writing postcards or reading and, sometimes, I'd scribble down ideas for stories and poems in my journal. Occasionally we saw each other briefly in the afternoon, but when it was time to go out for the evening, she and Nikos would disappear somewhere together, and we would go back to the concrete shell of your apartment above the unfinished bar. I usually crept back into the room long after she'd gone to bed, carrying my shoes, toeing the door open carefully and sliding quietly into my unmade bed.

One morning Lisa was sitting on the balcony when I came out of the shower, so I padded out to her, hoping for a debrief about her night, giving myself a mental high five she'd hit it off so well with Nikos because it made it so much easier for you and me to stay in our golden bubble.

'Morning.' I smiled brightly, rubbing the gold charm around my neck between my finger and thumb, but Lisa's face was set. She was looking pointedly out over the balcony rail, not at me. I frowned. She didn't seem her normal, carefree self at all.

'Is everything okay?' I was hoping everything was still good with Nikos as it might impact on my last few days with you if it wasn't.

She exhaled deeply, still looking across the road, ignoring me.

'Is Nikos okay?'

'Why wouldn't he be okay? He's always okay.' She sipped her water, 'Just like me, always fucking okay.'

'What do you mean?'

She didn't reply.

Puzzled, I pulled my cotton wrap closely around me, and returned to the bedroom, selecting a red top and a pair of denim shorts with a raw hem. She was definitely being frosty with me. Her eyes weren't meeting mine and her face was straight. Frowning in confusion, I wriggled into the shorts and wound my hair up. I wasn't a moody morning person, but maybe Lisa was. Why hadn't I noticed before? Idly, I wondered if it was her time of the month

'Are you cross with me about something?' Confused, I rubbed Ambre Solaire onto my legs for longer than strictly necessary before finally slipping into flip flops and returning to the balcony. 'Have I done something wrong?' I hoped this might snap her out of the weird mood she was clearly in.

Lisa emitted a long sigh.

'Well, as it happens, yes.'

She spun round to me, her face flushed. I felt my eyes widen. I'd never seen this side of her before, so I pulled out a plastic chair to sit opposite her. What on earth could all this be about? How could I have possibly done anything wrong?

'But we're having an amazing time and—'.

'No, Mel, *you're* having an amazing time but I'm being fobbed off on Nikos while you run around everywhere with Marios.'

'That's not fair.'

'It's true though. I'm supposed to be on holiday with you, but we've hardly done anything together. Instead, it's all about me fitting in around your schedule with him.'

I winced, wrapping my arms around myself. I was being thoroughly told off and it wasn't pleasant. I began to protest how she'd been quite happy with the idea of a blind date, but she interrupted me.

'All you're doing is making do with me until he finishes work. I hardly see you.'

Her voice was becoming shrill. I stared at her in dismay. She was quite right. I felt ashamed, embarrassed, the realisation dawning I'd been thoughtlessly selfish and there was little point in denying anything as it was all completely true. I hadn't deliberately set out for this to happen, but I hadn't considered her feelings either, in fact I hadn't really considered anything much apart from being with you and, yes, I'd been relieved she'd seemed to like Nikos because it made everything easier for me.

'I don't know why you bothered asking me to come out here at all,' she said. 'You'd have been perfectly okay on your own. I feel a bit used to tell the truth.'

I didn't like to remind her that I hadn't actually asked her. She'd technically invited herself along. I'd been worried she might get bored, but once you'd told me she was sleeping with Nikos, I'd assumed she was perfectly happy. I'd assumed quite a lot, really. I stared miserably over the balcony as the mountains, the hot, dusty road, and the Banana tree, all began to distort and swim in front of me. Running the side of my index finger under my eyes, I sniffed hard, looking despondently back at her.

'I thought you liked him.' It sounded a bit lame, under the circumstances.

'He's alright I suppose, as someone to pass the time with, but I don't want to just pass the time. I want a proper holiday.'

'But I thought everything was really good with you both, I mean, you're sleeping with him...' I hadn't meant to blurt it out. One of my failings, not thinking first before I speak. Lisa wasn't impressed. She glared furiously at me, her face turning even redder.

'Just because I've fucked him, doesn't mean I want to spend 24 hours a day with him,' she yelled right into my face. 'We can't all be like you!'

I was shocked at the velocity of her anger.

'Look, Mel, he's a nice enough guy, better than nothing, but I don't exactly live to see him like you do Marios, yet I feel obliged to hang around with him every single fucking day.' She paused her diatribe and looked me squarely in the face. She wasn't wrong. Something contracted within me. I felt inches smaller.

She hadn't finished either.

'The thing is, I knew you'd want time with Marios, but I'd really thought we'd be doing things together too. I was looking forward to this holiday, seeing the sights, you know, snorkelling, swimming...but not with Nikos, with *you*.' Her voice tailed off to a squeak as she scrubbed at her eyes. 'Oh, I don't know what I'm trying to say, it's all coming out wrong. I just thought we'd be spending a bit more time together as friends, that's all.'

I was horrified as her voice cracked and she began to blink back tears. I was praying she wouldn't full-on cry as I had no idea what to do with her. Lisa was usually so tough. It went with her job description. I'd never seen her upset before. It occurred to me how little I really knew her.

'Lisa, I'm so, so sorry,' I was desperate to make amends. 'Please forgive me.' I dragged my chair around to her side. I'd been busted, caught out taking her for granted, something I'd often accused Rob of doing to me.

'Look, I'll tell Marios I can't see him this afternoon and we'll go on that boat trip you fancied to Zenomeros, or something else if you prefer? Anything. Just you and me. What do you say?'

She ignored me, leaning down to inspect a chipped tile on the balcony floor.

'Please, I'll pay.' I was aware I was pleading. 'We could have lunch too.'

'Okay,' she finally agreed, sniffing hard and looking up at me.

Her green eyes looked damper, clearer, and brighter, like she'd put eye drops in. Unlike me, Lisa was one of those lucky few who can look pretty after tears.

'You promise?' she said.

'Yes, I promise.'

Inching into an awkward embrace, the plastic chairs getting in the way of a full body hug on the tiny balcony, we both agreed to go out to find somewhere completely new for breakfast that neither of us had ever tried before.

I was anxious about the holiday coming to an end, so I probably behaved differently towards you during those last few days. All my insecurities were surfacing. I could feel everything unravelling, like the raw hem on my shorts, as Lisa, and I perched on our packed suitcases outside the Beehive Apartments, waiting for you and Nikos to say goodbye.

You'd seemed a bit touchy, quieter than usual during our last couple of days, a bit lost in thought, so had whatever 'this' was finally come to an end? We hadn't talked about the future. Would this be the last time I'd ever see you? Would you want your gold chain back? The only thing for certain was I'd soon be going back to my grey, uninspiring life, with a hostile ex in the back bedroom, to a job I was quite frankly bored of, with nothing but memories. My throat had a ball of broken glass and barbed wire lodged in it, so I hardly trusted myself to speak when you wrapped me in your arms. Instead, I watched Nikos and Lisa kissing goodbye, seriously doubting she'd be swapping addresses or phone numbers with him. She'd had simply been having a lukewarm summer fling.

You, however, were a different matter. I knew leaving you was going to rip my heart out, but there was no option. I was going to have to say goodbye to you, but I was going to stay dignified. I certainly wasn't going to show you how much it hurt.

'*Ela, moro mou,*' you took my hand. Uncertain of what I was meant to do, I grabbed the pull handle of my case, ready to drag it behind me, but you shook your head.

'No, you leave it,' you said, pulling me into the shade of the bougainvillea. I looked up at you regretfully, feeling wholly deflated and hopeless. Was this to be the 'it's been great but' speech? I breathed in deeply, nails digging into the clinched fists I'd shoved into my shorts pockets, ready for whatever it was.

'Don't go. I don't want to lose you, so you will stay, yes?' You were searching my face for an affirmative answer, looking at me so hopefully my heart had initially leapt skywards. That's why you'd been so quiet. You did care. But then it plummeted back to the soles of my white, canvas espadrilles. How could I possibly stay? The only way would be to leave everything behind, to give up all I had back at home.

'Don't go, *moro*, I don't want you to go. I've been thinking about this, and you have to stay.'

I shook my head.

'I can't.'

You pulled me in, kissing my eyelids and my nose.

'Why not? You like it here. You like me. I like you.'

It was all so simple to you. This is where the age gap you denied existing really showed.

'Because I have a life in England.' I looked at you standing there, arms folded, demanding I make an instant decision, a hint of petulance in your voice, and rolled my eyes. 'I have commitments and a job, a proper job. I'm an estate agent. I have clients. I can't just… run away.'

'But I will find you somewhere to stay, and I will find you a proper job.

There are tavernas, bars, you could teach English.'

You had it all worked out.

'You can't leave a job in England just like that.' I clicked my fingers for emphasis, realising in a rush how exasperating you could be at times. 'I have a contract and there's this thing called 'notice' you have to give. They owe me money which I really need but they won't pay me if I don't go back.'

I knew you had little conception of what I was trying to explain and were unimpressed I was saying no to your suggestion. I was already learning you liked to get your own way.

'Don't you get any holiday with this job?'

I hadn't even considered what holiday entitlement I might still have left because I'd already taken quite a lot. It would be so awkward having to ask for more, and really selfish on the run up to Christmas, but perhaps there'd be a few days still owing. Maybe, with a few extra unpaid days, I could even stretch it out. It was worth a try. Why hadn't I thought of this before?

The afternoon sunlight was patching through the bougainvillea, dappling your skin.

'Well then,' you said, taking my grin as an unspoken 'yes' and beaming back at me after kissing me. 'You tell them you are taking holiday and you stay here, with me.' You squeezed me so tight I was scared you'd break my spine. 'We'll go to the Kiosk. You can call them now.'

'No, it doesn't work like that.' I laughed, as your face fell. 'But what I *can* do is fly back home now, see what holiday I still have, get paid, then come back.'

7

Little Lies

Lisa and I landed at wet, grey Gatwick and caught a National Express coach to Southampton, saying our goodbyes when she got off at the stop before mine. I continued on alone. Staring miserably at the tears of rain trickling down the window, I was in no hurry to get home.

Everything felt so cold, dark, and unwelcoming when I gingerly let myself in, raking my fingers through my damp hair and yanking my case over the threshold. I was never sure what to expect with Rob, but he wasn't in. I snapped the bare hall lightbulb on. The uncarpeted staircase creaked as I humped my case up to the bedroom, chucked the contents onto the bed, and dragged out any clean clothes to put away before tipping the rest into the laundry basket, ready to load into the washing machine later.

The bedside clock seemed annoyingly loud as it tick-tocked its way past midnight. I had to go into work in the morning, so I stripped off and quickly dived under an unmade pile of duvet still heaped exactly as I'd left it two weeks earlier, knowing my hair was damp and would look like a lampshade the next day. I hadn't closed my eyes for more than a minute when I'd heard scratching and clicking sounds outside. Shortly afterwards, there was the loudest, resounding crash downstairs, a lot of shuffling about, and finally the sound of someone swearing followed by a protracted 'Shush.' We were either having a visit from the noisiest burglars in the city, or it was Rob.

Annoyed I threw on my bathrobe and peered down over the bannisters. In the hallway, Dan's face loomed up as he mouthed 'sorry' and attempted to steer Rob by the shoulders through the hallway, into the kitchen.

With a deep sigh of resentment, I stomped back downstairs.

'Keep it down, will you, I've got work tomorrow.'

'He couldn't get his key in the lock. He's had a bit to drink so I'm making him a cup of coffee.'

By the look of Rob's glazed expression, it wasn't a bit, and a cup wouldn't be enough. He'd need a bucket of it.

Huffing with resentment, I filled the kettle and flicked on the switch, opening the cupboard in search of mugs only to discover they were all over the worktops instead, each full of something green and decomposing. A quick glance in the fridge revealed no more than a bottle of Smirnoff, a few yogurts, an uncovered tin of cat food and an out-of-date pack of bacon.

'There's no milk.' I said flatly, swilling away penicillin-type cultures from three mugs before wiping them with a tea towel. Yawning, I slumped against the worktop. 'You'll have to have black.'

Between us, Dan and I ladled a coffee down Rob who was brandishing a long-stemmed single red rose in a plastic sleeve, the sort gypsies tried to sell to tourists in Lathos.

'Ah, yeah, he got that in the club,' explained Dan, eyeing the bloom Rob had now slung onto the kitchen table.

'No thanks,' I said as he snatched it up again, wiggling it under my nose in what I assume he thought was a romantic gesture. No gesture was going to make the slightest difference now. I'd already made up my mind.

I turned away as Dan began steering Rob into the hallway, promising to get him up to bed. Finally, with Dan keeping him upright, Rob clattered upstairs leaving me leaning sullenly against the kitchen worktop nursing my mug and surveying the washing up mountain.

'He's really upset, you know.' Dan came back down to quickly finish his coffee. Leaning on the worktop, he gave me a look which seemed to convey a plea on Rob's behalf.

'He really wants another chance, Mel. Can't you find a way of working it out, you two?'

'No, absolutely not. It's over, I'm sorry Dan, I know this is tough on you as he's your friend too, but I'm not changing my mind.'

'Yes, but he's been telling me all about how—'

I could only imagine the latest web of fabricated disaster stories Rob must have spun to entrap poor Dan. I stopped him there.

'Honestly, Dan, I'm done.'

I watched him carefully rinsing his mug, before setting it upside down on the draining rack. Why couldn't I have fallen for Dan instead? It would have made life so much easier as we were already such good friends. He was literally the perfect man; attractive, intelligent, kind and funny and he only lived over the road, not over 2,000 miles away. But I'd never felt that way about Dan. I loved Dan, that much was true, but, like a brother. There was none of that essential chemical Factor X there.

He walked to the door then turned to me.

'Couldn't you find it in you to give him one, last chance Mel?'

Folding my arms, I chose to ignore his comment and swallowed a yawn. Creaks from the ceiling above told me Rob was now in bed. Hopefully he'd stay there. I fully yawned then, an inelegant, wide open one which made my eyes water, not making the slightest effort to cover my mouth in a ladylike fashion, partly because I was exhausted, partly because I hoped Dan would take a hint.

He hovered on the doorstep.

'Is this all because of that Greek guy?'

'No.' I jabbed thumb towards the ceiling. 'It's all because of that Rob guy'.

Dan gave me a hug as he left.

'Please be careful Mel…it's only a holiday romance. I'd hate you to do something you later regret.'

The thing is, I'd already done something I regretted. I'd married Rob and wasted far too much time on him to have more regrets about anything else. Even something as crazy as this.

I'd walked into work the next morning sporting a very dark tan, deliberately wearing a blindingly white top to further emphasise it.

'Looking a bit pasty, Mel. No sun out there?' Matt, our assistant manager, deftly missed the joke swipe I aimed at his head.

'Seriously, that's a stonking tan.' His gaze swept appreciatively over my bare, brown legs as he treated me to an eye-crinkling and somewhat suggestive grin. Matt was a bit like a young David Essex, with twinkling blue eyes, and the sort of direct gaze that usually made my stomach do a backflip. There was a time I'd found myself idly daydreaming about Matt, a time I'd have hugged myself inside at the delicious thought he might have actually been flirting with me. But now I jauntily sashayed past his desk without the slightest care. My head was filled with nothing but you.

The morning went by so slowly. My head wasn't in my work at all, and it was a massive effort to make it look as though it was during my handover with Alan. He was sitting at his desk, twirling his ludicrously expensive Mont Blanc pen when I entered, poring over a manilla folder bearing my name. The office was stuffy, and meeting was long. It required the utmost concentration, and a few clever suggestions too, neither of which I had at my disposal. All I could think about was you, us, Lathos, and my desperate need to get back there as soon as possible. I doodled suns and stars on my pad, wondering when I would have a chance to ask him about any remaining holiday entitlement as Alan droned on and on.

'...and the townhouse in City Row is still waiting on the survey report, so could you call the buyer's solicitor as a matter of urgency to see when they're expecting it?'

I remembered the early morning sunlight spilling across the water, the light spreading like golden threads across a satin quilt of barely rippling waves, the warmth of your arms around me as we'd sat in a beach café, coffees on the side, our toasted sandwiches sizzling on the hotplate ...

'Melanie!'

'Oh, god, sorry, what?' I physically jumped as Alan's voice cut into my lovely, soporific daydream, my face beginning to burn like the very hotplate I'd been thinking of.

'Have you even heard a word I was saying?'

'Sorry, sorry…I think I'm a bit tired, that's all.' I sat up and leaned forward, uncrossing my legs, trying to look perky and interested. 'Probably jet lag.'

'Let's finish this after lunch.' Alan huffed as he collected up the strewn papers, popped them into the folder and slapped it pointedly down in front of me. 'In the meantime, I suggest you read all of this, and make notes for discussion later.'

I nodded, murmuring an indistinct agreement while trying to look especially bright and alert.

'Oh, and hit the phones too.' He surveyed his clipboard. 'We're seriously down on sales this month.'

Alan's face was straight. Any sensible person would have then scurried off to the sanctuary of their desk and made a big, elaborate show of being Gold Star Salesperson. Any sensible person would have even worked through their lunch break to impress their boss, but sensible wasn't really my forte. I wasn't feeling particularly sensible at all right then, only lost, sad, disorientated, and missing you so badly it hurt.

'Listen,' he said, 'I know it's hard to come down to earth and concentrate after a holiday, but you do need to get your head back in the game, and quickly, because Nick's after blood.'

Nick Jackson, our terrifying director, would stalk into the office once a month in his black cashmere coat, carrying his slimline briefcase. Nick was the company's equivalent to God. Whether we got a pay rise or promotion, remained employed, or, indeed, lived or died, rested solely on the whims of Nick. Alan tapped his pen rhythmically on his pad for a moment then looked me straight in the eye.

'Our figures are well below those of Winchester,' he continued, 'But I know you can do this, Mel.' He leaned forward and fixed me with his chocolate button eyes. 'You're a good negotiator in fact I think you could be assistant manager when we move Matt up. I have every faith in you.'

Wow, the promotion carrot. This should have been a moment to make my toes curl with delight. Assistant managers got Vauxhall Cavaliers. But that was before us.

Smiling at me kindly, he stood up, patted my arm then began making for the door, as I gathered up the folder I had no real interest in. I had to move quickly.

'Alan, please could I have a quick word?'

He turned in the doorway.

'Of course, what is it?'

I took a deep breath.

'Um... I wondered...could you confirm how much holiday I can still take this year?'

I think I actually felt the shock radiate from Alan's chest, though his clipboard and straight to the centre of my solar plexus as he stared at me incredulously. I swear his eyebrows levitated an inch as his mouth opened then snapped shut again.

'Christ on a bike, are you serious?' he spluttered. 'You've only just got back. I do hope you're joking.'

I felt my face flush.

'Oh, no, um I actually only wanted to know what I had left as, er... there may be a few things coming up soon.' I hope I had loaded the mysterious word 'things' sufficiently.

He exhaled, his shoulders visibly relaxing as his eyebrows returned to their original position. In contrast, my stomach and other nearby muscles tightened considerably.

'Oh, I see.' He emphasised the word *see*, his face beginning to crinkle at what he'd considered a ludicrous idea. 'I'll check with HR, think it's about three days. I'll get them to send you a memo.' He took his glasses off and wiped them on his tie. 'Sorry, I thought for one moment you'd wanted to take more time off straight away. I'm off from next week myself.'

I shook my head most emphatically, making a few indistinct sounds which suggested a resounding 'oh, no', laughing with him at such a ridiculous misunderstanding. But he was quite right. I did. I really, really did.

HR didn't get back to me until the following Tuesday, by which time Alan was on holiday and Trevor from Fareham was looking after our office. As predicted, I was still owed three and a half days.

Alan being away was quite convenient, because I wasted no time in filling out a holiday request, asking for the Wednesday, Thursday and Friday of the following week off, along with half of the Monday after. Sneakily, I intended to further extend this with a day or two off 'sick' beforehand, and a conveniently 'delayed flight' home afterwards. I had it all worked out as I diarised a raft of fabricated 'appointments' for the Friday before my planned sick days. This creative jiggling would get me a whole, glorious ten days back in Lathos. I was a genius.

Feeling like a master criminal, I slid my holiday request under Trevor's nose along with some petty cash expenses, but he hardly looked up and signed everything off. Trevor had always been a bit of a pushover. By the time Alan returned, I'd be long gone and there'd be plenty of time in Lathos to practise my *thoroughly contrite face* for later. I popped in to see Mrs Burns at Thomas Cook on my lunchbreak.

8

It's Only Love

The descent into Aftonisi is often a hair-raising one. It's one of those airport landings pilots often cite as being tricky. The plane sweeps across bare, rocky ground as it descends over the party town of Loukada, but in a sharp 180-degree turn, it then skims the heads of sunbathers on the beach at Zenomeros. It's quite disconcerting and often results in a bumpy landing. My flight had been no exception, in fact the whole aircraft had given the pilot and crew a grateful round of applause when we'd touched down.

I watched the increasingly familiar vistas of the island through the coach window, shading my eyes against the brilliance of the sun. Red clay earth, sandy tracks and gnarled olive groves, all interwoven by the shimmering blue ribbon of the Ionian, blurred as the coach lurched haphazardly, the driver taking surreptitious swigs from a bottle wrapped in a brown paper bag.

Eventually we slowed to a donkey's pace, bumping over rough track towards the clearing by the Tropic Bar. It occurred to me this would the first time I'd be on the island completely alone. I'd have no one to rely on but you. No one else to talk to. A cloud of hyperactive butterflies began completing a Grand Prix circuit in my stomach.

You were waiting for me at the coach stop, bursting with news you'd found me an apartment to stay in, kissing me so vigorously, your lips nearly bruised mine. I glanced up at you as together we walked hand in hand down the small track to the beach. This was it, you and me alone, no Lisa, no Nikos. I felt strangely lost and insecure. Should I have felt excited instead?

You stopped on a corner, opposite a yellow OTE post-box, in front of small, two-storey concrete box of a building. It looked as though someone was living there. Chairs and a table were in the front yard, a bowl of currants, grapes and a small knife lying on the plastic tablecloth while a small line of washing fluttered between two palm trees. Seeing my probably quizzical expression, you pointed up to a wide balcony bordered by ornate white ironwork railings.

Without giving me time to think, you bounded up a flight of steps at the side of the building, dragging my heavy case effortlessly with you as I tiptoed my way uncertainly up behind, clutching the rail. Was this someone else's home I was supposed to be sharing?

Pushing the unlocked door open you strode across a sand-dusted marble floor as I hesitantly followed behind, passing open bedroom doors, noticing a proper bathroom. Unlike the crude showers at the Beehive Apartments, which had barely enough room to even shave your legs, this was an absolute dream, with a full-size bath and a shower attachment. It was luxury beyond words for Aftonisi.

'Ela, moro, come.' You were impatient to show me the rest.

We came to an open-plan pine kitchen where you began opening and shutting cupboards and drawers, proudly showing me cutlery, saucepans and plates as I gazed out of the window at waves gently washing the beach, a vastly superior view to my own kitchen window at home.

'This?'

You opened a door into large, bright bedroom. As far as furnishings went, it was basic, but huge, and flooded with natural light with a side view onto the beach. Before I could answer, you'd pulled me back up the corridor to show me the other bedrooms.

'You choose, moro,' you said, laughing at me as I investigated each of them, hesitantly at first, yet soon I was flitting about like a child hunting for Easter eggs.

The one you'd shown me first was simply furnished, just a pine double bed, a bedside cabinet, and a single wardrobe. Streaks of sunlight spilled through blue wooden shutters. I loved it, but I needed to be sure, so I peeped inside the bedroom next door, which was smaller, with twin beds. There wasn't much room to move as it was dominated by a huge wardrobe.

In comparison with the sea views from the others, the third overlooked the street. Presiding over one end, an ornately carved, ebony bed with a massive wooden headboard and, lurking at the other, a matching wardrobe on claw feet. The furniture wouldn't have been out of place in a Jacobean mansion. Everything smelled dank and musty as if it had been left unused for decades. I wondered if there was an equivalent of a charity shop on the island and tried not to think about whether someone had died in that carved bed.

I preferred the first room. Trying to keep my expression as neutral as possible in order not to offend you, I walked back to find you on the balcony which you were keen to show me, explaining each room led onto it through their own French Doors. A large table with plastic chairs occupied a shaded corner, but the rest was flooded with sunlight.

'This all belongs to my friend Pavlos's family,' you explained with a grin, throwing your hands open wide.

'Is it expensive?'

I hadn't brought much money and I couldn't expect you to pay for everything on a waiter's salary. I wouldn't want you to. You simply flicked your eyes towards the ceiling with a soft, hardly discernible tut and a small, upwards jerk of the chin, something I by then knew as the Greek way of indicating 'no'.

'*Dhen Pirazi*, it doesn't matter, you don't have to pay. Pavlos is my best friend, his father owns the kiosk and a restaurant, so he can afford it.'

'Are you sure?'

You lowered your head, a slightly angled nod. Again, a barely perceptible Greek gesture, this time the one for yes. All these small movements were subtle, signals I had to be observant to catch. There was such a lot to learn.

'So, you like?' you said, 'You want?'

Enthusiastically, I threw my arms around you.

'It's great, thank you. Yes please.'

'In Greek,' you demanded, somewhat bossily.

I hesitated. I always felt strangely shy speaking to you in Greek. In contrast, when I'd been with Lisa, I'd falteringly tried out phrases in restaurants, in bars, questions, simple words, quite happy to get them wrong and be corrected in order to learn. But with you, it was so different. Your approval meant everything. I didn't want to look foolish in your eyes because you constantly kept telling me how perfect I was. I didn't want to do anything to break the spell; to make you see me in any other way. The way Dad saw me.

'Well?' you insisted, with the little, characteristic foot stamp I was beginning to recognise as a measure of your impatience and exuberance.

'Um... *ine poli kala, efkharisto*. Er... *Parakalo?*'

'Bravo, *moro*,' You planted a firm kiss on my cheek. 'But you must say *orea*, great, instead of just good, *ne?*'

'Yes, I mean, *ne*.' I replied.

'You will be speaking it nicely in a few months,' You pulled me close, embracing me like a possessive bear, nearly squeezing the air out of my lungs. It was the first time you'd alluded to the fact you might want me to stay for longer. A throwaway comment you'd probably hardly noticed, but it made me glow inwardly. Indirectly, you'd mentioned a future.

Right outside was the sudden screech of a motorbike, and the sound of an engine switching off. Instantly, the staircase reverberated with thudding footsteps and a powerfully built Greek in sunglasses burst through doorway. There was also someone else, a petite, tanned blonde, wearing black shorts and a bikini top, clutching his hand as he dragged her behind him.

Instantly, you exploded into excitement. You and the visitor were embracing, back slapping, kissing on each cheek several times and shouting a loud stream of Greek at each other while I slunk back, unsure of what was happening. Instantly this pushed buttons with my classic British reserve. I wasn't used to this level of demonstrativeness.

The girl eyed me warily, giving a thin, self-conscious smile, which I politely returned. I had no idea what was going on, so I tugged at your hand, but you and the man were still talking excitedly, completely ignoring me. It was as though I'd become invisible. No one was being introduced but someone had to say something, so I finally took the initiative.

'Hi.' I stepped forward hesitantly. I couldn't be sure whether she spoke English. There were so many different nationalities in the resort she could have been from anywhere, but when she replied, she was English. We beamed widely at one another, the relief palpable.

'I've no idea what's going on here, have you?' I asked her with a grin, attempting to bond a little as she smiled back at me with perfect white teeth, shaking a head full of blonde curls. She wore no makeup except for vibrant red lipstick.

'Petros wanted to find Marios, so… here we are.'

So, 'sunglasses' must be called Petros, but I was still none the wiser. I looked at her closely as she tucked herself under his arm. She was very pretty, with wide blue eyes, full lips and high cheekbones, like a young Marilyn Monroe. The smile you treated her to was one of your most dazzling which instantly made me feel a little insecure, so I shuffled in a bit closer to you.

'Moro-mou,' you said, with great reverence, 'This is my good friend, Petros, back from Khalkidhiki.' Then the rapid machine-gunning of Greek between the two of you continued as I stood helplessly by, waiting for a gap in the conversation.

Petros was staring at me hard now. I couldn't see his eyes properly as he was still wearing sunglasses, but it was like he was appraising me, summing me up, somewhat quizzically as though deciding whether I was worthy of acknowledgement. I felt like I was undergoing a test.

'Hello,' I ventured. He was still clamping the blonde under his steely biceps as he continued to regard me unsmilingly. An age seemed to pass.

'Yassou.' He finally gave a somewhat curt nod, squeezing the blonde even tighter, his muscles visibly bulging under his tight cap-sleeved t-shirt, before looking down at her. 'I am Petros, this is Sairee.'

It was an unusual name, so I began to wonder if he'd actually said 'Sarah'. It was all a bit indistinct. I may have misheard.

'Hi… Sarah,' I ventured. 'I'm Melanie.'

'It's not Sarah. I'm Sherri.' She had a warm, genuine smile as she offered me a hand, and leaned in to plant a kiss on both cheeks. Then she laughed, rolled her eyes theatrically, and shook her head at Petros. 'Don't listen to him, he seems to have trouble saying my name properly.'

She turned back to Petros.

'It's Sherri, not Sairee.' She emphasised the shh sound. 'Sherri, with a shh…like in *shit*, remember?'

We all laughed. I was going to like her.

Sherri and I got to know each other quite well over the next few days and were fast becoming good friends, sitting in cafés, laughing, sharing stories, watching gentle waves on the beach crawl and recede until you came with Petros to find us.

She was a few years younger than me, from St Albans, and worked in her uncle's travel agency but he'd allowed her to take a six-month unpaid sabbatical. He'd said travelling would be good for her career. Enviously, I wished I could do that too, but I couldn't see how travelling would help my progression in estate agency. I wasn't keen on the unpaid aspect either.

As we sat together drinking frappés at a beach bar, Sherri explained she'd met Petros in May. She'd come back out in June to be with him, and they'd gone travelling to Khalkidhiki.

She'd been on holiday with her English boyfriend, Kevin, but had often noticed Petros cruising the resort on his red Kawasaki, tight vest tops enhancing his rippling brown biceps. They'd exchanged long, flirtatious looks over the bar where he'd worked until one evening, when Kevin was sleeping off a hangover, she'd gone in alone. It resonated a little with my own story about how I came to be there.

'One thing led to another,' she explained, as I wondered whether her comment was as loaded as it appeared. 'I couldn't stay with Kevin after that.'

To her acute embarrassment, however, the next evening, Kevin had proposed to her, right in the middle of The Grill House.

'He got down on one knee and everything with this little diamond he'd got from Ratners.' She opened her purse and took out a photograph from behind her provisional license. Handing it to me, she said how awful she still felt about it.

'It was so public, so humiliating,' she said, describing the horrible silence in the restaurant as everyone had hung on her response, broken only by the overzealous waiter prematurely popping the Champagne.

I looked at the dog-eared picture of a smiling Kevin, thick set, with liquid, dark eyes, an aquiline nose, broad shoulders, and what appeared to be a disproportionately wide neck. He looked like a body builder and was so dark he could pass as Greek himself, in fact he was not dissimilar to Petros.

'The strange thing is, I'd wanted him to do it for ages,' she said. 'We'd been together since school and I'd hinted so many times, even pointed out rings I liked in the Freemans Catalogue, but, when I saw him down there on one knee, I just felt embarrassed.'

She smiled somewhat sadly.

'He's lovely, but he wants to settle down and have children and I'm really not ready for all that. I'm far too young.'

She explained how she'd pretended to say yes to save him from public humiliation, but while they were enduring a round of applause and drinking the Champagne Kevin had arranged to celebrate their special moment, she'd whispered to him that there was something she needed to tell him later. Kevin certainly got his wish in wanting it to be an evening they'd never forget. He bought an early flight back home the next day.

She told me she was still writing to him.

'But only as friends,' she hastily added, probably noticing my expression of surprise. 'I'm not keeping him hanging on or giving him any false hopes. He knows I'm with Petros now.'

Listening to her, I been turning a microscope onto my own relationship with you.

I was so caught up in this delicious thing we were both bound up in, I hadn't really analysed it at all. What was it really all about? Admittedly it was exciting, romantic, the sex was great, but did I really know what I was doing at all? I'd broken up a marriage, jeopardised my career and divided the opinion of all my friends. Was it because I thought I loved you? Or just because I didn't love Rob. It occurred to me in that moment, I'd never loved Rob at all.

'Do you love Petros?'

Sherri was thoughtful for a moment.

'Yeah, I guess, I mean, I must do, or I wouldn't have turned Kevin down, would I?' Her arched brows drew together a little. 'Or, at least, I love *being* with him because he makes me feel so special. Kevin never did, besides, we're having so much fun.'

Tucking the picture of Kevin back in her purse, she took a long swig of her iced drink then, putting her sunglasses on, tilted her face upwards like a flower seeking the sun. I stared at the impossibly blue sea. Maybe that was it: having fun. Rob hadn't been fun for a long time.

That evening we met up with Petros and Sherri again. It was getting to be a regular thing, the four of us, sitting in a huddle at tables in our favourite bars, the air whining with mosquitos and throbbing with the hum of Cicadas.

The fragrance of thyme and oregano from the mountains would mingle with a sharp saltiness of the sea. Chaotic strains of Greek music would collide with thumping Europop, the rhythm of the waves and the crunch of the sand beneath our feet adding percussion. Omnipresent in the daytime, the mountains would gradually become shrouded in black, leaving their outlines barely visible; grey and lavender ghosts teasing their way through the darkness.

Coloured fairy lanterns were our only light. Crudely strung across trees, fences, gates, they'd swing drunkenly in the breeze, tracing our skin with multicolours. The soft darkness would be occasionally sharpened by a zap of blue light as an insect met its doom or little tips of red flaring in the dark followed by a drift of cigarette smoke.

All this was observed from the cocoon of your arms, locked within your warmth and strength, the natural scent of your skin and my perfume intermingling, making my head spin. The tangle of your hair against my face, your leg up hard against my knee, your hand stroking my thigh with a promise of the night to come.

Invariably, you would lace your arm across my shoulders, your hand finding mine, before silencing my words with your mouth. Our faces became hollow, shaded, charcoal-smudged drawings on grained paper, indistinct yet taking on completely new planes, depth and structure up close.

You would play with my hair, winding it through your hands, stroking its ends between a thumb and fingertip, telling anyone who would listen how beautiful I was, while stamping little kisses along the line of my neck and shoulders. You would call me *agapē mou*. You would take your index finger and, with a mock pout, pat it against your lips as a signal for me to kiss you.

If you ever needed to take your hand from mine, you would quickly replace it with the other as though you couldn't bear to lose skin contact for even a second. You would then whisper the phrase you'd taught me that night at the Tropic Bar, *pame sto spiti mas,* and we would leave the others, returning to what you called *our place.* Somehow, deep inside, I knew this was more than just fun.

9

Addicted To Love

Whenever we were alone, we would go somewhere on your bike. Your basic, Honda 50cc was nothing like Petros's Kawasaki and not particularly well looked after either judging by the dents and scratches. You thought nothing of dropping it to the ground, then later, jumping astride, twisting it noisily into life and speeding off through a rising screen of dust and grit with me seated behind, threading my arms tightly around your chest, my head pressed against the back of your neck, hair streaming behind. Thoughts of England were a whole lifetime away. Southampton no longer existed. Living for the day, the minute, the second, I was drowning in our intoxicating chemistry, weak with longing, governed by hormones, not reason.

I'd also met another English girl in Lathos, Elaine, your friend Sakis's girlfriend. Solidly built, with round brown eyes trapped behind highly magnified tortoiseshell glasses, her bobbed hair was that undefinable shade of fair which could best be described as colourless. With a straight and humourless manner, sensible, practical Elaine was not someone I'd have ordinarily gravitated towards.

Used to plain-speaking having been born and bred in a male-dominated farming community, Elaine didn't see the need for tact, diplomacy or indeed any form of subtlety. More used to drinking pints at the Young Farmers Club and sheering sheep at the county show than drinking cocktails in a wine bar or shopping on Oxford Street, she'd grown up in a totally different world to me. By the time I'd passed my driving test, Elaine was manning a tractor. We were born in the same year, but that was where our similarity ended. Elaine was more than happy to say exactly what she thought. I was far more guarded. Unapologetically herself, blunt to the extreme and unintentionally tactless, the upside was Elaine had no edges. She was genuine. With someone like Elaine, what you saw was most definitely what you got.

The three of us had, out of necessity, quickly bonded, forming a triangle, an exclusive group, the English girlfriends. It was, however, an isosceles triangle. Sherri and I were already close, two girls in parallel situations, thrown together under unique circumstances, drifting like dandelion spores from one disaster to the next, whereas Elaine was as grounded as an oak tree.

Always prepared for everything, Elaine was also practical. She'd brought painkillers, and laxatives with her 'just in case' and enough tampons to stock Superdrug, along with multivitamins, plasters, a torch, and even a compass.

'You never know when you'll need it,' she'd explained, tapping the glass, showing us where north was.

Whereas I didn't wholly connect with Elaine, I wasn't keen on her boyfriend, Sakis, at all. He seemed to have had a major sense of humour transplant and I cringed at how rude he often was to her. He certainly had no idea of manners or social pleasantries. When I'd been introduced to him, he'd just stared hard at me for a moment before turning away.

Older than you and Petros, he was always covered in a layer of plaster dust from his construction job. I felt sorry for Elaine having to spend the evening with a man who didn't bother showering after a day's work on a building site, but she didn't seem remotely bothered by this and even less so by the quite cutting remarks he often made at her expense, shaking it all off, like a fleece from a sheared lamb.

Sherri was the complete opposite, quick, bright and always drily funny, enjoying a liberal helping of naughty gossip every bit as much as I did. Together we became terrible gigglers, laughing openly at things only we seemed to notice, which seemed to increasingly annoy you. You'd once told us quite crossly we were behaving like children which made us laugh even harder. I already knew I'd really miss her when I went home.

The week was drawing to a close and I was on borrowed time, literally, but I knew Alan would still be on holiday in Cornwall, so I'd only have Trevor the Pushover to answer to over my illicit days off. I'd think of something.

'Why do you have to go?' You'd sounded somewhat sulky.

'Because I do.' I really didn't want to, but there was the pressing matter of money if nothing else. I needed to go to back to work to get paid.

'Just stay, *moro*,' you'd said, as if it were the easiest thing in the world. 'Stay here with me.'

'It's not that simple.'

But why?' you'd seemed frustrated. 'I don't want you to go.'

'Because I have a fight booked and I need to get paid. You know why!'

'You are making excuses,' you said, brows drawing closer as your gaze hardened but I ignored the comment, staring back at you with an expression matching yours. There was nothing I wanted more than to never go home, to simply tear up my ticket like you kept demanding, but it was impossible. I already knew 'tomorrow never comes' as far as you or, come to think of it, any other locals I'd met, were concerned.

'Think about it,' you said, in all seriousness, as you sat back against the beach wall with me between your outstretched legs. 'There is no such thing as tomorrow, only today, so why are you so concerned about it? Tomorrow is a myth.'

You slung a small stone across the beach. I watched its soft thud as it landed.

'Don't be ridiculous.' I picked up a handful of warm, fine sand and let it trickle through my fingers, like an hourglass.

'Look at all these people here.' You'd thrown your palms open wide to make a point as you gesticulated towards the sunbathers nearby. 'They're not thinking about tomorrow.'

No, of course they weren't. They were on holiday. If they had jobs, they were probably on a holiday they'd asked for *permission* to take. They weren't worrying about what Alan, or even worse, Nick, might have to say about going AWOL.

'Stay here with me,' you murmured into my hair as you pulled me in closer. 'Stay forever.'

I sighed, nibbling the skin around my nails as you played with my hair. I couldn't stay forever. I had to think of the future. If you didn't want to work one day, if you felt you had enough money for a while, you'd simply just stop, only to start again when you needed more. That's how it worked out here. It was all so simple for you. I was in the middle of a house sale and a divorce. I had to pay cheques into my bank account. It was all so complicated at home.

I couldn't help feeling jealous Sherri and Elaine still had more time left, knowing you'd see them each day yet I'd be back in England. I frowned. No, it wasn't a myth. Tomorrow was a real thing. It was clouding each day with its inevitability, and it wasn't a little cutesy, fluffy white cloud casting the tiniest shadow across my perfect blue horizon either. It was a great big, black, angry storm cloud of gargantuan proportion completely obliterating the view. If tomorrow wasn't real, how come it was all I could think about?

Back in the apartment, we lay on the balcony, watching the mountains ignite. As the fieriest red and gold trails of sunset fanned out like the tail feathers of a phoenix and the evening sky pulled on its cloak of amber and rose, I began to think. What was the worst that could happen if I stayed for just one more tiny little week? I was going to be in trouble now anyway, regardless of how much more time I took.

Three weeks later, I slunk back into the office, fashionably late for a Monday, trying to be as inconspicuous as possible although aware I was far too brown to achieve that. Darren's jaw was literally hanging, and Lucinda, the sales co-ordinator, nearly fell sideways off her chair.

'What the hell,' she said, her over-made-up eyes widening with a mixture of shock and excitement. 'Oh my God, you are in so much trouble.'

Darren leapt up, neatly steering me into the photocopier room just in time to avoid Alan who was heading for his office with a cuppa and a Bourbon biscuit.

'We thought you weren't coming back. Well, that was after we all assumed you'd been taken seriously ill, or were in hospital, or something.'

I looked at him guiltily.

'I'm so sorry...' I began.

'You *weren't* seriously ill, were you?' Darren was regarding me doubtfully. For a moment I wondered whether I should invent some really debilitating stomach bug, or a rare disease that was mystifying the doctors, when Alan's large form, clad in his best tweed suit, darkened the doorway.

'I think we need a little chat, Melanie.' He wasn't smiling as he led the way to his office. He usually called me Mel.

'Shut the door.'

Alan sat down in his big, leather, swivel chair and indicated to me to sit in the little plastic one opposite, which I did, fervently wishing I wasn't so conspicuously tanned. The only mystery disease I'd be able to invent now would have to be a tropical one. I crossed then uncrossed my brown legs, wriggling uncomfortably on the chair.

He sighed and made a long, protracted, puffing sound like a punctured football. By the jaded expression on his face and the resignation in his tone, he wasn't going to be fobbed off, in fact he appeared beyond angry and had veered somehow into the territory of being 'disappointed' which I really hated. I could deal with angry by being horribly contrite and making promises, but disappointed was a different thing altogether as, despite everything, I really cared about Alan's opinion of me.

'How was your caravanning holiday? Cornwall, wasn't it? Such a beautiful place, stunning coastline.'

'Didn't see much of it. Had to get Doreen to pack everything up double-quick so we could drive all the way back again because Nick asked me to. Do you know why?'

I did. Of course, I did. A large rock fell from inside my chest right down to my bowels.

His fingers tapped on the blotter. There was a bit of Bourbon biscuit caught in his moustache.

'Er, no?' I frowned, mustering as concerned and mystified a look as I could.

'It was because we were seriously down on staff,' he said, looking levelly at me, his eyes never leaving mine. His mouth seemed to have sharpened now and had become visibly narrower, the humour usually twisting its corners no longer present. 'Not enough people to man the office.'

I winced, gripping my hands tightly under the table. Shit. He'd had to cut his holiday short. I hadn't planned on that at all. I felt the heat rising through my silk blouse.

I started frantically trying to explain something about flight delays, misunderstandings, problems at home, no telephone I could use. I threw everything I could at the problem excuse by excuse as I scanned his face to see what, if anything, might be working in my favour but Alan remained impassive. I was fast running out of options but felt the need to keep on talking.

'I suppose it was a crazy thing to do, and I'm really very sorry but—'

'Do you know what I would do if it were up to me?' Alan leaned on his elbow, his chin on his fist, interrupting me before I'd a chance to finish.

I shook my head. I had a feeling I was about to find out.

'If it were up to me,' he said 'I'd think, well, she's a bloody good negotiator, we intend to promote her soon. She's only young and she's going through a divorce.'

I gulped, feeling grateful tears start to well. Alan was such a darling. I would be so much more respectful in future, I really would. That was close. I began to say something, but he silenced me with a lifted hand.

'However,' he continued. 'It isn't up to me, it's up to Nick. He was livid at you taking the piss, so we had a meeting and he said he'd pay you until the end of the month. I am genuinely sorry, Mel.'

I opened my mouth to say something, but I couldn't. Was he sacking me?

To my horror, tears began to prickle so I sniffed frantically, using the back of my index finger to stem the tide which was threatening to escape down my nostrils.

My mind whirred into action. Sherri had taken a sabbatical. Anything was better than this, even unpaid time off.

'Alan, I know this is a bit irregular, but what if I took a short...sabbatical? How would you feel about three-months, unpaid of course, so I could sort my head out? Then I could come back in the New Year, ready to start again.'

I was aware I was pleading but I didn't care. Pride was overrated anyway. I feared losing my job, but, most of all, I feared rejection. All my old insecurity buttons were being firmly pushed.

Alan fished in his desk drawer, and leaned over, pushing a small packet of Kleenex into my hand. I could smell his favourite YSL cologne, the one we'd all clubbed together to buy him for Christmas.

'If it were up to me, I'd say yes, why the hell not. She's an asset to us and, after all, we all do crazy things at times when we have personal problems to contend with. We've all been young and in love.'

Was he softening slightly? Taking in a deep gulp of air, I blew my nose loudly and somewhat unattractively.

'*However,*' he continued. He seemed to like saying that word. 'Nick would say it wasn't crazy at all, it was selfish and irresponsible. He would also say you're not young, you're nearly 30, and he would definitely say personal problems or not, you should have been more considerate.'

I squidged the damp Kleenex into a *papier mâché* ball, knowing much of this hypothetical conversation had probably already taken place. There was no more to add, nothing left to argue with, no room for further persuasion. So much for being able to negotiate. I stared miserably back at him. I'd always got on so well with Alan. He'd been my mentor in this industry, almost a father figure and he'd taught me so much, but, far worse, he'd always put his unwavering trust in me and showed so much faith in my ability. I was letting him down. For a moment, my first day flashed back when I'd had to undergo psychometric testing.

'*Well, well, I've not seen this for quite a while,*' he'd beamed, when he'd analysed mine. *'This is a manager's graph. We have a born leader here.'*

He stood up.

'I'm really sorry Mel but, with the greatest of regret, I'm afraid this is the end of the road as far as your career with Jackson and James goes.'

I nodded and stood up too. There was nothing more I could say. As he walked me to the door, he patted my shoulder, smiling ruefully at me.

'I do hope your Greek chap is worth it.'

Stunned, I walked back into the main office, aware of several pairs of eyes on me. Darren tactfully picked up the phone and began dialling, busying himself in anything to prevent having to engage with his red-eyed, mascara-smeared colleague. Lucinda was not cut of the same cloth. She regarded me with delighted interest as I clicked open my briefcase and began piling in my pen, notebook, and assorted bits of tat from my desk drawer. Lu loved a drama.

'Are you alright?' she asked with barely disguised glee as I ripped my stick-on furry gonk from my word processor and shoved my Bryan Ferry mug into my handbag.

'I'm fine.' I said sharply, popping my Filofax shut and chucking it on top of everything else in my case before flipping down the catches. I was anything but, however I wasn't letting her have the satisfaction of knowing the truth.

'It's all good.' I forced a smile.

'Can I have that?' she said, eyeing my gold embossed leather blotter opportunistically. I'd beaten her to win it in a target competition last year. I don't think she'd ever forgiven me.

'Help yourself.'

'If you want my advice,' she snatched it quickly off my now empty desk, oozing so much fake concern it was quite nauseating. 'If you want *my* advice, you should get yourself straight down to Alfred Marks and register for temping. There will be lots going in the run up to Christmas, like shop and factory work. If you want my advice, and you're not too fussy, they'll be able to find you something. They probably won't care if you've been...*sacked*...or anything.'

She was loving this.

'Lucinda,' I said with the sweetest of smiles, aware Matt was now watching this debate with interest, along with Darren, whose mind was clearly not on his sales call. 'If I wanted your advice, I'd have asked for it. So, with the greatest of respect, keep your great big, ugly, foundation-caked nose out of it.'

Her mouth gaped at this, and I had the satisfaction of seeing her turn puce under her bronzer, right up to her peroxided hairline.

I walked out of the office like a queen, head held high. At the door, I turned back, noting the genuine concern in Darren's and Matt's faces.

'Bye, guys, see you sometime.'

I blew them a little kiss.

Matt wiggled his fingers in a sorrowful wave as Darren made a telephone gesture with his right hand.

'Call me,' he mouthed.

I nodded, but I knew I wouldn't.

Face set, I tip tapped back up the road in my black patent stilettos and my pencil skirt suit. The lunchtime street was heaving with people, sixth formers from the comprehensive milling about, mums weaving in and out with pushchairs, buses hissing to a hydraulic halt, their doors swinging open with deep, mechanical exhales. The lady from the opticians was leaving the café with her customary morning Chelsea bun and heading briskly back to the shop. I usually spoke to her, but I walked straight past. She was part of my old life, and I had a new one to negotiate now.

As I rounded the corner, I felt a tiny pang of regret as I passed the little red Nova I normally used. I would have had the promised holy grail of a company Cavalier had I been promoted. All the negotiators either had little Vauxhall hatchbacks or a mileage allowance. I already had my own car, a nearly new Ford Escort, but rather than rack up the mileage and faff about with the complexity of the petrol expense forms, I preferred to use the pool car. It almost felt like mine anyway as no one else used it. I smiled at its registration number, the last three letters, GBY, were the reason I'd nicknamed it Gabby. Now they just looked like they read 'Goodbye'.

'Bye' I whispered stroking a regretful palm over its bonnet on my way past.

Then I noticed a familiar shape in a Donegal suit. Alan was unlocking his metallic blue Sierra and throwing his case onto the passenger seat, before heading off on an appointment. As I came up alongside, he held his arms out wide.

'Come here,' he said.

Putting my bag and briefcase on the pavement, I hugged him.

'Sorry,' I murmured into his tweed shoulder. It seemed so inadequate under the circumstances, but I really meant it and I think he knew.

'Me too,' he said, shaking his head. 'Damn shame. You were Branch Manager material you know.'

'I've really enjoyed working with you, you've taught me so much. Thank you for everything Alan and, for what it's worth, I really am sorry.'

'Please keep in touch,' he said, holding me at arm's length, smiling kindly as I nodded in agreement. 'I'd like to think we're friends now. Drop me a postcard or something once you're back on your island?'

'I will.' I promised.

As soon as I was home, I decided on my next course of action. I still had about a hundred pounds in my savings account, and I was being paid until the end month. It would certainly help, but I'd need more. Grabbing the yellow pages in the hallway, an advert caught my eye - We Buy Any Car for Immediate Cash. I also had a copy of Loot in my briefcase. Opening the salmon pink pages, I found a number for the free ads and quickly listed my overhead portable sunbed unit, my leather coat and unwanted items of jewellery, shoes, and clothing.

Within forty minutes, I was standing out on the pavement while a grunting primate in oil-stained jeans poked around under the bonnet of my precious white Mark III Ford Escort, the first decent car I'd ever owned. This was going to hurt. I knew I could probably put it in the paper and sell it for around £2,000. It was the only thing of real value I had but it had to go. I hadn't got the luxury of time. I was planning an escape.

He finally emerged, then walked all around, kicking the tyres, and pushed up and down on the boot to test the suspension.

'Hmm... one tyre's near the mark, you know—'

'There's nearly a year's road tax though.'

'Hmm.'

He said that quite a lot.

'So how much were you thinking?' He stroked his chin thoughtfully.

'Well, as I said when we spoke on the phone, I'd like about £1,800 for it.' He shook his head.

'Can't do it, love. I've got to make a profit, you know.'

'It's a lovely car.' I maintained eye contact with him, while inching the neckline of my silk blouse down a bit in an attempt to distract him with my cleavage. 'One careful lady driver.'

He said nothing, so I tried again.

'How about £1,700 then?' I'd definitely take that. I wanted a quick sale, and even though knew I'd get more if I sold it privately, waiting for buyers would take time. I hoped I didn't sound too desperate.

He shook his head, backing away from the car, jiggling his keys impatiently. Neither of us spoke. He might be a salesperson, but so was I...or at least, I had been. We appeared to have reached an impasse. Little spit spots of rain were beginning to fall from the clouding sky as he reached inside his jacket pocket and slowly pulled out a large, dog-eared wodge of notes.

'How about £1,400? I've got the cash right here.'

It was worth far more, we both knew it, but there was something about seeing the bundle of purple and brown notes all bound in a blue elastic band which made my heart pound and blood pulse in my ears. It was a lot of money.

'What do you think?' he fanned the bundle up and down with a thick, oily thumb, his eyes never leaving mine. Now he was up close, they seemed a bit too close together, which, combined with his overly long jaw, gave him a vaguely baboonish look.

He wafted the bundle under my nose. It literally smelled of power and one-upmanship, a slightly sour, cigarette-papery, metallic aroma, reeking of desire, desperation and control.

'My car's worth far more than that.' I said.

I knew its value. I was certainly not going to be selling myself, or my car, short to such a degree. Yes, I needed money, but I was not *desperate*. I felt disappointed and annoyed in equal measures. What did he take me for?

The following morning, I walked into Nationwide Building Society, deposited £1,400 into my savings account, then popped an envelope containing my green DVLA slip into the post box. Crossing the road, I stepped into the now familiar office of Thomas Cook to see Brenda.

10

Money's Too Tight To Mention

The flight had been half empty, because the previous day, there had been a magnitude 5.9 earthquake on a neighbouring island. At the check in desk, the airport staff advised against all but essential travel to Aftonisi and explained how passengers could get refunds or alternative flights but, undeterred, I explained my flight was essential. It was essential to me I saw you. I was so excited to get out into the Greek sunshine again and feel its heat on my face after two weeks in cold, damp Southampton.

Before I'd left, I'd been for an interview at Benningtons Department Store to work on the cosmetics counter for the run up to Christmas. I needed the money and loved the idea of getting paid for playing with makeup all day long, so I'd agreed a start date of mid-November.

I'd hardly seen Rob which had suited me just fine. I'd written a cheque for my share of the household bills and mortgage, and had paid it into the joint account. There'd been quite a bit of interest in the house, so I was hopeful we'd both have some money again soon. Ironically, it was on with Jackson and James as Alan had very kindly agreed to still honour my previous staff discount on sales fees

'I'll say it slipped my mind if anyone asks,' he'd said, with a little twinkle, giving my arm a fatherly pat. It felt odd being a client, a vendor, instead of an employee.

It had been a strange time, living a half-life without the anchor of a job but I'd managed to sell all the things I'd listed on Loot, giving me a little nest egg. All I'd thought about was getting on a train to Gatwick and flying back out to you and I was beyond excited this time it would be for a whole, perfect month.

You'd sent me wonderful letters again, full of plans and of hope.

'Come back in October and stay for as long as you like. In the summer you can work here. I have friends with bars, restaurants, and hotels. You can easily get a job and we can be together.'

I knew I wanted an English Christmas, but beyond that, I didn't care. I just wanted to be with you. I had the promise of money thanks to the Benningtons job, I'd banked the proceeds of my car and the Loot advert, and soon the house would sell, so I formulated plans and hugged then tightly inside like they were real, tangible things; a delicious secret which made me glow.

When I was settled in the apartment, I was thrilled to learn Sherri was also back.

'How long are you staying?' she asked me through a tight hug and a veil of her trademark Body Shop Vanilla scent when she and Petros came by. 'I'm here for two weeks then going back on the very last tourist flight out.'

'November,' I said. 'I fly back via Athens on the 17th and start a Christmas job on the 21stth.'

'A whole month. You are so lucky!'

I was, indeed. Beyond lucky. The job would take me through to lunchtime on Christmas Eve then I planned on cadging a lift to London with my cousin Greg and his family.

I couldn't resist telling Sherri all about how you'd suggested I came out in the New Year and got a summer job when the season started, hoping she wouldn't be too envious. I was still trying to work out whether I'd have enough money to last me until April, when she said something completely unexpected.

'Petros asked me the same thing.' Her face was flushed with excitement.

'We could both get an apartment together if you like, jobs too. Wouldn't that be amazing.'

I grinned at her. This couldn't be more perfect.

You'd seemed uncharacteristically quiet during dinner, as did Petros. Was something wrong? You'd both spent a lot of time at the bar, your heads melded together in deep discussion leaving Sherri and I sat together alone, wondering what we'd done wrong. Something didn't feel quite right. Then Petros went back with Sherri to her room at the Iliad Apartments after dinner leaving us alone together.

'*Pamē.*' You kicked your bike into life, and, with me clinging to your jacket, flew off up the road. You were still so quiet. As we zipped past bars and clubs, I noticed many were now closed so I mentioned it in an attempt to make you more talkative.

'It's the end of the season, *moro*, what did you expect?' There was an uncharacteristic snap in your voice. 'In two more weeks, there will be no beach restaurants open. Get used to it.'

You weren't usually so tetchy. I raised an eyebrow in the dark at your crankiness, rolling my eyes. It hadn't occurred to me the entire resort would change but, of course it would. The tourists would be gone, and it would become like a ghost town; a vastly quieter backwater locals would only pass through on their way to villages like Stavouna where they lived.

Back in the room, instead of ripping and pulling at clothes, we undressed quietly in the dark, barely speaking. You didn't seem the same, you seemed preoccupied.

Later, sitting on the balcony watching the stars twinkle through the vast blackness and breathing in that magical night air smell of heat and mountain herbs, the silence between us was heavy and loaded, like a truck full of quarry stone.

Time dragged like an anchor, then you turned to me.

'*Moro*, I have my papers.' Your expression was serious.

'Papers?' I stared at you, blankly. What were papers?

'My army service. Conscription.'

I knew you'd have to go one day as you'd explained once a Greek man was nineteen and until they were forty-five, they could be called up at any time for national service, but it could take years. I had no idea it would be this soon.

'When?' I felt like the breath had been knocked out of my body.

'Just after *Theofáneia*.'

I just stared back at you. *Theofáneia* was the sixth of January. You were going to be leaving me before we'd even really started.

'How long for?'

'Nine months.' You sounded resigned, yet resentful. 'I'll have basic training for six weeks then I will go to an army base in Kos.' You spat out a piece of matchstick you'd been chewing.

Nine months! That was a lifetime to me. Nine weeks would be bad enough and where the hell was Kos?

You'd seen my face by then, and tried to reassure me.

'*Moro*, by this time next year, it will all be over.'

Somewhat selfishly, my first thoughts were for me. In a matter of months, you'd be gone but what about the plans we'd made for me coming back in the summer? We'd talked about my working in a bar or restaurant. I'd just become used to this craziness, the backwards and forwards of it all, the flights out of Gatwick, the National Express coaches, the chaos, the hazy excitement of the future. Everything was anaesthesia for my issues at home. Was it all coming to an end? I didn't know how I'd survive without it.

'But I was going to come back out and stay for the summer,' was all I could manage before a great big stone lodged in my throat and my voice began to crack.

'I can't ask you to come now,' you said, miserably, pulling me in close and kissing my hair. 'It's not fair. I won't be here.'

My dreams were dying. All the things I'd planned, all my hopes and wishes, were vanishing, fading away in just the same way the furnace-hot summer was fading into winter and, just like the changing seasons, there wasn't a thing I could do about it.

'What if I came anyway, though?' I didn't know exactly where this was going but I needed to say it. The stone wall I was resting against felt cold and hard against my spine.

'You would be on your own here. I can't make you do this.'

'You're not making me. I want to.'

A spiral of panic was rising inside me.

You considered this for a moment, as you sat on the unyielding floor, pulling your legs in towards your chest, bowing your head onto your knees. Then, after what seemed like an eternity, you finally lifted your face.

'You know I can't make you do this. If you did, you would be here alone.'

'I don't care.'

I would rather be alone on your island, knowing I'd at least see you when you came back on leave, than be back in Southampton. Alone wasn't a physical situation, it was a state of mind. It seemed such a long time before you spoke again.

'But I don't know how I would cope, knowing you'd be here, and I wouldn't.'

None of that mattered to me. I hadn't thought for one moment about how hard it all might be for you because all that was important to me was following this crazy dream I was addicted to. I needed that high, I craved my drug. It would work. It had to.

I don't know how long we sat there, arguing, not reaching any firm decision, the sounds of the everyday Lathos drifting carelessly up from the roadside until you finally spoke.

'It wouldn't be easy. I wouldn't know when I'd get leave, or for how long.'

'Yes, but I'd be here, ready for whenever you came back,' I argued. 'Sherri said she's coming too so I won't be alone.' I dug my nails into my palms, fervently hoping Petros hadn't just had a similar conversation with her to make her change her mind.

My breath was tight and shallow. Why weren't you answering me?

Eventually you spoke.

'Okay, we could try. Maybe knowing you are waiting here for me will make me stronger.'

You seemed quite animated as you took my hand and pulled me over to sit between your legs, wrapping me in your arms. As far as evenings went, it felt perfect despite all the unexpected worry.

'When I am done, I will finish the bar, but I want us to run it together now. It will be ours.' You gripped my hand tightly in yours. 'Listen, I want to do this with you. Our bar, *moro.* I have never met anyone like you before. You are the only girl I've ever trusted, so I am asking you to wait for me. Will you do this?'

Your dark, gold-flecked eyes were searching for an answer in mine. You trusted me. My head was whirling. I'd be leaving the everyday life I knew far behind me. I hadn't really considered beyond the summer season before.

'Yes.' I didn't hesitate for even one second. 'Yes, I will.'

'You mean this?'

'Yes.'

'And when you come, you will wait here and be a good girl when I am in Kos? You won't let me down?'

You lifted the little gold charm you'd hung around my neck and looked searchingly at me. The answer was easy.

'I could never let you down.'

'Elsa said she would wait for Sakis when he was in the army she...' a pinch of distaste on your lips, 'but she was a whore.'

The word whore was a jarring shock. It jagged across our emotional conversation like a needle skipping the surface of a record, making me recoil for a second. I'd never heard you speak so disparagingly of a woman before, but I understood you were desperate to make a point.

'You must promise me.'

There was so much intensity in your eyes.

'I promise.'

Before I go any further, you need to understand something. In that moment, I'd really meant it. I didn't make promises lightly. I wasn't just saying what you wanted to hear. I'd meant it, more than anything I'd ever said before. In that moment.

11

Long Hot Summer

Waves were crawling up the sand then receding again, trailing tiny shells in their wake as we sat on the beach the next morning, the warmth of your arms around me as intense as the heat of the sun. Light glanced off the water, blinding me for a moment. You were looking at your Swatch and looking back towards the road. Then, a battered white truck turned off the track, veering directly towards us, spraying sand as its wheels spun. As it came to a halt, an older man in work clothes and dirty boots climbed out, leaving the engine running. A radio was blaring Greek music as he lazily meandered up to us.

You leapt to your feet and the two of you embraced, back clapping and hugging. You were chattering animatedly to each other, and looking over at me, so I stood up, suddenly conscious of my revealing bikini top and little denim shorts. I was glad I'd not been sunbathing as I would have been wearing far less. The strange man turned to me and slowly appraised me, looking me up and down, making me feel like something swinging from a butcher's hook as his eyes came to rest on my breasts for longer than I was strictly comfortable with.

Then he came right up close and pinched my cheek. It was wholly unexpected and quite painful. While I was reeling from this, a slow, partly toothless grin spread across his tanned face and he clapped me to his sweaty T-shirt with great enthusiasm, muttering something I only partly understood in Greek which included *omorfos kopella,* beautiful girl. He then prodded my one of my hips with a bony finger, grinned somewhat suggestively at you, and slapped you on your back, laughing loudly.

You were grinning at me.

Outwardly I smiled politely. I didn't want to offend, and you seemed to like him, but inwardly I was furious. Who the bloody hell was this?

You seemed amused at my shocked face.

'Meet your father-in-law,' you joked.

This was your *father*? I recovered my composure, and, quickly covering my cleavage with the spread of my palm, I said *yassou,* as politely as I could, while worrying *yassou* might be considered too familiar. Should I have said *yassas* instead?

My cheek was still smarting from the assault when your father then pinched me again, this time, he pincered the flesh from the upper part of my arm sharply between his thumb and forefinger before saying to me:

'Too thin, eat.'

Then he strolled back to his truck, hopped in, and reversed up the beach at a terrifying speed, disappearing in a cloud of sand, dust and Greek folksongs.

Soon I was constantly being stopped by other members of your extended family introducing themselves to me in broken English. These were mainly cousins, several rather confusingly also called Marios due to the Greek tradition of naming children after grandparents. But of them all, your father had somehow become omnipresent. I couldn't avoid him. Everywhere I went, he'd be there, wandering by, looking over, appraising me quietly. He kept his distance, but I'd be treated to the full wattage of his leering grin if we made eye contact. Thankfully, there was no more pinching.

'Your father pinched me,' I'd said, hugely affronted. 'He pinched my cheek…and my arm.'

I'd pulled a face to illustrate the point. You hadn't seemed remotely perturbed, so I'd rubbed my arm for added emphasis. I couldn't imagine my own father ever doing that. For all his faults, Harold Wright was a gentleman so he most certainly wouldn't have pinched anyone. With my buttoned-up, reserved, somewhat insular father, you'd have been lucky to even get a nod of the head. At best, if you were really in favour, you might have been afforded a handshake. The most I'd ever had from him was an awkward pat on the shoulder.

You'd just laughed.

'He likes you, *moro*,' you said emphatically. 'I like you.' And with that, you'd lifted me up and swung me around in your bear arms until I was laughing with you, until we fell in a heap on the sand, until you silenced my giggles with one of your kisses. What on earth would your father have done if he *hadn't* liked me?

The one elusive member of your family I had yet to meet was your mother. I had no idea whether she even knew of my existence, although I assumed so, given that your father and your older cousins now had me under constant surveillance.

Extended families were the norm in Greece, particularly on islands like Aftonisi where things were more provincial, whereas in England they were far less so. Greek boys were often expected to remain at home until they married and, even afterwards, their mothers were still very much in charge. Girlfriends were certainly not 'brought home' or, indeed, even introduced to mothers unless something very serious was imminent.

I did wonder what excuses you made when you stayed over in the apartment with me. I was very aware it couldn't be every night. Sometimes you left very late, and sometimes early, just the pink stain of dawn rising over the sea. Dragging your clothes on and quickly kissing me as I stirred through a half dream, you'd promise to be back later before rumbling off on your bike. I'd lie back in the crumple of our bed, still dented with your warmth, listening to your engine accelerate into the early morning light, the sound rising and falling, then growing fainter until it was no more than the indistinct buzz of an insect as you snaked your way up the mountain road.

I wasn't sure what your mother would have made of me, a woman several years older than her beloved eldest and a near-divorcee too; a woman in eyeliner and shorts who drank beer in bars and sunbathed topless on the beach. Only a few years earlier, such a woman would have been considered a *putana*, a prostitute. It certainly hadn't occurred to me at the time what a big deal it was that you'd introduced me to your father as I was still viewing everything through the free and easy lens of British culture where such a meeting would have been commonplace.

Did you actually realise at this point in our relationship, I wasn't really thinking beyond living for the moment...even if I wanted that moment to go on forever. I'd conveniently forgotten the past, I wasn't looking too far into the future, and I was enjoying the present, feeling freer and happier than I had for a long time. I had money in the bank, a job for Christmas, and there'd be something owed to me when the house went through. I wouldn't be legally divorced for another two years, but that didn't matter to me at all. Rob and I were over. The divorce was just a piece of paper. It wouldn't stop me being with you.

One late afternoon we were sitting with Sherri and Petros in a bar in Aftonisi Town, watching the sun slowly melting into the harbour, when Sakis pulled up on his bike with Elaine plumped on behind him. 'Yassou,' he said, unsmiling as always. His lower lip hung down, making him look like a codfish. Sakis had one of those unfortunate faces where nothing seemed to fit: eyes set a little too far apart, a forehead which sloped like a Neanderthal, and a fleshy mouth crammed with teeth which appeared to be trying to escape. I had no idea what Elaine saw in him. I couldn't find a single redeeming feature about him physically, but Elaine liked him which was all that mattered.

Elaine alighted from her pillion seat, legs striped with red sunburn, face glistening with sweat, hair somewhat dishevelled from the ride.

'Hey,' she greeted us. 'Sakis said you'd be here, so we came to find you. Thought we could all have some pizza?'

Oh God, not more pizza. I'd eaten nothing but cheese and tomato pizza for days. I might as well have been called Margarita.

You, Sakis and Petros all began chattering loudly in Greek, shouting out the odd sentence I understood as it filtered through to me. I found it amusing how Greeks always sounded like they were always arguing frantically, that it was all about to escalate when it was, in fact, just a conversation.

'We'll get pizza,' you decided, getting up and making towards Sakis, not waiting for my opinion. I already knew it was a foregone conclusion, I wasn't getting a choice, so I waited for Sherri and then we began to follow as you made across the street, your purposeful stride behind Petros's pumped form as he surged ahead, Sakis loping behind like an ape.

Elaine grinned at us both.

'Come on then.' She waited for us as we dawdled behind. 'I'm starving. I could eat a scabby horse.' Then, with an ungainly gallop, she caught up with Sakis, grabbing him by the hand to sling his arm around her shoulder, leaning into him as they walked, her sensible brown leather sandals scuffing the pavement.

'*Ela, moro, viasyni*,' you called back, so, Sherri and I hurried as instructed, picking up speed to trot along behind.

Aftonisi Town, with its elegantly arched Venetian buildings, paved walkways and profusion of manicured floral borders, was such a contrast to Lathos it might as well have been in a completely different country. In Lathos, you wouldn't be at all surprised to see a herd of sheep ambling aimlessly up the road, or a family of four all piled onto one moped, the smallest balanced on the handlebars. Donkeys were commonplace in the street.

Whatever transport method was available at the time was the one you took. The cars I'd seen in Lathos were battered, hand-painted heaps held together with little more than filler. They'd have looked perfectly at home in a stock car race, whereas those in town were the ever-present fleet of taxis or the latest, sleek models, many of which had foreign numberplates.

Glossy yachts studded the harbourside, their sleek, white prows and polished wood decks glinting in the sunlight, a contrast to the tourist boats crossing the horizon at Lathos, or the fishing boats anchored further inland, bobbing and dipping with the swell of the water.

We all headed to a pavement cafe where I scanned the extensive menu. The Ionian islands had been ruled by the Venetians for three hundred years and one of their legacies was a very eclectic cuisine, a hybrid of Italian and Greek, with a profusion of delicious pasta dishes. I really didn't want pizza, but I knew you'd be offended if I didn't have something. As you'd still expect me to eat with you again that evening, I chose the simplest option, Calamari.

Elaine had already decided.

'Having a Spag Bol,' she announced, 'None of that Parmesan muck though, it smells like sick.'

Exchanging furtive glances with Sherri, I saw you pull a face as you looked sternly over your menu at her. Elaine didn't have any conception of social niceties whatsoever.

She leaned over the table towards us while we sipped our Perrier and limes, seeming unusually bright eyed. For a moment I could imagine exactly what she looked like as a child. Sakis had lit up a cigarillo. Its pungent flavour invaded my nostrils so strongly I might as well have been smoking it myself.

Elaine's excitement was palpable, which was something unusual for her. 'You'll never guess what.'

Sakis's fleshy lips parted into what nearly passed as a smile as she beamed at him. I tried to work out what was going on from his wide, simian leer as he draped himself proprietorially over her shoulder, leaning in so close that Elaine appeared to have two heads.

She was about to speak when the waiter arrived with a tray full of plates, Spaghetti for her, pizza for everyone else and a sizzling plate of delicious, battered Calamari for me. I picked up a piece with my fingers and put it to my lips, but it was too hot. Regretfully I dropped it back onto the plate. The Calamari would have to wait.

'So, what's going on then?' I dabbed my mouth with a napkin.

Elaine gave a small, uncharacteristic squeak, as though she'd sat on something sharp, making a couple deep in conversation at the next table look up.

'Well….'

She wriggled in her seat, literally shimmering with excitement. Alarmed, my eyes darted from her to Sakis. He hadn't asked her to marry him, or something, had he?

'Go on...'

She took a massive mouthful of spaghetti and began slurping it up, the ends protruding like walrus tusks from her mouth.

'So, the farm shop had to let me go.'

Sherri and I frowned. Why was she pleased about losing her job? Surely it wasn't a good thing? I flinched inwardly, thinking of my conversation with Alan.

I instinctively put my hand on hers as she squelched through her pasta.

'Elaine, I'm so sorry.'

Splodges of Bolognese sauce were dappling the tablecloth now as she shovelled in more. I nibbled daintily at my Calamari.

'No, it's not like that. I'm taking voluntary redundancy. They're giving me quite a lot of money actually because I've worked there for ages.' She finished another mouthful then glanced at Sakis tentatively. 'Anyway, because I want to run my own business one day, I've enquired about going to university next year to study business.'

She paused to twirl more spaghetti. Elaine was literally glowing. I'd never seen her so alive.

Sakis was looking confrontationally at her.

'I keep telling you, help me to run *my* business, moré. You don't need to learn from books at school.'

'But your business is just holiday apartments, silly,' Elaine retorted, 'and you haven't even finished building them, so there isn't even anything for me to run yet.'

Sakis's expression darkened. He picked his teeth with the corner of a beermat.

'But nothing's decided about school is it, moré? You might not get in. It's a waste of time. We can use that money for when you're here.'

Elaine's earlier buoyancy disappeared as she sunk into herself like a deflated soufflé.

'Well, no, I haven't formally applied yet.' She flushed, wavering for a moment, glancing anxiously back at him. 'They did say I met the criteria though and I've always wanted a degree but nothing's definite. I'd only meant, I might...'

'No, you must, Elaine.' I couldn't help jumping in. I saw your eyes narrow momentarily but I didn't care. Sakis was annoying me, deliberately pissing all over her fireworks and I just couldn't let him get away with it. I shot him a look. 'A chance of university is a big deal, Elaine. Don't give up on your dreams. You could be the next...' I searched for female entrepreneurs to cite. 'The next Jacqueline Gold or Anita Roddick!'

Elaine flushed red to match her peeling nose.

'Do you really think?'

Sherri and I nodded enthusiastically, telling her yes, absolutely she could.

'Anyway...,' She beamed at Sakis as he continued to glare hard at me. 'The course doesn't start until the autumn so, first, I'm coming out here for the whole of the summer!'

I nearly swallowed my piece of Calamari whole.

'So are we!' said Sherri

'That's settled then.' Elaine splattered through another mouthful of spaghetti. 'We'll all get somewhere together. It will be fun.'

'This good, though,' you said to me later when I voiced my reservations. 'Now you'll have someone to be with when I am away. You will have friends here and won't be alone, so I don't have to worry so much.'

You were right. I'd never shared with girls before. I'd either lived with Mum and Dad, or with Rob, so this would be something completely different. A bit like a flat share but in the sun and, thinking ahead, you were right. A support network could only be a positive thing. I was a sociable person, I liked having friends and considered Sherri a good one now and even though Elaine still wasn't my type of person, I had seen a slightly different side of her today. We'd all be in a similar position. Sherri and I would have boyfriends in the army, so we'd understand each other, and as for Elaine? Well, I was hopeful there'd be *some* common ground. I'd have preferred it to have been just me and Sherri, like we'd originally planned, but that wouldn't have been fair on Elaine. I just hoped that Sakis wouldn't be around all the time.

12

Lessons In Love

In late October, once most of the holidaymakers had flown home, Lathos took on a very different persona. It vibrated with a completely different energy, barely recognisable from the holiday resort it had once been. The locals were always relaxed and unhurried anyway, with everything always put off until *avrio*, tomorrow but now this had all dialled down considerably. Everyone seemed even slower, lazier than ever, everything was sleepy and quiet.

It drove me mad. I was used to far more energy and action. In my opinion, this was the difference between living in a predominantly cold country as opposed to one which was so hot your skin literally fried like a charred aubergine on a barbecue at times.

When I'd lived at home, I'd always loathed Sundays. Sundays were endlessly dull. They represented the world coming to a complete standstill. Our town's identity completely changed on a Sunday, with no shops open and nothing much to do.

Dad was always at home on Sundays too, casting his brooding presence over everything, usually criticising me, not allowing me to question him. Questioning, in Dad's book, was arguing.

Little girls should be seen and not heard.

'You always have to have the last word, don't you, Melanie,' he'd complain, before shutting me down.

Dad used an expression when referring to my appearance, my efforts, anything I did, really: '*quite* nice' - with the emphasis on the first word, not the second. '*Quite* nice', rather than 'quite *nice*'. A whole world of difference in where the inflection was placed.

Sundays were never my favourite day, and now, Lathos seemed just the same, stuck on an endless loop of Sundays with no escape.

The beach, however, had taken on a new kind of beauty now things were quiet. It had become a meeting place for locals. The young teenage boys of the village turned a section into a bike run with a makeshift jump made from a plank of wood and a couple of old oil drums. It became where they all gathered with their bicycles and skateboards, sometimes an older brother came with a motorbike and the beach buzzed into life as a speedway, latticed with tyre tracks.

Just before dusk, village women would stroll lazily onto the beach, hitching their skirts to paddle, or to wade in modest bathing suits. Clustering together, they'd stand and chat until darkness fell, knee or even waist deep in the calm, dark sea until all I could see was the slope of their shoulders and their sleek heads nodding like seals.

Like pinpricks in a black veil, a sky full of stars would shimmer above us and the chatter from the sea would gradually quieten until all we could hear was the rhythmic swoosh of the waves and the occasional cry or shriek from someone who was still in the water.

Sherri went back to England at the end of the following week, on the last tourist flight out. It was the end of the month, Halloween, and we all went to say goodbye to her at the airport. Just you and me, Petros, and Elaine. Sakis was working on his apartments, and I can't say I was sorry. We asked a passing tourist to take a photograph of us all together with your camera. A bittersweet day.

'Look after Petros for me,' she instructed, giving me a warm embrace. She clung on for longer than I expected, her cloud of vanilla perfume enveloping me, leaving me feeling quite lost and alone once she'd heaved up her backpack, and given us all a cheery wave. Feeling strangely empty after she'd disappeared through departures, I turned to you, a lump in my throat. I'd miss her so much. I knew Elaine would still be there a little longer, but we weren't really *friends*, and she never did anything without Sakis. It just wouldn't be the same without Sherri.

You pulled me in close, searching my face as I blinked rapidly to prevent my view of the airport buildings blurring any further.

'Don't be upset, *agapē mou*,' you said, kissing me. 'Now I have you all to myself.'

I remembered what Sherri had said about looking after Petros.

'But will Petros be alright?'

I didn't really know enough about him to accurately gauge whether he would feel upset without Sherri or whether he'd simply be off on his red Kawasaki, after other women as soon as the plane had taken off.

'Of course.'

'But he'll wait for her, won't he?'

I'm not sure why I said that. Maybe I was feeling the presence of my 'insecurity troll' who lurked within me, making me feel anxious. I'd named it after a troll toy with a fat little belly and a big nose I'd had when I was a child. I'd taken it everywhere with me until Dad had teased me, saying it looked just like me. Being ten and impressionable I'd been devastated. I never played with it again.

'What do you mean, *moré?*'

It was one of those language confusion moments.

'I mean, does he love her, or not?'

'Of course,' you said, most emphatically.

'Of course, what?' I felt frustrated by this barrier in comprehension between us.

'What?' You'd sounded confused.

Oh, good God. I rolled my eyes. This was exasperating.

'He likes her.' You replied dismissively at first, then, as you caught my expression, you hastily corrected yourself. 'He loves her, she's a very beautiful young girl, how could he not?'

I felt horribly insecure. In the corner of my eye, my troll was waiting. Perhaps it was the word 'young'. I was acutely aware of our age difference. It was constantly scratching away under the varnished surface of us, always there, this barb. Or perhaps it was the way you'd emphasised Sherri was beautiful.

I couldn't help myself.

'Do *you* think Sherri is beautiful?'

As soon as I said it, I regretted it, inwardly cursing I'd said anything at all, hoping you couldn't read my expression. With a bit of luck, I'd pass it all off as a language misunderstanding. I fought to keep my expression neutral because I had one of those faces that showed exactly how I felt.

'You can't hide it *moro*,' you'd once said. 'It's on your face, everything you're thinking.'

You looked at me for a moment. I didn't really understand fully why I felt so vulnerable as you'd given me no cause to doubt you. You were nothing like the *Kamaki*, the men who deliberately went out each summer in search of women with just one goal in mind, to have sex with as many as possible then compare scores later. Notches on the bedposts.

You took my hand and pulled me in close to you, holding me tightly for a moment.

'Yes, she's beautiful,' you began, 'but she's only beautiful because she's young.'

All my buttons were being pushed faster than the most industrious stenographer.

'But I'm older than her–'

'But you will always be beautiful because you have something that will last. Something that's not just about being young.'

I bit my lip, wrapping my arms around myself. What did you know? You were twenty-one.

'Listen,' you said. 'It's like this. There are many pretty shells on the beach.'

'So, you're saying I'm just a shell on the beach?' I teased, couldn't resist it, keeping my voice deliberately light, making it a jokey comment. But something was starting to nibble at my insides. There were thousands upon thousands of shells here, on the beach, in the sea, everywhere.

You looked as though you didn't really know what to say. Perhaps you were trying to let me down gently, or wanted to say something you couldn't translate easily.

'Yes, you are like a shell.'

I said nothing, resisting another opportunity to roll my eyes and say 'charming' again, but my flat expression must have registered because you continued.

'But you a special one, because you have a…' You seemed to be searching for a word Eventually you said it in Greek. 'You are a shell with a *margaritari*, a pearl inside.'

Within a week the end of the month came. It was cooler now, more like early English springtime and it was so peaceful sitting on the tourist-free beach with you, breezes drifting across the sea and glints of November sun patching through the clouds as you stroked my face and kissed me, lifting the little gold charm on a chain you'd given me and kissing that too.

'Mine,' you said, holding my gaze, smiling deeply into my eyes.

'Oh, you want it back?' Playfully I pretended to unfasten it.

'Not the chain, *moro*,' you said as you play-wrestled me back to the sand. 'You.'

Sometimes we'd sit there until the enamel blue of the sky became inflamed by the most spectacular orange and red sunset, turning everything, the water, your eyes, and the planes of your face, a deep copper gold.

Then, at this late hour, we would go to eat at one of the smaller, less inspiring, often brutally bare places where only locals ate; places with a scant selection on display you would just point at to be served. Sometimes *Stifado*, a mutton stew, Octopus in sauce, or *Patstitsio*, a kind of lasagne and moussaka hybrid made with large tubes of macaroni. My favourite was *yemista*, oil-glossed oven- baked tomatoes and peppers, their split skins stuffed with meat, rice, and fragrant spices.

Most of these unimposing little eateries were located up rocky mountain roads near the neighbouring resort of Alomenos. I'd lean in behind you on your bike as we bumped over sparse gravel and clay roads, speeding past the dark foliage of cypress trees standing like sentinels on rocky outcrops, often waiting while a herd of sheep lazily clipped across the road. We'd laugh as they bleated, vocally voicing their disapproval at your revving engine, taking all the time in the world. Then you'd lurch away again, the bike whining against the gravel as it continued upwards, the still air giving way to sudden pockets of cold that took me by surprise, making me nestle in closer to you. I'd feel the heat of your body and the strength of your warm hand as you pulled mine in tighter around your waist.

For a moment, as another slap of cold air stung my face and legs, I felt an inexplicable pang of nostalgia for winter in England, for the smoky coal fire at my parents' house, for the red and gold table laden with roast turkey, for the whole tinselled, sequinned, gaudy sparkle of Christmas. But most of all, for snow.

'Does it ever snow here,' I whispered, leaning in towards you.

'Sometimes,' you said. 'Up in the mountains, but there are people who have never seen snow.'

'No way,' I exclaimed at what seemed an impossibility to me.

You laughed. I felt it ripple through your chest, through your warm denim jacket, through to my heart. I didn't want this to end. But something would have to change. Christmas was coming, then the army, so the end of what we had now was coming too.

I knew our time was limited. All this would soon seem a lifetime away, but, melting against you, I tried to let the thoughts go. Leaning my cheek against your shoulder, I closed my eyes and batted the unwanted intrusion away. How often did it snow in England at Christmas anyway?

13

Never Tear Us Apart

In the flick of a gecko's tail, it was my last week. To say I felt unanchored, lost, and really confused about the future was putting it mildly. All I knew was I'd soon be back in Southampton. Benningtons would no doubt be heaving. I'd be so busy I'd hardly have the time to write letters to you and with the kiosk rarely open, how could I even ring you when I wanted?

I missed Sherri's bright bounciness. Elaine was always off somewhere with Sakis, although I'd managed to have another word with her about how rude and dismissive he was to her. I just couldn't understand it. Elaine was quite capable of being outspoken with us but with Sakis, she was a mouse. The more we got to know her, the sparkier she became, but when Sakis was around, she completely changed. I still couldn't help feeling a little resentful towards her. Sakis had already done his army service. Elaine wouldn't be left alone.

The weather was turning slightly cooler and cloudier, and with the novelty of the odd day with great, big splots of rain, the size of tiddlywinks counters, pelting our skin without warning, making everyone run for cover. One afternoon the previously innocuous blue sky we'd taken for granted darkened dramatically to a deep, industrial shade of grey and a massive crack of thunder reverberated across the resort. Within seconds, great needles of rain began to stab the earth, pitting the sand until it looked more like a sheet of hammered metal than a beach, drumming against the stone floors, the concrete roofs and balconies. Palm trees began to brace against the wind as everyone ran to find shelter under any awning, doorway or projection available, wet skin gleaming like vinyl. You'd grabbed my hand and pulled me under a doorway, our soaking wet hands sliding within each other's, hair plastered our faces, shoes drenched. Fork after fork of gothic lightning strobed the sky as thunder cracked over the sea with ever increasing intensity, echoing like a cannon against the mountains.

You'd laughed as more thunder rolled overhead.

'It rains like this in England too?'

'Nothing like this,' I'd said, clinging to you, feeling terrified and excited in equal measure, secretly enjoying the drama. Despite everything, you made me feel safe. It was like being in a video game.

Within minutes, the rain began to change its rhythm. The endless staccato drumming slowed to a gentle tap, the battleship grey sky resumed its usual shade of blue and I began to feel the heat of the sun once more. It was as though someone had turned floodlights on across the resort. The road, the track, the marble floors all began to shimmer and steam as the water dried up. It was over.

We went back to my apartment and put towels on the damp balcony chairs, our feet up on the railings, watching the street below.

'Everything's so quiet,' I'd sighed, pointing at one of the now closed bars just across the road.

'Ah, it's winter now,' you'd said with a laugh. 'This is normal, island life. You must get used to this, *moro*.'

In my mind, this was not winter at all. November was autumn. I'd tried to discuss this with you once, but you claimed there was no such thing as autumn. Certainly not in Lathos, anyway.

'Summer is when the tourists come, and we work, *moro*,' was all you'd said, 'Then the tourists go, we pick olives, its winter, and we stop work'. It was all so simple to you. I explained autumn was one of my favourite times of year. In England, all the trees turned gold, red, copper. Their leaves fell, rustling underfoot, the air was crisp and cold, mists descended, smoke from bonfires and log burners was everywhere, and the pre-Christmas build up was setting in. I tried to explain that new term feeling of excitement that would rise giddily within me, tried to explain autumn started in September; that winter didn't begin until December, but you had absolutely no concept of what I was trying to say.

The thought of blackberry picking, making apple crumble, crunching through fallen leaves on the roadside, was making me feel quite melancholy. I sighed as I leaned over the railings. It didn't seem all that long ago we'd all sat across the road under Helios Bar's shaded vines, drinking Metaxa in the hum of a warm, dark evening.

I'd gradually become used to the language you all spoke. Not every word made sense, but things were gradually forming, assimilating, clarifying. It was as though someone was drawing back a curtain. I was beginning to understand. My listening skills meant I would catch more and more conversation, but my understanding was far better than my spoken or reading ability. Everything was always delivered way too fast for me, but I was determined to at least get by.

The sigh must have been louder than I had intended.

'Ti simveni, what's the matter, moro?'

'Ah, its nothing,' I shrugged 'Dhen xero, I don't know. I just miss how things used to be.'

I pointed across the road to Kerry and Panayiotis's now closed bar. Goats were bleating in the field behind the supermarket, somewhere, further up, the buzz of a motorbike, and the insistent bark of Mr Mavrakis's Vizsla. The sea breeze was rustling through the dry fronds of the palm trees, a world away from busy Southampton streets with their traffic jams, petrol fumes and surges of office workers crowding the chewing-gum studded pavement. You just gave me a squeeze, tapped at your lip with a fingertip so I would reach up to kiss you, and led me back through the balcony doors into my room, closing the shutters. The room was warm and dark, shutter light latticing our naked skin as you pinned me beneath you, your sweat drenching me, my mouth bruised by the crush of your lips.

Afterwards, we opened the shutters, drowning in late afternoon sunlight, but then you dragged on your clothes, saying you had something to do but would be back soon.

'Get dressed quickly. Be ready for when I get back'.

I scurried around, showering, selecting a favourite outfit of a red, ankle length cotton skirt and a cropped black bodice. Where were we going? It was too early to eat. After drawing on strips of black eyeliner I found my denim jacket as it got cold on the bike sometimes before brushing through my now dry hair, so it fell around my shoulders. Usually just boring brown, it was becoming lighter with sun streaks. I wondered how long I'd hang on to those free highlights once I was home.

Sitting at the kitchen table, I put my INXS tape into my portable stereo, thankful it also took batteries because the electricity kept dropping out, when you bounded exuberantly up the stairs like an excitable puppy.

'*Pamē*, let's go.' You grabbed me by the hand.

I made to pick up my jacket and bag.

'You don't need,' you said, pulling me down the stairs from the apartment and out onto the street, where, right in the middle of the road, which had been very quiet since the end of the season without tourist cars or coaches, was Petros, Elaine and Sakis, Pavlos, and Nikos, all sitting around a plastic table. Your friend, Dionysus, was pouring out glasses of amber liquid from a tall, angular bottle which could only be Metaxa.

'Wait,' you said, racing back up the stairs two at a time, returning with my little Sony stereo, plonking it onto the wall opposite us and pressing the play key.

'Yammas,' you announced loudly to the table. Never Tear Us Apart blasted out as you handed me a glass of Metaxa, raising yours. I sipped the aromatic, golden liquid, the warmth filling my veins as our eyes locked. You never failed to surprise me.

'I bring the summer back, for you,' you said, kissing me. '*Agapē mou.*'

By then I was feeling pleasantly pissed, like all of us were, I suspect. It was such a lovely surprise. Such a golden afternoon. It had been just a little gesture, but one which was so thoughtful, making me feel so special. I glowed inwardly. You'd arranged all this for me. I only wished Sherri could have been there to make it really perfect.

The light was failing, and we were beginning another bottle of Metaxa.

'I love you,' I whispered as you pulled me in, snuggling me into you as everyone laughed, talked, joked. It was such a natural thing to say. It just felt right. However, despite everything you'd decided for us after the army, way you treated me like a princess; through all we had been to one another, all those letters full of longing and, despite the way you constantly called me *agapē mou,* my love, we'd never, actually said *Those Words* to one another. But now, in an unguarded moment, sitting in the half light, drinking Metaxa on an empty stomach, just days before I was due to fly home, I'd blurted them out.

You just stared hard at me for a moment as I held my breath, but you didn't respond. Colour bled out of the golden afternoon like a watercolour in the rain. It was as though my blood had turned to concrete and solidified within me. You were very quiet. I don't know what I'd expected, but I hadn't expected silence. I looked sideways at you, but you still said nothing, you just squeezed me tighter, kissed my hair absently and continued talking to Dionysus.

A cloud crossed the sun, everything felt colder. One moment, I'd been so happy, the next, I'd wanted to crawl back into the apartment. I don't know whether it was the shock of what I'd said, the even bigger shock you'd said nothing in return, or the fact I was well on my way to being very drunk, but I just wanted to be on my own.

'I'm going back up,' I announced, feeling horribly embarrassed.

'Okay, I'll come with you.'

'No, don't, you stay.' I slung your hand clumsily from my thigh and stood, scraping my chair, wobbling a little. Standing up somehow made everything different. The Metaxa hit me like a truck, and I felt very out of control. My head spun. Had I just ruined everything?

I stumbled on the staircase, aware of a sudden ripple of laughter.

'*Opa,*' cried Dionysus.

Forcing a brave grin, I grabbed the stair rail, glancing back to see you looking confused, getting up and following me, despite me telling you quite firmly not to.

Back in the room I slumped onto the bed, mortified, as you held back in the doorway. It felt like I'd kept a cupboard stuffed with all the things that made me insecure but by saying those words in an unguarded movement, I'd opened it and they'd all come tumbling out. Now they wouldn't fit back in again.

'What is *wrong* with you?' Your hands flew high with exasperation.

Good old blunt Greek delivery. I knew you'd probably meant nothing; it was just a figure of speech, but the words twisted inside me, stinging like lemon juice on an open cut. What *was* wrong with me? I was an idiot, that's what was wrong with me. An idiot who'd badly misjudged a situation, misjudged an entire relationship. If it even *was* a relationship at all.

'Nothing.'

You just shook your head and sat down heavily next to me, staring straight ahead as I bit the skin around my thumb, surveying the polished stone floor; brown, cream, gold, little flecks of metal. Nothing more was said for what seemed an eternity. Outside I could hear the plastic table and chairs being dragged back into the Athenian bar.

'Okay,' I'd had enough. 'If you must know, I feel like a complete prick now.'

'What?'

Hurt and anxiety were beginning to rise up like ink through blotting paper. My troll was squatting on the bed between us, grinning in delight. *'He doesn't care. He doesn't love you,'* she taunted, sticking out a big, ugly tongue. I took a huge and painful gulp, swallowing down tears I didn't want you seeing.

This was it. My stomach was starting to liquefy. I had to say something.

'I just told you out there I loved you.' I began, swiping at my cheek with the back of my hand.

'Yes?' You sounded puzzled.

I took a deep breath. I might as well go for it. Nothing to lose now.

'But you didn't reply, so...do you? Love me, I mean.'

I would never have started any of this had I been completely sober, I'd have had far too much pride. All my protective barricades should have been up, but alcohol has a way of loosening your defences. For a moment, that annoying wartime expression Dad often used flew into my head. *Loose lips sink ships.* Well, I appeared to have torpedoed mine.

'Of course,' you said, shrugging. You seemed genuinely confused.

'But you've never said it.'

'Listen, *moro.*' Your expression grew serious. 'They're just words. I'm not like the *Kamaki* boys who tell every girl this.' You frowned hard at me. This really wasn't going the way I'd expected. 'Why do you even need to ask? Have I not shown you enough?'

Your body seemed tense, under your skin I could see a little knot of muscle as your jaw ground. Your brows drew closer. Were we having a row? I wasn't sure what the hell was going on now. The side table, the wardrobe, the open door to the kitchen all began to dance, sway, and distort.

'I want you to go home,' I announced, somewhat dramatically. Deep inside I hoped this would force a reaction. Maybe you'd say sorry. I was secretly hoping for a scene from a romantic novel. This was the part where you'd sweep me into your arms, Mills and Boon style, and silence me with a kiss, but instead, you simply got up, walked through to the kitchen and stood in front of the window, your arms folded. Stubbornly, I remained on the bed examining the folds of my red cotton skirt.

'Okay, I'll come tomorrow,' you finally said, unsmilingly. 'When you feel better.'

No kiss. Nothing. You just left.

I threw myself across the bed sobbing, listening to your bike whining off into the distance. You were right though. If I really thought about it, you had shown me, repeatedly how you felt. I knew in my heart you loved me so why was I hell-bent on ruining it? Surely showing was better than telling? Why was it so necessary you said those stupid words and why was it so important to me; important enough to tear everything apart for? To fully understand, I'd probably need to drill down through the rubble of my relationship with Dad, and I just wasn't going there.

My troll was dancing on the bed now, taking great pleasure at all this. 'You're just not good enough,' she jibed, jumping up and down, up, and down. 'Not *quite* good enough.'

That night, I'd slept in my clothes, something I only ever did when I was really upset. It was as though removing clothes would strip away any remaining protective armour, leaving me even more vulnerable than ever. In the morning, thanks to the Metaxa, my head was banging. My eyes were uncharacteristically puffy too. Dismayed, I grabbed a couple of teaspoons and shoved them in the ice box along with some used tea bags for soothing my swollen lids.

Pulling my crumpled red skirt off and dumping it in a heap on the floor, I removed my bodice to reveal skin latticed with scar-like crease marks. Cursing inwardly, I wrapped myself in my little towelling robe and after cleaning my teeth and washing my face, I padded back into the bedroom to sit cross-legged in front of the wardrobe mirror with my makeup bag. This was going to take some work. As I began examining the dark thumbprints and puffiness around my eyes, you were in the doorway.

'Don't look at me!' Alarmed, I leaned back, turning my face away. 'I look awful.'

Shit. After everything, you were now going to see me with swollen, shiny eyelids and dark circles.

You smiled.

'You look beautiful.'

'I look all blotchy and horrible.'

'You don't,' you laughed. 'But you drank a lot of Metaxa so I'm thinking maybe you don't feel too good?'

That was a gross understatement.

You walked over and sat on the bed.

'I feel so stupid.' I looked at the floor, feeling horribly hungover. What a combination. I had no coffee or paracetamol. My sinuses were buzzing from all the crying. Someone was playing a drum kit inside my skull and there was every chance I might be sick too. Feeling like shit didn't even begin to cover it.

'*Ela*, come here.'

I slid over to you, hiding my puffy face in your shoulder.

As you wrapped me in your arms, I felt the sting of fresh tears, but I forced them back.

'What you said, yesterday...' you began.

Oh God, not this again. I was impaled on a spear of acute embarrassment. What now?

'What you said. I...I liked it. I really liked it.'

The world stopped spinning for a moment, righted itself and when it began again, everything felt more balanced. I found myself smiling with relief. You liked it? Were you saying what I thought you were? You did love me. Deep inside, I felt it, anyway, but this made everything better somehow.

Then you held me at arm's length and looked right into my reddened eyes.

'We start over again?'

I nodded.

'And you feel the same?'

'*Moro*, don't be stupid, you know I love you.'

You sounded so indignant for a moment, but then you smiled. It was like the sun coming out. Pulling me in, you kissed me, making the room spin again as my robe slid from my shoulders and your hands explored my body, your lips on my neck.

14

Always On My Mind

Elaine had gone back home. The first we knew of it was when Sakis turned up without her on the back of his bike.

'I expect you'll miss her,' I said, expecting a positive response, but his dark eyes seemed to register absolutely nothing. A bead of spittle had settled at the corner of his fleshy mouth.

'She comes after Christmas,' he shrugged, settling down at the kitchen table and making himself comfortably at home as I made the effort to be as pleasant as possible, swallowing my feelings of dislike. He was your friend. I had to try.

'I don't think Sakis likes me,' I told you when he'd gone, 'and I don't think he likes Elaine much either.'

'How you mean, *moro?*'

I could tell your defences were up by the tone in your voice.

'Well,' I took a breath. 'She's coming here for the whole summer just to be with him, but all he does is criticise her and tell her what to do, and he didn't seem remotely bothered she'd gone home. He's not supporting her in any way. Did you see his face when she mentioned university! I just think she could do so much better than him.'

You'd been listening intently, but not speaking.

'Do you think he's got someone else?' I added, chucking another pebble in the pond for good measure as I collected up coffee cups and glasses to put them in the washing up bowl. 'An Aftonisian girl, maybe?'

'This is crazy talk, *moro*.' You were laughing at me now as I ran the tap and squirted in some Fairy Liquid. 'You don't know what you're saying. He's told me he will make a life with her because she's a good girl. He trusts her. He's happy.'

But was Elaine happy and could she trust *him*? That seemed to be of no consequence whatsoever. I was gradually learning romance, love, relationships on the island were perceived a little differently to how they were in England. Here it seemed to all be about how women could be proven trustworthy. Having a 'good girl' who was worthy of 'trust' seemed to be the top priority among men here. A gold star accolade. The compliment didn't need to be returned. I particularly didn't like the way Sakis always scowled at Elaine whenever she mentioned university, so I made up my mind to speak to her about it. I'd never forgive myself if she missed her opportunity just because of him. Someone needed to make her see sense.

Finally, my last full day had come.

'You will come back, when?' you demanded, sitting on the bed, watching me ram all my things into my suitcase.

'Soon, but I do have to work,' I explained, sorting out what was going into the huge, canvas travel bag I would take onto the plane with me. You didn't like it, but I needed money because it gave me choices, freedom, it meant I could do more things I wanted next year, like coming back for the summer season. I felt a bit irritated you didn't get it. I had to work for my money. It didn't grow on trees, whereas, technically, yours did. Olive Picking season had arrived.

I don't think you ever fully understood work and money. You seemed to get by, and you'd never go without because you had a huge extended family to look after you. You were the favoured, indulged, first born. The only son, who always got his own way. Greeks cared about family more than anything. I felt momentarily ashamed of how difficult things currently were with my parents. Mum was glad I was getting divorced but hated me flying out to Greece all the time and she just couldn't understand why I wanted to work in a department store.

'You should get a proper job, not just play about with makeup all day,' she'd replied when I'd told her about the Benningtons job. 'You had a career with prospects at Jackson and James, but you just gave it all up for no good reason. Why are you always so irresponsible?'

I may have omitted something - the minor, teeny weeny point about being sacked. I'd left her to assume leaving Jackson and James had been my choice. Underneath the sniffy response, I could tell she was desperately worried. As a woman who was usually very intuitive and perceptive, she seemed to think there was something to worry about, but this time she was wrong. For the first time in my life, I knew I was doing exactly the right thing. I just wished she hadn't been so disappointed that I wouldn't consider working at their local estate agency. As for Dad, well, true to form, he was usually disappointed in me anyway, so no change there. I'd always fallen short of his expectations. He'd been disappointed from the moment I'd popped out and he'd realised I wasn't a boy.

Work wasn't my only priority. I also needed to get back to see Rob about the house and I wanted to catch up with my friends.

'I'll come after Christmas.'

'But you will be here for New Year and for... *Theofáneia*?' The word hung in the air. You hadn't mentioned the army, but we both knew it was approaching, darkening the sky like a thundercloud, heavy with its inevitability.

'I will.' I wasn't sure exactly when I'd get a flight, but at least I could afford it. I had the money squirrelled away from my adverts on Loot and the sale of my car.

You'd bought a carrier bag with you to the apartment.

'These are for Christmas,' you said, lifting out something in tissue paper and a small, dark blue box. 'But I want you to have them now.'

You placed the delicate paper packet into my hands.

'This,' you said solemnly, 'was chosen for you by my mother.'

You'd been watching me closely as I gazed through the huge glass doors at the sunset staining the sky and you turned to me.

'You love my country,' you said, seriously, proudly, as I felt your lips against my hair. I wasn't sure if it was a question or a statement, but I nodded anyway.

'Yes, I do,' I said, and squeezed your hand, looking up at you. I could see myself reflected in your eyes. Every minute was precious, I wanted to stretch them all out, like a never-ending piece of elastic, to last forever. I didn't want to leave this place. It occurred to me in that moment I loved your country, but it was becoming increasingly difficult to separate how I felt about you from how I felt about Greece. I hardly knew you. Perhaps I was only 'in love' with the idea of you. In a rush, I realised something unexpected. I had somehow fallen in love with the 'me' I was when I was with you, when I was in Greece. I was beginning to really like that person and I didn't want her to change. I was far happier and more accepting of myself in her skin, so I didn't want any of this to come to an end.

For a moment, I wondered how I'd feel about you if we'd met somewhere different, at a different time. How much of what we had was bound up in the magic of this wonderful place and the freedom it represented? How would you feel about yourself, about us, if you had to live in grey, wet Southampton, wrapped in layers of winter clothes, enduring one day of rain after another? Would it change you? Would you even want to adapt? Or would you be just like those poppies at the roadside, beautiful in bloom, but shrivelling and dying as soon as they were picked? The answer was something I didn't want to acknowledge.

When I was finally on the plane from Athens back to Heathrow, I was lucky enough to get a window seat, so I slumped with my head against the glass and tried to sleep. It was impossible though. I put all the strange, confused tangle of thoughts I'd had in the airport down to just momentary madness. It occurred to me my troll might be sneaking around somewhere, trying to make her presence felt, stirring her stick, muddying the water. Well, I just wasn't having it.

'*Fuck off,*' I hissed at her, telepathically. '*I'm stronger than you*'.

The next few weeks were mercifully so busy, so hectic I barely had time to think. The Benningtons job was surprisingly fun. I'd always loved makeup and skin care, but I had no idea I'd be so much in my element advising people and demonstrating products. It also had the added benefit of being a sales job with targets, something I thrived on, so I quickly realised I'd found a job I not only enjoyed doing, but one I was good at. In a different life, if I'd been able to afford to, I'd have taken the job full time, but it only paid a basic salary of £5,000 plus a somewhat meagre product allowance and commission structure which certainly didn't compare with what I'd been used to at Jackson and James. Besides, I didn't need a full-time job. I was going back to Greece.

I got on well with all the other consultants, but I clicked the most with Helen, a chic redhead who worked in perfumery and was always followed by a trail of the latest 'it' perfume, Georgio of Beverley Hills. It was pungently loud, with equally strident yellow and white striped packaging. Perfumes were supposed to whisper, but this one howled like a banshee and every time Helen walked by it hovered in the air above her like wasps around a jam donut.

Byzance by Rochas, with its curvaceous blue and gold glass bottle, was my favourite. It's oriental top notes had an undertone of something indefinable that made me nostalgic, reminding me of the Johnson's Baby Shampoo we used to have at home. I'd always loved perfume and the way memories can be sparked by the faintest drift of it.

The Body Shop's Vanilla oil would now always remind me of Sherri, and, through her, I'd become hooked on White Musk, which she'd introduced me to. It was sweet, yet sexy, without being obvious, its softness balanced by something which took me straight back to school, reminding me, somewhat weirdly, of pencil-shavings. It was far cheaper than Byzance, so it became my second choice. It was also all I could afford now.

Working in cosmetics was quite convenient as we were allowed to take home old testers and broken items, sometimes at a greatly reduced cost, sometimes even free when Agnes, the department manager, agreed and signed them off, or, when we popped them illicitly into our makeup bag or a pocket. That was always a tricky one. We never knew when we'd have our bags checked as we made our way through the staff exit and you needed a signed docket to take anything out, but the odd eyeliner or lipstick sometimes made its way into my bra before I ran the gauntlet of Fat Dave from Security and his walkie-talkie-carrying sidekick, Martin.

Helen announced she had a brand-new bottle of Byzance she could sell to me for £10 if I liked, so I went home with her that evening where she produced not one, but two, huge unopened bottles. Not only that, but she had a bathroom shelf that looked like the Benningtons stockroom: bottle upon bottle of shrink-wrapped Opium, Miss Dior, Oscar de la Renta, and so many more, as well as skin creams, makeup, and bath products, all stood in rows in their cellophaned boxes.

'Just don't ask,' she'd said with a sly chuckle, opening a dressing table drawer to revel even more. I didn't. I just slipped her a £20 note and went home on the bus, grinning from ear to ear. I had no idea how Helen did it, but I wasn't complaining, and she'd said she could get anything else I liked with a little advance notice.

I'd been puzzled how she did it though. I seriously doubted Helen had the brains to be a criminal mastermind, so in the end I just had to ask.

'You know Martin?' she said. 'Let's just put it this way, he'll always turn a blind eye to whatever's in *my* bag.'

It took me a few seconds.

'What, you and Martin...really?'

Martin was tall, thin ,with a dodgy moustache. He reminded me of that keyboards player in Sparks. He never seemed to smile. That's all I knew of him.

'Yup,' she chuckled. 'On the quiet, obviously. He's no catch, is he?'

'How long's *that* been going on for?'

'Few months now,' she said. 'To be honest I'm really not that into him. I'd have probably let it fizzle out ages ago if it wasn't for all the perks I get.' She gave me a wink. 'I think of it as a supply and demand thing.'

Letters flew between us, mine saturated with Byzance as usual, then one day you sent me three photographs. One was of us with Sherri and Petros on the day she went back to England. I smiled at our happy, carefree faces, my dark hair was up in a high ponytail, I was wearing my red and white vest and black shorts, Sherri was in jeans and a pink, puff sleeved top, a pair of painted wooden parrot earrings swinging from her ears. Her blue backpack was at our feet. Behind us loomed Petros, his skin several shades darker than ours, making him look more Asian than Greek. I missed Sherri and wondered what she was doing for Christmas.

Another was one of us both together in town, sitting in a café. I stared long and hard at this one. Did I look as though I was several years older than you? I didn't think so, but paranoia was starting to kick in. To be fair, I'd been surprised when you'd told me your age as I'd really assumed you were older, and people were always saying I looked much younger, so I hoped we met somewhere in the middle. It was only a handful of years anyway. At least it was the same decade, and wasn't it you who'd said age was just a number, it was how you felt that mattered? I could see faint lines around my eyes, but, then again, I could see them around yours too as you crinkled them at the sun.

The third was the biggest surprise. It was you, grinning, standing with your strong arms protectively encircling an attractive woman in a floral dress. Thin and petite, with black wavy hair, sharp cheekbones, and olive skin, she stared into the camera with serious dark eyes, as you dwarfed her with your broad frame. On the back, you'd scrawled *'with my mother'.*

15

Father Figure

Time flew by and I kept busy. I'd seen an advert for a correspondence course in copywriting and, although I couldn't really afford it, I'd stuck it on my credit card anyway. I wasn't too worried. I'd have money to come from the house. It kept me occupied in the evenings and I discovered I was rather good at it. I even wondered if I could make some extra money from writing advertisement copy one day.

I was hopeful the house would soon sell. By this time, knowing there was little significant equity in the property anyway, I just wanted it gone and to have the money I was owed. Alan was our agent. He'd make sure we got the best deal but, by then, to me, it was just a house. My head and heart were already dancing away to when I'd be with you again. My life was now in Aftonisi. The army would over in no time. It was just a blip, a small moment in time I'd hardly remember one day.

There were various forms I'd needed to sign. They were just one step closer to my new life, so when I'd sat down with Rob at the kitchen table, with Dan acting as witness, I was just keen to get it over and done with. To tell the truth, I'd barely glanced at them. One of them was to allow Rob to deal with the sale alone in my absence as I would be off abroad again. Any fees would be taken directly out of the sale so neither of us would have to find extra funds to pay them, and half of what was left would then come back to me. I signed as instructed. I'd already spoken to Alan, and he'd told me that, as our agent and as a friend too, he'd keep an eye on everything and try to steer Rob. He knew I was in a difficult position.

Rob seemed to be very contrite about his previous behaviour during the few weeks I was back and had behaved relatively well under the circumstances. It was such a relief for me we could at least be civil as I'd been feeling so guilty. Somewhere deep inside I still cared about him. I didn't want to be married to him any more, but I didn't want him to be unhappy either. I hoped he'd find someone else one day, someone who could help him exorcise his demons, someone who would love him in a way I never could. It occurred to me we should have only ever been friends. I'd been impulsive and headstrong when I'd agree to marry him. It had seemed a good idea at the time but it had soon become clear that Rob wanted a drinking partner, not a wife.

'If things don't work out,' he said as we sipped coffees and ate warm, sticky Pain Au Chocolates one morning. 'You could always come back, you know...'

'How do you mean?'

Even as I said it, I known he'd meant back to him.

'Well, back here, to…Southampton, you know.'

I took deep breath in.

'I won't be coming back Rob.' I needed to make myself clear. 'Not to Southampton, not to you. The house will be sold. I'll be in Greece.'

I looked at his expression, trying to work out whether he was fully taking this on board.

'I'm sorry if that's hurtful, but you do understand, don't you?'

He looked a little crestfallen, but, to his credit, responded with nothing more than a shrug.

'Yeah, I know.' He nodded firmly, his voice full of enforced buoyancy and cheer. I smiled tightly back at him. Phew. Dodged a bullet there.

'We'll still stay friends, obviously.' Guilt was making me gabble. Rob had done little over the years to be considered a friend.

He was quiet for a moment.

Then he hit me with it.

'So... as we're going to stay friends, I can still come out and see you, like, for a holiday, can't I?' His brows raised expectantly.

What? Was he completely nuts? I'd rather stick needles in my eyes and pull out my fingernails with pliers.

'Yeah, maybe.' I said, turning away.

He wandered to the fridge, poked his head in for a moment, then grabbed a beer. It was a bit early for that type of thing, even by Rob's standards, but I was in no position to moralise under the circumstances. I shook my head when he waved one at me. I'd hadn't even finished my coffee.

Levering off the lid with a bottle opener, ironically, the one shaped like a naked god with a massive penis he'd bought in a gift shop in Aftonisi, he dragged the kitchen chair over to me. Straddling it the wrong way round, he leaned over the backrest.

'So, about Greece.' He swigged his beer. 'Had this idea the other day. Thought maybe I would...erm... buy...a jet ski with my share of the house and start a little business over there, just for the summer. In Aftonisi, I mean. Then I can see you, make a bit of money, get a tan. What d'you think?'

He seemed particularly enthusiastic now as a growing mania seemed to take hold, his eyes dancing as he watched my face for a reaction.

What? He was joking. A Jet Ski? He'd never even been on a Jet Ski before.

I had to shut this down quickly.

'No, Rob. Absolutely not. Just forget it. I think it's best you concentrate on building a new life here. I'm with Marios now.'

I stood, picking up my bag, mentally congratulating myself for not wildly overreacting, proud of preventing everything from escalating into something unpleasant. Hopeful I'd stopped this mad idea in its tracks, I made for the front door, with Rob muttering from the kitchen.

'Well don't come crying to me when it all goes tits up...'

I stepped out onto the drizzly, December Street, wrapping my coat tightly around me.

'...which it will...'

121

I shut the door.

'...deluded bitch.'

So much for the *entente cordiale*.

At last, Christmas was finally over. That was not something I ever thought I'd hear myself saying as I usually loved Christmas, but this one had been difficult.

My aunties and uncles, cousins, and their families, all converged at our house on Christmas Day, which was lovely, but, by the evening, I was sick to the back teeth of all the questioning over what was happening about Rob and the house, and I was even sicker about being interrogated over why I'd decided to give up a 'perfectly good' job in estate agency. I tried to just deflect as much of the attention as possible onto other things, which, with noisy, excitable children running around wasn't too hard. I just tried my best to keep my head down, tucking into Mum's home-made mince pies and the obligatory box of Mon Cherie liqueur chocolates which had become a family Christmas ritual.

Those of us who weren't in a turkey coma went for an afternoon walk along the riverbank; Uncle Dave, Dad, and me, with Cousin Greg following up behind, supervising his children. We strode alongside the river, our noses damp from the cold, our warm breath pluming ahead in the frosty air. These were moments I would savour as it would be so different soon when I was back in Greece.

'River's kicking up a bit,' observed my uncle, wrinkling his nose as I nodded in agreement. We were getting closer to the weir with its spiked grid of river pipes laced with weed. He grabbed Greg's eldest as he ran past, propelling him along in front which left me, somewhat awkwardly, lagging, alone with Dad. I always found it so hard to be with him, we rarely had much to talk about, so an uneasy silence ensued, broken only by the odd burst of forced small-talk and a flurry of ducks quacking.

'So, Melanie, you're off out *there* again day after tomorrow?' he finally said, stating what I felt was unnecessary considering we'd already dissected everything earlier over the Bucks Fizz. Dad liked stating the obvious. On my twelfth birthday he'd strode into my bedroom first thing, yanked the curtains apart, peered out of the window at his handiwork in the garden and announced, 'now you're in your thirteenth year.' Every year thereafter, he'd done the same. No matter what age I'd achieved, he liked to remind me I was technically a year older. Dad liked to chart the passage of time. He was always in a hurry to get to the finish line.

'...to see your young man, I understand.'

'I am,' I said, injecting as much purpose as possible into the conversation. I folded my arms tightly around myself, partly as protection from the cold, partly as protection from Dad, as I trudged onwards.

I bristled inside. Dad didn't do nice, fluffy conversations. Where was this leading?

'When I was in Norway...' he began. Oh God, what was coming now. Hopefully not a war story. Dad had been in Norway as part of Operation Doomsday with the 1st Airborne forces and had liberated the county from the Germans. We often had to sit through the same old tales. He'd stayed there for several years afterwards as he'd become involved with a Norwegian girl, someone my mother still rather snippily referred to as 'that foreign woman.'

'When I was in Norway,' Dad repeated, 'I had this girlfriend, Toni, I think you might remember me mentioning her?'

I nodded. Yes, I had. I'd heard all about it from Mum too.

'She was older than me.' He stated the fact bluntly.

'Oh, really?'

I hadn't realised that.

'Yes.' He kept looking ahead, not at me. His nose was now glowing red from the cold and his glasses were misting up. 'Yes, ten years older. Didn't put me off, mind you, still loved her, despite that.'

I didn't really know what to respond.

'Yes, I loved her a lot.'

It seemed strange to hear Dad not only recalling something which involved emotions and feelings, things which were certainly not his forte at all, but also mentioning the L word. He'd never told me he loved me, or

123

Mum, according to her. He seemed to pause then. Perhaps he'd thought better of being too candid. I was his daughter, after all.

'Of course, I was still a young man then, Melanie,' he added hastily, tucking the ends of his plaid scarf inside his coat. '…it was all a very long time ago.'

We marched on, weak winter sunlight glancing off the brown river, the silence deafening us. The only sound, the trudging of our wellingtons on the muddy river path.

'Your age gap with this Greek chap is about the same, your mother informs me'.

My defences were well and truly up now. I felt a massive iron portcullis clang down between us.

'Seven years, Dad,' I reminded him. 'Just seven, in fact, only just.'

'Still a few years older though, aren't you?'

His hazel eyes regarded me sagely for a moment before he thrust his hands into his pockets and kept walking. Where were Greg's usually omnipresent children right now when I could do with a distraction? I saw them careering around up ahead, with Greg chasing them, pretending to be a monster. Too far away to have any convenient interaction now.

I didn't answer. My nostrils flared. Round of applause for Dad. I was livid he was bringing this up.

'Anyway, what I was trying to say was… just be careful.'

Was he showing a modicum of fatherly concern for me?

He stopped walking, turned, and looked at me fully in the face, not something he did often.

'She turned to me once when we were out walking, much like we're doing now, only it was a warm, sunny day, very bright as I recall. The sun was full in our faces. She turned to me, and do you know when she said?'

I shook my head.

'*Harry, I think I've had my best years,*' she said, just that.' He seemed to pause mid-sentence, pondering it all for a moment, lost in a trance of time, but quickly snapped out of it clearing his throat awkwardly. He pulled a few Quality Street from his pocket, unwrapped one and offered me the others as an afterthought. I shook my head.

'Anyway,' he continued. 'I looked at her face, in the bright sunlight, properly, I think, for the first time ever and I noticed all these...little lines around her eyes, and on her forehead...her jaw had this sort of...slackness, a lack of definition I'd never noticed before and I thought to myself, '*yes, I think you probably have.*'

I gulped, staring back at Dad wordlessly. Poor Toni, that was just so sad, but poor Dad too. He'd never shown me his human side ever before. The only emotion I'd ever seen from him was when Watford lost the FA cup to Everton four years earlier. Something prickled in my nose.

'Anyway, it ended shortly after that.' He kicked a few branches out of his way. 'I just want you to be aware of what can happen, do you understand?'

I made fists in my pockets, digging my nails into the leather of my gloves. I was one hundred percent not going to cry in front of him. I couldn't quite make out what was happening here, but if he was attempting to show some fatherly concern, this might be my most significant Christmas ever.

Laughing myself out of the tide of emotion threatening to engulf me, I found myself spontaneously tucking my arm through his, even though it felt awkward as hell.

'Don't worry Dad, I'm *far* too beautiful for that to happen.' I joked theatrically, pulling a silly face.

Dad laughed. I wasn't sure whether in disagreement or because I'd made a feeble joke. I could feel his body stiffen and brace as we continued to walk arm in arm. He didn't do affection or bodily contact, so I just knew he was hating my gloved hand against his coat sleeve, my arm through the loop of his.

Predictably, he pulled away after a few more steps, patting my shoulder like you would a dog that wasn't yours.

'But, in all seriousness Melanie,' he said, 'Toni actually *was* a beautiful woman, yet even that didn't stop me from seeing our age difference when it was finally pointed out to me. So just bear that in mind, okay?'

Now feeling like a cross between a grossly misshapen old hag and a child snatcher after that little missive, I made my excuses and sprinted ahead to catch up with Uncle Dave and Greg, who was trying to stop his youngest from launching himself down the muddy riverbank into the water.

Then I saw her. Near the large ridge of Oak trees at the end of the path, there was a movement. It was little more than a shadow at the corner of my eye. But it was her, nevertheless. My troll, poking her tongue out in glee.

Thanks a lot Dad.

As agreed, I spent Boxing Day with Dan, his latest girlfriend, and Rob. I'd like to say including Rob in the equation was a selfless, altruistic gesture on my behalf, but to be brutally honest, it was a calculated move to keep everything as light and pleasant as possible, making it easier on me.

The following day, I took a National Express coach to Heathrow and flew out to Athens to stay overnight in Glyfada on the Athens Riviera. There were no direct flights to the island as the tourist season had ended so my plan was to take a taxi to the nearby port of Piraeus then a coach to Kyllini and a ferry over to the island. The journey was going to be a gruelling one of around six hours, not something I was especially looking forward to as a lone traveller in a country whose language I'd yet to master.

The next morning, I hopped on the coach to Kyllini and got a front seat, right behind the driver with a panoramic view through the front windscreen. An elderly Greek man plumped down in the seat next to me, as I smiled politely, wriggling closer to the glass to accommodate his bulk. Taking my Greek phrase book out of my bag, I studied it intently. After a few miles, he turned to me.

'*Anglika?*' he enquired.

'Yes, English.'

He pointed to my phrase book.

'You learn Greek?'

I smiled

'Trying to.'

I returned to the book, hoping he wasn't expecting a long conversation as I was quite tired, but he persisted.

Theodoros, a widower who'd just spent Christmas with a daughter in Athens, was travelling to Korinth to stay with another. I told him all about where I was headed and why, omitting the awkward fact I was still married to an Englishman. He reminded me of Alan, with his moustache and kindly brown eyes. Doros, as he instructed me to call him, took it upon himself to test my Greek, so, I practised my faltering skills on him to enthusiastic cries of 'Bravo'.

'You are speaking nicely, now,' he beamed.

'Better with your help.'

'Ne, kalytera,' he said with a little sideways lowering of his head.

'Kalytera?' I enquired.

'Kalytera, it means better.'

Kalytera. I liked that. It was a good word. My Greek was getting better. Life was getting better. I would add kalytera to my growing vocabulary.

It'd stared in wonder from the coach window when we'd crossed the famous Korinth Canal then stopped for a short break, so I decided to quickly walk back over the bridge to look down at it.

The air was fresh and the breeze strong, with thundering juggernauts rumbling past, their might and strength emphasising the vastness of the drop to where the Aegean Sea met the Ionian. I had never seen anything like it before. It was hard not to be caught off-guard by such a precision feat of engineering; a deep slice hewn out of multi-layered striped limestone in every shade of brown, grey, cream and gold. There, at the very bottom of this truffle-coloured layer cake of rock was a narrow ribbon of sparkling blue, dotted with cargo ships the size of rice grains. By the time I returned to the coach to continue my journey, Doros had disappeared into the crowd.

The rest of the journey to Kyllini passed quickly and soon I was below deck on the ferry, breathing in the diesel stench while feeling quite proud of myself for completing such a long, protracted journey all on my own. After around forty minutes, the outline of the coast of Aftonisi came into view. I would soon be back with you.

16

I'm Not Scared

I had somehow assumed I would go back to where I'd last stayed but I found myself back at the Beehive Apartments

'There's a problem with the water,' you explained with a shrug, leading me into a massive studio, your face shining with expectation. It was a beautiful room, vastly superior to the ones before.

'You like?' you said, arms wrapped tightly around me.

'I love it, thank you. Please thank Nikos for me.'

'It's better, yes?'

'*Kalytera.*' I nodded feeling quietly pleased with myself at trying out some unsolicited Greek.

'*Kalytera,*' you said in delight. 'You are learning good Greek!'

Excited with my new knowledge, I told you all about Doros and my impromptu Greek lessons, but your face clouded, darkened, your expression became set.

'*Moro*, you cannot just talk to strange men on buses.' Your voice was tight. 'It is not right.'

How ridiculous. I was most indignant at this, and I told you in no uncertain terms what I thought of your reaction.

'Okay.' You conceded brusquely. I think I'd surprised you with the force of my response. You didn't like me arguing with you. 'But it's not correct to talk to men you haven't been introduced to. It is wrong. This Doros, he would not expect his daughters to behave like that.'

'Behave like what?'

'Speaking to strange men. You shouldn't do that.'

'Why ever not?' Folding my arms, I glared at you.

'Because you have to wait until…until you have permission.'

'What?' I felt a surge of heat rise up through me as I braced my hands against my arms, my voice rising in indignation. 'You are joking, right? You're saying I actually need *permission* to speak to someone now?'

'Just to strange men, well, to any men. You can't just go talking to men on your own, *endaxi.*'

'Oh, okay. So, I need permission now to speak to Nikos, to Petros, to Sakis, even the man in the fucking supermarket–'

'It's not all your fault. You are a foreign woman, you still have much to understand of our system—'

'Do I need permission to talk to you?' I grabbed your arm as you turned away from me. 'What if we're in a bar one day and you have to leave me on my own for a moment, then I see some of your friends. What do I do, ignore them?'

I was furious. By the tone in your voice, so were you.

'Yes. If that happens, you do that. You just sit there, *moro.* You don't speak to anyone until I return, *kataleveno?*'

'Not a chance.' I yelled back. I was shaking now.

'I can see you're not in a good mood, so I will give you time to think about what you did wrong.' Your mouth pulled into an ugly slant. 'You have a lot to learn. I'll come later.'

'Don't bother.' I shouted, banging the door hard behind you.

Unpacking my things, I slammed them into drawers, shutting the wardrobe doors with a resounding bang, huffing at the ridiculous things you'd said. Kicking my suitcase up against the wall, I slung my toiletries bag onto the bathroom shelf then paced back to the balcony. Gripping the rail hard, for a moment I felt like crying.

In an attempt to relax, I had a shower, smothered myself in body lotion then perched on the bed in a towel with my mirror and makeup bag, trying to make sense of your reaction. I tapped my fingers against my leg, my breathing tightening as I thought of your reaction.

Suddenly, there was a knock on the door. I really hoped it was you, back to apologise, but also, I equally hoped it wasn't. I didn't want another row. I'd waited for so long to see you, I wanted everything to be perfect. We didn't have much time. Soon you'd be gone to the Army.

It occurred to me you might not be happy for me to open the door in a bath towel, but it would take too long to change.

'Hang on, one minute…um…*ena lepta…*' I shouted. Tucking the towel tightly around me like a tourniquet, I edged the door open, sticking just my chin through the gap.

Standing there, grinning, was Sherri.

I literally pulled her into the room and gave her a massive hug, inhaling her vanilla scent.

'When did you get here?'

'Yesterday. I'm just upstairs. Did Elaine get hold of you?'

'No.'

Sherri walked to the bed and sat down, her face shimmering with late afternoon sunlight as I returned to my makeup bag and began drawing on eyeliner.

'She tried ringing you over Christmas, more than once, and left a message on your machine?'

'Really?' I frowned, adding a flick of black at the corner of each eye. I hadn't received any messages. Rob hadn't said there was anything on the answerphone.

'What did she want?'

Sherri's eyes were shining like mirrors.

'She's contacted Pavlos's Dad.'

'Why?'

Sherri was nearly levitating with excitement.

'She's negotiated us a really cheap monthly rent for that massive apartment you had in October, the one on the corner. Basically, he's agreed to a six-month let with three months up front and, best of all, no deposit. It's ours from the end of March!'

This was fantastic news. We'd all discussed looking for somewhere after New Year so it had never even occurred to me Elaine would take it upon herself to do it on her own and so much earlier than we'd planned. Clever Elaine. This is where her organisational skills were very useful.

'Really, that's wonderful!' I loved that apartment, so the idea of a whole six months there was perfect. I easily had enough savings to pay my share of the first three months. All we needed now were jobs and, from what I'd been led to believe, that was the easy bit.

Sherri must have read my mind. She walked over to the balcony and lit up a Marlboro, leaning into the light as the sun dipped towards the mountains. The cicadas were going crazy now, the air rattling with their constant, maraca-like vibration, a symphony of whirrs and buzzes.

'Petros says there are many bars and tavernas that would love pretty English waitresses for the summer.'

'Really, and where on earth will they find those?' I joked, walking over, and pulling a puzzled face as Sherri mock-punched my arm. Sherri's soothing presence lightened my mood so much, I'd almost forgotten what had happened earlier.

I'd been a waitress and a barmaid during college so I had experience. Sherri apparently didn't.

'I'm going to be just shit,' she laughed. 'I've never waitressed before. I'm clumsy so I'm pretty sure I'll drop things and I'm bad at maths, but how hard can it be? Anyway, I'm pretty and I'm English so they'll love me. I'll get away with it.'

Sometimes Sherri's confidence astounded me.

Apparently, Elaine had already paid Mr Mavrakis herself, so we just needed to reimburse her. This was the best news ever.

Hugging this amazing, exciting news to me like a precious gift, I quickly dressed in a top and jeans, with Sherri reclining on the bed, chattering excitedly about her Christmas, about Petros, but mainly about how much fun we were going to have together next summer.

I sat down next to her on my bed

'Have you seen Kevin?'

I tied my hair up in a high ponytail then put on the drop earrings I'd bought with my Benningtons staff discount.

'Just once, at Christmas. He bought me a present, and he gave me this back.' She pulled a little red embossed ring box from her bag and handed it to me. I just gaped at the little twinkling stone set in a gold band, nestling in a bed of white velvet.

'Sherri, is this your engagement ring?'

She nodded, biting her lip.

'He told me to keep it whatever happens, but when I'm home after the summer, he said he'll come over. If I'm not wearing it, then he'll know. It's up to me.'

I fluffed my hair up and walked through a cloud of Byzance.

'God, Sherri, what a dilemma. What about Petros? What are you going to do?'

Something clouded her face for a moment, then she forced a big grin.

'I'll worry about it later.' She snatched the box back, shoving it into the depths of her handbag before pulling out her compact mirror and her red lipstick. 'Anyway, let's forget about it for now. Far more important things to think about.' She blotted her lipstick, smiled at her reflection then grabbed me by the shoulders in excitement. 'Do you realise, next year we're coming out here for the whole summer.'

When we met you waiting with Petros, your face lit up as you grinned at me. I must admit I was so relieved everything seemed alright again, so I mentioned nothing about what happened earlier. It was just one of those things.

You hugged me, pulling me in close for a lingering kiss before I hopped onto the back of the Honda. The cooler air came as a surprise, in fact it had rained earlier in the afternoon, but this was still nothing remotely like

December in England so there was still much to be grateful for. All the Ionian Islands are particularly green, something I hadn't fully appreciated until many years of travelling later, as they'd been my first experience of Greece, but I soon learned the lush, verdant landscape didn't happen by accident. It came from a plentiful supply of wintertime rain. I have since been to other islands which are dry, arid, and dusty in comparison.

There was a suspicion of summer warmth still rising from the fragrant earth as we rode along, bumping over rough track and stony ground, before curving off the main route onto what just about passed for a road, finally cutting up a narrow track bordered by a tangle of Olive trees. You drove with just one hand on the bike, the other reaching around to find mine as I held on tight to your denim jacket, pressed in close against your body, feeling your heat. To the left, glittering turquoise flashes of the sea flickered between the trees, to the right, blackened hillside where the sun had finally sunk low and disappeared. Finally, we reached a brightly lit taverna filled with local people. The air was blue with curling cigarette smoke, the aroma of chargrilled meats greeting us.

Shrugging off my jacket and blinking under the glare of bright, fluorescent lights, I slid onto the bench next to you. Unlike the tourist bars, this place was devoid of atmosphere with no music. It was purely somewhere to eat; a pit stop. I reached for your hand, but instead you frowned at the black top I was wearing.

'I can see your mole, *moro.*' You spoke somewhat testily, your eyes flickering to my chest before you glanced around the busy room.

I had a small, very dark, mole on one breast I'd jokingly called my 'marker'. I'd pretended it was useful because if I saw it, I'd know my top was too low, but I hadn't really meant it. It had been a joke. I thought you'd realised that.

Unbelievably, you continued to stare pointedly at my mole, before raising your eyes, hard and glittering, to lock with mine. Still no smile. Outwardly I was calm, but inwardly, my gut burned with leaping flames of molten anger.

For a moment, I remembered something I'd seen in Lathos when I'd been with Rob. We'd been talking to a friendly Finnish woman late one night in a bar. A business owner in Helsinki, she'd given everything up for Tinos who she'd met several years before on holiday. She was an older woman, in her forties; blonde, elegant, and intelligent.

I'd really enjoyed talking to her as she'd perched on her barstool, bronzed skin gleaming, cigarette casually waving, telling us all about her wonderful life on the island. A little later, with the conversation in full flow, a bearded Greek man had approached. Tinos, we'd assumed. But instead of joining in the conversation, a heated dialogue had begun between them in Greek, the volume escalating with every word, his hand slapping down on the bar for emphasis. I'd no idea what they were saying but she appeared to be trying to diffuse something. Eventually, she'd turned away from him with an exasperated roll of her eyes.

Then it happened. It only took a second, but he'd grabbed her by the hair and, with one hand, had dragged her off her barstool. Her piercing cry was like the shriek of an animal as he pushed her ahead of him, out of the bar, still gripping her hair. Several tourists had gasped in shock, but the barman just continued calmly wiping glasses, not a flicker registering on his face.

You continued to glare. I could hardly believe how you were behaving, but to keep the peace I inched my top up until the offending marker was hidden.

'Kalytera,' you said to Petros, with a barely perceptible nod, treating him to a wide grin, refusing to talk to me from that moment on unless I spoke to you in Greek.

By then, my shoulders were defensively squared off, my stomach uncomfortably tight, and my mouth blotting-paper dry. My breathing seemed to have become suspended. Everything had momentarily frozen.

Then, you smiled that slow, lop-sided smile, tapping your lip with a very precise index finger to specify I should kiss you as directed, so I leaned in obediently, dazzled by the binding sunlight of your approval. I'd never felt like kissing you less.

Back at the room, I ripped off my earrings and let my hair down from its ponytail.

Kicking my shoes across the room I threw myself onto the bed.

'What the fuck was all that earlier?'

'What?'

'The mole, making me only speak in Greek…and what you called my *bad behaviour* with the man on the bus, that's what.'

I folded my arms.

'I thought you'd like to show me the good Greek you learned from your new boyfriend Doros.'

You had never been like this before. You were like a different person.

'What's wrong with you?'

You said nothing, just scowled from the corner of the room, a dark shadow hovering over what should have been a bright evening, my first back on the island. I got up and snapped on my Sony, jumping as The Scorpions track, 'Rock you Like a Hurricane' blasted out, louder than I'd intended. It was too aggressive when something softer and more soothing was called for. You jumped up, angrily slammed it back off then slumped onto the bed next to me. Childishly, I got straight back up again to move away from you.

Snatching my hairbrush off the dresser, I dragged it through my hair.

'I was going to tell you something that made me really happy earlier, but, by the way you've been tonight, I really don't see the point now.' I brushed rapidly, shooting you as lofty a look as I could muster.

You still said nothing which was wholly frustrating. I could have put money on you coming round at that point, or at least showing some interest in what I might have to say, hopefully even offering me a highly deserved apology.

Undeterred I continued raking the brush through my hair, making it crackle with static.

'Elaine's spoken to Pavlos's Dad, and we're going to rent the corner apartment for six months next year…' I sat down next to you again, watching your face for a reaction but there was nothing discernible I could read.

I persisted, my voice loaded with sarcasm.

'Wonderful, isn't it?'

Fuck's sake, how long were you going to carry this on for?

'No, this is not a good idea,' you finally said. 'I don't think you should come now.'

My easy-to-read face must have shown how I felt as an indescribable wave of shock and hurt overwhelmed me. I could feel myself begin to shake inside. Surely not just because I'd spoken to a strange man on the bus and had worn a low-cut top. This was madness.

My troll plumped herself down between us, eyes darting like a fox's from me to you, loving every minute. I couldn't see clearly any more, your form was blurring and changing shape.

You tried to pull me in close, but I stiffened against the circle of your arms.

'Listen *moro*, I won't be there, so I can't protect you from…from strange men, from anything that might happen. I keep thinking about it. It will drive me crazy when I am in the army, knowing you are here, alone—'

'But you said it would make you stronger.' I pulled away, my voice rising indignantly. 'You wanted me to do this. It was your suggestion.'

'But anything could happen if I am not here.'

'Listen,' I gulped. I had to pull this back. I had to. I'd burned my bridges now, so I had no choice. This was supposed to be my new life. 'I think you're just worrying because you only have a few days left and I understand that, but if you're suggesting I can't be trusted, then you are so wrong. I'd never, ever do anything to hurt you. I want to do this, I was looking forward to it, and… I thought you were, too.'

…and I've lost my job, sold my car, ended my marriage - well, to be fair, that part wasn't your fault - upset my parents, in fact I've completely dropped a massive nuclear bomb right in the middle of my life, and all for you. And now you're doing a U turn? Well, thanks a fucking lot.

It seemed an eternity before you finally spoke again.

You grabbed both my hands, staring into my eyes with such intensity it scared me.

'But how do I *know* I can trust you? I have to know. I've never put my trust in a girl before; this is a big thing for me.'

'You can trust me, I promise.'

'But Sakis trusted Elsa when he was in the army, yet—'

'So, what are you saying? I'm not her, you're not Sakis. That's just stupid!'

'I *want* to trust you.'

'Well, trust me then.' I knelt on the floor between your knees and looked up at you. 'I'm the one who usually feels insecure, not you. I've left so much behind for you so why won't you trust me?'

You stared at me for what felt like ages while I hardly breathed at all. I couldn't read your expression and there was nothing left I could say now, so I waited until you finally spoke.

'Okay,' you eventually nodded. 'Okay, maybe it can work, somehow. Maybe we can try.'

You pulled me in and held me so tight, smothering me in kisses. That was so close. I felt my exhale of relief travel right through my body as I melted against you. I could only imagine how strange and unsettling the prospect of going into the army must be to you, particularly with me still here.

'I just need to know you will be a good girl,' you said, lifting my chin with a finger.

Once again, that famous priority. To have a *good girl* waiting at home. I forced a little smile as you squeezed me in, tighter than ever, but I was anxious now. I'd have to somehow prove you were right to put your trust in me, whatever it took.

You kissed me, but afterwards, I must have still looked concerned, doubtful, unsure, because you laughed.

'Don't worry about me, *moro*,' you said. 'I only ever treat people the way they treat me, you know this.'

17

Is Your Love Strong Enough

New Year's Eve was a time when I felt surprisingly lonely, without an anchor, away from everything familiar and, for the first time, like an afterthought, a dirty secret to be hidden away and left to my own devices until you returned. From what I had gathered, a lot of cards would be played all day and long into the night, which seemed mind-numbingly boring. It was so different to what I'd been used to which usually involved dressing up, parties and alcohol.

With Petros's family not even aware of Sherri's existence, everything became slightly awkward. During the swell of tourist season it was easy to stay under the radar, but, in December, two English girls in Lathos stood out like tattoos on a nun. Largely confined to Sherri's room, we read magazines and drank copious quantities of Nescafé, making plans for the summer while toasting bread on the two-bar electric fire Petros had brought to keep her warm.

It would soon be 1989, a year I could hardly wait for as it represented so much. It would be the year I'd move to the island, initially for six months, but after that, who knew. It seemed incredible we were nearing the last decade of the 20th century.

I danced inside at what the evening might have in store, my very first

New Year's Eve in Greece, but it was suspiciously quiet. Undeterred, Sherri and I were determined to uphold British New Year's Eve traditions, so as soon as dusk fell, we opened a bottle of Verdea in her room and drank it from two chipped mugs after dressing up to the nines. Sighing, I wondered what my friends in England would think of my glamorous life in off-season Greece.

'I will come for you later and we'll go to see Nikos,' you'd said. 'He is making us a party.'

I knew Nikos had been playing cards for hours with his family and drinking ouzo so I doubted it would be the party of year. Looking over at Sherri, I smiled resignedly, finding it hard to hide my disappointment as she gave me a wry grimace in return.

At home in Southampton, there was usually a real party somewhere, but the best bit about New Year's Eve in a coastal city was when all the ships sounded their horns at midnight in a clashing cacophony of beeps and hoots while the sky exploded and crackled into life with deafening fireworks. It was certainly more atmospheric than in Lathos.

I wondered who else might be at Nikos's party as we all walked downhill. It was gone ten, and the road seemed worryingly quiet for a New Year's Eve. Through the vine covered archway to his Taverna, I could see Nikos waiting alone, upside-down chairs on his tables, newspapers pasted on the inside of his front windows. My heart sank.

'Hello, hello, my very, very good, dear friends.' Kissing us all in turn on both cheeks, before slapping us each hard on our backs, he'd undoubtedly had a few Metaxas to pass the time. His reddened eyes danced alarmingly. 'You want dancing?'

Jigging his way over to a radio which had been humming quietly in the background, he immediately turned it to the highest, ear-splitting volume.

'Yammas.' He yelled over an explosion of Greek music, slopping red wine into glasses for us. He necked his in virtually one gulp, nodding at us to do the same. Neither you nor Petros seemed to have any problem with this. Sherri and I tried our best, but it was very strong and really bitter.

Nikos must have spotted my easy-to-read expression.

'You don't like?' he said, genuine concern colouring his features. Greeks are traditionally very hospitable, wanting their guests to be happy and I knew it was very insulting not to eat or drink whatever was offered so I tried to be polite, but Nikos had other plans.

'It's no good, eh?' Knocking me off-balance with an enthusiastic slap on the arm, he gave me a big grin. I was learning Aftonisians really seemed to like slapping, and pinching, even spitting sometimes to ward off evil spirits. 'We get more, yes?' And with that, he simply dropped the bottle to the stone floor where it smashed into a fountain of glass fragments and red wine as Sherri, and I, just gaped in shock. Picking up another bottle, he tried a sip directly from it before pulling a face.

'*Ochi, ine kakos* - no, it's bad,' he announced, smashing that one too. 'I get *my* wine.'

Picking up what looked suspiciously like a clear plastic container full of wee, he began sloshing out varying amounts of what transpired to be Nikos's special home brew

'Is now good?' he yelled, glassy eyed, treating me to a blast of alcohol breath. 'Or this?'

He waved another bottle at me.

Not wishing for more glass on the floor, any more than I wanted to be rude, I shook my head

'No, really, it's, um, lovely…er, thank you, *efkharisto.*'

Politely sipping, I glanced around what had once been a lively, traditional taverna. Now it was just a soulless open space, with tables topped with chairs all pushed to the side and a mop and bucket in the corner. Refracted beams from the headlights of occasional passing cars arced across the papered windows and the only light was from the few candles Nikos had shoved into empty wine bottles to create his idea of a party ambience. I glanced sullenly at the bar laden with full ashtrays, noticing the bowed head of Nikos's mother as she played cards with his uncle and some other elderly Aftonisians. I smiled politely at her. It was hardly the night of my dreams.

I peered into the cloudy liquid I was drinking. It tasted okay, a bit sharp maybe but I wasn't sure about all the little black specs floating in the glass.

'What are these little bits?' I asked you, taking one more sip as I slid my teeth experimentally over yet another little grit, trying to work out what it might be. Maybe local herbs?

'Is this…*rigani?*' I lifted it to the candlelight. 'Or another herb?'

You grabbed my glass to inspect it.

'No, they are just little flies, *moro,* from the barrel.'

'What!'

I pushed the glass firmly away as you offered it back to me.

'I can't drink flies!'

'It's okay, *moro,*' you said, dismissively. 'They're dead.'

Nikos was now right up close to us.

'Bravo. Now we dance.'

Soon he'd pulled us all into a line and was showing us the moves for some traditional Greek dancing, but just before, there was a small demonstration from Petros who, rather impressively, danced on upturned wine glasses, to many cries of *Opa!*

Thanks to Nikos censoring many of the bottles he'd selected, the floor now resembled a crime scene, blood red wine running between the grout lines, smashed glass crunching underfoot with wild, chaotic dancing adding to a sense of imminent danger. I soon sat down. The last thing I wanted to do was slip over in all that mess.

'How are you feeling about the army?' I asked you, when you joined me, knowing the time was drawing near. I'd purposely booked a flight for the next week, before you'd leave. It was bad enough saying goodbye to you when it was me leaving, but I just couldn't face it the other way around, having to watch you walk away, watching you disappearing, taking the sun with you, leaving me cold, empty and alone.

Your expression was resigned, your eyes uncharacteristically blank as you shrugged, pouring more of Nikos's wine, offering me one. I shook my head. One mouthful of flies was enough for me.

'I have no choice, but the quicker I go, the quicker I'm back with you.'

'Are you scared?'

Something flashed in your eyes, and you made that little, barely perceptible head lift with a soft tut.

'What is there to be scared of, *moro*? I'm worried, of course. I don't know what to expect, but why would I be scared?' For a moment, your voice was filled with confrontation, brimming with confidence, inflated with pomposity as you lifted your chin and fixed me with blazing eyes. 'I am a Greek man, not a stupid boy.'

'Have you spoken to Petros about it? I mean, is he... *worried* too? Do you know anyone else who is going to Kos? Can you find out, maybe?' Looking back, I was thinking of how I'd feel if it were me. I'd need a support network, someone to talk to, something to keep me optimistic, forgetting that you were far more likely to close down, to withdraw and just mark time until your return.

'Look, *moro*, it doesn't matter what he thinks, what I think, or what anyone else thinks. We go to the army. Nothing changes that.' You drained your glass and helped yourself to another.

I decided to leave the subject of the army alone. It was strangest New Year's Eve party I'd ever attended. Scowling, you continued to drink Nikos's home brew in silence, and I just sat there, until Sherri pulled me to my feet.

'It's quarter to, nearly time,' she said. I checked my watch, wondering if there'd be a countdown to midnight like in England, a build of excitement, but it all seemed a crashing anti-climax.

'*Ela*, you must all come, now.'

Nikos began rounding everyone up, handing each of us a pomegranate and shepherding us all outside onto the dusty roadside to stand under an inky sky, shrouded by a blur of mountain ridges.

Then it was midnight.

All at once, everyone seemed to be hugging and kissing, back slapping, spitting away evil spirits, as gunshots cracked the night air open. You seemed to have shaken off the blackness clouding you earlier.

'Happy New Year Mel.' Sherri pulled me into an affectionate hug.

'*Kalí Chroniá*.' I replied. It was finally 1989. The year of hopes and dreams. The Year of the Snake. I was looking forward to calling mum from a payphone to wish her a Happy New Year. She'd hear a voice from the future, I'd hear a voice from the past. I'd be treading a path between two time zones.

I waved my pomegranate at you.

'I don't think I can eat this now,' I whispered, not wishing to be rude about Nikos's gift, as you kissed me and wished me a Happy New Year in English. 'I'll keep it for later.'

You laughed.

'You don't eat it *moro*, you break it, for good luck. The more mess you make, the more luck you will have and if you get juice on you, it's even luckier. So, be lucky, *moro*.'

It certainly made a change from Auld Lang Syne.

As we all clustered in the darkness, Nikos brandished his pomegranate then hurled it hard against the taverna door to bring his family luck for the rest of the year. It split into pieces, spraying fragrant seeds and juice.

Sherri's bounced then broke open on the floor.

'*Opa!*' Nikos seemed very happy with this.

With each smashed pomegranate, Nikos's mother clapped, and his uncle's gunshots rang out into the darkness.

'Now you,' he said, after I'd watched you and Petros smash yours. 'Now throw this to bring good luck.' He winked at me. 'Today is also *Agia Melaina's* day, so special luck for you, *moré*. Make a big smash to bring luck for your Marios in the army too.'

Saint Melanie's day. It was a sign. I took a deep breath, watching your face soften, then closing my eyes for a second, I made a wish, the most fervent, desperate and heartfelt wish I'd ever made. Everything had to be perfect. I needed you to be okay in the army, I needed us to survive whatever 1989 would bring, I needed us to get through whatever came next. I needed the future you'd decided for us more than anything.

I hurled the pomegranate.

It completely missed and rolled away.

18

Heaven Is A Place I'm Moving To

1989

January and February passed in a blur. I wish I could say I remember everything about those months, but I hardly remember a thing apart from flying home just days before you went to the army. I didn't want to think about you leaving. All I could think of was counting the days down until I flew back out to the island again.

The Christmas job at Benningtons had ended and I'd been offered a permanent job on Cosmetics, but it couldn't have come at a worse time. I only needed something to tide me over for a couple of months until I moved to Greece.

The old, irresponsible me would have accepted it anyway, knowing full well I'd be off like a cork from a highly volatile champagne bottle the moment it suited me but, wishing to keep my reputation intact in case I ever needed Benningtons again, I came clean.

To my surprise, HR offered me something else; a job in the accessories department until Easter, which I gratefully accepted even though I knew I'd be absconding a little earlier than they'd expect. The money wasn't as generous as before, but it would save me having to find something else and

I wouldn't feel like the new girl either. I couldn't believe my luck.

I soon discovered there was a reason the job seemed too good to be true. The new role mainly involved stocktaking socks. Lots and lots of socks. There'd been a certain cachet to being a beauty consultant but being a lowly accessories assistant was something completely different.

The worst indignity to bear was that a new beauty consultant had been appointed, so the whisper was I hadn't been good enough for a full-time job. It was exhausting trying to constantly explain and endure all the doubtful expressions. I mean, no sane person gives up a cosmetics job in favour of sorting socks and knickers for eight hours a day, and what lunatic would go running off to a Greek island for someone who wasn't even going to be there?

Each day I had lunch in the cafeteria with Helen who was always so glamorous, whereas I'd just look dishevelled from sitting on the stockroom floor, firing Kimball tags into multi packs of sports socks. I consoled myself with thoughts of the glamorous existence I would soon have on a paradise island in the sun.

I can't pretend I hadn't been ridiculously excited when I finally arrived at Heathrow Airport with a massive suitcase, an equally massive holdall and a massive tote bag too.

I'd taken a train to the airport and slumped in a window seat, surrounded by my assorted baggage, feeling nerves growling in the pit of my stomach, gnawing at my insides like a hungry rat. Now and again, I'd pull myself away from hypnosis induced by staring out of the window, watching stations, fields, buildings, all pass like a smeared watercolour, as the excitement built. All my nerves were tingling with anticipation and my thoughts were like a box of wasps. I was really doing this.

Once the doors of the departures hall slid open and I'd stepped inside, a sudden jolt of reality hit me unexpectedly like a stray ball in a rounders game. What was I doing? I looked down at my fingers curled tightly around the handle of the luggage trolley. For a moment, I felt like turning around and running, then I remembered the long-term plan, the goals you and I had talked about, the future, the bar, a new life.

Get a grip, I thought. *You wanted this. Look how far you've already come. This is the last hurdle now. You can do this.*

All around me were swarms of people heading in myriad directions to hundreds of different check-in desks operated by numerous airlines. Everywhere was a blur of energies and bodies, a heady mix of travellers, lights bouncing from the overhead panels onto the airport floor, bleeding colour from everyone until they looked transparent. I surveyed the constantly changing information panels. I just needed to find Sherri then we could check in.

While I was walking up and down, scanning the busy crowd for her, I thought of you. You'd written to me several times since I'd returned to England. Each letter was longer and more detailed than the last, but all were full of how much you were longing to see me, how much you missed me. You told me of your basic training on the mainland, and how difficult it had been. You certainly weren't getting enough sleep and were physically exhausted.

I pictured you laying back on your bed, wearing khaki, wearing army boots, writing to me, and wondered if you were allowed to pin up photographs as I read and re-read how you crawled under nets wearing full combat kit and had to load and unload rifles in a set time. According to your letters, everything was noisy, foreign, alien to you. The commanding officers always shouted, and everyone hated being there. I'd lived for those letters, but they also made me sad. It was so different from your previous lazy, sun-filled life now swapped for a hot, relentless existence of regimented army drills. You told me you would soon be transferred to Kos. I wondered how this would change you while hoping fervently it wouldn't. I didn't want things to be different.

Somewhere in my core I truly believed if I willed you to remain just the same, then you would, which shows how naive I really was. How could someone not change in a situation like the one you'd been thrown into? I didn't like change one little bit, which is why I'd tended to hang on even through adverse situations, like being married to Rob. It had little to do with tenacity, strength and optimism, and an awful lot to do with fear, therefore what I was doing was a huge deal for me, a bigger deal than you could have ever known.

Although I didn't realise it straight away, your letters were subtly changing too. They were becoming less about me, about us, and gradually turning into long, complaining missives about how hard you were finding everything. At least you would have 18 days leave during your service and, if you excelled in certain areas, you might, at your commanding officer's discretion, be awarded another ten days. I wasn't religious at all, but I prayed so hard you would excel.

Finally, I caught sight of Sherri, dragging a large grey suitcase, her familiar blue nylon backpack weighing down her slight frame, a handbag over one arm.

'Oh my god,' she exclaimed as she threw her bags to the floor and we fell into each other's arms, literally hyperventilating with excitement. 'This is really it.' Her face was glowing as I beamed back at her.

'Wow, is all that yours?' She eyed my mountain of baggage in alarm.

'Well, it is for six months, isn't it?' I replied, a little defensively. She didn't appear to have anywhere near as much as me. Now I was doubting the wisdom of that last minute dash around the Chelsea Girl sale. In the harsh airport lighting, the reality was beginning to hit home. My bags were certainly drawing attention, suitcases big enough to smuggle bodies in and a giant holdall too.

On the flight, I tried hard to only concentrate on the growing feeling of anticipation and excitement not the equally strong one of terror too. I knew from the conversation I was having with Sherri she felt the same, however, the bite of fear was part of the fun of it all. The sharp stabbing inside hurt with a savage ferocity but at least it made me feel alive when the alternative was a long, lingering death by dullness and routine in Southampton which I was just not prepared to accept. Looking back now, I was so naïve to assume it would all work out simply, easily without problems.

The tingling anticipation of the journey was marred by just one thing. You wouldn't be there. You'd be on Kos, an island just off the Turkish coast which you told me was hotter, drier, and far less green than Aftonisi. I hadn't even heard of Kos before. It was still an island though, so I hoped it might have some similarities to Aftonisi, not that you'd get an opportunity to see much of it, but at least it had a coastline. Poor Petros was going to a camp on the mainland, close to the border with Albania.

During the flight, Sherri and I chatted about our plans. Even though we'd paid the first three months' rent by bank transfer to Elaine so she could sort everything out with Mr Mavrakis, we both knew three months would go quickly. We'd need to find jobs to afford the next quarter's rent.

'There will be a lot of bars and restaurants who will want staff for the summer,' Sherri had reassured me, but now we were three quarters of the way there, 35,000 ft above the Mediterranean and under an hour from landing, it seemed like just another reason for my stomach to lurch uncomfortably. I'd put my trust and faith in the fact the house was on the market and there'd already been a flurry of interest. Soon, there would surely be an offer. I knew I wasn't owed much, but there'd still be a few thousand pounds coming my way which would go a long way in Greece. The thing Rob and I had remained in total agreement about was getting the best possible deal for the house.

Something lodged uncomfortably within me for a moment. Rob could be so unpredictable, and he was still drinking heavily according to Dan, but the thoughts were no more than an annoying mosquito to bat away. With Alan guiding him, everything would be just fine. My shoulders crept back down from where they'd lodged up near my ears and my breath streamed back through my nostrils, slowly and steadily. I was worrying far too much, something you always said as you quoted me that irritating song *Don't Worry Be Happy*.

'Shall we get a voddie?' I felt a smile edge its way across my face. I'd finally decided we were on an adventure, and it was time to celebrate. Everything instantly felt much brighter, and I was really looking forward to whatever was to come. Sherri was my closest friend now. We were two girls with an exclusive bond, a connection through a unique set of circumstances and we were going to look out for each other.

'Let's do it.' Sherri's eyes were shining. 'It feels like we're on holiday.'

A moment later, we were happily clinking our little plastic cups to a resounding *Yammas*.

19

This Is The Right Time

By the time our chain-smoking taxi driver from the airport had lurched around hairpin bends at terrifying speed, I was regretting the vodka. He'd merrily steered in and out of the path of several oncoming vehicles, launching us like crash test dummies when he'd randomly slammed on his breaks, so we were relieved to see the resort finally come into view.

Peeling my shaking legs from the hot leather seat, I thrust a handful of Drachma at him, then watched him speed away, a rosary chain waggling from his rear-view mirror. We were now standing in the centre of Lathos, just below the balcony of our new home where Elaine was hanging over the railings, waving frantically and yelling our names.

'Hey,' she bellowed, running down the steps to help us, and soon we were all sat around the kitchen table, staring awkwardly at one another and making polite conversation. In the glaring afternoon sunlight, the kitchen looked just the same as I'd remembered, yet also slightly different. It was like going into neighbours' houses as a child; a suspicion of grounded familiarity in the shape, size and layout, yet everything interlaced with the foreign atmosphere and smell of someone else's home.

With Elaine's discarded sunglasses on the kitchen table, her flight bag lying open on the floor and her sweatshirt slung over a chair, it felt like she'd already stamped ownership on what I'd come to think of as mine. I flicked my eyes over the clothes spilling out of her bag. It was hard to accept we were all going to be living together; that, by default, two women who had been complete strangers a few months ago were now my closest support network, my new best friends. We had become a family.

'Have you been here long?' I asked her.

'About an hour,' she said. 'Sakis picked me up earlier in the truck. He's gone to get cigarettes.'

I'd forgotten about Sakis, our largely unwanted house guest. All previous thoughts of him had vanished like a hangover after aspirin, but now I was only too aware he and Elaine came as a package.

'I thought you'd like that one,' she said to me, pointing at the room I'd had last year. I was greatly relieved as I really loved its double aspect balcony doors and blue wooden shutters. It already felt like home, as it had so many memories of me and you.

'We're in here.' Elaine pointed at the one next door, the smaller room with twin beds and one balcony door, as I prickled inwardly at her saying 'we'. Her suitcases were already open on the bed. The only good thing about that room in my opinion was the huge wardrobe, but I seriously doubted Elaine would have all that much use for it as I eyed what she'd laid out regimentally on the bed covers: shorts, t-shirts, sensible sandals and hiking boots. Sakis seemed to only wear the same top and shorts, or jeans. That wardrobe was wasted on them.

'Sakis liked this room best and as he'll be staying over most nights, I've pushed the beds together,' she added. 'Hope that's okay?'

I fixed her with a bright smile, trying hard not to think about their headboard being back-to-back with mine, just a thin wall separating us.

'Absolutely.' I forced my best happy face.

'So, Sherri, that's yours, then,' she jabbed a finger towards the dark, street-facing room with the ornately carved, ebony bed.

Soon we were all chattering excitedly while organising our rooms, hanging up clothes, sticking up photographs, investigating cupboard space.

'I've made a note of where the electric meters and the fuse box are,' said

Elaine, predictably sensible as ever, although, to be fair, it was good at least one of us bothered about things like that. She was looking particularly pleased with herself when she told us she'd brought a mini screwdriver set and a first aid kit with her, and I wondered idly whether she'd been Head Girl at her school. If not, she had almost certainly been a Girl Guide.

'Sakis is also getting us some tea, coffee, milk and loo rolls from the kiosk,' she said, adding. 'I think we need a kitty for all the bits we will be sharing like washing up liquid, milk, sugar, all those things?'

'Um, yes,' Sherri said, nudging me. 'We should.'

I nodded, still a little irked about Sakis.

'Oh good,' Elaine grinned again. 'I'll work out how many Drachmas we'll each need to put in.' By virtue of being there an hour before us, Elaine had taken charge.

She opened the fridge.

'We can share all the stuff we put in here, but not this.' She pointed to a bottle of Smirnoff Blue Label. 'That's just mine, for emergencies.'

Sherri and I exchanged quick glances. With an inward smile I wondered what sort of emergency Elaine thought vodka would help with. Perhaps she hoped it would make Sakis look more attractive.

I suppose, on reflection, every house share needs an Elaine to take care of the practicalities because if it was all just left to me and Sherri, any necessary funds for groceries and loo paper would have gone on wine, chocolate and English magazines.

Soon we'd settled into everyday life in Lathos. *Trias Kharis*, Mr Mavrakis called us The Three Graces, the three daughters of Zeus, the handmaidens of Aphrodite.

'*Yassas Khari mou*,' he would often wave up to us from the street if he saw us congregating around our plastic table and chairs with instant coffees and Caramelo biscuits, or a shared bar of Ritter Sport, and we'd hang over the railings waving back, relieved to have such an amiable landlord. He often bought us grapes or a bunch of wildflowers, sometimes a tray of sticky *baclava* from his restaurant. He called us his English daughters. As far as

Mr Mavrakis was concerned, we could do no wrong.

From our vantage point, we could look down on the terracotta tiled bars and houses leading uphill towards Stavouna, the entire street bathed in early spring sunshine, with the fragrance of herbs drifting on the breeze, each wall studded with pink and purple bougainvillea. Our railings were shaded slightly by an overhanging pitched roof, and we were sheltered by palm trees so we could all observe life below virtually undetected.

With little to do before the season properly started, we frequently visited Nikos. His mother couldn't speak English but still made us very welcome with a cut glass dish of *gliko* and a glass of water, while we waited for him to finish his gym sessions. She would appear through the overhanging arch of clematis which led to their colourful, sunlit garden, beckoning us over, motioning for to us to sit on elaborately carved dining chairs she'd dragged outside especially for us. Handing us a pile of out-of-date English magazines, she would then busy herself, hanging out her washing while treating us to slightly awkward smiles whenever we made eye contact. As we could do little more than exchange pleasantries, and she only seemed able to say *please* and *sorry* in English, it was always a relief when Nikos emerged from his weights room in the basement, and we could finally communicate with her.

Cars or taxis occasionally wound their way uphill. Grit lorries from the quarry sometimes stopped in the middle of the road, their drivers having long, animated conversations which sounded to the British ear like an escalating, aggressive argument. As the week went on, bars, tavernas, shops and the kiosk sprang into life preparing for the first tourists. Windows were cleaned, tables were hosed down in the street and the rumbling of delivery lorries became more frequent.

Every morning, we'd sit in the Athenian Bar in the same window seat, ordering the same breakfast: black coffee, a freshly baked bread roll with butter, and a Greek Yogurt laced with dark, syrupy, aromatic local honey topped with a small handful of chopped walnuts. If we stayed longer than usual, we'd also order a milkshake and thumb through leftover English magazines, invariably with Princess Diana emblazoned on the covers. With rumours of a rift in the marriage, she was looking increasingly thin and unhappy. I felt sad for her. Only a few years earlier, she'd been a wide-eyed, fairy-tale princess but now her dreams were as crumpled as the taffeta dress she'd worn down the aisle.

We weren't the only foreign nationals in Lathos. We'd also met an Australian man who'd made Lathos his home and owned a small boat for tourist trips around the hidden coves. One afternoon, he took us to Agia Maria to see the somewhat unimpressive shipwreck. I'd found it underwhelming when I'd first seen it with Rob, complaining it was just a lump of rotting iron, not the romantic pirate ship I'd imagined. There were far more imposing shipwrecks on other bigger islands like Corfu and Zakynthos, and the bay itself was an inhospitable rocky wasteland, but now, bobbing gently in the swell of the water on a simple fishing boat, watching the sun glint off the wreck's rusted hull, it had a certain charm and beauty that was probably easier to appreciate from the sea.

'It's actually more interesting than you might think,' the Australian insisted, cleaning his nails with a penknife. 'The ship was wrecked in the 1960s by smugglers carrying illegal contraband. Folklore says a local family, big in crime, with mafia connections, arranged everything and made sure the insurance paid up, so no one was out of pocket. The islanders call it *Sidira Kyria*, The Iron Lady.'

He must have caught our expressions.

'It's not named after your prime minister,' he laughed, jemmying the tops off a few beers on the side of his oar rest, before offering us each one. With a chuckle, his leathery face cracked open into a grin as he opened his Golden Virginia tin and began rolling a joint. 'The island imported no tobacco or cigarettes for at least a year after that and now we have a tourist attraction, so everyone is happy.'

He pointed up to the etched rock face jutting out across the bay to where a small, ruined chapel was clinging precariously to the sharp incline with little more than willpower.

'That's where the smugglers hid their contraband.' Closing his eyes, he took a long draw on his joint before offering it to each of us in turn. 'Church is always a good place for hiding things.'

Following that, I saw Agia Maria in a different, somewhat romantic light, a bit like Jamaica Inn, but in the sunshine.

For the rest of our first weeks, we just lazed about on the beach under the watery sun and a sky of blue marble, hypnotised by the waves, getting to know one another better.

Elaine grew up in a farming community and had worked in a farm shop from the age of sixteen until her redundancy. She was torn over whether to get a professional qualification or to stay and help Sakis run his apartments. Sherri wanted her own travel agency one day. I told them of my ambition to be a published writer and even read them some of my poems, but I didn't mention how obstructive Dad was and how he'd trampled on my dreams.

Dad was a subject I was reticent to broach. Both Elaine and Sherri seemed to have fathers who adored them, so I kept quiet, feeling alienated from all their happy family discussions, strangely jealous of something I didn't fully understand.

I also couldn't help but feel a little envious Elaine had Sakis there. She'd never have to worry about the spectre of the army shrouding them, but least Sherri could share my anxieties as she was in the very same position. I don't know how I'd have coped without her being able to understand exactly how I felt.

'We should all go out on the lash,' Elaine announced one night, painstakingly struggling with yards of magnetic tape as she rewound her Duran Duran album with a pencil. 'Make the most of it before we're all working.'

So, all three of us wandered down to Helios Bar, Sherri and I in denim ra-ra skirts, eyeliner, and lipstick - mine glossy pink, Sherri's bright scarlet. I didn't have the confidence for such a bold shade and envied her for that. Elaine went barefaced as usual, clad in sensible shorts, a t-shirt, and her ubiquitous brown sandals. We'd already had vodka and cokes in the apartment and stuffed ourselves with crisps. Elaine had eaten half a family-sized pizza.

The heat of the night was closing in as we scanned the chalkboard in the bar.

'Well, I'm having a Depth Charge,' Elaine announced, hanging over the counter, trying to explain to Panayiotis what it was.

'That looks absolutely vile. Won't catch me drinking shit like that.' Sherri exchanged a superior glance with me as Elaine asked for a shot glass of Drambuie to be dropped inside her pint.

'Won't catch me mixing my drinks either,' I replied. 'I'm sticking to vodka.'

Sherri slapped a mosquito out of the air.

'We could try a vodka *cocktail*, though....' She was eyeing the menu, reading out the options. 'What about a White Lady?'

Panayiotis shovelled ice into two glasses in readiness.

'You want this in too?' He'd poured in vodka and Cointreau but was now waving the bottle of Drambuie he'd used for Elaine's drink. Sherri looked at me. She hadn't been quick enough with the mosquito. A bubble was forming on her shoulder.

I shrugged.

'Guess so, why not?'

With a flourish, Panayiotis threw a generous slug of the whisky liqueur into our glasses, each decorated with plastic monkeys and a paper umbrella.

'Oh, I love this one,' yelled Elaine, as music flooded the bar. 'Poison Summer!'

Tunelessly, she began singing along to Don Henley's Boys of Summer.

I watched her, a slow smile spreading over my face. Elaine was unselfconsciously howling her way through the track singing completely the wrong words.

'Doesn't even make sense.' Sherri giggled. 'I mean, what's a Poison Summer when it's at home?'

I shook my head, smiling over at Elaine.

Sipping my drink, I pulled a face at Sherri. Adding Drambuie hadn't been such a great idea. Her expression in response spoke volumes.

'I know!' In a flash of inspiration, I lifted my glass. 'Panayiotis can put this on his menu, call it Poison Summer, sell it to unsuspecting tourists.'

Sherri grimaced.

'Only to ones he never wants coming back.'

Laughing openly, we both watched Elaine jigging to the chorus. She'd already necked her Depth Charge and was now ordering something else.

'Another?' Sherri was bright eyed now, slamming her empty glass down on the bar and pushing back her curls.

'Okay,' I agreed, 'But without the Drambuie. That stuff's like paint stripper.'

'It's your turn...' Sherri was yanking up her boob tube which had slipped when she'd leaned over the bar.

'Two more Light Wadies but hold the Drambuie,' I yelled at Panayiotis, briefly standing to disentangle my knickers before sitting back heavily on my bar stool.

Sakis had just walked in, so I wiggled my fingers at him, but he ignored me.

At first, Elaine launched herself at him, laughing, but soon he was walking away. I noticed she'd grabbed his arm, but he'd thrown her off, his hands up in the air and he didn't look happy. He was pointing across the road. When Elaine eventually came over, her eyes seemed bright, prickling with unshed tears.

'What's the matter?' I asked.

Her face was straight.

'It's Sakis, he says we should be at home, not out drinking.'

'What?' I put down my glass and stared at her. 'Are you serious?'

'He's not very happy—'

'That's his problem.'

'Well, it's mine too now, and I don't want to cause trouble because—'

'Elaine! You were drinking in bars all the time last year, we all were, and he was alright about it then, so what's the big deal?'

I threw my hands open in that gesture you often used.

'I know, and I told him that, but he said it's different now.'

Sherri hung over my shoulder.

'Oh, come on Elaine, that's daft. Have another drink.'

Elaine looked defeated.

'No, I'm going back up. You coming?'

I hesitated. I remembered what you'd once said about sitting on a chair, waiting, about not talking to people without permission.

Sherri's eyes darted from me to Elaine.

'Mel, come on,' she pleaded. 'We haven't been out long.'

The bar was filling up now with a mixture of tourists and locals, the heat intensifying with the falling darkness. I noticed the tightness in Elaine's features, the pinch of her mouth and how her earlier, carefree shine had become dulled. She was already walking away. I couldn't let her go on her own, so I began to follow with Sherri dragging reluctantly behind.

Sherri grabbed her arm.

'You do know this is quite ridiculous, don't you, Elaine? He's just being a controlling prick. We were always out before. It's just the same, so why—'

'But it's not the same, is it?' She shrugged free from Sherri's grasp. 'Sakis said we live here now, we're no longer tourists, there are rules.'

After that, with little money left as we hadn't got jobs yet, we stopped going out. Instead, we shared simple meals of pasta in tomato sauce we'd made on the hob, or slabs of pizza washed down with a cheap bottle of wine, while playing music on our balcony.

Sometimes, one of the Mavrakis boys would find me and announce you were on the telephone, and I had to come now. It would feel so strange, taking a call on a payphone at the edge of Mr Mavrakis's counter, crammed up against the dusty display racks of leather sandals and plastic flip flops, while he talked and gesticulated with a friend who was standing virtually elbow to elbow with me.

Your voice sounded thin and distant, as though it had diluted and lost all resonance across the miles stretching between us, the occasional sound of coins being added by you would interrupt us. Always you asked me what was happening at home. Every phone call ended with you telling me to be a good girl, you would be home soon, you loved me. You said all the right things, but with each call, you sounded more strained, distracted, detached. I was reacting to the alien tone of your voice and had begun to sound the same. The army was changing you, changing us. I could sense it.

Sofia, Mr Mavrakis's shy wife, would visit weekly to bring fresh towels. These were always a mismatch of colours and sizes, usually old and threadbare, which we suspected were beach towels left behind by tourists. She would tap the open door, whisper 'plyntirio', laundry, then dart in apologetically to strip our beds, leaving our mattresses bare. All our linen would then be washed by hand outside, with an old-fashioned wash board and a mangle, and pegged on a plastic line across the beach track behind the apartment to billow like a Spanish galleon in full sail. By evening, we'd find everything neatly folded at the foot of our beds. I'd sleep that night with my face buried in the pillow I'd brought from home, the evocative scent of sun, sea and herbs infusing Sofia's freshly laundered, sun-dried pillowcases.

On the wall next to the bed, I'd stuck up photographs with little blobs of Blu-Tack. Looking down on me were my parents under the rose arch in their garden, my cat draped over the sofa, me sitting on the bonnet of my now long-gone Ford Escort, a couple of me on my own that Lisa had taken on our trip, and a table load of us, including Helen from work, Lisa, and Dan, all sat in a wine bar for my 'bon voyage' drinks. I smiled at the memory, taking in all our happy faces, the table littered with bottles, the flash rebounding off our eyes making us all look like red-eyed devils.

I'd also affixed a picture of you and me in Helios Bar. Did I look older than you? I thought I felt the presence of my troll, beginning to edge into the room but I didn't give her the satisfaction of acknowledgment. Instead, I gently stroked your gold charm around my neck like a talisman. At least you were phoning me. I just wouldn't have been able to cope without speaking to you even though I was constantly see-sawing between elation when you phoned and deflation when you hung up. I pictured your tanned, handsome face, your strong brows, and your ever-ready smile. It must be strange for you too, queueing to use a pay phone surrounded by other soldiers with only a finite amount of time in which to call. No, everything would be okay. *Don't Worry, Be Happy.*

20

Heaven Is A Place On Earth

The thought of finding work was never far away, even though we still had a little time left before our money ran out. I tried not to think too hard about it but the need for getting a job, being settled for the season, was an intrusive thought that was hard to ignore. Everyone had said it would be easy to find work and there were signs in many of the hotel windows for kitchen workers, but I wanted something better, something Sherri and I could do together just like we'd always dreamed. I decided to go up to Dimitri's Place and see if Jenny needed anyone, idly thinking how I'd feel that much closer to you if I could work where you once had.

Dimitris was slitting open large boxes of paper napkins in the kitchen, a cigarette in his mouth, as Jenny swept the patio when I walked in off the beach, leaving footprints and a spray of sand over her recently cleaned path. A couple of early morning tourists were sipping frappés by the bar, but apart from that, it was quiet. A radio gently hummed in the background, a gentle Ionian breeze blew, and waves rolled back and forth near the beachside tables where I'd first met you.

'Hi Jenny, remember me?'

She stopped for a moment, then recognition flooded her.

'Yes, of course,' she smoothed her hair back from her pale face. 'How are you?'

I remember you once saying rather disparagingly that her skin was like milk. It was still as white as I remembered, she was clearly not a sun lover. I felt incongruously brown next to her. She leaned on her broom for a moment, shading her eyes with her hand.

'Everything okay?'

'Yes.' I hesitated. 'I just wondered…whether you had any waitressing jobs or bar work coming up? I'm here for the season with my friend and we're both looking for—'

Dimitris walked over, interrupting our conversation.

'No, it's okay, we can manage, Jenny has my brother, Stathis, to help.' He stood protectively by, wiping his hands down his jeans before compressing Jenny's narrow shoulders with a strong, tanned arm and peering hard at me.

'This is Mel,' Jenny smiled up at him as he regarded me with suspicion. 'You know, the English girl with Marios.'

Dimitris ran his eyes cursorily across my top and down my shorts to my tanned legs.

'Yes, I know you,' he said, 'You were here last year…with a man.'

God, he remembered Rob. A rush of heat spread from my chest right up to my neck and face, as I felt pearls of perspiration dotting my forehead.

'Um, yes…I, um—'

'Your husband.'

I said nothing. This was awkward.

'We don't need anyone.' His expression was tight, guarded, a curl of disapproval on his lips. 'We only employ family.'

Jenny smiled apologetically as he stalked back to the kitchen.

'Sorry about him.' Her laugh was a little thin, a twitter laced with discomfort. 'He didn't mean to be rude, he's just old fashioned. Traditional. I'm sorry if he embarrassed you.'

'No, it's fine, please don't worry.'

Family? As far as I knew, Marios wasn't related to Dimitris. We both just looked at each other for a moment.

'I hope you find something,' she said. 'There'll be plenty going soon, honestly, it's just that we're rather small, but I can ask around if you want.'

She looked a little lost as she stood gazing out to sea. It made me feel sorry for her.

'Jenny, when you get some time off, would you like to maybe come to the beach with us? We usually go down there,' I pointed to the wall beyond the Iliad Apartments. 'It's just me and my friend, Sherri. You'd like her. She's English too. You'd be very welcome.'

I smiled my warmest. It occurred to me I needed more friends to survive the island alone, without you, and now it looked like Jenny could really use a friend too.

'Thanks, but I never sunbathe these days,' she said. 'Dimitris thinks its lazy. I don't really get time anyway, and there's my little boy…well, that's if his *Yia Yia* ever lets me near him.'

Something in her voice made me dig deeper.

'Can I ask you something, Jenny?'

'Sure.' She busied herself sweeping under bar stools, while Dimitris huffed and heaved boxes around in the kitchen, casting us the occasional mistrustful glance.

'I won't keep you long but…'

I found myself telling her about how difficult it was not to do or say the wrong things, about some of our silly rows and how there seemed to be an unspoken set of rules to follow.

'Did you find it hard at the beginning?'

She took a deep breath and leaned on the bar.

'It depends on which beginning you mean. If you mean at the beginning of the relationship, no. It wasn't hard, it was magical. He treated me like a queen. I'd never had anything like that level of attention before. So, no, it wasn't hard at all.'

I nodded slowly in agreement, completely empathising with every word she said.

'But if you mean once I'd settled in Lathos off season, yeah, it was hard. I'd been assistant manager in a building society. I'd had a life, money, responsibilities, but as soon as I married Dimitris, I was just his wife, only another foreign woman, a no one really. My opinions held no weight. I felt quite indignant, so I kicked hard against it for a while, until I finally played it their way. It was either that or go home.'

'But surely, I mean, it's the 1980s not Victorian times so couldn't you—'

'Look Mel, we fell for Greek men, and you don't need me to tell you what they're like, how romantic and attentive they are, the way they bowl you over and make you feel so special in a way that English men never do, but you can't exist on romance alone. You soon learn they expect things their way. There are rules and there's little negotiation. There's a set culture here in Aftonisi that you must adapt to if you want to fit in. It's a good life, really, it's just…different.'

'I know, but why—'

'Just remember, its better to fit in than stand out and be noticed for all the wrong reasons. In the beginning, we had so many rows before I finally learned that.' Jenny looked up, her eyes serious. 'A lot of English girls come out here, they fall for local men. They think it's going to be as free and easy as England, only in the sun, but when the holiday's over, real life begins. Then they find Aftonisi too hard and go home. It's not all sun, sea and sex you know. There's the other S too.'

'And what's that?'

'The most important one, the only one that really matters; the System'.

Dimitris was heading our way, so Jenny picked up her broom again and hastily began sweeping over an area she'd already swept before.

The next morning Elaine thundered up the staircase and burst into the apartment in a great flurry of excitement.

'Got some news about our jobs.'

Her face was red from the exertion of running as she slumped into a kitchen chair, gasping before giving her arm pit a quick sniff.

'Fuck me I'm sweating like a cheese.'

Sherri and I exchanged quick glances. I was glad you were not there to see that little display. You expected women to be feminine.

'What...how?' I pulled up a kitchen chair and sat next to her, my elbows on the table, chin resting on my knuckles. This was very exciting news indeed.

'So...,' she began. 'I was speaking to that Kerry earlier.'

Kerry was a no-nonsense girl from Birmingham who was married to Panayiotis at Helios Bar across the road. I wasn't that keen on her.

'Kerry and Panayiotis have got some new rental apartments up near the quarry and they want chambermaids. When I told them about my Saturday job doing all that at the Drovers Arms, they hired me for the season.'

She paused to beam at us.

'Well, that's great, well done.' I tried to sound enthusiastic, but I couldn't. I didn't want to be a sodding chambermaid. I didn't fancy working for humourless Kerry either. How typical of Elaine to just volunteer us without asking.

'Only thing is...' she continued. 'It's day work in shifts so I'll only see Sakis at night now.' Still grinning broadly, she pushed her damp fringe back off her face and began cleaning her glasses on the corner of her t-shirt. 'Main thing is we'll have money coming in.'

That certainly wasn't what I'd had in mind. Maybe I was being idealistic, and beggars couldn't be choosers, however, I'd had this vision: days of sunbathing, swimming, learning Greek, exploring the island with my new friends but when the warm, dark fragrant night fell and the resort came alive with music bars and buzzing tavernas I wanted to be working. I didn't want to be left to my own devices in the evening, when everyone else was out having fun, sitting around alone, missing you. I needed to be busy.

'I didn't really want to work all day—' I began, but she cut me off in her usual blunt manner.

'It's not for you two. It's just for me.'

'But I thought you said you had news about *our* jobs.' I was confused now.

'I do,' she said. 'Kerry said someone called Lynn, at Mayfair, is after bar staff and waitresses but she's opening soon so I said I'd send you down there quickly.'

Bar work and waitressing sounded a lot more fun than stripping beds, emptying bins, and mopping floors. Things were looking up. The first flights had already come over and it was getting a busier in the resort daily, so the timing was great.

At just after midday, Sherri and I set off up the beach to the seafront entrance of Mayfair. The weak springtime sun was flinging spears of light through a pastel sky striped with vapour trails from planes, as a welcome breeze caressed the waves, teasing them up the beach.

'I'm interested to know what Lynn's like.' I padded along next to her, leaving footprints embedded in the damp sand. 'She's probably English with a name like that. I hope she's nice.'

'I'm more interested in what she'll pay.' Sherri gave a dry chuckle, lifting her gypsy skirt high around her thighs, wading along the shoreline. 'I'm not working myself to the bone for nothing.'

Soon we came to the restaurant and stepped hesitantly off the beach, through an archway which led up a crazy-paved path to a patio. Behind this was a palm-fringed bar which looked more Polynesian than Greek, with a selection of tables and chairs scattered around.

A tall, sullen-looking, bearded man wearing glasses stood guard at the entrance, leaning on a broom, a fag dangling in his hand.

'Hi,' I smiled as brightly as possible as we both bent to put on our flip flops. 'We're looking for Lynn?'

Sullen Glasses said nothing, just took a long draw on his cigarette, eyeing us up and down laconically, returning my expectant gaze with blankness.

'I'm not sure he understood you,' whispered Sherri to me as we stood there, making awkward eye contact with him. 'Maybe he doesn't speak English?'

I tried again in Greek.

'Um…er…*pou ine Lynn, parakalo?*'

He gave us both a dull stare, the ash now piling up at the end of his cigarette, ready to fall.

'Perhaps he's a bit…you know, simple?' Sherri said to me, her eyes still fixed on the man's.

'I do speak English, you know,' he snapped back.

He gave a sharp jerk of the thumb towards the kitchen where a woman in jeans was scuttling about behind a counter.

'Thank you...' I was about to say it in Greek too, but he'd already strolled off, leaving a stack of ash standing to attention on the path.

'Hi, are you Lynn?' I called out.

The woman ambled out from behind the servery, wiping both hands down the front of her jeans and peering at us both enquiringly. She had distractingly prominent front teeth, bright red hair pulled into a ponytail and a Scottish accent.

'I am, who's asking?'

I explained what we were there for.

'Ah, you're the two girls with Marios and Petros, the army widows.' She gave a warm laugh, grabbing each of our hands in turn and pumping them up and down enthusiastically. 'You two *must* be in love to come out here without them. Nice to meet you.'

She regarded us both with dark blue eyes.

'You waitressed and worked bars before?'

'Yes,' I responded enthusiastically, watching Sherri do the same, knowing full well she was lying.

'Good, because I really haven't got time to train beginners,' Lynn said. 'I run this place. Yorgos is my husband. He's the chef.'

She indicated towards Sullen Glasses who'd stopped sweeping now and was staring into space. 'There's also Yiannis who looks after the bar, so you may need to help him too. Deserts are always ice creams which you serve from here.' She pointed at an ice cream fridge with lots of empty plastic containers lined up bearing exotic names like *Caribbean Rum Punch, Chocolate Decadence* and *Strawberry Shortcake Surprise.*

'Okay.' I felt excited, knowing I was going to like this sort of work.

'If a customer wants to buy you a drink, you can take the money but tell Yiannis first so he can account for it or drink it if you like, just don't get pissed.'

Sherri beamed at me.

I'd heard something vague about needing Health Papers to work legally in Greece.

'Don't we need papers though?'

'Well, yes…and no. You technically need certification after three months, and your employer is supposed to pay for it, but it's expensive and means lots of form filling, so hardly anyone does it. You've not been here long, have you, so I wouldn't worry.'

'But what happens after three months though? Won't we get arrested or something?'

Lynn laughed deeply.

'Well, *technically*, you could.'

She seemed to like that word, technically. I gulped inwardly. I didn't like the sound of arrested at all. I'd seen Midnight Express and although this wasn't Turkey, I was pretty sure a Greek prison wouldn't be dissimilar.

'You only need to worry when the police come in checking, but there's a way around that anyway.'

'Really?' Well, that was a relief. I exhaled the breath I'd been containing. 'Do they come in often?'

'Yeah, quite often.' Seeing my concerned expression, she playfully shoved my arm. 'Don't look so worried. All you do is sit at the nearest table, grab one of your customer's drinks and just act like you're with them. Simple. Just get them more drinks later.'

'And that's alright?' I could hear the doubt creeping into my voice. I wasn't sure this was such a good idea.

'It's fine, don't you both go worrying now. In all the time I've been here, I've only ever seen one - okay, maybe two - arrests.'

Yorgos had ambled over and was giving the patio a cursory flick with his broom while regarding us over his glasses. Lynn shouted to him in rapid Greek which I assume was a resume of our conversation because I caught the word *Astynomia*, Police. At this, Yorgos grinned, somewhat nastily. It was the first time I'd actually seen him smile.

We must have still looked very straight-faced because Lynn turned to face us, head cocked to one side, arms folded, the faintest suspicion of uncertainty sharpening her features.

'Look, do you want these jobs, because it's going to get busy soon, and I don't have time to mess about?'

Mutely, we both nodded.

Okay, three shifts,' she used the fingers on one hand to tick them off in the air. 'Lunchtime 11am-4pm, Evening 7pm-12pm, oh, and the early one, 6am-11am, that's the Shit Bin Shift. Anything else, Yorgos and I can take care of.'

I was trying to process this rapid delivery. Except for the vague possibility of ending up in a Greek jail, it all seemed pretty good to me. At least we wouldn't be stripping beds or mopping floors like Elaine.

'Why's it called Shit Bin Shift?' Puzzlement was creasing Sherri's forehead. I was glad she'd asked because I'd been wondering too.

Lynn just gave a throaty chuckle.

'You'll find out,' she said.

At last, we had work and money coming in quicker than we'd expected.

We ran into Nikos on the way back who was delighted. He wanted to take us into Aftonisi Town to celebrate but was worried about his ancient car as, in his words, it had a 'little problem'.

'You can drive?' He looked at us both expectantly.

Sherri shook her head.

'I can,' I said, regarding the car doubtfully. Nikos didn't seem to want to drive his own car, which worried me a little. It looked more suited to stock car racing and, since I'd last seen it, he'd somehow sawn the top off, creating a home-made convertible which he appeared enormously proud of.

'This is good,' Nikos seemed very happy and wasted no time in getting me ensconced in the driving seat. The 'little problem' turned out to be something major to do with the clutch but Nikos was determined, so we made our way into town with me driving, Sherri in the back, and Nikos crouching in the footwell using pliers to operate the clutch whenever I needed to change gear.

'I have heard from Marios,' he announced as he took a rest from changing gear, and I flew along in fourth. 'He asked me if you were being a good girl.'

'I'm always a good girl.' I replied, puzzled for a moment why you would ask Nikos. Didn't you trust me?

It was early April, and the sun was getting stronger. With its growing warmth came the excitement of Pascha, the Greek Orthodox Easter, biggest of all Greek celebrations. Leaning over the balcony railings one afternoon, we'd noticed quite a few open-backed trucks full of bleating lambs all destined to end up on a spit for the celebration.

Nikos was very keen we accompany him to Aftonisi Town on the night of Easter Saturday, so he drove us in his cousin's truck, and we stood alongside him in the Square outside the Church of Agios Stephanos, where a huge crowd had gathered to hear the *Pappas* recant the Gloria. With all the lights off, it was as though there'd been a universal power cut. Everything was enveloped in a deep black velvet darkness.

It must have been about 11.30pm and the blackened street had become interwoven with a procession of children holding lit candles all making their way towards the church under the priest's hypnotic incantations. Suddenly, everyone seemed to have candles. I really missed you. This was my first Greek Easter and I wished I'd been able to experience it with you. Tears began prickling. It was just so emotional, so incredible, so evocative but it also made me feel so totally alone and insignificant. It was as though I was on the edge of something I didn't truly understand.

Sherri must have noticed as she unexpectedly put an arm around my waist, so I did the same, and, leaned into her. Wrapped in each other's arms, we stood in awe watching what was happening around us as the bells of Agios Stephanos, and every church nearby, began chiming in harmony, ringing out across the town along with what seemed like a million voices calling out *Christos Anesti,* Christ is risen. Nikos turned to us, his face shining, candlelight flickering in his eyes.

'*Christos anesti,* my friends, *Christos anesti.*' Sherri and I just smiled back hesitantly demonstrating our characteristic British reserve. What were we supposed to do or say now?

Nikos must have read our minds.

'Okay, now you say *Alithos O Kirios*,' he prompted, making us repeat it after him until he was satisfied with our pronunciation. Apparently, it meant *truly, the lord is risen*, and was what you said in response. He seemed very happy indeed when we did, shouting *bravo* so close to my ear he nearly deafened me. Soon, we'd forgotten our shyness and were happy to say this to anyone who greeted us.

It was the most wonderful, joyous experience, set against a backdrop of the inky night sky which had just exploded in arcs of vivid, crackling, jewel bright colour. Soon there was a strong smell of sulphur in the air and unexpectedly loud bangs at ground level as children let off firecrackers in the street to excited cries of *Kalo Pascha.*

'Isn't that rather dangerous?' Sherri said, leaping away from one which landed rather too close for comfort as we followed Nikos back through the square to the truck, where he invited us back to his home for a meal. We thanked him, but said we were both tired. The fact Nikos had mentioned a soup his mother was making from the entrails of a lamb was possibly the strongest deciding factor in us declining.

After a few weeks of working at the restaurant Sherri and I were very used to our new work routines. Wading through the waves, shoes in one hand, to cut across the beach opposite and arrive at the restaurant before sunrise certainly beat fighting my way to work through the heaving Southampton traffic. My previous existence as an estate agent now seemed like another person's life on another planet far away. Even the brutally early morning shift was a pleasure when I could watch the sun rising over the sea, draping a chiffon pink glow over the pastel horizon, gradually infusing everything with golden light. Sometimes I'd just be overwhelmed by Aftonisi's beauty.

There were more tourists around Lathos by late April, but as it was still early in the season, it was mainly couples or older visitors who preferred the scenic splendour of springtime while the island was still verdant, and the fertile earth had yet to bake into hard clay. Each day the resort shone with the promise of a blisteringly hot summer to come and each coach that arrived was fuller than the last. I smiled to myself, remembering how the first intake at the very beginning of the month had been greatly misjudged by local teenage boys who'd doused themselves in Lynx for a drive-past of the bars on their mopeds. No doubt they were expecting lots of pretty girls to impress with their battle cries of '*Opa!*' as they pulled wheelies in a dust cloud. Instead, all they found was a handful of bemused octogenarians quietly sipping coffees.

21

It's Alright (Baby's Coming Back)

One Sunday I was sitting in the window seat of the Athenian Bar, alone, sipping my coffee while feeling vaguely disappointed because there'd been no fresh bread deliveries.

I chewed my slightly stale Saturday bread roll as I flicked through Friday's newspaper, which was full of the aftermath of the Hillsborough Stadium tragedy, when Sofia Mavrakis burst into the bar.

'*Ela, grigora,* Come quickly. You have telephone call.'

Jumping up I ran after her into the kiosk, squeezing past all the leather sandals and last year's sun creams that had been left out on a rack to stew in the heat. Never buy SPF from a resort kiosk. I picked up the receiver, excited to speak to you.

It was Rob.

I could instantly feel a tightening in my throat, my stomach contracting at just the sound of his voice. The line crackled.

'Everything okay?'

'So, we have an offer on the house.'

We were on the market for £60,000 so I was hoping it would be close to that. We needed to clear £48,000 to discharge the mortgage and all the debts Rob had built up. Anything else would pay for the solicitors and estate agency fees and what was left over would be split between us. Alan had been confident we'd get close to the asking price and had said anything around £58,000 upwards would be a good offer.

Rob's voice was a little indistinct, but I heard him mumble something.

'Sorry,' I said. 'Thought for a moment you'd said £52,000.'

'I had.'

'Rob, that's not nearly enough!'

Something began to grip me, a feeling of unease crept through to my core, squeezing at my insides.

'Yeah, I know, but listen, Mel, you'll really like this...'

I had a strong feeling I really wouldn't, as my hand tightened around the receiver. Sofia glanced at me as she stacked cigarette packets. My expressive face must be giving the game away, so I forced her a bright smile before continuing.

'Go on.'

'So, I'm going to accept it.' Rob said. I genuinely think he expected me to be pleased.

More crackles.

'Why, for God's sake, Rob, are you mad? That's way too low—'

'No, no, listen,' he interrupted. There was a pause as his breath hissed through a cigarette. I could imagine his expression. 'This bloke's a builder, right. Always flashing the cash. Met him in the Royal Anchor. Wants to turn the house into bedsits...anyway, he's cut us this *really* good deal.'

I admit to having more than just a little pang at that point. My beautiful house turned into bedsits when I'd hoped for a family who would continue to restore it, to love it as I had.

'What deal?'

'Okay, so... I tell Alan we accept, and it all goes though for 52 grand, right?' Another draw on the cigarette. 'But then this bloke bungs us another six grand in cash on the q.t when we exchange. Genius, eh?'

'But I don't see why he can't just pay us £58,000 like a normal buyer?'

'He's explained it to me, and it all makes sense,' Rob was speaking faster and faster now. 'That's three grand each upfront. It saves us paying so much agency commission, and we get cash on exchange, so we don't have to even wait for completion for all our funds. Oh, and he's going to give me first refusal on a bedsit too.'

'And Alan's okay with that?'

I could hear the doubtfulness in my voice and the tightness in his.

'Well, I haven't actually said anything to him yet…but it's not up to Alan, isn't it?'

Something wasn't right here.

'I'm not sure about this, Rob,' I began. 'I mean, what's in it for this builder?'

'Christ's sake, I've just explained.'

I knew that tone of voice. I could imagine his frantic, wide-eyed expression, fag waving around, jabbing a finger into the air for emphasis.

'No, you haven't. You've only told me what's happening, not why?'

'It's just something about tax, cash flow, you know, all complicated business stuff, something about money he's trying to keep under the radar, but he's loaded. Got a Rolex. Bought me an Indian at the Maharajah Star and that place is proper expensive.'

I tried to quell the feeling of panic beginning to accelerate with my heartbeat.

'What's his name?'

Maybe I'd heard of him. Maybe Alan knew him.

Another draw on the cigarette. He was chewing gum now. I could hear it squelching wetly down the line.

'Um Dean…hang on, think it was Roger.'

Rob could be a such an exasperating dick. I felt my blood pressure rising as I snapped back at him.

'Well, which one is it?'

'Dean Rogers…or was it Roger Dean? Anyway, one or the other…'

Rob began to ramble on, extolling the virtues of 'Dean or Roger'.

'Look, I'll call you tomorrow.'I wasn't wasting any more of my day on this. 'Just don't speak to that Dean or Roger bloke, until I've phoned, okay?'

I'd ring Alan. He'd know what to do.

'Right.' Rob seemed slightly distracted now, like something else had taken his attention, his voice was fainter, as though he'd moved the receiver further away.

'Fine, speak tomorrow,' I nibbled my cuticles, and clenched my jaw. Alan would sort this out. Thank God for Alan.

A pause, more crackles. Sofia was gabbling in Greek to a friend, ignoring the customer standing patiently next to me waiting to buy a bottle of Nivea Factor 10. His shoulder rubbed mine. There was no such thing as privacy in the kiosk.

'Mel?'

'What?'

'When are you coming home?'

It was like I'd just gone on an Awayday to London not moved over 2,000 miles away, like we were still a couple.

'I'm not.' I hung up.

I walked back towards the bar, my head a washing machine of thoughts. Rob was so erratic, so volatile. I decided to ring Dan after I'd rung Alan. Perhaps he could talk some common sense into him, even though I knew Dan found him as unpredictable as I did. I thought back to my 'goodbye' drinks at the wine bar in March when Dan had pulled me to one side.

'I need to just ask you something Mel,' he'd said. 'Please don't be offended or anything but Rob's not...abusive in any way to you, is he?' I remember jumping inwardly as he continued. 'I mean, everything you're doing, getting divorced, moving to Greece for this younger guy, it's all a bit *extreme* isn't it, unless there's more to things than you're letting on?'

I'd found it hard to meet his eyes.

'Oh no, absolutely nothing like that.' I had laughed, reassuring him, watching him look visibly relieved. I'd smiled back at him, changing the subject but I'd felt too ashamed to say more. Rob wasn't abusive in the way Dan had meant, but there had been many insidious attempts at control I should have seen as red flags. Now I felt stupid for ignoring them, for putting up with Rob's behaviour for so long. What did that say about me?

In Lathos, there'd been one afternoon when we'd been walking back to the room and were nearing a shop. I'd been thirsty and wanted a bottle of water.

'Why waste money, there's one in the room?' Rob had argued.

'But I'm thirsty Rob. We can share it on the way back.'

'I'm not paying extra. There's one in the room.'

I tried not to make too much of a fuss. I knew he'd had a few beers and was what I called 'on the turn'. I'd pulled at his arm.

'Come on, Rob—'

'I said no.'

Jutting his chin, he'd continued to march uphill, pretending he couldn't hear me. I remember my frustration with him had quickly turned to elation when I'd discovered a few forgotten coins in my bag, so I'd quickly darted in and bought some water anyway. After taking a few sips, I'd caught up with him, offering the bottle.

'Go on, you must be thirsty too.'

Our eyes had connected for a moment as he'd snatched it off me.

The insistent heat of the sun was baking my arms, scorching my skin, it's brightness like a relentless spotlight on me. He had his aviators on now. I could see my face reflected in their void as I smiled up at him, hoping to keep the peace. He took a few large gulps.

'I said we had one in the room, didn't I? I told you not to buy one.'

Despite being spoken to like a child, I'd felt only relief. I'd diffused what could have so easily become one of his blacker, alcohol-induced moods.

He'd swilled the last of it around his mouth.

He'd spat it straight back into my face.

The following day, Sherri and I were working the evening shift together. I really enjoyed evening shifts. It was like getting dressed up for a night out but knowing you'd be paid for it.

Yiannis the barman had been younger than I'd expected, probably about my age, with cropped black hair, lots of gold chains and an insolent stare. He never seemed to smile at me at all, but he was all teeth whenever Sherri was nearby. I got the distinct impression he didn't like me, but he certainly liked Sherri and had begun following her about like a puppy.

'Don't you find Yiannis a bit annoying,' I asked her after yet another time I'd noticed him trailing around behind her, his eyes following her lasciviously wherever she walked.

'Oh, he's okay,' she said, glancing back at him, a flush spreading over her face, a half-smile on her lips.

I raised an eyebrow.

'Oh, not like that,' she replied with a chuckle. 'We're just friends.'

May arrived and with it, my birthday. Greeks are not big on birthdays. They prefer to celebrate their Name Days, the day commemorating the saint whose name they share, so when my birthday dawned it, all felt a bit of an understatement.

'Happy Birthday my lovely,' Sherri burst into my bedroom with a card and a small, gift-wrapped box containing my favourite White Musk Oil from the Body Shop along with a few bath-oil pearls.

'Thank you, they're perfect.' I hugged her tight after slitting open the envelope and propping her card on my bedside table.

'There's something else for you,' she beamed. 'Come on.' She threw my little cotton bathrobe at me, then, pulling me out of bed, propelled me into the kitchen and pushed me down into a chair.

'Ta da!' Elaine burst in, wearing shorts and one of Sakis's t-shirts. She'd gone out earlier to buy my favourite hot roll, a portion of butter, a yogurt, and a small pot of deliciously sweet, dark, sticky local honey.

'Happy Birthday,' she boomed, presenting them to me with a Nescafé and giving me an unexpected peck on the cheek. 'Big surprise for you today.' I could tell she was simply desperate to say something, but I noticed the warning glance Sherri shot her.

'Surprise?'

'Oh…it's nothing much, just something for later.' Elaine busied herself making her own coffee and one for Lord Sakis who was still languishing in bed. I loved surprises when they were for other people, but particularly disliked ones involving me, so I resolved to practise my *Its-Just-What-*

I-Always-Wanted face for later, should I need it. Hopefully I could draw on my acting ability.

Elaine was working all day at the Sunrise Bar, but Sherri and I weren't needed until the evening, so we wandered into the resort to see who was around.

'Let's go to the beach for a bit,' Sherri suggested, and soon we were lying on the sand, soaking up the sun.

Nikos came to find me, presenting me with a large Oleander blossom.

'*Chronia pola*, my dearest friend,' he sang, crouching in the sand to embrace me enthusiastically, slapping a massive kiss on each cheek as he attempted to position the bloom in my hair.

'How old you are now?' He enquired in his broken English.

I laughed. That would be a rude question in England, but this was Greece, and, furthermore, this was lovely Nikos, and I was quite fond of him.

'Twenty-eight,' I laughed, enjoying the attention of this special, birthday morning, my first in Greece.

'*Ikosi octo*, twenty-eight,' he exclaimed. He looked at me seriously for a moment, shaking his head and whistling through his teeth. '*Po po po*, twenty-eight is very old indeed.' Then he burst out laughing as I leapt up, chasing him along the beach, while trying to hang on to the Oleander bloom.

After Nikos left, Sherri checked her watch then got up, dusting down her denim cut-offs.

'Wait here,' she said. 'Got something for you.'

Was this my birthday surprise? Feeling thoroughly spoiled, I sat back against the wall by the Iliad Apartments hoping I wouldn't need my rehearsed grateful face. I watched the waves gently crawling up the beach and receding, fully appreciating the beauty around me; the lemonade morning sunshine, the sparking turquoise sea, the sensation of my legs making indents in the pale golden sand. I sat there, idly stirring the sand, cupping it in one palm and letting it trickle through my fingers into the other. The sun burned through the crest of proud Cypress trees. A petal dropped from my oleander bloom. Sherri had been gone ages.

I must have been in some sort of trance, hypnotised by the growing warmth of the sun, the waves, the beach, because I thought I saw you for a moment, or at least, someone who looked a bit like you. Then I leapt to my feet. It was you.

You sprinted over the sand to me.

'Baby *mou*.' Your arms were around me, your lips on mine, your back-crushing bear hug of an embrace nearly squeezing the air from my lungs as you lifted me up. '*Chronia pola*.'

'Oh my God, I'd no idea.'

You were grinning at me.

'It's a surprise.'

It certainly was. In more ways than one. Your beautiful black curls had gone and what was left had been drastically shorn into a brutal short cut making you look older, harder, more severe. I found myself staring at you in shock.

'My hair?' you ran a palm over it. 'You like? I had the best army hairdresser.'

'When did you get back?'

'Earlier, I came as soon as I could.'

'How long?' I hardly dared ask.

'One week'

My heart was doing cartwheels. One week. This was the best birthday present ever.

You took my hand and pulled me up the beach towards our apartment where you pulled the shutters and we hurriedly undressed, tugging at buttons and zips, t-shirts over heads, shoes kicked across the floor. It was only when we stood facing one another that I got a good look at you. You looked tired, worn somehow, but the biggest shock had been your hair. It had changed you quite dramatically, making your profile different, your jawline more prominent. You were different. Any softness you'd previously had in your body had hardened, your muscles were more pronounced, your legs solid, like granite, your palms were calloused. I glanced at you warily, feeling shy. It was like I was with a stranger, and I didn't know quite how to behave.

You must have sensed this.

'I'm still me,' you said. 'I'm just the same, nothing's changed.'

I tried to quell something rising inside me as I gazed back at you. Yes, it was you, but whatever you said, something had changed, you weren't the same and I wanted the other one back, the one before the army.

22

Wonderful Life

All too soon, your week's leave was over.

'I will be back soon, *agapē mou,*' you said kissing my hair, my eyelids, my lips while we lay entangled in bed just before you were due to return to Kos. I was desperately sad you were leaving, but also happy nothing had really changed between us as I'd feared.

We'd had a couple of minor spats, but nothing serious.

Sitting in a bar, Black's song Wonderful Life had come on.

'This is a really beautiful song, *moro,*' you'd said, playing with my hair, expecting an affirmative answer.

Perhaps I should have just agreed with you.

'So, what, you're some sort of music critic now?' you'd snapped.

Our eyes had locked, mine in surprise, yours glitteringly hard, as we stared each other down. Wasn't I allowed a different opinion? You were like a stranger for a moment.

It was over in a second, but I was beginning to learn you didn't like me disagreeing with you, about anything. Just one of your character traits. I'd assumed you were getting edgy about returning to camp so I chose not to dwell on it, particularly as it might be a long time before I saw you again.

The next day, when you left in the early morning, I felt stronger somehow.

I had my new friends. I had my job. I had the sunshine. Choking back tears I watched you go.

This is what you wanted, I reminded myself. *You knew there would be days like these.*

In no time at all, springtime on Aftonisi was over, and the island had accelerated full throttle into a hot, sultry June, full of tourists, beach days and working nights. After one busy shift, I'd planned to walk up to the Sunshine Bar with Sherri to meet Elaine for a drink, but Sherri had been too tired and wanted to go straight home. So, I went alone.

Elaine was stomping her way down the hill, scuffing up dust with each footstep.

'Hey,' she boomed good-naturedly, giving me a cheery wave. The heat had flattened her hair into a helmet and there were damp patches under the arms of her blue t-shirt. 'Could fuckin' murder a pint. Been working since six and my throat's dry as a badger's arse.'

Poor Elaine had been on her feet all day, stripping beds, mopping floors, and emptying bins before serving behind the pool bar. So, we settled down at the first bar back along the road, Elaine with a pint, me with a vodka.

'So, you like the job, then?' I was really enjoying mine. I relished the evening shifts, when the tempo changed, the light softened, and the fairy lights and lanterns laced the decking with jewel-bright colours. I loved the sensory overload of vibrant orange sunsets, the burring cicada army in the pine trees, even the sizzle of Yorgos's open hotplate. I thrived on the urgency of getting orders out to the tables, and happily chatting to new people every week.

'Yeah, it's good,' she said, gulping her man-sized drink. 'Some of tourists are pigs though, so messy.' I smiled to myself, thinking of how Sakis had gradually scattered clothes and fag ash all over Elaine's room to the extent that Sherri and I now referred it as 'the skip' or 'the floordrobe' when she wasn't around.

Together we sat with our drinks, enjoying the buzz of activity in the busy bar, chatting about nothing in particular until she nudged me, drawing my attention to the English wife of the Greek owner.

'That could be you one day,' she said, a degree of palpable excitement in her voice. 'You know, working with Marios, in your very own bar.'

I put my drink down for a moment, watching the woman scurry around, frantically wiping tables, clearing ashtrays, taking payments, and collecting plates, while her husband simply leaned louchely on the bar, talking to friends, eyeing girls, waving his cigarette.

As the harassed woman continued to rush about, I watched her unshaven husband clicking his fingers for attention, an impressive beer gut straining over his jeans, and smiled inwardly. Marios wasn't a slob like him. He'd never make me do everything. He'd said it would be *our* bar so I'd be his equal, his partner. He respected me.

Thoughts of equality, respect and partnership made me decide to talk to Elaine about Sakis. I started off gently, taking another sip of the vodka, feeling its welcoming warmth flood my veins.

'How did you meet him?'

'Came on holiday with my pal Carol and we were at a bar and got a bit pissed,' she explained with a grin. 'I saw Sakis and thought, *phwoar*.'

I couldn't imagine anyone thinking *phwoar* about old fish lips, but it perfectly proved the adage that there was someone for everyone.

'Anyway.' She took another slurp of her pint. 'Caz dared me to go and speak to him, but I went one better.' She rolled brown cow eyes, which appeared even rounder now when viewed through her highly magnified lenses.

'Guess what I did?'

I had no idea.

She gave a deep, snorty chuckle.

'I decided I was going to snog his face off, so I went over and stuck my tongue straight down his throat.' My face was probably displaying its usual transparency. 'Ended up having a knee trembler round the back of Helios Bar.'

I wasn't expecting that, and thinking of Sakis, I could only imagine he'd made the most of a rare opportunity as he certainly wasn't your average

Greek god. More like a Greek cod with those lips. I couldn't help but smile to myself, thinking of the fun I'd have later, regaling Sherri with this juicy little morsel.

'Marios said he had Swedish girlfriend once?'

'Yeah, Elsa.' Elaine seemed unbothered about Sakis's past and equally unfazed by my nosiness. 'He was only about 20, but she was ancient, at least 10 years older. Bit of a cow if you ask me, screwed some other bloke when he was away in the army, but apparently it wasn't serious and he'd wanted to finish things anyway, so it saved him the job of dumping her.'

We sat in silence for a moment, but then I seized the opportunity.

'Elaine,' I began. 'I hope you won't mind me saying, but he's quite rude to you, isn't he? I hate the way he speaks to you sometimes. You really don't have to put up with it, you know. You should try giving it back to him, see how he likes it.'

She drained her drink.

'He's a funny bugger sometimes, I know, but it's okay, I can look after myself. I don't want to get him all at it because he's lovely to me sometimes… you should see him when he's had a drink.'

'Yes, but—'

'Mel, you don't know him like I do.'

I nodded, sipping my drink. That much was true.

'And you're planning to go to university?' I thought I'd better engage her in something else. 'That's so exciting.'

'Well…' she began, picking at a beer mat. 'I'd like to, but Sakis isn't keen. I did say he could come to England with me for a bit, but he wants to stay put here. He was really pleased about my redundancy pay though.'

I pressed my lips together tightly. *Yes, I bet he was.*

I stared at her. She looked so much smaller and less defensive when she looked back at me that I felt a surprising rush of protectiveness towards her. I needed to make her see sense. It made me realise how much time I'd wasted on Rob. For the first time, I began to think of my own future too. Maybe I could write as well as work with Marios? He wouldn't expect me to just work in a bar when I had other potential.

'You can't give up on your dreams, Elaine. What about running your own business?'

Resting her chin on her hand, she leaned in.

'I might be able to defer for a year if I get accepted... there's also an opportunity to study in Athens, but Sakis says my Greek isn't good enough, besides, he wants me to run those apartments of his once they're finished.' She fixed me with her Coke-bottle gaze. 'What would you do?'

I probably wasn't the best person to ask. I had a history of impulsive, irrational decisions. Elaine was the sensible one. I was the one who'd given up a career, a home, and a husband, to impulsively run off to Greece.

'Well... you'll have your redundancy pay, so, whatever you decide, you have real opportunities now. Just don't make any rash decisions. If Sakis really cares about you, he'll understand. If you want to go to university, just make him see exactly how much it means to you. Have it out with him. You have to think of your future.'

The small frown on her face was beginning to smooth and her blank expression was beginning to animate, so I carried on. God, I loathed Sakis.

'You deserve to follow your dreams. He'll still be there if he loves you, won't he? Don't let him talk you out of it. You could even come back after university, get his apartments up and running for him, then do something else for yourself?'

She didn't answer.

I wanted to shake her.

'Talk to him.'

'He won't like it, though—' She sounded doubtful, wavering, so I interrupted her.

'Look, Elaine, man up. You're a strong woman. You're clearly intelligent enough to go to university. He should be proud of you, so just bloody well do it, then go and start that business empire.' I smiled encouragingly at her, all the while feeling fury towards Sakis bubbling up inside. 'You know you'll only regret it if you don't.'

Emitting a loud belch, Elaine checked her watch as we got up to leave.

'You know what,' she seemed visibly brighter. 'I think you're right Mel.

185

I'll have it out with him later, like you said. That's not a bad idea.'

The next morning, I couldn't wait to tell Sherri about Elaine's dilemma and the additional little nugget that she was more spontaneous than we'd realised, so I tapped on her door, but instead of waiting like I usually did, I walked straight in. I could see the curve of her body under the sheets, her blonde hair fanned over the pillow.

'Morning.' I opened her shutters as I called out to her. 'I've got the kettle on, and I've got the funniest story to tell you...' The words died on my lips. Not only did Sherri's flushed face pop up, but Yiannis's did too.

Sherri was still a bit flustered as we sat together on the balcony later. She took a long, drag on her Marlboro, leaning towards the railings.

'I know this looks bad,' she said, fidgeting with her rings, while sighing out a plume of smoke.

'Do you really like him?' I stared directly into her blue eyes. I'd thought she'd been happy with Petros. She'd left Kevin for him and had been prepared to wait for him while he was in the army.

She averted her gaze and wouldn't look back at me properly for what felt like ages.

'I guess I'm just enjoying the attention,' she finally said.

'But what about Petros?' Something felt like it was slipping from my grasp. Sherri and I had been in the same situation. The army widows, Lynn had called us, but now I felt abandoned, marooned, setting a solo course when previously I'd had a sailing companion. Everything was changing. The sand was shifting under my feet.

'Oh God, I don't know.' She stabbed out her Marlboro on a saucer, then resting her forehead on her hand, stared hard at the table. 'I still have feelings for Petros, I mean, I still like him, but... I like Yiannis too, I mean, I *really* like him. Petros is away, but that's the problem; he's away. You get it, don't you Mel? Yiannis is here, Petros isn't. Does that make sense?'

Sadly, it did. I looked at her hopelessly, at a loss as to what to say.

'Okay, so, what would you do if they were both in front of you right now?' I ventured. 'Who would you choose?'

Sherri's gaze flickered to mine.

'It's complicated.'

'You're not kidding.'

'Yiannis knows about Petros, so it's not like I'm hiding anything from him. Does it sound awful to say I really want to see how I'll feel when Petros is back and they're both here? I think it's the only way I'll be able to decide.'

It made perfect sense to me, but I still felt desperately sorry for Petros. From your letters, I knew how hard it must be for him in the army, being away from everything he knew. You'd told me my letters and phone calls were all that kept you sane and you'd go mad without them. Surely that was how Petros felt too? I felt horribly conflicted, but Sherri was my closest friend now and I had to be supportive.

'You won't tell Marios, will you?' She gripped my wrist for a moment. 'I'm going to see Yiannis in secret for now, so please don't say anything. I just need a little time to work it out, that's all.'

'Of course, I won't.' My eyes darted towards Elaine's closed bedroom door. Keeping things quiet would be hard in here, Sherri must know that. I would do all I could to keep her secret but something I couldn't easily define was making me feel uneasy. Petros was your friend. Was I being disloyal to you by being loyal to her? Loyalty was a big thing to you. I wasn't technically *lying* to you, yet I was keeping something from you. I was aware of the dull ache of guilt, yet, surprisingly, something else was snaking its way around my insides too, something I really wasn't expecting. Sherri was stepping on board the train of a brand-new love affair whereas mine had been temporarily derailed. She would be out having fun; I would still be alone, going to bed early, feeling lost. The realisation came like a slap around the face. I was jealous.

We sat in silence for a moment. Sherri was playing with her little love-bead bracelet, snapping the elastic thread up and down so much I thought it was going to break.

'There's something else too,' she said, biting at her thumbnail before raking scarlet nails through her blonde curls.

'What?'

187

'One minute.' She got up and darted off to her bedroom, returning with a blue airmail letter which she thrust at me.

'Just the last bit, but promise you won't say anything, okay?'

I nodded in agreement and tentatively took it from her while she perched opposite me, hugging one knee in, rocking back and forth on her chair, her eyes never leaving my face. It was from Kevin, which was unexpected enough, but I felt my jaw slacken and my mouth hang as I read it.

'Sherri, he's coming out here!'

'He wants us to try again.' She bit the skin around her thumb. 'What do I do now?'

'Can't you stop him somehow?' I felt an upsurge of anxiety on her behalf, but it was simple really. All she had to do was ring and stop him coming.

Neither of us spoke for a moment but I noticed she was still avoiding my gaze. Then it all came to me in a rush.

'You *want* him to come, don't you?'

She grabbed her pack of Marlboro and lit another, inhaling deeply.

'Please don't judge me. I know it's a mess; *I'm* a mess, but I need to be sure who's right for me.'

'Does Petros know about Kevin?'

'God, no, that would be horrendous.'

How could Sherri possibly think this could stay quiet with Sakis coming and going without any notice, and everyone knowing each other's business. Technically she had three men on the go now. This was madness.

'And Yiannis?' I hardly dared ask.

'Yes, but he thinks I want Kevin here to finish things properly, face to face.'

This was going to be very interesting indeed.

I didn't have long to think about how to help Sherri with her dilemma as I was soon to have one or two of my own. That afternoon Sofia came to find me.

'Telefono,' she said. 'Ela, grigora.' I did as I was told and came quickly to the kiosk and picked up the phone. It was Alan.

'Mel, I thought you should know your husband has unwisely accepted what I consider a frankly ridiculous offer on the house from a local builder, a Mr Roger—'

'Dean.' I interrupted. 'Roger Dean?' Something had cut the strings to my heart, and it plunged at speed like a lift in a skyscraper. I hated there was an element of dishonesty towards Alan I'd somehow been obliged to collude with.

'Yes, how did you know?' I pictured his expression, his thick eyebrows drawing together, the habit he had of rubbing a thumb inside his collar when confused about something. A little twinge of nostalgia pinched me hard for a moment.

'I think Rob *might* have mentioned him.'

I felt horribly compromised now, given the situation. Really stuck in the middle. Alan didn't sound pleased, so I attempted to sound confused, as though I knew nothing, while praying my guilt wasn't transmitting down the line. Damn Rob.

'Well, I felt you needed to know the offer is below value and against my advice, but Robert's instructed we take it off the market.' Alan sighed. 'I know you've agreed he acts in proxy for you but, as a friend, I wanted to ring you as I wasn't sure how the communication was between you both.'

I stared hard at the rack of leather sandals to my side and the billowing sarongs in the window as he continued talking. I knew Alan had my best interests at heart. He was more than just a former employer and mentor, he was like a father to me but, but I'd managed to divorce myself mentally as well as physically from far more than just Rob by then.

I cared a lot about upsetting Alan, but now I was thousands of miles away, the house was just a house. It already felt like it belonged to someone else and in a different lifetime. I didn't even care all that much about Rob's dodgy deal with the builder any more. I knew there'd be something left from the proceeds, and I reasoned with myself that Alan would still get *some* commission. The quicker all remnants of my past life with Rob were laid to rest, the better. I had no more head space for dramas at home. Everything I needed now was in Greece.

I finally hung up, promising I'd write and agreeing to a coffee with him when I came home. Alan had told me he was planning to leave Jackson and James to launch his own agency before the new year and would like to employ me again if I'd like. I'd responded enthusiastically because I didn't have the heart to say I'd only be back for a short break at the end of the season. I'd be running a beach bar with you next year. I hugged that delicious thought to me like a warm puppy.

I walked back out onto the street, a shimmering mirage of sun and dust rising through the fierce heat, a fine veneer of wind-blown sand against my skin. The sunlight was fluorescently bright in my face, and I hadn't got my Foster Grants on. I just needed to soak myself in the sea. It felt like a way to let everything go, to wash away all thoughts of Rob and the issues of the house. A symbolic baptism of sorts. Although I had my bikini on under my shorts and top, I didn't have a towel, but I just didn't care. I wasn't far from home. Laying back in the buoyant water, like a starfish, hypnotised by the unbelievably blue canopy suspended above me, watching the landscape gently rise and fall to a background hum of chatter, laughter, and the occasional motorbike engine, I felt reborn.

23

Every Breath You Take

By mid-June there'd been a massive rise in tourists, most of the English ones with decent tans as the weather had been uncharacteristically good at home. Sherri and I often sat on the beach before our shifts with tourists we'd got to know, one being a heavily built German called Klaus. He'd ridden into town the previous week on a big, black motorbike with all his belongings in panniers and in a massive roll on the back. He was distinctive because, unlike the Greeks, he wore a helmet and a sensible leather jacket while on his bike.

Initially he'd sat alone, quite a distance away, surveying us with sharp little eyes, his balding head and round face reddening right to the roots of his thick beard. Day by day, he edged closer. As he was always polite and respectful, we didn't mind him sitting and chatting with us.

'Don't you think it's a bit creepy, the way he looks at you?' Sherri said one day when we were paddling in the shallows in just our bikini bottoms, leaving Klaus minding our stuff.

I hadn't really noticed.

'I think he likes you,' she warned.

'Don't be daft, he's ancient. Besides, I keep going on about Marios non-stop, so he knows I'm not available.'

'I can't be sure, but I think he was taking pictures of you earlier.'

'No, he wasn't!'

'Well, okay, but just be careful.'

'I think he's just lonely, anyway, he'll be gone soon.' I laughed, splashing her, before throwing myself into the waves to swim.

The following evening, after a walk to the Kiosk to buy cigarettes, I'd returned with Sherri to the apartment to share chocolate and a bottle of wine, before getting ready to meet Nikos for a drink. Wandering into my room, I noticed my bedside drawer was wide open.

'Sherri, have you been in my drawer?' I couldn't think why it was open.

'No.' She was laughing at my accusation.

'But it's wide open.' I protested. 'I never leave it open.'

'Well, you must have.'

We both laughed but deep down I felt uneasy. I always closed it. Rummaging through the tangle of underwear and swimwear, I checked everything was there. Among the predominantly black contents, it was easy to see something was missing.

'Someone's had my purple thong!'

'Well, it wasn't me.'

'Well maybe it was Elaine then.'

'Unlikely, I mean, she's more a Marks and Sparks big knickers type. Can't see her in your thong. Sakis is more likely to wear it than she is.'

I giggled.

'Maybe it *was* Sakis. I wouldn't put it past him.'

We were both laughing so much we hadn't seen Elaine standing there.

I felt heat rushing through me, flushing at being caught speaking out of turn.

Elaine's face registered confusion.

'What wouldn't you put past Sakis?'

Her eyes sharpened as she wiped her glasses on her shorts. She wasn't smiling.

'Nothing, we're just being silly. Just a joke.'

My face felt well and truly on fire now.

The next afternoon, I'd put my Simply Red album on. Elaine and Sakis were out, and I was getting ready for shift with Sherri, standing in front of the full-length mirror outside her bedroom. Wearing just a bra and knickers, I was hitching a skirt up over my brown thighs when the light darkened. Behind me, in the mirror, was Klaus, his helmet under his arm, wearing his black leathers. My heart sprang in my chest as I whirled round.

'Hello.' His eyes looked particularly bright. 'I have come to say farewell. I now go to Italy.'

I tried to speak but my voice had somehow turned into a strangled little squeak. How did he know where to find us? Quickly bobbing down, my heart still knocking, I scooped up my lacy cardi from the floor, clutching it like a barrier in front of me. Klaus the friendly, harmless loner from the beach seemed a lot bigger and infinitely more threatening when dominating the doorway, smelling of alcohol.

I found my voice and replied with enforced jollity.

'Klaus, you gave me a fright then, how did you get in here?'

Sherri was now at my side.

'You left it open for me.' Klaus waved a thick palm towards the open doorway, beamed at her, then grinned even wider at me, his little rodent eyes almost disappearing inside his pink, inflated cheeks.

'How did you know where we lived?'

'Each day I watch you.' He seemed very pleased to point this out. 'I came yesterday too. I waited, in there.' He pointed towards the kitchen. 'But you did not come.'

I glanced quickly at Sherri. Klaus was the size of a truck, and he was blocking the exit. Anxiety tightened inside me.

He was inside our apartment yesterday.

'I like those photographs of you, ' he said to me, pointing towards my bedroom. 'I may have one?'

'Sorry, no.' My mouth was as dry as polystyrene, adrenalin flooding me.

He looked crestfallen for a moment.

Stepping closer, he pulled out a small Instamatic.

'Then your friend can take one for me, of us together.'

'I don't think so. My boyfriend wouldn't like it.'

'Okay, I have others.' I inched back as he extended a hand to towards me. Where was the usually omnipresent Sakis when we needed him? 'I like having things to remember you by. You remind me of my Therese.'

'I do?' I tried to keep the conversation genial, but inside, I was shaking. Sensing the need to be very careful, I became aware of a veneer of sweat forming around my waistband as his unusually bright little eyes bored into me. The knot of unease inside pulled tighter.

'Yes, my lovely Therese, my *Liebchen*. When I first see you, I know you are her, back again. Everything is just the same, a miracle, and I say, that's my Therese, she has returned to me.'

'Listen, Klaus.' Sherri spoke carefully. 'I'm sorry, but you can't come up here like this, just because you think Mel's like some girl you knew.' A soft breeze blew through the shutters as we both glanced at one another then back at Klaus.

'Therese was not just some girl,' his face creased with puzzlement, his eyes never leaving mine. 'She was my love, my fiancée.' He took a deep breath. 'She died...but now she has come back.'

The smile he radiated towards me was one of pure rapture. He wasn't seeing me at all. He was looking at Therese. I began to wonder whether some of this was my fault. Elaine would never have been so friendly towards Klaus on the beach and even Sherri had warned me. Had I encouraged him? Why did I always think male attention, no matter how dubious or flawed, was always welcome?

'I think it's time you left, Klaus, because we need to go to work now.' Sherri pointedly checked her watch.

'Then I will walk with you, Therese.' He beamed happily at me as if all he'd just said was perfectly acceptable and not strange at all. For a moment, I felt horribly trapped, but maybe there was a way to get him out after all. I forced a smile.

'Well, we're not dressed yet, so why don't you wait, down there for us, and we'll be out in a minute.'

I pointed down to the boundary wall we shared with the elderly Greek widow who lived below us. It seemed that no-one spoke for the longest time, until Klaus finally nodded and marched outside, a beatific smile lighting up his face.

As soon as he had gone, we threw ourselves against the door, exhaling loudly, staring at each other in absolute horror. Prickling with sweat, I quickly locked it. Thank God he'd gone. I turned to Sherri.

'Oh my God, he was in here yesterday, are you thinking what I'm thinking?'

'Yep, bet you anything he took it, the fucking pervert.'

Peeping through the kitchen window, I could see him on the wall, drawing on a cigarette while gazing up at the perfect blue sky, his helmet on the ground by his feet. Then I saw something else, Sakis strolling past, heading for the staircase.

'*Yamo to,*' he cursed, rattling the handle in annoyance. Once we'd unlocked it and dragged him inside, we began telling him everything in a garbled rush, begging him to get rid of Klaus.

'And tell him to give Mel her knickers back too,' Sherri's eyes flashed with indignation.

Sakis's bottom lip just hung for a moment, his eyes darting from me to Sherri, listening to our frantic gabbling. A moment later, he marched back down the stairs.

Still from the safety of the kitchen, we watched the conversation he'd begun with Klaus quickly become animated with Sakis throwing his arms up and down, pointing and shouting. Finally, Klaus got up and walked away. When Sakis sprinted back up the stairs. I could have hugged him. The feeling of relief cascaded like a waterfall through me as I shook my head in disbelief, grinning at him.

'You are a hero, Sakis, thank you.'

'Why are you laughing about it, *moré?*' He looked directly at me, ignoring Sherri, his lips ruched tight, eyes sharp as gravel.

'We're not, we're just pleased he's gone,' I said, feeling horribly exposed for a moment in just a bra and a skirt. I opened the fridge to reward him with a well-deserved beer.

'Thank you so much Sakis, we both really appreciate it.' I even toyed with the idea of giving him a kiss on the cheek as I handed him the Amstel, but thought better of it, so I smiled gratefully at him instead. In that moment, I resolved to make more of him as a friend. Perhaps he wasn't so bad after all. Maybe all he needed was to be included more, for us both to just be a little friendlier and more tolerant towards him.

I wasn't prepared for what came next.

'You, *moré*, are a stupid woman.' His eyes were black pits of animosity as he ignored the beer, jabbing his finger in my direction with barely restrained fury. 'You invite that German man into the apartment, you flirt with him, you walk around everywhere with no clothes on, and then you wonder why you get into trouble. You are no different to that Swedish bitch.'

When he'd gone, Sherri and I sat in stunned silence for a moment before I spoke.

'Told you he doesn't like me.'

'No shit.'

'Why the hell does Sakis always think the worst of me? He seemed to really hate me earlier. He didn't say a single word against you, only me.'

I had lived for my weekly phone call from you and the letters you sent, telling me of new friends you'd met, complaining about how awful your commanding officers were. Your last letter said you may have a surprise for me and to just be patient, which I hoped meant you may possibly have some leave.

Then one Wednesday afternoon, while I was getting ready for evening shift, Elaine stomped up the staircase and burst into the kitchen.

'Hey,' she spat through a fistful of crisps as she slumped onto a kitchen chair. 'Sofia said you have a phone call. Think it's Marios.'

I threw on a beach dress and, quickly, with my hair still wet and my makeup half finished, sprinted to the kiosk to pick up the by now familiar receiver lying on a pile of newspapers.

'Hello...?'

It *was* you.

'Baby *mou*, listen, I don't have long. Can you buy a ticket to Kos for

Saturday? I have only the weekend. It will take too long to get back, so you come to me. I will get you a room, *endaxi?*'

'My head was whirling. Go to Kos? I was trying to think what shifts I was supposed to be doing and whether Lynn would let me have time off.

'*Moro,* can you do this?' I pictured you: broad shoulders, shorn hair, army fatigues, waiting while others jostled impatiently behind you. I heard you feeding in more coins and muttering *yamo,* as you fumbled with the telephone. 'For Saturday, to the airport, *ne?* Just get one way, it's cheaper to get the return here. Just ring tomorrow with times. I will sort everything.'

I heard a few voices in the background then the line went dead. I clipped the receiver back onto the rocker, grinning like an insane woman. I was going to Kos.

When Lynn confirmed I could take an unpaid weekend off and she would cover with Sherri and Yiannis so long as I promised I'd be back for the Monday night, I was so excited I kissed her.

'Woah, steady,' she laughed as I launched myself at her. 'Save your strength for the weekend.'

That night I literally danced through my shift. I was so hyper I must have served twice as many customers as anyone else, feeling like I was on roller-skates as I whizzed up and down from the bar, to the tables, to the kitchen. Sherri was so happy for me and enthusiastic for my trip, even offering to lend me her blue backpack, despite how she must have felt herself, knowing Kevin was arriving soon.

'Bet you're so excited,' she said as we passed each other by the servery, me with empty glasses, Sherri with two plates of *taramosalata,* one decorated with a generous stack of Yorgos's fag ash. Laughing, I helpfully brushed it away. I was walking on a carpet of clouds, my head already on Kos, with you.

I couldn't wait.

The next morning after Shit Bin Shift, I took a trip into Aftonisi Town. I'd never been there on my own before, and certainly not on a local bus, so it was a bit of an adventure. I'd become acutely aware of being watched in resort. There was always a member of your family close by wherever I went but, as an only child, having time to myself was as essential to me as breathing. Up until then, I'd had none, living in a flat with two other girls and, increasingly, with Sakis too, so I enjoyed wandering the streets, on an agenda that was mine alone, with no time constraints.

After going into a travel agent to buy my ticket to Kos, I treated myself to soap made with local honey, then ventured into a small boutique where a very thin, overly made-up Greek girl was leaning on the counter. I smiled but to no response, so I just thumbed through a rail of colourful, silky garments as she chattered in Greek with another customer, ignoring me. One was a beautiful red dress in my size which I held up to the mirror, but my troll was standing behind me. I put the dress back and bought a pair of shorts and a vest top instead.

Once back in Lathos, I headed up the road towards home. Sofia was throwing wet bedlinen across a taught washing line with strong, brown arms, so I waved.

'*Yassou Sofia, ti kanete?*'

She smoothed her apron down.

'*Poli kala.*' She clamped a plastic peg between her teeth before anchoring the edge of a bedsheet and eyed my bags. The afternoon sunshine was strong and the breeze soft. Her washing would be dry in a very short time. She deftly pegged up the other side of the sheet, then bent to squeeze water out of a pillowcase.

'Shopping?'

'Yes.' I pulled out the top and shorts, which Sofia appraised as *poli kala.*

'Ah, but not the red dress.' She sounded vaguely disappointed.

It was only when I was inside the apartment it hit me. *How the hell did she know about the red dress?*

24

Like A Prayer

Landing at Aftonisi was hair-raising, but Kos was in a different league. With a very short runway leading directly to the sea and framed by a jag of nearby mountains, it left very little room for error and was a terrifying descent. I dug my feet into the aircraft floor bracing my thighs tightly as we dropped from the sky like a stone, leaving my stomach still miles above. Through the window as we taxied to a halt, the island seemed very different to Aftonisi: far less green, with brutally sparse clumps of tough grass dotted through the sand, and just the occasional tree clinging to a landscape of sand and rock.

I could hardly contain my excitement as I left the arrivals hall and hailed a cab for the short trip to the town which was to be my home for two nights. You'd given me an address, told me everything was paid for, and you'd join me soon.

As the taxi crawled along a harbour studded with millionaire's yachts and elegant café bars, it became clear the resort was far more sophisticated than Lathos. It was also hotter and dustier, hardly surprising given Kos's geographical position as one of the closest Greek islands to Turkey, gateway to the middle east.

With a swing in my step, I hoisted Sherri's backpack and entered the hotel.

I could hardly believe I'd soon be with you. I was looking forward to seeing your new island, but I was still a little nervous after our recent phone calls when you'd been so distant. I reminded myself it was hard for you being in the army, but it was hard for me too.

In my room, I closed the wooden shutters to keep out the blazing July sunshine and the many insects that plagued the island. Sitting on the bed, I ran a palm over the intricately embroidered cover, watching the light dance through the shutter slats, spilling fragmented lines of gold across the heavy cotton, when there was a knock at the door. It was you. You rushed straight in entrapping me in a massive hug, as I leapt into your arms, wrapping my legs around you. The warmth of your skin enveloped me, the taste of cigarettes and chewing gum on your lips, the warm sea breeze in your hair.

'Baby *mou*,' you whispered into my neck as we fell together onto the bed, shards of light embellishing our skin with zebra stripes, your hair turning amber in the sun, mine spilling down onto your face as you pulled me on top of you. Everything was going to be alright.

Later, you announced you had to go to meet your new friend, Tomas, who was going to have dinner with us both this evening. He was an officer, a career soldier not a conscript, and someone I got the distinct impression was very important to you. You wanted to show me off.

'I will give you an hour alone to get ready,' you smiled. 'Wear something pretty. Tomas has a girlfriend here too, a Russian girl, Jana, who will call for you at seven so you can both meet first, then come to us find us.'

I spent time in the shower, washing my hair, then drying it and applying my makeup with care before selecting your favourite black cotton dress with the hook and eye bodice. Finally, when I was happy with how I looked, I stood in front of the full length mirror. Nervously, I wondered what Jana might be like. Something appeared next to my reflection. What a time for my troll to make an appearance.

'*She's going to be far prettier than you,*' she taunted, one eyebrow raised.

'Piss off,' I yelled angrily as her reflection evaporated. 'Just leave me alone.'

There was a sudden, loud, and precise knock at the door. She was earlier than I'd expected. With one last glance in the mirror, I edged the door open.

Outside stood a vision in blue. She was tall and slender with long, dark hair falling like a curtain over one eye, and wearing possibly the shortest dress I'd ever seen. It barely covered the cheeks of her bottom. Extending an arm tinkling with gold chains and bangles she pulled me in.

'I am Jana,' she said, in a thick Russian accent, blowing smoke sideways before kissing me once on each cheek then back once more on the first. Although she appeared somewhat intimidating, her smile was warm. I knew I was going to like her. It was a great relief.

'Hi, come in.' I stood back to accommodate her jangling gold as she swept in on a spike of exotic perfume, haloed with cigarette smoke, swooshing her hair over one shoulder. Her eyes were rimmed with Kohl.

'You were talking to someone?' She waved her cigarette airily. 'I am interrupting?'

As her gaze grasshoppered around, I felt myself flush.

'No, I...er...just had the radio on.'

I was glad the room was dark. That troll had to go.

I couldn't help but warm to her as we chattered non-stop, strolling together along a picture-perfect harbour, framed by creamy ornamental stone buildings, a strong contrast to Lathos with its plain concrete boxes and iron rods projecting from most roofs.

I found myself telling her all about Rob and how problematic he was, even his latest news which had been a massive setback for me. Rob had gone to see Roger Dean on exchange and had asked for our promised cash backhander, but the builder had simply laughed and slammed the door on him. Rob's get rich quick scheme had backfired, leaving us both out of pocket. I hadn't told you about that yet.

Tomas was Jana's second army boyfriend, the last one had been a conscript, but their relationship had failed when he'd returned from the Army.

'Why?' I asked. 'What happened?'

She stopped for a moment and pulled a pack of cigarillos from her bag, gold clanking at her wrist as she offered me one, which I politely refused. Lighting it, she inhaled deeply, her eyes momentarily closing as her chin tilted towards the sky. Then she marched ahead in a cloud of smoke.

'Let's just say, some people find it hard to be good when they're apart.'

'Oh no, Marios isn't like that. I really don't—'

'No, I mean me, I found it hard.'

She gave me a naughty grin as my eyes widened.

'So, you…?'

'What can I say,' she laughed. 'I like sex. Anyway, then I tell myself, no more army boys, but Tomas is different.'

'Marios is different too. I met him before the army, and we have plans for when he gets back.'

Jana fixed me with heavily mascaraed eyes.

'In my experience, when they get back, they change.'

Where did that leave me? I felt you'd changed already.

Jana steered me into a busy waterside bar where you were waving to us from a table and as you stood, so did a tall, serious man, with watchful eyes. By his bearing and build you would be in no doubt Tomas was a soldier. He stood at our approach, his back straight, his chin squared, appearing defensive, guarded and aloof. I wondered whether he was ever off duty. After the introductions, you then both spoke very rapidly in Greek as I sat by helplessly. I could only catch one word out of five.

Tomas had softened as the evening had worn on, aided by Jana being so friendly and open. We'd drunk a lot of wine, eaten souvlaki and shared a fresh fruit platter as the sun had dissolved over the harbour. With the searing heat, the loud music and the coloured lights swaying on the awnings, it was a magical setting. You seemed very close to Tomas which made me happy. You had a friend on the island. When we'd finally said goodbye to them both, Jana and I had embraced, promising to keep in touch somehow.

Feeling pleasantly pissed, I'd held your hand as we ambled back up the harbourside, watching the gentle undulation of brightly lit yachts on the black water, an aroma of delicious, chargrilled food in the air, an audible sizzle from the open hotplates. There was a large video screen outside one bar playing the video for Madonna's new single, Like a Prayer, so I lingered for a moment to watch but, surprisingly, you pulled me sharply away.

'*Putana,*' you sneered at the screen as Madonna gyrated high above us, the song ringing in our ears. We continued walking. It was only a small comment but for some reason it seemed to carry immense weight. Was this the army's influence creeping insidiously under your skin? Something jarred inside but I decided not to overreact.

You stayed with me all night, a rare treat. It was so wonderful having your skin next to mine, to hear you breathing, to feel your chest rising and falling as you slept but I remained wide awake. My head was full, and my mind wouldn't rest. A mosquito droned in the dark, airless room so I padded across to the balcony and watched the globe of the moon suspended in the sky. Something didn't feel right.

Images from the harbourside filtered through my mind. Good girls or whores, was there nothing in between? *They all change when they get back.* Jana's words were pole-vaulting across my brain. Perhaps I was just tired. Shaking the thoughts off like raindrops from a folded umbrella, I carefully crept back into bed and curled around you like a cat. You moved your arm to make way for me and I fell asleep with my head on your chest.

The next day, you hired a bike, and we rode around the island, discovering a fascinating archaeological ruin. The unspoiled site was little more than columns and foundation stones lying abandoned in overgrown scrub grass, with none of the slick capitalism of the sites in Athens which just added to its charm. There was no one else there. It was as though it had been abandoned by time and we'd just chanced upon it by accident. Clutching your waist as we roared away towards the beach, I felt blissfully happy, the warm breeze in my hair, the sun kissing my bare legs. Finally, we found a deserted cove, little more than a narrow strip of beach consisting of mainly boulders and stones, and, stripping off all our clothes, ran into deep, buoyant, bath-warm water to swim. Lying back on the towel you'd bought for us to share you pulled me in and kissed me. Our eyes met. Why not? There was no one around.

Later, luxuriating in the sun like two, basking lions, we stretched our limbs, sleepy from its heat. The beach was empty, or so we thought, until a nearly naked, elderly man appeared. Quickly we rolled onto our stomachs as he clambered over the rocks in his plastic sandals and headed towards us with a cheery wave. Feeling exposed and awkward, we remained face-down on our tiny towel as he loomed above our naked bottoms, making small-talk, clad only in a string-thong which left nothing to the imagination. Once he'd rounded the corner and disappeared, we laughed so hard, gasping for breath, before running hand in hand back into the water. At that point, I was probably happier than I'd been for weeks.

The following day I was sad as I knew I was flying back.

'I will pay for your flight, my treat,' you said.

We found a travel agency and I sat glumly in the office while you spoke to the clerk.

'We want two tickets to Aftonisi, for tonight.'

I stared back at you, hardly believing what you were saying.

'I wanted to surprise you, *moro*,' you explained with a kiss. 'I still have five more days.'

Once you finally returned to Kos, I felt so deflated. We'd snatched a few, precious days then, once again, you were gone. Life consisted of massive highs making me deliriously happy followed by plummeting lows leaving me feeling dejected and miserable. One of these was losing my job at Mayfair.

Lynn hadn't been thrilled when I'd asked for more time off as I didn't want to work when you were still on leave and, unlike my previous bosses at home, she was no pushover.

'Sorry,' she'd said. 'A weekend is one thing, but a further week is quite unacceptable. I need someone reliable.'

Work had been a welcome distraction making the hours just fly by. It had become my life. I'd rarely gone out after shifts, as I was always mindful of being watched, particularly after the trip to Aftonisi Town. Your father often cruised the street in his truck looking for me, and your cousin had regularly visited the restaurant to chat, his eyes darting all over me as I attempted to pull my skirt down to what I hoped he'd consider a decent level or cross my arms over my cleavage. With no work, I was lost and cut adrift. Now I felt awkward even going near Mayfair after what was effectively a sacking, despite Lynn saying it was only a business decision and she hoped we'd stay friends.

It left me far too much time to just think about every minute detail of our conversations and to inflate any imagined problems which were probably of my making. Each day was as endlessly long, hot and sunny as the last, but every perfect day had now become something to endure rather than enjoy. I tried to fill my time by scribbling in my notebook and writing short stories, but I was becoming increasingly disoriented. The only positive thing was the house had sold, thankfully just in time as house prices were plunging again.

I tried to concentrate on my correspondence course as it was something to keep me occupied but, even with that distraction, everyone else seemed to be forging ahead while I was struggling to even stand. It was like trying to remain upright when paddling against a strong current. Everything was shifting beyond my control.

Everywhere were reminders of you and me, of us, of the colourful world we'd once inhabited, but it felt increasingly like a dream now, as though I'd been suspended in time, left on ice, my life on hold again until you returned. All the colours had bled away, leaving just a grey landscape. I was spending more and more time alone, while the rest of the resort seemed to be having fun. Even sunbathing was too much effort. I already had a deep, glowing tan which was maintained by just walking around, so the beach had lost its appeal. Elaine was always busy working. She'd even managed to get a third job, and Sherri was usually with Yiannis. I felt left out. I'd often find her on our balcony, draped over him, a glass of wine in her hand. She'd chat happily with me, while running her hand over his cropped hair as he nibbled at her neck, but as soon as Elaine and Sakis pulled up outside, they'd quickly dart into her room and shut the door. How they kept everything quiet I'd no idea but, by some miracle, they did.

25

The Boys of Summer

One day, while gazing over the balcony, I noticed a young Greek in mirrored sunglasses riding a Suzuki. Barefoot, with black curls, a flash of gold at his strong brown wrist, he opened the throttle and the bike leapt like a stallion as he roared off. His passenger, a girl with long, dark hair, was clutching his waist, and laughing. His profile was so like yours that it shocked me. Watching them disappear, their bodies melded together, his strong thighs gripping the bike and her slim tanned arms holding him tight, something caught in my throat. It was exactly like seeing an image of you and me. I couldn't have felt more alone.

I was reading Cosmopolitan on the beach one morning and eating a slice of melon that Mr Mavrakis had given me, when Astrid, the Danish Thomson rep, strolled over.

'I need to show you something.' She scanned her clipboard, her tone making me feel uneasy. 'This is your husband, right?'

She pointed to the name Robert J Cassidy on her printout.

My eyes widened, and my heart began to race unpleasantly. Surely Rob hadn't booked himself onto a flight and a transfer into Lathos? I peered closer. It was no mistake. He'd threatened to come out on holiday but I thought I'd convinced him otherwise. He knew I didn't want him to. What the hell was he doing? After Astrid left, I raced to the Kiosk and tried to call him, but, to my shock, the line had been disconnected.

As a complete reaction to all this angst, all I could think about was calling you. Even though I was nervous because you weren't expecting my call, I dialled and waited until a male voice barked *'parakalo'*. I asked for you in my best Greek. If you weren't there, my Greek was now good enough to leave a message, but you came onto the line.

'Oristē?'

It was such a relief to hear your voice. I found myself immediately spilling out all the issues with Rob and his planned trip. Just telling you made me feel infinitely better. Finally, I could feel my shoulders relaxing, but the feeling was short lived.

'And you expect me to do what?' you said when I finally paused for breath. 'I am here, not there.'

I pictured you throwing your hands up in exasperation.

'I just—'

'He's your problem, not mine. Look, *moro*, I have no time, I have to go. It's not my turn to use the phone.'

Click. The receiver went down at your end, leaving me with just the dialling tone. My heart plunged to the floor as my head swam. The hot, airless kiosk, with the smell of sun-warmed leather, and all the garments rustling and swinging in the window, suddenly felt heavy and oppressive. I just needed to get out of there, so I rushed outside onto the street, a growing feeling of panic rising. Why on earth were you so horrible just then, why was Rob coming out here and what the hell was I going to do now? My vision began to blur. Clumsily, I backed off the kerb right into the path of a motorbike which squealed to a halt.

'Yamo to panagia!' the rider cursed in anger, glaring at me though mirrored sunglasses.

'Oh my God, I am so sorry.' I hadn't been looking at all, all my attention had been on how angry I was with Rob. To my horror I burst into tears. The next thing I knew was the rider had slammed his bike onto its stand

and was taking me by shoulders.

'Hey,' he said, his eyes searching mine. 'Hey, it's okay. I am not dead; you are not dead. *Ti simveni*, what's the matter?'

'Sorry, sorry, it's been a bad day, that's all. I'm really, really, sorry.'

He was regarding me suspiciously.

'You okay now?'

'I'm fine thanks.' I sniffed. I wasn't, though. I was acutely embarrassed, furious with Rob and heartbroken about your dismissive reaction, but I wasn't going to let this stranger know. I turned away, feeling more of an idiot than ever.

'Hey, you want a frappé?' he called out, as if iced coffee cured everything. I looked back at him. He'd balanced his mirrored sunglasses on top of his black curls now, dark brown eyes glinting as he regarded me, a strong profile, thick brows, a stubbled jaw. My heart lurched. He looked so like you in that moment in his white vest top, with his tanned, muscular arms, with his innate arrogance and pride. Then it dawned on me, this was the man I'd seen a while ago with a girl on the back of his bike.

His name was Andreas, and he lived in the neighbouring village of Alomenos. He was the same age as me and worked for his family.

'So, they have a restaurant?' I wasn't familiar with the bars and tavernas in Alomenos except for Cassiopeia, the lively music bar just on the outskirts of Lathos that everyone knew.

'Many,' he laughed. 'They have business interests all over the island, bars, a club and tavernas too. I look after insurances and take rents.' My vision strayed to his strong arms, the thick fist he'd curled around his glass, the silver skull ring he wore. I imagined everyone paid on time. Nobody would be likely to argue with someone so powerfully built, so confident, so persuasive.

It was far easier practising my growing Greek vocabulary skills on him than it had ever been with you, and I enjoyed learning as he corrected me. I found myself explaining all about Rob, the divorce and I told him about you, all of which he took in his stride. I even told him a little about Dad, mainly how we didn't really get on.

'I actually don't think he likes anyone all that much,' I added, trying to make sense of it myself as I spoke. 'He's not a 'friends' person either. He's a bit of a loner, really.'

'But a father always loves his child.' Andreas said, as a little knife twisted inside my gut. 'My father is, to many, a hard businessman, but to me he is gentle, he is good, he loves me. He would do anything for me, and I for him too.'

We sat in silence for a few seconds. Andreas was one of the lucky ones. If your own father doesn't love you, you always believe you're damaged goods; broken, shop-soiled, never enough. Only ever *quite* nice. This was getting unintentionally heavy, so I changed the subject.

He told me the girl on his bike was from Cyprus, but they'd recently broken up.

'What happened?' I asked, leaning in.

He paused for a moment.

'She wasn't a good girl.'

There it was again, that preoccupation with being good, or were things were getting a bit lost in translation? Something I couldn't quite register crossed his face as his jaw clenched and unclenched, a knot forming at his temple, his eyes narrowing. It occurred to me she might have dumped him. He'd probably been hurt and didn't want to say more.

'Enough about her, she won't come here again.'

'Break ups can be messy,' I agreed, sipping my drink. 'My family and friends all warned me about Rob, but I didn't listen.'

No one had been able to see the attraction with Rob, but they didn't understand how something had resonated within me when I'd met him. He'd worn his damage on the outside, like an old overcoat, so I hadn't needed to dig deep to find it. Problematic men like Rob were catnip to me, and much in the way dogs can smell fear, Rob had sensed the damage surrounding me too, like a cloud of cheap perfume. It was like invisible ink, unseen by most, but glowing bright as day for those with the special, ultraviolet light.

'Always listen to your family.' Andreas leaned closer towards me. 'Family is everything, okay? Family takes care of you. You keep them close and do what you have to, for them. Loyalty to family is everything.'

I gazed across the road towards the apartment. I hadn't called Mum and Dad for a while, and I owed them a letter too. I couldn't imagine being in such a loyal, devoted and close family. For a moment my vision blurred.

'Hey, you okay?' He briefly touched my arm, just a small imprint with his fingers, but it felt like I was being marked out somehow. I looked down, almost expecting to see the sizzle of a branding iron.

'Yes, fine.' I smiled at him. I was absolutely not going to dump all my issues on him. I'd done that to Rob, years ago. At the time it had felt such a relief to speak about everything, quite cathartic, but in baring my soul, I'd given him ammunition. He'd found my weak spot. That wasn't ever going to happen again.

'You should come to Ionia one day, it's my father's biggest restaurant.' Andreas smiled, showing perfect teeth. I watched the curve of his lips as he slipped a cigarette between them and flicked his lighter, thick, gold chains jangling at his wrist. 'You are very beautiful. I'd like to show you off.' He drew the smoke in, his eyes roaming my face. 'I want you to meet my father, my brothers, my uncles.'

'I have a boyfriend, in the army,' I reminded him, but he just smiled, fixing me with his penetrating eyes, a challenge in their depths.

I ran tip of my tongue across my teeth, holding his gaze, enjoying his obvious interest, letting it wash over me, wave by wave. It was so easy being with him and I was entranced by all his physical similarities to you, but all the time we were sitting together I was on tenterhooks that your father might drive past or someone who knew you might see me, even though, by British standards, I was doing nothing wrong.

I offered to pay for my drink, but he just tutted softly, lifting his chin.

'I never pay in here,' he laughed with a dismissive shake of the head. 'Never.'

'Another family business?' I enquired, smiling back at him, remembering the deference of the waiter who'd seated us and the exceptional service we'd been given.

Smiling, he ignored my question, looking towards the sun, golden light illuminating his handsome face. Again, my heart jumped. He was so like you in that moment.

'You want to get a proper drink one day?' he said, briefly grabbing my hand as I got up to leave.

I paused.

His hot fingers were still on mine as he persisted.

I looked down at him. Through half-closed eyes, he could almost be you. 'Maybe.' I gave him a little half smile.

Why did I do that?

26

With Or Without You

Back at the apartment I told the girls about Rob's impending visit. Sherri had already dealt with Kevin coming out earlier, so she understood exactly how I felt.

'All you can do,' she advised, 'Is keep patiently explaining to him it's over. That's what I did with Kevin. Do nothing he could misconstrue, be open with Marios, and make sure everyone knows you didn't ask Rob to come. It will be fine. He'll get it and we'll all be here to help you.'

I had serious doubts. Sherri didn't know what Rob was like.

When Kevin had arrived, I'd been intrigued to meet him, but Sherri had said he wanted nothing to do with any of her new friends.

'It's best I don't introduce you,' she said. 'He blames you and Elaine that I'm still out here because without you both, I'd have never come for the summer.'

I'd frowned for a moment. Petros had been the reason, not us, but maybe it had suited her to tell Kevin that.

Kevin booked himself into a hotel in Pervasi where she'd spent some time with him, but, on his last day, he'd come to Lathos, and they'd sat on the beach, deep in conversation. Yiannis and I shared the lunch shift, me rushing about covering for Sherri, Yiannis exuding a poisonous, black atmosphere at Kevin's arrival. I'd caught Kevin's eye just once, feeling desperately sorry for him, but he'd returned my hopeful smile with a hostile stare.

After she'd seen him off at the airport, Sherri had telephoned Petros, saying she didn't think they should continue with the relationship, which, according to her, he'd taken well. All she'd felt was relief.

Instantly, Yiannis became a fixture in our apartment, so, now, each evening, I not only had to put up with Elaine and Sakis's headboard banging my adjoining wall, I also had to deal with shrieks and giggles coming from Sherri's room as I ran the gauntlet to the bathroom.

'She's a quick mover,' observed Elaine drily, on the first morning Yiannis had visibly stayed over. Little did she know, I thought.

Soon, the day Rob was due arrived and I was as wired as a telephone exchange, literally twitching at my own shadow. Dusk fell, a lavender smokiness descended over the mountains making them virtually invisible and the cicadas' humming grew louder. All the lights in resort gradually flickered on, and tourists filled the road as they wandered from bar to bar. I still wasn't working, but instead of getting my customary early night, I tapped the balcony railings, chain smoking Marlboro and keeping watch for the Thomson coach. Finally, it rumbled up to the crossroads and the doors swung open. Out stepped Astrid, in her bright blue uniform, her normally tousled white-blonde hair in a neat bun, looking every inch the professional tourist rep. As she stood, ticking off the new arrivals and the driver began dragging suitcases from the hold, I hardly dared breathe. Tourist after tourist climbed down. But not Rob.

This was the coach's last drop off and Astrid's work had finished for the evening so when I saw her walking to her parked moped, I raced down the stairs to her.

'Astrid, where is he?'

I'd spent most of the evening hyperventilating in worry about everything, so I really needed to know.

'What...your ex?'

'Yeah, what's happening? Has he gone to a different resort?'

I held my breath. That would be the best-case scenario. Astrid had already told me he hadn't booked accommodation. It wasn't unusual. People often just turned up and found somewhere to stay afterwards, but, as this was Rob, anything could happen, and he was unlikely to get off a flight sober. I wouldn't put it past him expecting to stay with me.

She looked at me apologetically, shaking her head.

'Sorry Mel, he was an NS.'

'A what?'

'A no-show.'

My mind was racing. Maybe he'd jumped in a taxi.

'What, you mean he wasn't on the coach?'

'I mean he wasn't on the *plane*, Mel.'

I stood gaping at her. He'd paid for the flight. It must have cost him over £100 so what the hell was he playing at?

'We did wait,' she said. 'Sorry, I'm shattered. Going to bed now, *Kalinichta*.' She kicked her bike into action and puttered uphill, out of the resort.

'*Kalinichta*,' I replied, dazed. Rob never failed to cause problems. He could still manage to upset me even from over 2,000 miles away. All I could assume was it had been a drunken mistake, either booking the flight or missing it. Naturally, I felt immense relief, but I was also furious he'd put me through all that worry. It even crossed my mind he'd done it deliberately. Either way, I couldn't wait to tell you. I fell into the blissful darkness of my bed and sank into the deepest sleep, knowing how relieved you'd be, hoping it would make you happy.

I rang you the next day, knowing you'd be pleased Rob hadn't turned up.

'Listen' you said, before I'd finished speaking. 'I can't help with your problems from here so don't keep telling me about them. Just wait until I come back on leave.'

'Sorry?'

'I don't think you should call me here again. I've told you before how hard it is for me when I'm here, and you are there, *moro*. I don't tell you how bad the army is, so don't tell me your problems. I can do nothing. Wait until the end of September, it's not long now, then I will be back.'

That was nearly two months. What were you saying? I felt my stomach fall to the floor and my head spin, tears threatening to spill. I was already all over the place after the drama of the past week. All I needed was some reassurance, but now you were saying I couldn't even phone you. I was lonely enough already, but now this...?

'I will write to you,' you said. 'I will call you when I can, but you don't call me, okay? You must understand, this is too hard for me. I cannot stand it when you always tell me about things I can't control. It makes me angry. I am here and can do nothing, so don't call. Wait for me instead. *Kataleveno?*'

'But—' I protested.

'Listen, *agapē mou*, it's easier for me like this. I can forget problems this way. Just do this one thing for me, be a good girl. The army will be finished soon. You just wait for me to call you, *endaxi?*'

It was me who ended the call this time. I'd hoped by slamming down the receiver, it would make you reconsider what you'd just said. Best for *you*? What about *me*? I was here virtually alone. I needed support. Furious and upset in equal measure, I loitered by the sun cream and cigarette lighters, waiting for the payphone to burst into life. Surely you'd ring back. But you didn't, so I eventually slunk out into the sunshine, feeling like the end of the world had come.

'Right,' Sherri said when I told her everything, 'We're going out tonight. I'm not working, so you and I are going to have some fun, okay?'

'But I haven't got any money left.'

I'd spent most of my savings on the ticket to Kos and the stuff I'd bought in town. I hadn't got a job any more and I needed what was left of my money for rent and food. I had a credit card for emergencies, but I wasn't going to touch it unless it was a matter of life or death as the interest rates were astronomical. Being virtually broke was not a position I enjoyed. I needed a job.

As luck would have it, salvation came in the unexpected form of Elaine, who'd been working three jobs: for Kerry at the Sunrise Bar, at Taverna Thalassa, and cleaning at the Solomos Hotel. Elaine liked making money but, unlike us, she rarely spent it, however she'd just splurged on hiring a bright orange Mini Moke until the end of September.

'My mum's coming over with her friend and I want to spend time taking her around the island, so why don't you do my lunchtime shifts at the Taverna?' She gave me a wide grin. 'You can also use the Moke too if you want, just keep the petrol topped up and don't prang it. I won't need it for two weeks. Mum's hired a car.'

Hugging her, I knocked her glasses skewwhiff. I would be working again, and I'd have a car. My stomach turned little cartwheels.

They say luck breeds luck, and within a day, two other jobs just fell into my lap too. The Ampeli restaurant, preceded over by the terrifying Mr Manasis and his dour wife, Maria, wanted a new evening waitress. They had a reputation for hiring and firing, and I knew Mr Manasis shouted all the time because we could often hear him from our balcony, so I was a little reticent, but needs must. I called in that evening. Unsmilingly, Maria flicked me a cursory glance.

'Come tomorrow, tie up your hair, wear black.'

That was it. I was in.

The third job was most unexpected. When Sherri had said we were going out, there'd been no arguing with her. My lack of money hadn't put her off.

'I'll stand you a few drinks,' she'd said. 'I know you'd do the same for me.'

The chosen venue had recently opened just a little past Ampeli but on the opposite side of the road. Noisy and raucous, it was a Mecca for belligerent, drunk lads, partly because the drinks were cheap, but mainly because the ageing owner, Spiros, was a drunk with no control over the bar whatsoever. If you got there early, everything was reasonably orderly, but later it descended into complete anarchy with people helping themselves to drinks from behind the bar and fights often breaking out. Spiros would appear oblivious to the escalating chaos, sometimes taking to the floor with a cane and a top hat to execute a little Fred Astaire dance routine. It was aptly named the Wild West Saloon Bar. You could just imagine someone being hurled full length down the bar on their stomach accompanied by a shower of glass.

While we took advantage of the cheap drinks, dodging the groping hands of a stag party of Irish lads, Spiros came over.

'I want to ask you girls something,' he bellowed in our faces over the din. 'If you like to want food here, what food you want to like?'

Not exactly the Queen's English, but I got the gist.

'What, inside, like in a restaurant, or as a takeaway?' Sherri asked.

Spiros pondered, with an alarming wobble. There was no way he could make this a restaurant, it was total pandemonium inside and you could hardly hear yourself think.

'Take it away.'

'Pizza?' I suggested. He didn't look interested. 'Hot dogs...?' As soon as I saw Spiros's puzzled expression, I knew that was unlikely to hit the spot. 'What about chips then, or burgers...maybe, crêpes, or something?'

A big, stupid grin spread across his face like sticky icing on a bun.

'*Tiganita!* Is cheap and easy, and you can make, *ne?*'

I'd thought he'd said *Ti Kanete,* how are you, instead of the Greek word for pancake, so I'd nodded and replied, 'good, thank you' which had somehow caused Spiros to think I'd agreed to sell pancakes. From having no job, I'd somehow ended up with three: Elaine's lunchtime shift at Taverna Thalassa, three weekday nights at Ampeli under the close watch of Maria, and regular late shifts making crêpes. Spiros had gone straight out and bought a hotplate because he'd been convinced I was an experienced crêpe maker, quickly setting up a little stand for me outside Wild West and supplying me with a jug of batter, lemons, strawberries, sugar and a squeezy bottle of chocolate sauce. I'd nearly refused, until he'd said something which appealed to my better judgement.

'Each night, you take out 2,000 drachma, just give me back the rest.'

Spiros was usually very drunk when I handed him the balance of the money, so he'd sometimes take out another 2,000 drachma for me, so I was often paid twice over.

27

Love Is A Battlefield

I couldn't wait to tell you, so when you finally phoned, I was literally bubbling with excitement about having money again. You seemed pleased about the Ampeli job and my copywriting course but working at Wild West Saloon Bar selling crêpes was a different matter.

'No,' you said. 'You must stop. It's a job for a gypsy, not a good girl.'

'What do you mean?'

'You will leave. *Moro*, if my family learns you work there, they will say you have no pride. It looks bad on me for allowing it.'

I didn't bother mentioning your cousin often bought crêpes from me.

'What's wrong with working there?' I demanded.

'Spiros is not so good, everyone knows this. He doesn't know how to….' you seemed to be searching for something. 'To stay nice.'

'Stay nice? Spiros's always nice to me.'

Very nice, when he sometimes pays me twice.

'Nice, you know, sober, *moro*. Tourists get drunk, but Greek men should stay nice.'

I felt my shoulders becoming tense. Spiros was a hopeless drunk, everyone knew it, but he was harmless. I had no idea you despised drunks so much. In a flash, I could now see why you'd first noticed me during my holiday with Rob. Without him, would you have noticed me at all?

'Well, I'm sorry, but I need the money and I like the job...'

...and you aren't going to tell me what to do.

'Well, I *don't* like.'

You sounded like a petulant child.

Feeling wholly deflated and irritated, the call ended with you under the impression I would be leaving the crêpe-making job, and me more determined than ever to continue.

The next day as I headed uphill to the Taverna for my lunch shift, Spiros darted out of Wild West Bar.

'Why you want to leave?' he demanded.

The awnings on the bar rustled with a soft sea breeze, strong sunlight already burning down on the crown on my head.

'I don't understand.'

'I hear you don't like.' Spiros smelled sour: of curdled milk, whisky and stale cigarettes. There was a smear of ketchup on his greying vest. As his lips turned down, his brows followed. Why would he think this? Had you tried to stop working me there, somehow?

'There must be a misunderstanding.'

He looked perplexed for a moment, lifting a chin dusted with black pepper stubble, tiny lines on his face crazing like broken pottery. His gold tooth glinted in the strong sunlight. Up close, despite his pouched eyelids and slack jaw, I wondered if he was really as old as I'd thought or had years of alcohol abuse aged him prematurely? I thought of Rob.

'So, you still come tonight?' He sounded doubtful.

'Yes, of course.'

'Bravo.' He punched my arm before sprinting back inside.

So, I continued making crêpes, and earning good money, all the while feeling increasingly annoyed at you, frustrated by this power you were somehow trying to wield over my life and independence. I was caught between desperately wanting to please you, to be your *good girl*, but not wanting to lose myself in the process.

Our next phone call was particularly fraught.

'You are still making the crêpes, you must stop.'

'I will do what I like.'

'You will not. You are my girlfriend. I will not have the shame.'

'Oh, shut up, for God's sake, this is ridiculous. No one cares. Even your cousin buys crêpes from me.'

After that, everything accelerated rapidly.

'You want to embarrass my family?'

'You're being ridiculous.'

'You'd stop if you loved me.'

'You wouldn't ask me to if *you* loved *me*.'

'When I call again, you will have left the gypsy job, *endaxi*?' The tight anger in your voice was palpable.

'I can't believe you're telling me what to do—'

'I have the right.'

'How dare you.'

You didn't reply.

I hung up, shaking, leaving the kiosk close to tears of anger. Returning to the apartment, I could see Sakis and Elaine sitting on her bed as I stomped past, slamming my door. Walking out onto the balcony I gripped the rail tightly and let out an exasperated squeal. Then, from the corner of my eye, I saw Sherri on Yiannis's lap. They both jumped and looked up.

'Everything alright?' she asked.

'Sorry,' I said and made to return to my room. There was no privacy anywhere and no place to think either. For one tiny moment, I regretted being there at all.

Sherri hopped off Yiannis's lap and followed me in.

'You want to get a drink?' she smiled, smoothing down her t-shirt which he'd clearly just had his hands up. 'We're about to get some food at Grill House then we're going Kristos's bar after work.'

She sat down on my bed, smiling up at me.

'Come with us. Kristos is having one of his full moon parties. Please say yes.'

Kristos was a young, affluent Athenian with family ties to the island who'd recently come over for the summer to run a music bar, right on the beach, not far from where the breeze block shell of our future bar lay. On each full moon, he'd held a beach party with non-stop music and the hypnotic beats of a bongo player who drummed like he was possessed. Lit only by the moon and the flicker of flaming torches in the sand, there was something magical about his parties. I'd loved the feeling of the world spinning away from me after a few vodkas, the sand shifting under my feet, to a beat connecting with something primal deep inside me, but instead of agreeing, I shook my head.

'You don't want me. I'll get an early night.'

Yiannis had followed Sherri into my room and was making himself comfortable next to her on my bed, his trainer-clad feet up on my clean sheets. I shot him a glare. It was my room, not his.

Sherri reached for my hand. 'We *want* you to come with us, don't we, Yiannis?' He took a moment to answer, his loaded expression forming a solid wall between us, but he finally conceded.

After they left, I showered, changing into a short, black, frilled skirt to show off my tanned legs, a black halter-neck top, black flat pumps, and scooped my hair up into a high ponytail. Adding big, cheap, golden hoop earrings the size of bangles I'd bought in the kiosk, I crayoned on a slick of Sherri's favourite red lipstick she'd left behind. If I was going to be accused of being a gypsy, I might as well look like one.

Making my way out onto the darkening street where the resort was starting to hum into life, the July heat hit me. It was relentless, even at night. I thought I'd acclimatised, but I felt hot and restless, on edge. The Don Henley track which Elaine was convinced was called Poison Summer was drifting over the road from Helios Bar. Stroking your gold chain and charm around my neck, a sudden vision of us together in Kos, laughing and carefree, filled my head. I knew what I had to do. Despite your orders, I headed for the kiosk and waited for my turn at the payphone before eagerly dialling. I just needed to hear your voice, to be reassured all was well, that you loved me. I wanted to say sorry but also to make you understand I needed my own life too. I held my breath, fiddling with Sherri's lipstick in my pocket as the phone connected.

You seemed to take ages to come to the phone, so long I nearly lost my nerve and hung up.

'I'm sorry,' I said, exhaling at the sound of your voice. 'I don't want to argue. I just wanted to let you know I...I love you and...and...er...well, just that, really.' I closely examined the telephone receiver. It could do with a good clean.

Once I'd said it, I felt like an idiot. The words landed heavily, like rocks. I stood there, winding the chain around my neck, feeling the comforting smoothness of the little cornucopia charm between my fingers, aware my troll was popping her head around the corner of the kiosk and watching with interest.

Say something...

It seemed ages before you replied.

'Okay,' you finally said. 'I have to go now, there's a queue.'

You sounded a little clipped, short with me. It wasn't what I'd expected so I waited to see if you were going to say more. You didn't.

Was that your way of reminding me you'd told me not to call. A nasty little spike of angst stabbed me through the gut as a pulsing band of pressure began to tighten around my head.

'Are you still angry with me?' I demanded, knowing it would be far better to just shut up. I fed in more coins. You remained quiet.

'Hello?' I said, irritated after enduring another pause. Why did I never learn to shut up? Mr Mavrakis, closing the till, glanced over, eyes narrowed, lips pursed in suspicion, so I flashed him a reassuring smile, watching his expression towards his *English Daughter* soften.

'No, *moro,*' you said. 'Just... disappointed.'

Disappointed? The word sliced through me like a paring knife. I'd have preferred angry. At least there would have been passion behind it. But disappointed? The very word transported me back to childhood admonishments, to Dad's disinterest, to never being *quite* enough.

'Do you love me?' I suddenly asked, feeling weak, as if all the bones in my body had turned to water. Emotionally I was battered, bruised, bleeding.

My troll was laughing and pointing.

'*Yamo to, moro*, this again!' Your voice had risen. 'Why do you always ask? What am I doing wrong? Why won't you believe I love you? What more do I have to do? I am here, trying to get through these days, but you won't do as you are told, and you keep asking stupid questions. Don't you understand how hard all this is for me?'

'What about me?' I gulped. I swallowed down the massive boulder of tears constricting my throat, refusing to cry. I'd just done my makeup and I was supposed to be going to work. Sod you. I sniffed and pinched my damp nose between thumb and forefinger.

'You are not the one in the army.' You were shouting now. '*Yamo to*, you have no idea what it's like.'

No, I didn't. But you didn't know what it was like for me either. I was being constantly watched by your family, trying to always do the right thing, working hard, and going to bed early when all my friends were staying out late, having fun, falling out of bars. I was letting a whole, glorious summer slide by as though it never even existed. Maybe I should have thought more about how hard this might be for me too. For one, brief, moment, I wished I'd never come at all, and we'd just stuck to writing romantic airmail letters across the miles.

'I only wanted some reassurance.'

I wasn't proud of pleading, but I had nothing to lose any more. We both clearly felt sorry for ourselves, but neither could give the other what they wanted.

'I don't want to speak to you on the phone again as you will only upset me, I will upset you.'

'But—'

'Look I don't need this shit, *moro*. I don't want either of us to say something we will regret, so it is best we say nothing more until September.'

'Well, fuck you,' I yelled, knowing it would make everything 100% worse. Good for you if you could compartmentalise everything and pretend all was well until the end of September, but I couldn't. Sofia's eyes were wide circles now, her mouth hanging slack as she pretended to tidy a display of disposable cigarette lighters. This would be all over the resort before I'd even started my shift. Slamming down the phone with force, I marched straight out of the kiosk and stamped up the hill to work.

I necked quite a few shots at work that night, often using the tenet of one for you, one for me, when serving a customer. I also quickly swigged the dregs of various bottles left on tables as I returned with them to the kitchen. On an empty stomach and in the persistent heaviness of the hot, airless night, it had a lethal effect. I was angry pissed. Not a good combination. At least I managed to glide through my shift appearing relatively unscathed, although I spent most of it looking out for Maria and hiding by the ice cream fridge when she came by.

Finally, after adding my armour, Sherri's bright red lipstick, I wandered down to Kristos's bar, staggering on the soft sand in the dark, to find her with Yiannis.

'Are you okay?' asked Sherri, probably noting I was anything but. Immediately, a song I really liked came on, *One Nation Under a Groove*, by Funkadelic, so I kicked my pumps off, threw my arms above my head and began to dance, spinning, turning, throwing my head back and laughing.

Sherri danced with me for a bit, before wending her way back to Yiannis's side. I saw her wrap herself around him as I circled my hips, the music dictating my moves. Letting my hair down from its ponytail, I shook it around my shoulders, continuing to move to the beat, feeling my breath coursing through my lungs, the coolness of damp sand under my bare feet contrasting with the oppressively hot night air. For the first time in ages, I felt alive, free, uncontrolled. I had no money on me, so I grabbed a bottle of mineral water from the bar, shouting to Kristos over the music I'd owe him. He didn't seem to hear. The last thing I needed now was more alcohol. I just wanted to dance. Dancing had always been 'my thing' when I was younger. It transported me to happier times and made me feel like me again. It made me forget.

The beach was pulsating with shadowed bodies gyrating to the beat, indistinct faces lit with flare light, the insistent bass of Mory Kanté's *Yeke*

Yeke thumping through my chest. Flames wavered and flickered in the blackness. Sherri was throwing her head back, laughing at something Yiannis had said. My perspective and spatial awareness had been altered thanks to the earlier alcohol as I gazed at the huge, yellow moon. I must have been looking up too much because I felt really dizzy and overbalanced.

'*Kalispera*, pretty girl,' I felt a rush of hot breath right at my neck as a pair of strong arms steadied me, kept me upright. I tried to register who'd stopped me falling, pulling my gaze quickly back into focus. White vest top, black curls, a flash of gold. It was Andreas.

28

Need You Tonight

I was instantly reminded of how like you he was, in fact, in the dark, he could have been you. The you before you were weighed down with the army, the one who hadn't begun pushing me away. For a moment, I had a crazy instinct to throw my arms around his neck, to rest my face against his cheek, to feel unfamiliar lips on mine. Alarmed, I rocked backwards, leaning away. What was I thinking?

He took a swig from his bottle of beer, his gaze never leaving mine, lights from the flares dancing in his eyes.

'You want to get out of here?' He flicked the stub of his cigarette into the sand and held out his hand.

I'll never be completely sure why I did this but, I nodded, picked up my shoes and, slipping my hand into his strong, warm grip, let him pull me along the beach close to the water's edge, into the darkness where all the lights had disappeared, and it was hard to see. The party was now far behind us. Everyone was too busy having a good time to notice two figures fading along the blackness of the shoreline.

I don't think we spoke much at all as we walked. Eventually we crossed up onto the road to where his bike was waiting. I bent to put on my shoes, but when I stood upright, his eyes locked onto mine and he pulled me into his arms. I was so aware the scent of his skin was infused with something different, alien, something metallic I didn't recognise layered over the cigarettes and cologne. For a moment, I breathed him in. There was something enticing and exciting in unfamiliarity.

'So, where you want to go now?'

I'd totally lost track of time, but it must have been gone 1.00 am.

'I have a boyfriend, you know—'

'I know.' He cut me off in that characteristically Greek way, slightly confrontational, slightly dismissive. 'But he's not here. I am.'

'I just…'

'Look, I like you, okay,' he said, breathing close to my neck. 'I'm not in the army, I have done with all that *skata*. I can read you, *re*, it's summer, you want to have some fun. I think you need someone, so why not me?' He called me *re*, a shortened form of *moré*, a general greeting between friends. For a moment he looked so like you it blindsided me, took my breath away. I really wanted him to be you. So much.

I stepped back.

'Sorry.' I shook my head.

His arms clamped tighter.

'I want you,' he murmured into my hair, his hands exploring the curve of my hips, cupping the cheeks of my bottom, pulling me in tighter to him, guiding my hand towards his zip. The warm breeze was laden with the heady scent of jasmine.

'I think I want to go home, actually.'

It seemed wise under the circumstances. I was dangerously close to doing something I might regret in the morning, and I was only yards from the apartment.

Okay,' he shrugged. 'But I think you should let me make you happy. What do you say?' His finger traced my cheek as he looked enquiringly at me. Somehow, I could sense he was someone used to getting his own way which strangely made him all the more like you than ever.

'Like I said, I have a boyfriend—'

'But he's not here, is he, *moré*?'

He gripped me by both shoulders but just as he moved in to kiss me, I neatly sidestepped, turning my head. He just laughed.

'You like to play, do you? Okay, we'll play your way...for now. I shall come for you tomorrow, in the morning.' It wasn't a question.

'You're not sure yet?' He gave a deep, throaty chuckle. 'We can go somewhere quiet, no pressure and no eyes. I'll be outside your place at eleven.'

'But you don't even know where I live.'

'I do,' he said. 'I have seen you often, up there on your balcony.' He pointed up to the apartment.

He was very self-assured, arrogant, entitled. This was someone used to having exactly what he wanted. He'd clearly been watching me. Maybe that should have rung warning bells. But it didn't. If anything, it made him more intriguing, and a little spike of excitement begin grow within me.

'Okay, but *I* will meet *you*.' I said, taking back the control I felt I needed. 'I'll be outside Cassiopeia Bar at eleven.'

That morning, I hurriedly got ready, then skipped down the steps into the orange, open-sided Moke, clunked into gear and rumbled up the road. I hadn't got a lunch shift that day so I could take my time in getting back. Heading towards Alomenos then curving along the dust track that followed the sequinned band of sea, excitement and nervousness rose within me, but also guilt. The guilt shot through me like a bolt, but it didn't stop me, it made me feel alive. Going somewhere other than Lathos made it so much easier, and no one would expect me to be driving Elaine's Moke. For a moment I clutched the steering wheel, feeling light-headed. What the hell was I doing? I'd thought it through a million times already and had convinced myself I was doing nothing wrong but as I met my own eyes in the rear-view mirror, I knew I was kidding myself. Where did I think this was leading?

Olive groves, stone walls and dusty tracks all flashed by. By British standards, I was simply meeting a friend, it was nothing. Nothing at all. Even if this 'friend' was very attractive, looked very like you, and clearly wanted far more than just a drink. It wasn't like I was going to get *involved*

228

with him, or anything, was it? He might not even turn up, in which case, I'd have just had a little drive in my friend's fun car. No big deal. It was just a casual drive, an innocent meeting, a way to feel good about myself. I was swimming with the tide, no expectations.

Already, the day seemed brighter, more exciting, less predictably tedious as I pulled into the sandy clearing by Cassiopeia Bar. This was how summer days on the island should feel, uncomplicated and fun. However, my stomach skipped and jumped when I saw Andreas in his mirrored shades, leaning on his bike, a black Iron Maiden t-shirt clinging to his impressively muscular torso. I couldn't help my face breaking open into a wide grin that matched his as I jumped out of the Moke and ran to him. Swimming with the tide? I was already in over my head.

Andreas was surprisingly good company. He was attentive, courteous and respectful, with a smile as open and unselfconscious as a child's as he drove me around the island, pointing out the prettiest beaches, his favourite bars, the tall iron gates to his impressive family home, his old school.

We stopped outside a beautiful, whitewashed church.

'My family worships here,' he said, as a black-robed *Pappas* raised a hand in greeting. 'They pay many drachma each year for its upkeep. All our family weddings, funerals, baptisms are held here.'

I leaned into his back as he shifted the bike into gear, heading for a remote bar he knew, closing my eyes as his hand reached back to rest on my bare thigh. From behind he could have been you.

Drinking directly from the icy glass rims of our Amstel bottles under trees which were alive with bees and butterflies, he let me speak to him in Greek, making me laugh rather than cringe at my mistakes. Then, with sunlight dappling the wooden table, in the shade of an ancient vine, I told him all about my copywriting course. I also mentioned how distant and withdrawn you'd become, but he simply said if he'd been you, he'd never have let that happen; you were an *ilithios*, a *malaka*, he'd have put me first. Passionately he slammed his huge fist down on the table for emphasis, making me jump.

As he fed me pieces of melon from his fingers, and lit my cigarettes from his own mouth before offering them to me, I knew I was playing a dangerous game but that was part of the excitement, the fun, the thrill. I'd been so bored, so stifled by waiting, worrying, and exhausted by all the long-distance arguments we'd been having. After all the excessive attention from your family and friends who evidently tracked my every move, this new freedom in places where no one knew me was beyond exhilarating.

Nothing felt better than warm air breathing softly on my skin, the sun infusing my bones as we roared through red clay and up dusty mountain tracks. I was holding on tightly to a handsome, attentive Greek in mirrored sunglasses who knew my situation but didn't judge me. I didn't have to pretend or lie when I was with him. I was as free and unconfined as the breeze in my hair. This is how island summers should be.

When we'd eventually parked up to walk to a shop, he'd unexpectedly wound my hair tightly through his fingers and, dropping his cigarette to the ground, had pulled me in close, kissing me hungrily in the shade of a doorway while a stray cat rubbed against our legs, purring for attention. I felt something disconnect as his lips parted mine and he'd pushed hard against my hips. A small piece of me had lifted, detached, dissipated as his tongue greedily explored my mouth. I knew then everything had irrevocably changed.

When I finally drove back into Lathos, the earlier excitement had evaporated. My chest was tight, a cold trickle of guilt running down inside me. I desperately needed to find Sherri. She would understand, given what had happened with her own love triangle, but first I pulled over and stared at the sea, watching foamy waves lapping the beach, palms waving in the breeze. Tourists were shrieking and splashing in the water. Everything looked just the same, but it wasn't. I'd just kissed another man.

What was I doing? I can't lie, I'd been ridiculously flattered by the attention from Andreas after life had seemed on hold for so long. I'd ached with the need for someone to be there for me each day, my insecurity craved it, and you were so far away, physically and, so it seemed now, emotionally too. I didn't feel you had any more left to give me, but maybe that's what I wanted to think. Perhaps it was me with the problem, not you, because although I felt undeniably guilty, I also felt every nerve had sparked into life, the sun was shining brighter, every colour was more vivid. Was it a sign?

I should have felt ashamed, but the memory of that kiss brought a shudder of desire not conscience. Andreas had told me to leave you to be with him, promising he'd protect me; he would make me happy. I half believed him. I liked how he made me feel, how I was when I was with him. Free, uncomplicated, wanted. With Andreas, nothing was supercharged with emotion like it always was with you. It was easy, relaxed, the stakes were lower, the power balance had tipped. I felt in charge, sensing he liked me more than I liked him, and he made me laugh. I'd even laughed when he'd shown me the knife he always carried for protection, shaking my head incredulously as he'd pointed it for emphasis, saying he wouldn't allow anyone to ever hurt me.

'I don't need protecting, silly,' I'd said, smiling up as his fist clenched around the handle. Laughing, he'd thrust it back into his pocket.

'Tomorrow, I will take you to *Sidira Kyria* on my boat,' he'd said. 'It's not the only shipwreck in Greece. Other islands have more impressive ones, but *Sidira Kyria* has a special place in my family's heart.'

As I sat wrestling with every emotion, trying to make sense of it all, I watched a young couple wander past, holding hands, wrapped around each other as they strolled towards the beach. Then it hit me. Life was just too short. A song was drifting out from a nearby bar, 'Love the One You're With.' I had to decide whether loving you or loving myself was now the most important thing. In the past I'd always deferred to someone else, moulding myself into what I thought they'd wanted. It had never once been about me. I turned the ignition. I wasn't going to waste a drop more of this golden summer. It was now my turn. I was going to start loving myself. I was going to start living again.

Sherri hadn't been as shocked as I'd expected. She'd understood, just as I'd hoped she might. Surprisingly, she then confessed she was having doubts over Yiannis.

'I'll wait until the end of the season and see how I feel then,' she said. 'It's easier that way. But you must phone Marios. Don't put it off, Mel, do it today before someone else tells him.'

'He doesn't want me to phone him any more though. I'm supposed to wait until he phones me now because he says it's too hard for him if—'

'Sod that.' Sherri's hands were hands on her hips. 'I can come with you if you want, for moral support.'

I took a deep breath.

'No, this is something I need to do on my own.'

I was shaking when I dialled. This was a momentous decision. I was breaking up with you. I don't expect you to understand, but anything was better than being suspended in this strange half-life, always second-guessing what was going to come next, wondering if you still loved me. I was too old for you and too old for games. I thought of Dad's story about Toni. How long would it take for you to see my face in the sun? I was so sure you were drifting away, and I just wasn't going to wait for that to happen. You weren't due back until late September, but I had already decided absolutely and unequivocally I was leaving Aftonisi before that. But first, I'd have fun with Andreas, just like Sherri was having with Yiannis. So long as I never had to ever see you again, I could do this.

You'd seemed irritated when you'd answered the phone. Another cut, another blade in my heart.

'I thought I'd told you not to call me until—'

'Just wait, I need to say something.' I took a deep breath. 'I don't think this, us, is working any more. You clearly aren't happy, neither am I and….and…'

Your voice became emotionless. It was like you already knew.

'What are you trying to say?'

This was so hard, in the kiosk, with people around.

'I'm trying to say I don't think this relationship is fair on either of us any more. With the distance, the army and everything…' my voice tailed off. Even as I said it, I began to wonder what on earth I was doing.

'So, what, you're breaking up with me?'

I could imagine your expression. I didn't reply.

The pause seemed to go on forever. I scrambled in my purse to add more coins scared we'd get cut off before I'd finished, pressing my lips so tightly together they hurt. My heart was knocking in my chest, blood pulsing in my ears, my legs shaking. I honestly think at that moment, if you'd reacted differently, I'd have lost my nerve. I'd never have gone through with it. But, with a resident troll in the apartment and with my many unresolved issues, I was like a runaway express train. There was no stopping me.

'I think it's for the best.'

The bomb had dropped. The sky had fallen. The world had titled on its axis. There was no going back now. Your voice rose, your breath heavy against the receiver.

'Who is he?'

Oh, God.

'There's no one else.' I lied. Andreas was a distraction, but never anything long-term so what would be the point of even mentioning him.

I clung on tightly to the receiver, my mouth dry. I felt sick.

'Come on, *moré*, this is me. At least be honest. I know you, and you don't like to be alone.' I winced as you accurately identified the insecurity I tried so desperately to hide, and you had called me *moré*, not *moro*, a subtle variance, but a gulf of difference. Something inside was telling me I owed you the truth, but I just couldn't.

'There's no one else.'

The line went dead.

Walking out of the kiosk mechanically, I gulped in lungfuls of air, trying unsuccessfully to stem the flow of tears but when I reached the apartment, I ran up the stairs sobbing and collapsed into Sherri's arms, literally howling. What had I just done? What the hell was wrong with me?

By morning it was all over Lathos. People wanted to know why we'd broken up, so I let everyone think it was a mutual decision, because of the army, the distance, but Sherri and Elaine knew the truth.

Sakis walked into the kitchen when I was with the girls, telling them everything in minute detail but even as I explained about Andreas, and how I felt I was losing you anyway, it felt all wrong, like something I should never have done. Sherri shot a warning glance at me as Sakis drew up a chair and, wrapping his arm possessively around Elaine, listened intently. His mouth hung open, a chimp-like grin beginning to form.

'So, *moré*, what's this about you and Marios?' He'd clearly heard more than I'd intended so I had no option than to tell him.

'This why I saw you in Alomenos with Andreas Laskaris?' His mouth turned down at the edges, the distaste in his expression obvious. Inside me, a small stab of shock. I hadn't noticed him. Perhaps he'd seen the Moke and had first assumed it was Elaine.

'You can't say anything,' Elaine warned. 'It's...complicated.'

Well, nothing I was going to say would make any difference now, so I just squirmed in my seat, looking up at him.

'I'd really appreciate it if you don't say anything, Sakis, particularly not to Marios. I need time to sort my head out. It's not serious with Andreas, it was just a drink.'

He just shrugged his shoulders, looking straight past me, through the window, out to the sea.

When everyone was out later, I had an unexpected visit from Andreas. He ran up the stairs and grabbed me by the shoulders as I stood in the doorway and kissed me. Within moments, we were a mass of tangled limbs and sweaty skin, the bedsheets scrunching beneath us, the pine bedhead hammering Elaine's adjoining wall. It was over within a matter of minutes. After all the raw, visceral desire had subsided, the silence between us was deafening.

29

Notorious

I continued to see Andreas in secret for the next few days, but when the drama was finally old news, I had no excuse to stop him staying every night. Each time he kissed me, stroked my skin, pulled me to him in our bed, I closed my eyes and saw you. I still have no idea where my head was really at. It was easier to just go along with everything. Outwardly I looked happy, inwardly, I was a mess. I'd lost control and was just drifting, floating like seaweed on the tide.

If I'm honest with myself, Andreas should have been nothing more than a one-off, however, he clearly thought otherwise. He began describing me to his friends, as *yineka*, his wife, and telling me he would come to England with me for Christmas. Christmas seemed as far away as the moon right then and the idea of Andreas sitting at our family table while Dad carved the turkey almost made me laugh out loud at its ridiculousness.

It was little more than a ripple in a pond to Elaine who was as unbothered by a new man in the apartment as she'd been when Yiannis became a permanent fixture. These things happened. Sakis, however, remained quiet. He said nothing. Although he was your friend, he only really cared about himself anyway.

To my surprise, he'd seemed to know Andreas well and had embraced him enthusiastically when he'd seen him huddled over the kitchen table on the first morning he'd stayed over. Were they old school friends? They clearly knew one another from somewhere which made me uneasy. Now Sakis's dead eyes would follow me as I walked from room to room, his expression fathomless. He'd once shown a flicker of unwanted appreciation, his eyes alighting on my legs, my breasts, my hips, as I'd walked around in my bathrobe, but they now seemed to be shadowed with distaste, disapproval, disgust.

I tried to push the little twinges of misgiving firmly aside. Ignoring my instincts, I tried to enjoy the freedom I'd missed by having a boyfriend in the army, as I perched on the back of Andreas's bike on our way out. I always made sure we headed out of Lathos but the flinch of awkwardness in the possibility of seeing any of your family or friends was never far away.

Andreas took charge. He always decided where we would go, what we would do. We ate where he wanted to eat. Sometimes he collected his rents while I sat at the table, drinking Metaxa, picking at sumptuous fruit platters, enjoying fresh prawns, moussaka, stifado, whatever Andreas had ordered, feeling thoroughly spoiled. Each night, somewhere different. Each night, wherever we went, he was treated like a god, and, by default, the spotlight also shone on me. The Laskaris name was a golden key.

The taverna he'd chosen that night was one of the bigger ones on the outskirts of Pervasi. A lively bar with pop music playing instead of Greek songs and a restaurant with a cluster of tables draped in white linen, edging their way towards the sea. I gazed around at the perfect setting, the blackness laced with coloured fairy lights, the air alive with cicadas, the rhythmic sound of waves grazing the nearby beach. It would be hard enjoying meals at the Italian in Southampton again after all this.

The waiter brought our food: two plates of carbonara, and a bottle of local red wine. Andreas had ordered. I didn't get a choice, but I really didn't mind. In some ways it was good being with a man who knew exactly what he wanted, and I liked carbonara.

He trapped my hands within his massive paws, staring deeply into my eyes.

'You are very beautiful,' he said, kissing my fingertips one by one before glancing at the Omega Seamaster he always wore. 'You're my good girl.' My hands remained imprisoned for a moment, his eyes magnetising mine, then he planted a heavy kiss onto my lips. I pulled away. The food was getting cold.

Carefully, I began twirling my spaghetti, watching him stab at his, twisting a heap carelessly on his fork, slinging it into his mouth, his sharp white teeth scraping the prongs as he hurriedly devoured it. His eyes flickered to his watch again. For a moment, as I sipped my wine, I remembered the day I'd met your father, the way you had been constantly glancing at your Swatch. Was Andreas waiting for someone? I checked the little gold Rotary I'd had for my 21st Birthday. It was nearly 10.30 pm.

The restaurant was busy. Every table was full, and someone nearby had ordered an elaborately dressed lobster which had just arrived, studded with lit sparklers on a large platter. People were clapping but Andreas barely glanced up, instead he pointedly checked his watch once more then beckoned the waiter back. A rapid, high-volume dialogue ensued but instead of being the usual wall of noise, my Greek was getting better. I could make out some of the conversation. Andreas was expecting something and seemed annoyed the owner hadn't brought it. I smiled to myself listening to him forcefully demanding *tora, viasyni.* It was so typical of him to want whatever it was now, and quickly, for everything to be perfect. Andreas didn't like being kept waiting. I caught the man's straight expression, feeling a little sorry for him, wondering if he'd perhaps forgotten to bring a dish Andreas had ordered.

Everything was so loud; the pop music invaded my thoughts, and the people at the lobster table were now singing Happy Birthday with other tables now beginning to join in too so I began to sing along, but Andreas just scowled, tapping his plate with his fork, face set. It was hard to ignore the snake of anxiety beginning to coil inside. I stopped singing and continued with my carbonara.

Andreas's eyes flickered to the bar. He ate a few more mouthfuls, then checked his watch again.

'*Malaka*,' he finally muttered under his breath.

I felt my eyes widen.

'Is everything okay?'

Silencing me with a glare he steepled his fingers, his scrutiny intense as his eyes scanned the darkness. I followed his gaze. He seemed to be looking directly at the owner who had noticed and darted into the kitchen. Andreas slowly shook his head, his jaw clenching and unclenching.

I pulled at his sleeve, but he barely looked at me. Something was happening but I couldn't fathom what, so I pushed what was left of the spaghetti about my plate as though disturbing it, stirring it, would somehow diffuse the strange atmosphere and make everything alright again.

'Shall we order a dessert?' I spoke brightly, smiling my sunniest. Neither of us had finished our main course yet I hoped it might relax the unexpected tension hovering between us, but Andreas was completely ignoring me. Tearing the napkin from his lap, he slung his fork down, nostrils flaring. Throwing what was left of his cigarette to the ground, he scraped his chair back and got to his feet. Hesitantly, I stood up too, assuming we were leaving.

'No, you wait.' His words were harsh, not open for negotiation as they lacerated the night air between us. 'He won't be disrespect me like this. Stay there. Eat. This won't take long.'

Sitting back down, I watched him stride across the lawn, making towards the owner who was now behind the bar. They both seemed to be arguing, however with Greek men, it's hard to tell. How had this man disrespected Andreas? Had there been something wrong with the food, perhaps? I glanced over at his nearly empty plate of carbonara and abandoned fork. He hadn't said anything and mine had been lovely.

Trying to quell the vortex of alarm spiralling inside, I smiled tightly at the family who'd ordered the lobster, twisting more spaghetti, trying to normalise this anything but normal situation, but the heavy, parmesan-laced creamy sauce was now making my stomach lurch. Andreas was yelling right into the owner's face, pushing him back towards the till, then waiting with arms folded while the man opened it. On the stereo system, *Don't Worry Be Happy*. I had completely lost my appetite.

Calmly, Andreas walked back to our table where I plastered on a bright, Oscar-worthy smile, as though I'd not seen anything.

'Is everything okay?' I'd assumed Andreas had demanded a refund but the huge, bulky wodge of drachma he tucked inside his jeans pocket was far more than the meals were worth.

'Everything is good now, *yinkea mou*.' he said, patting his jeans. Threading his hand behind my neck he drew me in close to kiss me, then pulled me to my feet. '*Pamé*, we're leaving.' He shoved the table aside. 'I can't eat any more of this *skata*.'

Muting any negative instincts, I concentrated on trying to recreate what I couldn't have with you, someone to wake up with, to have fun with, just having someone there. By some miracle, no one in Lathos really seemed aware Andreas was firmly established in the apartment by then, only that you and I were over, although Sofia's eyes now refused to meet mine and Mr Mavrakis had stopped waving to me as he passed by. I was no longer his English daughter. Now he just regarded me blankly, unsmilingly, disapprovingly. I was relieved the rent was up to date.

Then one afternoon, just after I'd finished my latest copywriting lesson and was scribbling in my journal on the balcony, Sakis came back and threw himself proprietorially onto a nearby chair. Picking at his thumbnail with a bottle opener, he paused to light up a cigarillo, the pungent smoke drifting across the railings.

'Marios, he wants you to telephone.'

As soon as I was put through, you seemed different, tense, your voice tight. A cold, darkness gripped inside me in contrast with the relentless sunshine streaming through the kiosk.

'I've been hearing things, so you will tell me the truth'.

'His name is Andreas Laskaris.' I barely whispered. 'He's from Alomenos, but it happened after us. All this is not because of him...he's...he's just a friend, really.'

'Friend,' you snorted. 'I know him and his family. He is *trelos,* you know, in the head. They all are.' You began to chuckle softly. Another snort. 'Are you are so stupid you don't know this?'

I frowned. *Trelos.* I knew that word. It meant crazy. You were just angry, throwing barbs into the conversation, something to unsettle me.

'Why, Melanie?'

'I didn't set out to do this on purpose… I was lonely, you were being so distant, and he was nice to me.' How pathetic it sounded out loud. You weren't replying so I found myself rambling on to fill the silence. 'I thought you didn't care any more, and—'

'—and you wanted sex so badly you couldn't wait?'

You spat your words out like pistachio shells.

'No! It wasn't like that.' I scratched around for more justification. 'I only noticed him because…because he looked like you.'

The last words fell like hailstones. Why did I say that?

'He looked like me, is that your best excuse, a crazy man looks like me? He's not just crazy, *moré,* he's dangerous.'

Another snort. You'd never sounded more like a stranger than you did then.

'Well, I hope you will be very happy with your *trelos andros'.*

I suppose it was no more than I deserved.

I kept myself busy working while Andreas went most evenings to the restaurant in Alomenos, convincing myself I was happy, but why was everyone so guarded about the Laskaris name? Something had already began niggling at me. It was as though I'd got something out of my system, and now I was beginning to regret it. I'd scratched an itch and been left with a graze. I'd been scared you were slipping away and, true to form, I'd jumped before I was pushed.

Andreas was hugely possessive, more than you had ever been. Why had I not noticed before?

'You are mine now, so you never look at Marios again,' he'd demanded.

I'd brushed it off. I'd thought he was being dramatic, nothing more, but now I wasn't so sure. Frying pan and fire came to mind. So intense as well. Constantly talking about the future, wanting to come to England with me in October, and pestering me about having babies. Like most Greeks, he wanted a lot. We'd only been together a matter of weeks, yet he'd demanded I stop taking my contraceptive pill, so I'd hidden them in Sherri's room. He told me he loved me constantly, words I'd craved from you, but which left me impassive when delivered by him. Blundering words which crackled with pretence when he made me repeat them back.

Sometimes I could almost switch off and attempt to enjoy being with him, basking in his attention, but I became aware he constantly watched my face, as I spoke, as I ate, as I drank, always smiling wider and brighter whenever I caught his eye. He was always touching me, stroking me, trapping my hand under his.

I noticed a livid graze across his knuckles one evening as he lit our cigarettes.

'How did you hurt yourself?'

I ran my fingertip tentatively across his hand. He drew it back into a fist.

'It's nothing, just work.'

He flashed me that smile again. A self-assured, entitled, shark of a smile, blindingly white.

I sometimes sat on the edge of the bed, watching him sleep, with a growing disquiet, his strong limbs stretched out against Sofia's cotton sheets, his dark curls on what had once been our pillows. His face looked almost angelic in repose, yet he slept with a knife and there was something in his eyes I couldn't fathom. *Trelos*, you'd called him. I'd thought it was just retaliation, anger, but it was now beginning to disturb me, nibbling at the edges of my consciousness like a rat in a trap. The more I looked at him, the less he looked like you until I couldn't see the resemblance all.

I'd only wanted a selfish, summer distraction; I'd wanted to feel adored. I'd only wanted to replicate what I couldn't have with you, because I was lonely, yet it was becoming increasingly obvious Andreas wasn't you at all. I didn't know what I was doing any more. I'd made a stupid mistake, one

I'd have to rectify somehow but, above all, I couldn't shake the thought you were due back at the end of September. It terrified me. I just couldn't hang around for that. I'd never be able to face you again after everything, so I began to formulate an idea. Even though I had no real plans for my future, I'd go home. Back to England. I'd make sure the rent was paid until October; I couldn't let Sherri and Elaine down, but my time in Aftonisi had just run out. I'd tell them later and ask them to keep quiet, but by mid September, I'd be gone. I'd give Andreas the slip. I didn't know exactly how, but I would find a way.

30

Could You Be Loved?

One afternoon, a letter arrived from Alan saying he and Trevor had left
Jackson and James and were opening a new agency on the outskirts of
Southampton.

'I am sure you're very happy on your paradise island with your Greek
man so you probably won't consider this, but we'd love to have you here
as Assistant Manager,' he wrote. 'I'll match your pay at Jackson and James,
company car too. Just let me know before the end of the month, Mel, before
I have to advertise, and for God's sake, if you do decide to come back, *please*
don't let me down again.'

Gazing out over the street, feet up on the railings, the intensity of the sun
on my legs, I considered everything. Had Alan thrown me an unexpected
lifeline? I folded and unfolded his letter in my hands. Something else I'd
have to hide from Andreas. Just like I'd hidden the little silver olive leaf ring
you'd given me. He'd insisted I threw it away, but I just couldn't. Not yet. It
was all I had left of when we'd once been happy. I wasn't ready to let it go.

The heat I usually enjoyed now made me feel completely drained and tired.
Everything around me felt devoid of life. I looked down on the tourists
milling about below, clutching inflatables as they wound their way back
from the beach, sitting outside bars, drinking, shouting, laughing their way

through their perfect holidays. They were enjoying what was now to me just relentless, cruel, unforgiving sunlight, an inescapable spotlight that only served to highlight all my misgivings.

My thoughts whirled on spin cycle.

It was my turn to buy a few supplies, so I sprinted down the stairs, crossing the road to the supermarket to help take my mind off my dilemma. Aimlessly, I wandered around, as the owner stacked packets of washing powder, leaving sprinkles on the shelf after ripping the delivery open. Suddenly, I thought of Mum and realised I needed her. It had been a gnawing ache for a while but now, surrounded by familiar groceries in a foreign shop, the drifting scent of washing powder, it was a sharp stab. I really wanted to hear her voice. Even though I knew I had to go home, I still wasn't sure about Alan's job offer. I'd got myself into a bit of a predicament, she'd know what to do for the best. I also fervently hoped she'd help me out with the flight costs as I was getting very low on funds.

I crossed back over to the kiosk. No-one was using the payphone and thankfully none of the Mavrakis clan were about so, taking a deep breath, I dialled.

Dad answered.

'Hello, Dad.' I tried to sound breezy, as I asked for Mum. The last thing I wanted was to be caught in some awkward dialogue with him. Any dialogue, really.

'Who's this?' His voice sounded thin, indistinct over the miles.

Why did he always ask that? I was his only child, after all. Instantly, I prickled with annoyance.

'It's me, Dad. Melanie.' I tried to smooth the snappiness from my voice and make it as neutral as possible.

'Oh, yes, sorry, just watching Countdown.'

'Is Mum there?'

'No, at pottery…you know your mother, always got hobbies on the go. This one's blasted pottery. Making a fruit bowl, if you please.'

'Oh, right…'

A pause.

'Will I do instead?'

Oh God, how awkward.

'Um...'

I wanted to make my excuses and say I'd call her back, but now I felt obliged to chat.

'Er...of course, don't be daft.' I took a breath. 'Thing is, Dad, I'm thinking of coming home.' I heard the catch in my breath and began digging my nails into my palms, hard. I was not going to cry.

'Righty-ho,' Dad sounded a little confused.

I found I couldn't speak any more.

'Melanie...is everything okay?'

No, it's not.

'Yes, of course.'

I grappled for a tissue, sniffing hard before blowing my nose.

'Have you got a cold?'

'No, I'm fine.' I said, aware I sounded anything but, as I noisily blew my nose again. The kiosk was oppressively hot now as I shoved another handful of drachmae in at the pips.

Although Dad was silent again, I couldn't remember having such a long conversation with him in ages.

'Are you in some sort of trouble?' He sounded softer, surprisingly less judgemental than usual. I felt my eyes well up.

Stop being nice to me.

'Melanie?'

'I've broken up with Marios.' The rawness of the words ripped at my throat, their enormity probably sinking in for the first time ever.

'Ah, thought he'd get fed up with you.'

'No, Dad. It was me, I finished with him.'

'Oh.'

His response sounded so loaded I felt defensive so I continued airily, hoping he wouldn't ask for details.

'I've actually met someone else...but it's not serious, so, basically...I thought I might come back before the season ends. If I can scrape some money together.'

Instantly I realised he'd think I was only phoning for a handout. To be fair, I would have asked Mum outright if she'd answered, but this was Dad. I didn't want him thinking I was weak. Weakness was something he'd always made clear he despised. When he answered again, it was as though he'd chosen to ignore my last words, concentrating only on our breakup.

'Probably for the best, like I said, what with you being older—'

'Don't, Dad.'

'So, when are you coming back then?'

'I don't know exactly, but before the end of the month…probably. It all depends on a few things.'

Like, if I can afford to.

'Are you going back to Southampton, or coming here?' His voice seemed a bit metallic, indistinct, crackling across the miles. 'How the devil did she get nine letters?' He was clearly still distracted by Countdown.

'Look, don't worry, you're busy. I'll ring Mum later.'

'Melanie…'

'What?'

He cleared his throat.

'Look, I know we've never exactly *connected* in the same way that you and your mother do, but I still worry about you, just the same, so if you need to come back, use your Access card, okay?'

I gulped hard, tears scraping the inside of my throat, my chest aching as I pictured Dad's face turning puce at this level of intimacy.

'What I mean is, put the flight on the plastic and we'll worry about it later.'

'But it's a lot of money, Dad, it's about 400 quid.'

He made a long, whistling sound.

'Oh, that *is* rather a lot, Melanie.' He was quiet for a moment while I chewed the inside of my cheek. 'You do get yourself into some scrapes, don't you? Jetting off to Greek islands. Running after foreign men. I mean, you're nearly thirty, aren't you? It's time you grew up a bit.'

I knew it had all been too good to be true. Dad and I never usually had proper two-way conversations, and certainly not without Mum as mediator.

'If you do come back Melanie,' he added. 'There's this new thing called Poll Tax that Mrs Thatcher's bringing in, so you'll have to pay for that too. We can't be expected to pay yours as well.'

'I probably won't Dad,' I replied, stiffly. 'Come back to yours, I mean. If I do, it will only be for a couple of weeks, not long term.'

'I shouldn't have to be bailing you out at your age—.'

'I didn't actually ask you to, Dad.'

I'd been planning to put it on Access anyway and had resigned myself to paying it back over a year. Sod Rob and his stupid deal with that builder. I was even less sure about Alan's job offer then, but I needed options and had to get away before you came home from the army. I just had to.

'Stick it on the card anyway,' Dad interjected, quite unexpectedly. 'I'll sort it out for you. Let's just get you back safely. Your mother would never forgive me if you were in a fix, and I didn't help.'

Suddenly, an image of him in his gardening pullover, his face red from bending over and pulling up potatoes, leaning on his fork, formed, and I felt an unexpected rush of emotion. Tears were flowing freely now as I sniffed and spluttered my thanks, not caring that several tourists were watching me dissolving into a blubbering mess.

'Thank you, Dad, thank you so much.' I looked around. I'd been hogging the payphone for ages, and I wasn't sure how welcome I was in the kiosk any more, even though I knew the Mavrakis family preferred money to morals. 'I've got to go now.'

'Melanie?'

'Yes, Dad?'

'Are you crying?'

'God, no.' I swallowed hard. 'Look, I'd better go—.'

'Melanie, you do know I...' He cleared his throat. 'Look, I'm not very good at this sort of thing, but I want you to know that whatever you might think, I do...'

I took a deep breath. It was now or never.

'I know, and I love you too Dad.'

I replaced the receiver and, crying openly, ran back up to the apartment.

Whatever had happened then was momentous to me. To anyone else, it would just have been a conversation about money but to me, it was a defining moment. Something heavy and cumbersome I'd carried for years had shifted. What had once been a solid lump inside had become fluid, suffused with lightness. I felt something lift and dissipate. Love takes many forms and not everyone shows their emotions the same way. The events of the past few months had certainly taught me that. Maybe, when I was home again, things might be different.

I hadn't had long to process this because Sherri raced in as I was putting the groceries away in the kitchen.

'Mel, you to need to sit down,' she said, out of breath. Her tone was serious, and she wasn't wearing her usual smile, in fact she looked uncharacteristically solemn.

I frowned.

'What's happened?'

'Let's just say September's come around a little early.'

Once Andreas knew you were back, he demanded I never spoke to you and kept far away from you.

'I forbid it.' He paced the bedroom, face set.

Once again, I didn't know when to shut up.

'I don't intend to speak to him, but you can't just tell me what to do—'

'Don't answer back or disobey me,' he roared, drawing himself up, jutting his chin, eyes blazing as he followed me into the kitchen. 'I am Andreas Laskaris.'

I almost wanted to laugh at how ridiculously pompous that sounded.

'If any woman disobeys *me*,' he said, eyes sharp and cold like stones, as he turned to Sakis who'd just walked in, 'I punish her.' This was all said in English, so I would miss nothing.

That afternoon, I went to see Nikos. He was one of the few who was still my friend after our breakup. I asked him about Andreas's reputation and why you might have said he was crazy.

248

'*Moré*, I don't know for sure,' he said, rotating his signet ring as he spoke. 'But wherever he goes, there is trouble. There was a big problem with his last girlfriend.'

'Yes, he told me she wouldn't come back again.' I remembered that first conversation, with Andreas, wishing now I'd asked him more. 'I got the impression he was upset when she decided to go and didn't want to talk about it.'

Nikos shook his head.

'She didn't decide, *moré*, she didn't get a choice. You don't argue with the Laskaris family. They made her leave.'

I stood gaping at Nikos.

'What do you mean?'

'Look, I don't know everything, but I know this Andreas, and he's...*trelos*, you know, like in the head, and the family are trouble, they are not good people. They made her go back to Cyprus even though she still had a proper job here, at the airport.'

My head was whirling. Surely Nikos would have told me earlier. Surely even Sakis, who knew Andreas, would have said something if this were true?

'What do you know about his family Nikos?'

Nikos ripped up his Rizla paper and snapped a matchstick in half.

'What has *he* told you about them, *moré*?'

'Not much. I know they own restaurants, bars and a nightclub in Pervasi.' A random thought came to me. 'Andreas said he collects rents for his father. That's about it, really.'

Nikos snorted. He leaned towards me, his voice lowered, muttering at first in Greek, too fast for me to understand.

'*Moré* it's not rent, it's payment for services from Andreas's family. Let's put it this way, it's not a business transaction, it's more a *syndromi*.'

'A what?' I felt my brows draw closer. It wasn't what Nikos was saying, it was the guarded way in which he was saying it.

'It's like a subscription, *moré*, er...an insurance payment, *asfalsi*.'

I must have still looked puzzled.

'*Moré*, don't make me spell it out for you. You are not stupid. Businesses pay insurance to families like these, okay, or they will not thrive, *endaxi?*'

I felt my mouth part and my eyes widen. Surely, he didn't mean what I thought he did. I laughed despite everything.

'Come on Nikos, that's a bit dramatic. You're making it sound like it's some sort of…protection money.' I expected Nikos to also laugh, to reassure me, but instead his eyes didn't meet mine. I felt the smile freeze on my lips.

'I cannot say,' his voice was little more than a whisper now as he leaned towards me, his roll up clinging to his lip as he finally met my gaze. 'But they are *adelfotita*, a brotherhood, and certainly *enklimatias*.'

I knew that word, it meant *criminal*.

'That can't be right, they're respectable people, very religious. Andreas told me his father and uncles are always going to church. They even make regular donations to it. You've got it wrong. They're not criminals, they're generous, successful businessmen.'

'Businessmen.' Nikos snorted. 'Yes, they're men with many businesses, but they're not businessmen and they go to church, because church is where their type meet. It avoids suspicion, *moré*. By the time I knew who you were with, that his name was Laskaris, it was too late. If I'd said anything, I'd be in trouble, *katalaveno*. It's really not my place to start trouble with the Laskaris family. I have my own family, apartments, a taverna to think of.'

Just as I was searching for more to ask him, Nikos spoke again.

'As for Sakis, he doesn't have a good opinion of you.'

'But why?'

This day was getting better and better.

Nikos flipped open his cigarette tin and offered me a roll up which I took, leaning in closely as he lit them both with his Zippo. Drawing the smoke in deeply, he regarded me as I stared back indignantly.

'It's not your fault, *moré*,' he said, placing a hand on mine, 'but he's never liked you. He says you have too much to say.' He seemed to be considering something for a moment, taking another drag on his skinny roll up. 'He's always…*mistrusted* you because you're like Elsa.'

'Who, that Swedish girl he was with?'

Elaine had mentioned her and so had you.

Nikos nodded.

'You look just like her.'

I frowned for a moment. How could I have possibly looked like her? I'd assumed Elsa was like Astrid who was so obviously Scandinavian. Swedish girls, weren't they all blonde, like that girl in Abba, like Britt Ekland? I was so dark I could have easily passed for Greek myself.

'Wasn't she blonde?'

'No, *moré*, she was dark, and very like you. I think Sakis must have had a big shock when he first saw you, and now he says you're a cheat, just like her.'

There seemed little point in explaining it was all a technicality because I hadn't really cheated on you, not by British standards, but I felt sick and hollow inside.

'But Elaine said he'd planned on ending things between them anyway. She said it wasn't serious—'

'No, *moré*. Sakis thought it was. He wanted to marry her. He was *pligoménos*...you know, heart wounded...destroyed. Really bad after what she did.'

'You mean broken hearted.' I corrected.

'Broken, yes.' Nikos agreed. 'I think it made him scared of loving another woman until Elaine, but now he's worried he'll lose her too, and all because of you.'

'What do you mean, because of me?' A little spark of indignation flared inside me as I glared hard at him.

'*Moré*, Sakis is happy with her because she's a good girl. She won't cheat on him, or give him the broken heart like Elsa, but you've encouraged her to change, to argue, to go to school, maybe even go back to England and leave him, and he doesn't like it.'

My face must have instantly shown my feelings because Nikos put a hand on my arm, his expression serious.

'I tell you this, *moré*, so you can learn your lessons and not interfere.'

I was completely stunned as we hugged goodbye, knowing he'd meant

251

well. It wasn't his fault he saw everything through a simplified lens with everything either black or white, no shades of grey. I had to accept there was a cultural difference and a lifestyle one, too. The islanders I knew lived in a quiet, idyllic paradise with an existence akin to rural life in England, but I'd been born and raised in West London. Our opinions and perspective could never, ever really be the same.

31

Careless Whisper

Making my way back up the sand, my head was littered with very unwelcome thoughts. Even Nikos, whom I considered a friend, hadn't explained about Andreas to me earlier, but more upsetting, he clearly felt I needed to learn some sort of lesson; to be more subservient and acquiescent. I'd initially thought he was telling me everything because he'd felt I should know as a friend, not because he felt I should learn by it.

The beach was strewn with sunbathers, all probably thinking what a perfect life it would be, living on a Greek island. For a moment, I envied their simple, uncomplicated holiday making and naivety of thought. The nuances of life here were far more complex than I'd ever realised. Since coming out here, I had lost my status. I wasn't a local, or a holidaymaker, I was only a worker, and an illegal one at that. In the last six months, everything had turned upside down, leaving me feeling like I was hanging by the seat belt in an overturned car, pinned the wrong way against the roof, the only way out to come crashing back down again. Frowning, I ran back up the steps and stepped back inside the cool of the apartment.

Sitting at the kitchen table to think, I tapped my nails against the wooden surface, drumming an impatient beat while trying to piece together fragments of something I didn't quite understand. Andreas had said

Agia Maria was important to his family, *Sidira Kyria* was a special place. Something kicked hard inside, a remnant of the day trip with our Australian friend. My tangle of thoughts snaked their way to Sakis. It now made sense why he tried to keep Elaine away from Sherri and me as much as possible. In my view, I'd had a breakup, it happens, but Sakis saw me as a cheat and a threat, reinforcing his dislike of foreign women.

Then I remembered Andreas pushing against me in the gift shop doorway, his palm sliding under my top, his tongue in my mouth and how my initial twang of conscience, the spike of guilt, had quickly been replaced with the real thrill of illicit excitement as I'd tasted another man's lips. I'd known exactly what I was doing. Perhaps Sakis's suspicions hadn't been completely unfounded. Maybe I was like Elsa after all. Instantly I knew how you'd found out about Andreas. I bet he hadn't been able to contain himself.

I got ready for my shift with a heavy heart. You hadn't been due back until the end of September. I'd planned to leave before then. Now what was I supposed do? How could I ever face you again? Horribly aware of what an idiot I'd been, the overwhelming force of how I still felt about you hit me like a cricket bat. I had to find you.

Leaving the apartment, I wound my way through the early evening tourists, searching, scanning, all my senses alert to the sight of you but you weren't in any of the familiar places so eventually I gave up and went to work. Usually, I enjoyed working at Ampeli, but that evening I got orders mixed up and took dishes to the wrong tables.

'What's wrong with you, *kopella?*' hissed Kostas, the Head Waiter, as I brought back yet more plates originally destined for different tables. 'You're making a lot of mistakes.' He glared at me as I apologised. In Kostas's eyes, I wasn't even worthy of a name. He only ever called me 'girl'.

By the end of the shift, I was exhausted in trying to keep my mind on work instead of the awful fact you were somewhere on the island. Then, just before midnight, a large, noisy crowd of locals appeared, funnelling through the gateway, stampeding across the terrace like cattle. There must have been at least thirty of them. Greek families or groups of friends often ate late, but I was tired and wanted to get back home so my heart sank. I knew they'd have us all running about like spinning tops, ordering massive amounts of food, making a terrible mess, littering the table with beer bottles and the floor with napkins, cigarette ends and ripped up beer mats. So much for getting off on time.

Kostas greeted them deferentially, treating them like royalty, pushing several tables together into one as he seated them, pulling out chairs, nodding genially. I sighed. They would probably stay for ages now, and I would be expected to stay too. Usually, I didn't mind too much, they often tipped generously, but this time it was different, because the group he'd seated had included you.

I felt the blood drain from my face and my tongue turn to jelly when I saw you sitting there. That one glance told me everything. I still loved you. I'd never stopped. I felt such a magnetic force pulling me. Could you feel it too? What the hell had I been thinking these past weeks? It was so hard not to rush to your side as I watched Kostas walk over with menus, all the while chatting and nodding politely. He then walked briskly back to me.

'Drinks, *kopella*.' Snapping his fingers, he pointed to your table and disappeared into the kitchen. My heart nearly stopped. I was frozen to the spot. I couldn't go over. How could I?

You turned in my direction, staring long and hard at me, your gaze unwavering, so, for a moment, my heart jumped with expectation, but it was short lived. The look you cast me was one of distain, then, with your eyes still on me, you waved Kostas back over. I hesitated. Was I supposed to go now to take the drinks orders, or wait? I saw Kostas bend, his head inclined towards you, nodding, then you both looked back over. I couldn't read your expression. Maybe you were asking for me. Something inside me leapt.

Smiling, I began crossing the shadowed garden towards the seated group, all the while, digging my nails into my palms. I might as well get this over with, but as I neared the candlelit table, Kostas gripped my elbow, propelling me back to the patio.

'Do you know what he asked?' he said, glaring at me.

I shook my head, trying to keep my composure.

'He asked why we had a dirty prostitute working as a waitress and weren't we afraid the customers might catch something.'

I didn't finish the shift that night. Kostas sent me home after nerves got the better of me and I dropped a full bottle of Mateus Rosé, which exploded all over a customer's dress. The only other table left anyway was yours and I clearly wasn't welcome there, so I'd been heading for the kitchen to get my bag when, without warning, you were there.

We were on either side of a table by the servery when our eyes locked. I looked straight at you, and you back at me, your eyes hard, mouth distorted with scorn. Who were you? It was like I didn't know you at all. There was such a gulf between us, your expression of derision, the curl on your lip, you exuded pure hatred. Despite everything, I knew this was my chance.

'Can we talk, please?'

'Filthy whore, *putana*, don't come near me.'

In one angry move, you completely upended the table, and it landed upside down on the concrete, a loud crack as it fell, two chairs tumbling over. You picked up a third and hurled it as I leapt out of the way, your face contorted with anger.

'*Yama sou, skyla,* fuck you, bitch.'

Kostas told me to go, face white with fury, so, shaking, I grabbed my bag while he stood with his arms folded. I was too shocked to cry. Why was no-one helping me? You'd behaved aggressively and violently towards me in front of everyone, but somehow I was the one in trouble, not you. In England, after a break-up, you're free to live your life. Not so in Aftonisi. For the first time since I'd arrived, I felt unsafe.

Back in the apartment, my mind was still racing as I tried to make sense of it all. Andreas was already sleeping so I quickly got ready for bed, slipping in quietly so as not to wake him but after a short while, he stirred and I felt him reach for me in the dark, pulling me towards him, his lips against mine. I remained limp, deliberately slowing my breathing, pretending to be asleep and praying my heart rate would quieten, but he wasn't taking no for an answer as he stroked my skin, twisting around my curled form, kneeing my thighs apart and pushing inside me. The way I was able to completely detach myself from the situation reminded me exactly of how things had been with Rob last year. At that moment, I couldn't have wanted anyone less.

In the morning he questioned me about whether I'd seen you, so I had to say what happened as it was likely to be all over Lathos anyway.

'Stay away from him,' he warned, stabbing the air with his finger. 'If he comes near you again, I will kill him. Leave the job. My family has money. They will look after you now.'

'Thank you, but I need to earn my own money. I promise it won't happen again.' The room had shrunk, the ceiling felt lower, imaginary bars were springing up against the windows.

'I will be angry if you go near him.'

Sensing the need to calm him, I gave him a reluctant kiss as he made to leave for his shift, but he pulled me in close, crushing my lips against his, kissing me with such force my head jerked back.

'As I keep telling you, I have more than enough money.' He stared long and hard into my eyes. 'You don't need to work.'

'I know, and it's very kind of you, but I want to pay my way,' I summoned up a smile, hoping I'd loosened the tightness in my voice convincingly. 'I really enjoy working and you already treat me so much. I'd like to treat you for a change.'

That evening I arrived in the restaurant, my chest tight and my mouth dry. My heart seemed to have risen to my collar bone. It pulsed unpleasantly as I walked toward Kostas who was deep in discussion with Mr Manasis.

'*Kalispera.*' I tried to look relaxed. Neither of them acknowledged me but I was aware of their eyes following me as I put my bag in the kitchen and sailed back out into the restaurant with a fixed smile. Brushing an imaginary crease from my skirt, I took a step forward.

'*Yassas,*' I greeted them cheerfully. 'Which tables are mine tonight?'

'None, we don't need your kind in here.' Mr Manasis folded his arms, his mouth a hard line.

'That wasn't my fault last night. I am so sorry, but it won't happen again.'

My heart was jumping around uncomfortably, like a trapped bird trying to escape a cage.

'And you can guarantee this?' Kostas had such a sneering, imperious look on his face it was almost comical.

I was about to say that, yes, I could, when Mr Manasis interrupted me.

'We don't employ *putana*, it's bad for business.'

At that moment, Maria came out of the kitchen holding my bag at arm's length like it was contaminated. She pushed it at me.

'Go away,' she said. 'You're no longer required.'

I stood mute for a moment then something ignited inside me making me shake with fury. To prevent it showing, I crossed my arms over my bag, hugging it tightly and, lifting my chin, stared back into her cold eyes.

'I'm not leaving without the money I'm owed.'

'Come tomorrow.'

Maria looked derisively down her sharp nose and turned on her heel, so, calling on every ounce of dignity I could muster, I walked out.

'No work, no money, big problem.' Kostas smirked, clearly enjoying it all.

Mr Manasis shrugged, an ugly sneer on his lips. 'Prostitutes can always find work, even ones like her. Not everyone is fussy.'

This was all in English, for my benefit.

Trying to forget the cruelty of their laughter, I hid in the apartment, watching drunk tourists from the safety of the balcony, scanning the heaving crowds, desperately looking out for Sherri, until I saw her walking back from her shift. She wasn't with Yiannis, so I rushed down to meet her.

'I'm in so much trouble,' I gulped, biting the inside of my cheek to fight back tears as we walked up the stairs together. I told her about my altercation at Ampeli.

Sitting on the top step with me, she pulled me in to her, rubbing my shoulder as we both sat staring down at the beach. Blackened waves were dancing with coloured lights from beachside tavernas and Bob Marley's

Could You Be Loved was drifting up from a nearby bar. It occurred to me the irony of those lyrics under the circumstances. I dropped my head to her shoulder. If nothing else, I'd made a true friend. A friend for life.

'Why didn't you wait, Mel? She turned to look at me. 'I mean, Marios wanted you to start a new life with him, the bar and everything, didn't he? It was never like me and Yiannis, only a bit of fun, was it? Why didn't you just…wait?'

Why *didn't* I just wait? What could I say? What was there to offer in explanation except for the plain simple truth. I'd been selfish. I'd felt insecure, I'd got bored with waiting. I'd been jealous of all the fun everyone else seemed to be having. I was sick of a summer on hold, of being a good girl, but the main reason was I'd felt you were slipping away. I needed to find some degree of control. If I was going to lose you, I'd lose you on my own terms. How shallow, stupid, and immature it all sounded now. Why didn't I wait… I really didn't know. What a spectacular lack of judgement. If I hadn't gone through so much drama earlier with Rob, if Dad had shown even a modicum of interest in me, if….

'I've made such a big mistake. I can't believe I've been so stupid. I've ruined everything now.'

'You still love him?'

'I wish I didn't, but as soon as I saw him again….'

Sherri rubbed my arm, smiling sadly.

'But what about Andreas?'

'What about Andreas?' I snorted, aware it was so easy to completely forget he even existed until someone mentioned him. 'I don't want Andreas.'

'Well, you'll have to tell him, then.'

'How?' I wailed. 'It's not that easy… you know what he's like.'

I'd found Andreas's possessiveness and intensity hugely flattering at the start. He'd made me feel so special, so wanted, so valued, but now I was feeling increasingly trapped and Nikos's words were haunting me.

'Yeah, I know what you mean,' Sherri said. 'He *is* a bit…scary, isn't he?'

'Oh God.' I sunk my head onto her shoulder. 'It's such a mess.'

We sat in silence for ages until she spoke again.

'Look, try speaking to Marios again. Yes, he's angry now but he'll calm down later, you'll see.' She rubbed my shoulder encouragingly. 'Then tell Andreas once you've both sorted yourselves out. Maybe you can tell him together?'

I was doubtful about that. Sherri hadn't seen the way you'd looked at me, the things you'd said. I would never have dreamt you were capable of such explosive fury, especially as you'd seemed so calm and accepting of our breakup on the phone. It was only then I'd realised how much I must have hurt you.

'It's a good thing, in a way,' she eventually said. 'I mean, anger is still passion isn't it. He wouldn't be angry if he didn't care. He's getting it all out of his system. At least you can see he's going on instinct now, on feelings. It's not like he's ignoring you. I think this actually might be a good sign.'

I sat there quietly, thinking. Maybe she was right. A flicker of a smile cruised my lips. Perhaps all we needed was a little more time.

The next morning, I marched into Ampeli, my head high. The place was heaving, the breakfast shift underway, lots of busy tables full of tourists eating full 'English' breakfasts, ironically with the very un-English additions of processed German hot dog sausages and a random pile of fried peppers, aubergine and oregano. Maria was carrying two coffee jugs, fussing around the tables like an overfed pigeon. She ran her eyes slowly up and down me. Ignoring her, I made straight for Kostas.

'I'd like my money, please,' I said, mustering as much confidence as possible.

'You wait here.'

He disappeared into the kitchen and soon returned with Mr Manasis who gave me a cursory glance. The table you'd turned over was upright again, a small vase of flowers now in its centre.

'You want money?'

'Yes please.' I tried to be polite, ignoring his supercilious expression and contemptuous tone as I trotted behind him.

Snorting derisively, he punched the till open, took a mixture of notes and coins from the drawer, then slammed it shut.

'Here.'

As I reached to take it, he flung it all at my feet before jerking his chin back to spit on it with full force. Notes fluttered in all directions, coins scattered and rolled under the tables.

Cutlery was now poised midway to several pairs of lips as diners gaped at the free entertainment they were getting with their breakfast. Why had I even imagined he would make it easy for me.

Refusing to appear as humiliated as I felt, I bobbed up and down, scooping up notes, chasing spinning coins, while carefully avoiding his glob of saliva. Then, biting back angry tears, my gaze fixed straight ahead, I walked out. On the way up the path, I aimed a savage kick at Maria's beautiful, hand-drawn chalk board and was rewarded to see it topple face first into the dust. I might have even broken it.

'Whoops,' I said as I stepped out onto the road. 'Clumsy me.'

32

Would I Lie to You?

Without my job at Ampeli, I was now left with just the occasional shift Elaine could spare as she'd found managing three jobs a little tricky. I was grateful to her. With that, and the crêpe making, I could just about cope. We'd paid for rent up until the end of the month, I could afford to eat, so all I had to worry about was trying to sort things out with you.

That evening, when I did my crêpe shift, I caught sight of you, but you were not alone. You were hand in hand with a dark-haired girl but as soon as you saw me, you looped your arm around her neck, pulling her in close, lingering over a long, passionate kiss. My heart sank, complete misery and emptiness flooding me. Looking over her shoulder directly at me, you smirked.

'You come to Alomenos and wait for me,' Andreas got out of the shower, his skin glistening as he wrapped a towel around his middle. He clearly didn't want to let me out of his sight. 'I will bring you back later to make crêpes.'

I followed him into the bedroom where he sat on the bed, fed his rings one by one onto his fingers, and lit up a cigarette.

'It's okay, I'm with Elaine tonight,' I forced a bright smile, standing by the shutters, half hoping I might see you outside. 'But I'll see you back here after your work.'

'But what are you doing, where are you going?'

'Just getting some food, having some quiet time together.'

'I don't want you going near Marios.'

'I won't,' I said. 'I've nothing left to say to him. It's over. I only want you.'

I saw his face soften a little. It was so easy to lie to him.

'Come here,' he said, pulling me towards him, his hands skimming my body. He was still damp from the shower as he kissed me. 'You don't talk to him; you don't even look at him, you cross the road if you see him, *kataleveno?*'

I nodded compliantly and went back to the balcony as he pulled on his jeans and a shirt, ready for work. I knew he was worried, and I suppose he had every reason to be, but I didn't care at all. All I could think about was you, as I scanned the street below again, wondering where you were. I really needed to talk to you. Surely you couldn't still be so angry? I even wondered if the recent drama had all been for the benefit of your friends as it was so out of character for you.

Andreas came back out to say goodbye, his eyes contracting in suspicion when he saw me looking down on the street

'Melanie, come here,' he demanded. 'I'm going now to collect rents.'

Roughly he pulled me into his arms and kissed me hard, pushing my hair back with his huge hands before clamping me possessively to him. '*Kopella mou,*' he murmured, '*yineka mou,*' as I hung limply in his embrace. I felt numb towards him; it felt impossible to respond, but I knew he'd notice, so I decided to draw on all my acting ability. After all, I had a Drama O Level.

'Don't forget you're mine now, not his,' he hissed into my hair, his thick fingers encircling my wrist. 'I don't want you near him again or I will be angry.'

His face was set as he ground his cigarette out before stalking back into the bedroom, banging the shutters.

'You really don't need to worry,' I called to his retreating form, thinking about what Nikos had said: *He's crazy.*

As soon as I saw his bike flying up the road, I sprinted into the shower. I was planning to meet Elaine at The Grill House for dinner because it was rare she had an evening without Sakis. I needed a distraction, and I couldn't bear the idea of seeing you with that girl again.

Padding out of the bathroom and back to my room, wrapped in a towel, my hair up in a clip, I sat on my unmade bed and peered into the mirror. I looked tired but it was my eyes that surprised me. I could literally see the effect all this was having on me embedded within my irises. A spiral of pure pain had wound its way into the very core of me, it was there, a tangible thing, staring back at me in the mirror.

Pulling a particularly short, white dress from the wardrobe, I slung it on the bed, determined to make you notice if I saw you again. Tonight, I was going to make a big effort. Smoothing moisturiser over my face, I began digging in my makeup bag, barely glancing up when I heard someone walking into the kitchen. The door was always open; it was probably Sakis or Yiannis.

It was you.

I jumped, reaching for my wrap, feeling horribly exposed in the towel, even though you'd so often seen me in much less. But this was different. This was a different you now, a different me.

'So,' you said, leaning against the door frame, your eyes travelling the length of my body. 'All this… for him.'

That sneer again.

'What are you doing here?' I asked, pulling the wrap protectively around me.

You eyed my makeup bag.

'That stuff won't make *you* beautiful.'

Troll one, me nil. All my insecurity flags were flying high.

Then you glanced at the white dress on the bed and raised an eyebrow.

'And dressing like a slut. *Bravo moré, bravo.*'

You began a slow handclap.

'Did you want something?' I hoped I didn't sound bothered as I stared at you with as much dignity as I could muster. Even then, all I really wanted to do was to throw myself into your arms, for everything to be alright again.

'From you? I've already had everything,' you mocked, voice scornful. 'He can have my leftovers.'

I tried not to react. I could sense under all the anger, you were probably hurting as much as me.

'What are you doing here then?'

I concentrated on my moisturiser as I looked into my mirror.

You said nothing but you walked over, and, to my surprise, you came to sit next to me on the bed. I hardly dared breathe or move as your fingers began tracing my collarbone. Wordlessly, I stared at you as the hypnotic, feather-light movement of your fingers continued. Then, with the quickest flash of a hand, you ripped the gold chain with its cornucopia charm from my neck. It happened so quickly I didn't even register the pain at first. My gasp of shock seemed to be coming from someone else, not me, as my hand flew to my throat.

Your face contorted. The broken chain was in your fist.

'You don't deserve this.'

Then you were gone.

The next morning, Andreas left early to help his father with family business. Once he'd gone, I sat in the kitchen with Sherri and Elaine, explaining everything.

'What a dick.' Elaine plumped coffees down for us all, her eyes round with concern. 'He's made a mark on your neck.'

'I thought we were about to make up.' I stroked my bare neck; I could still feel the welt.

'Does Andreas know about this?' Sherri sounded nervous. Andreas's presence had completely changed the dynamic of the apartment. He seemed to have very strong opinions about everything, and you never knew when he was going to voice them. Having Andreas around was like owning a pet rattlesnake.

'No, of course not.' In my heart, I knew I'd have to finish with him whatever happened, but, for now, it was far easier to leave things as they were. I thought of Rob for a moment, and it occurred to me there was a pattern in my behaviour. I'd worry about Andreas later.

I was taking a sip of my coffee when we heard footsteps thundering up the stairs and you burst into the kitchen.

'We don't want any trouble.' Elaine stood protectively in front of me as I jumped up and backed away.

'I'll get Yiannis.' Sherri was instantly up, banging her cup down on the table and moving towards the door.

'No,' you said to her. 'Please Sherri, it's okay, I only want to speak to Mel.' Then you turned to me. '*Moro mou*, I need to speak with you, now. Please. It's important.'

You didn't sound threatening, just desperate to talk, your eyes pleading. In my naivety, I admit, even then, I still hoped you and I could work something thing out.

'Okay,' I was still wary of you though. 'Just five minutes.'

'I'm out here if you need me,' Sherri didn't look happy about this at all and Elaine gaped at us both, her jaw slack.

You followed me into the bedroom and shut the door as I sat on the bed then you immediately came to sit at my side, taking my hands in yours.

'*Moro mou, agapē*, I am so sorry, I can't believe how I have been, how I have behaved, can you forgive me?' Your eyes searched mine with such intensity I nearly crumbled, but I held back. How could I trust you after all you'd said and done?

'Please, Melanie *mou*.' You lifted a hand towards my face, but I flinched.

I could see your eyes travel to the red mark on my neck.

'I won't hurt you; I'm sorry. I didn't plan to do that. I was…just angry when I saw you were still wearing it.'

I said nothing.

'I want things to be okay with us again. Don't you want that?'

When I still didn't answer, you slumped forward, your head in your hands. You looked so defeated and, in that moment, I knew I couldn't bear it any longer. Then, somehow, I was in your arms. As you held me so tightly, all I could think was *it's over, it's finally over.* The relief flooded through me like a burst dam as I soaked up your embrace, tiny kisses raining down on my head, your heart beating against mine.

'Why...?' I began, but you silenced me with a kiss. Unlike your usual long, lingering kisses this was different, the briefest, lightest touch, like the brush of a feather, a snowflake against my lips.

'But what about that girl?' I was acutely aware things were now very different between us. There was Andreas, and you had clearly moved on too.

'Girl?'

'The one outside the bar...'

'Ah, her...' You paused for a moment before grinning wolfishly at me. 'She's good, but not as good as you. Less *experienced*.'

I winced. The comment felt like a slap, out of place, crude even, given this magical moment but maybe I deserved it, under the circumstances. I must have looked a little uncertain because you laughed that familiar, warm, rich laugh, pulling me closer.

'Don't look so serious, *moro*,' you said, crushing me to your side as I braced at your comment. 'We will go out tonight, baby *mou*, there is a lot for us to talk about.'

I felt myself beginning to smile, breathing deeply again. You wanted to take me out. You wanted to talk. You called me my baby again. Was it going to be alright? Inside, I was dancing, I was a mass of butterflies, party streamers, golden sunlight, glittering stars. You wanted me again. I didn't think about Andreas for even a millisecond. He didn't exist any more. Nothing existed outside this sphere of golden light that surrounded us.

'I will come for you tonight. There are things we need to say, things we need to do.'

I nodded enthusiastically as you stood up, hugging the thought of seeing you again to me like a delicious secret but then my heart sank for a moment. It was going to be awkward telling Andreas we were back together, but I'd find a way. Maybe I should find somewhere public to tell him? It might be easier on him, easier on me too.

'Wear something nice,' you said, pulling me back in. 'Something you know I would like.'

I smiled happily back at you as you tilted my chin up to you with one finger, but instead of returning my smile, you glanced across the room, towards the shutters. Perhaps, like me, you were also wondering about Andreas, where he might be, whether he would come back. Then, with lightest kiss on the top of my head, you were gone.

I literally danced around the apartment, feeling a spiral of excitement radiating throughout my body, glowing with ecstasy and when I looked in the mirror, I was amazed to see that shard of visible pain lodged in my iris was now gone. I had never felt such pure happiness and relief. I was being given a second chance; you were sorry. It was all I needed. Every single desperate prayer had been answered. All I had to do now was find a way to tell Andreas, but I'd worry about that later. I'd sit him down and explain. I would talk to you about us maybe telling him together. Perhaps that would be the best way. We'd make him understand. He'd have to.

The girls were thrilled for me. Elaine gave me the biggest, tightest hug, saying she was so happy for me, most unlike her.

'Please don't mention this to Sakis, he'll tell Andreas and I need to tell him myself.' I called after her as she went back into her bedroom. 'He deserves that much.'

Sherri said she'd help me to do my hair before her shift.

'Ironic, isn't it. You're getting back with Marios just as I'm about to finish with Yiannis.'

She picked up her She Magazine and thumbed through it dismissively.

I was actually a bit shocked. Sherri had played Kevin off with Petros, then dumped Petros for Yiannis and now she didn't want him either. For a moment, I wondered whether Kevin really had blamed me for her staying in Lathos, or whether she'd just wanted me to think that. I stared at her, realising Sherri was quite a selfish person and only really did what suited her, however, I could hardly talk. Maybe we were two of a kind.

'I only took six months off my job,' she said. 'Everything's been so much fun, but when the lease is up, I've decided I'm going home. My uncle has said he'll make me manager and give me the flat above the shop. He says all my travelling experience will help towards the role, so... I'm going.'

'Does Yiannis know yet?' My heart had sunk a little. Her plans had certainly taken the edge off my excitement. It wouldn't be the same without Sherri here.

'I don't know how to bring it up, but I have a plan. When I'm ready, maybe I'll tell Lynn. She's a terrible gossip, so it's guaranteed to get back to him.'

I was about to reply when Sherri shot me a warning look. Elaine had opened her door and was wandering out into the kitchen, heading for the fridge.

Andreas came back briefly, but I could hardly look him in the eye. I knew it would be the last time he'd return my smile and it felt so wrong when he kissed me, his hands roaming my body, his lips on my skin. It felt like I was cheating on him, with you. I suppose I was.

'I will see you tonight, after work,' he loaded the comment, making it sound suggestive after we'd shared a long kiss I could have won an Oscar for.

'Definitely.' I purred, knowing I was about to upset everything, but nothing else mattered now. I knew what I wanted, and I was dancing inside at getting a second chance.

Once he'd gone, I soaked in the bath before slavering myself in body lotion, dousing myself in Byzance, and emphasising my eyes with mascara and eye liner. Sherri brought in her curling tongs, and we turned my wavy mop into tumbling mermaid curls. And I knew exactly what to wear. The black broderie anglaise dress with the hook and eye bodice, your favourite. Stepping into my best black silk panties edged with pale pink lace and slipping the dress over my head, I then opened the little blue box I'd hidden at the back of the wardrobe and slipped the silver olive spray ring onto my index finger. Eventually I was ready. I turned this way and that, admiring myself in the mirror. My skin was gleaming and tanned, my hair shone, my eyes were bright as I carefully hooked up my bodice, but only so far, pushing my breasts up a little, leaving more cleavage showing than usual.

This was a night for window dressing. I wanted to show you exactly what you'd been missing. We were drawing a metaphoric line under all that had gone before. This was the start of tomorrow.

33

Cruel Summer

Left alone in the apartment, the time ticked by so slowly. I could hardly breathe, the suspense, the excitement, the need to be with you, it was all too much. I kept tapping my newly painted nails on the balcony rail looking out for a glimpse of you until, finally, nerves got the best of me, so I opened the fridge and necked some of Elaine's emergency vodka straight from the bottle. Just a few mouthfuls, but it blurred the edges, taking some of the anxiety away, making me feel more confident. I knew not to touch her vodka and she'd even marked the bottle, but my needs were greater in that moment. I carefully topped it back up with water.

Minutes later, I was sat behind you on your bike, my arms wrapped around your waist, leaning into your warmth as we flew through the heavily scented August air. You took my hand in yours, pulling my arm tighter round you. Nothing was going to wipe away the crazy smile I could feel creeping across my face ever again.

I was a little surprised when we eventually we stopped at Mayfair, feeling it was a little public under the circumstances.

'Don't you want to be seen with me, then?' you said with a laugh as I held back on the pathway. 'Are you ashamed of me, *moro mou?*'

'Don't be silly,' I said, gripping your hand tightly.

You called me my baby.

Blondie's *Heart of Glass* was playing, and the place was heaving as we strolled in. I was aware of several pairs of eyes on us, but, brave from the vodka earlier and the warmth of your strong hand, I didn't care who saw. Everyone would know soon enough. Some of your friends passed us on their way out. Your exchange with Pavlos was rapid, his eyes dancing from you to me as indistinct words rang over my head. Dionysus slapped you on the back, grinning. Clutching tightly at your hand, I smiled my brightest, watching you all laugh loudly. A tiny niggle made me worry about being seen, but Andreas was out collecting rents and wouldn't be back for hours. I felt braver with you beside me. I'd tell him later. He deserved the truth.

You must have been nervous like me, more so, perhaps, as you quickly downed a whiskey at the bar. I'd never seen you drink whiskey before, but the army must have made its mark on you. Did you know I was nervous too? I think you must have, because I heard you asking for all my vodkas to be really large. Yes, the army had changed you. You were a man now, any shred of the boy that had still been within you had long gone. In the candlelight, your roughly cropped hair made you look older, it emphasised your strength, your masculinity, your powerful build. I was so in love with you at that moment, I felt dizzy.

I sat the table, trying to hear what you were saying above the wall of music, slowly becoming aware I was talking far more than you. Your eyes skimmed me, watching my mouth forming words, roaming my face, scanning my bodice, my skirt, my breasts, before returning to meet mine. I was tingling with excitement as I knew we would soon be somewhere quieter, somewhere where we could really talk, properly making up in the best way we knew.

I glanced up at the spray of twinkling stars as I got back onto your bike again. Cicadas were humming in the trees along the roadside as lights, buildings, bars and the petrol station all flashed past. I remember reaching for your hand like you usually did for mine, but this time your hands remained firmly on the handlebars. Then you slowed down and turned onto an unmade road I didn't recognise. I was intrigued. Where were you taking me?

Hopping off the bike, you fished in your jeans pocket for a key then walked up a pathway to what appeared to be some sort of holiday apartment building, but there were bags of cement outside, a bucket and a few paint cans. For a moment, memories of our first night flooded back - the flight of unfinished stairs, the cement, the trowels, your mattress on the floor.

Waving the keys at me, you said you'd borrowed them from a friend. These were his apartments, you said, most were still unfinished, but he was letting you borrow one he sometimes used. I slipped in through the communal doors with you, noticing the smell of wet paint, your hand tightly gripping mine as you pulled me behind you up the stairs. You stopped outside a room, knocked the door loudly and waited, before turning the key in the lock. Was there someone inside? I must have looked confused because you laughed and threw your arms around me, your lips hitting mine in an enthusiastic kiss as you explained you were only knocking to make sure your friend had left.

The scent of wet plaster invaded the sparsely furnished room: twin beds, side tables, a double wardrobe, and a small, noisy fridge. Behind patterned curtains, I could just about see the outline of French doors leading to a balcony. Everything was so clean, so sterile. The floor tiles were pristine, not a mark.

You didn't want lights on. Instead, you went to the window, edging the curtains and the balcony doors open just enough to let the moonlight in, as I tentatively stood waiting. More romantic, you said, as I sat on the bed, feeling shy, overwhelmed by the situation. Crossing to the fridge, you asked me if I wanted a beer. I shook my head, but I slipped off my sandals and lay back, propped on one side, watching you moving like a panther, back and forth. You seemed nervous. The outcome of the evening clearly mattered a lot to you.

You came to sit next to me, facing the balcony as I touched your arm, looking up at you in the low lighting, the curve of your face, the brightness in your eyes, feeling the warmth of your skin, aware of how strong, how muscular your arms were. You had been trained to kill, to fight, to be a soldier. I tried to read you, tried to decode the expressions that crossed your face like shadows running from the sun. You seemed to be unable to say anything but one of us had to

'Do you want to go first, or shall I?' I began.

You hunched forward, your head hanging.

'I don't want to talk,' you finally said, 'Actions, not words, so, no talking.'

'I never meant to hurt you, I swear,' I whispered, sitting up and running a hand down your arm. I felt I still needed to clarify this. I wanted you to understand how sorry I was. I'd never stopped loving you.

'Go on,' you said. You were still sitting there, your face set, eyes narrow. You'd opened the beer, but you weren't drinking it. Instead, you were picking off the label, little curls of white and gold falling like confetti to the tiled floor.

'I was so messed up.' I whispered, my guilt smothering me, its heavy thickness, sticky like tar, clinging to my skin. I reached for your hand. 'It was so hard without you; I hadn't realised how hard it was going to be, but then, you went cold on me. You stopped me phoning you when I needed you most, and—'

'So, it was all my fault you fucked Andreas?'

I stalled for a moment, feeling ashamed, dirty, exposed. The wire suspending my heart was clipped savagely with pliers. I felt it fall away as I looked into your eyes.

'I thought you'd given up on us, and...'

Lines creased your forehead as you snatched your hand back.

'What about me?' Your voice rose in volume, hardened in tone. 'I was struggling, but you betrayed me.'

I knew I had no real defence to that.

'Look, I don't want a row, I thought we were here to...to make up. I thought you wanted me again...' I felt so vulnerable saying that. My voice tailed off.

You didn't reply. You simply kicked your shoes off.

'Come here, *moro mou*,' you said, throwing yourself back onto the bed, pulling me over on top of you. 'No more talk.'

My baby. You called me my baby.

I can't begin to explain feeling of sheer relief, the lightness infusing me, because you still wanted me. All that had gone before was over. This was the start of something new. We could get through this. My hair draped over your face as you kissed me, not gently, not emotionally, but roughly with what almost felt like anger, before spinning me over and pinning me under your weight. Even then, I smiled up at you, deliriously happy we were even there, together. Dreams do come true sometimes. Perhaps this was my time to be happy at last.

You began to tug clumsily at the hooks on my bodice.

'Hey,' I laughed, trying to help. You were going to break them.

'Hurry,' you said, dragging the dress over my head, tossing it impatiently to the floor, before pulling my hand to the undone zip of your jeans. I stood up to remove my black silk panties, dropping them onto where my dress was pooled on the floor like a slick of black oil in a sea of white tiles.

'Stay there,' you instructed. 'I want to see you.' The moonlight was bright, spilling in through the windows, highlighting the white of my tan lines against the golden brown of my skin. Your face was a dark hollow, your features indistinct, as you lay back on the sheets.

'Turn round,' you instructed. I did as I was told, aware you were appraising me.

'Nice arse,' you finally said, with a low chuckle. I felt uncomfortable with that. It wasn't like you, but you were in the army now, after all. Instead, I turned back to face you, lifting my chin, smiling at you as you locked your gaze onto me.

'Tell me you love me,' you demanded. The moon seemed even brighter as it pierced the darkness like a stage light, the balcony door creaking in the soft sea breeze.

'I love you.'

'You betrayed me, but you are sorry now, for what you did?'

'Yes,' I whispered. 'Of course.' I nearly argued at the word 'betrayed' but thought better of it. I sensed you needed my humility, my acquiescence, my assent. I was happy to comply. Anything to make things work between us again.

'Louder.'

'I'm really sorry.'

My words sounded hollow as they rang in the corners of the room.

'For what?

'For what I did.'

'For your mistake?'

'Yes, for my...mistake.'

The word mistake sounded so inconsequential, so trite, but I didn't like to argue it was so much more than a mistake. It wasn't something I'd done lightly. I didn't feel it was the right time to add how messed up I'd been, to explain how your distance and coldness had pushed all the wrong buttons in me, or how much my own insecurities had made me act in a way that someone with more self-worth might not have. You didn't need to know by pushing you away, I'd been trying to protect myself from what I'd thought was inevitable pain to come. You didn't need to know my background, my issues. You only needed to know I was sorry.

'And for betraying me?'

I nodded.

'Say it, then.'

'I'm sorry for betraying you.'

You didn't reply. Instead, you patted the bed, so I climbed gratefully back on, stretching out next to you, knowing the worst was over now, basking in the golden light of your approval. You were still wearing your jeans, but you'd pushed them right down now and were clearly not in the mood for more talking as you grabbed a handful of my hair, pushing my head down.

Moments later, running your hands over my body, you instructed I should get on top of you, so I enthusiastically responded. Part of me was in that room with you, but another part was somewhere else, still incredulous that this was happening, that you and I were finally back together. It was nothing short of a wonderful a miracle. Pulling me astride you, you sat upright, pushing my hair back, biting roughly into my neck, my shoulder, my breasts, laughing as I yelped, shocked at the pain.

You were in charge not me, moving me as you wanted, savagely, urgently, aggressively. None of this was what I'd expected. I wasn't enjoying it, but I wanted to make you happy. The simple, pine bed legs juddered on the tiled floor, a sudden breeze making the curtains on the balcony door billow. I remember I kept wanting to wind myself closer to you, for all this to be softer, to have a connection with you, but you kept insisting I stayed upright.

'No,' you said, sinking your teeth into my neck again, really hard. 'I need to see you. I want to remember everything.'

You still had your t-shirt on.

Then it was over.

Completely over.

To my surprise you immediately pushed me to one side, wriggled into your jeans and got up. Crossing the room, you flicked on the light, transforming everything into a cold, blue fluorescence. You laughed as I blinked, screwing my face up against the unexpected flood of light, feeling exposed and naked in the unaccustomed brightness. Colours appeared: a green picture frame, blue patterns on the curtains, the blood red of the fire drill poster, the deep golden pine of the wardrobe door.

'*Tora*, now,' you shouted, with a clap of your hands, as I frowned in confusion, making to get up, but you hadn't meant me, had you? You'd meant Dionysus, squatting like a toad, eyes glassy, inside the wardrobe. You'd meant someone else, someone I didn't know at all, who was now grinning, pushing their way into the room from the balcony, sweaty, dishevelled, doing up their zip. You had also meant Yorgos, Lynn's sullen husband, Pavlos Mavrakis, whose red-rimmed eyes suggested he'd been smoking dope, and you'd meant Nikos, the only one with the grace to look awkward, his eyes barely meeting mine. You'd also meant others I vaguely recognised. One by one they all piled in.

The next seconds passed like a nightmare, broken shards of kaleidoscopic pictures that made no sense, shouting, laughing, high fives, a plan well executed, my dress thrown at me, my sandals kicked across the room, my silk panties passed around, a trophy. At first, I couldn't move at all until I fell when you shoved me roughly from behind.

'Whore,' you spat, aiming a great glob of saliva right into my face.

I was dragging my dress on, watching myself from above, watching a graphic movie, too stunned to cry, as I watched the woman below. Who was she? It wasn't me, it wasn't me, it wasn't me.

And then I ran. Out of the open door. Down the staircase. Falling out into a thick, heavy blanket of night as, like charging bulls, everyone thundered past.

The sound of motorbikes revving, spinning on the sand, three or four bikes, two up on each. Yours turning in a spray of grit as I overbalanced, falling to my hands and knees in the gravel. Pavlos Mavrakis leering up from behind you as you pulled back your chin and spat on me again with such force before lurching away. Your face contorted with hate and rage, a terrifying mask of incandescent fury.

'Never come back to Aftonisi!'

Tooting horns, laughing, catcalls, a roar of engines. Finally, silence. In the void above me, light years away, cold, hard, harshly glittering lumps of rock that had died a million years ago.

I don't know how long I was there. I can't remember. I only remember complete blackness. My awareness of space, time and existence had completely frozen. Everything within me had stopped functioning. I had no idea where I was. Somewhere off the main track, somewhere near the beach, somewhere between the resort centre and the hills of Stavouna. All I remember is gulping in air, staggering in the direction I thought we'd come in, the sea to my left, the main road up ahead, blinded by tears, vaguely aware of blood running down my leg where I'd fallen.

My head began to spin, I felt faint, felt sick. I remember bending over, vomiting, then vomiting again. Where was my bag? Then I heard a bike. Terrified, I whirled around. Was it you again? Then, the relief in realising it wasn't you, it was someone else, someone on a big trial bike. I stumbled into the road to flag them down.

It was Kristos.

I remember him slowing, stopping, staring at me in horror, asking me if was alright and me replying that, no, I wasn't. Instantly, he was saying 'Get on.'

I don't remember much of what happened next, as I clung tightly to his jacket, occasional flashes of light, blue, red and white relieving the blackness ahead, curving round uphill, past Tropic Bar, past the Beehive Apartments and up a little mountain track until we came to a small, yellow-painted house with wire fencing where a chained mongrel barked wildly.

The door opened into a kitchen, a tray of *yemista* on the table, a bowl of fruit, some cheese covered with a little glass dome.

He turned to me, his features painted with confusion, with helplessness, his eyes following mine as I anchored my gaze onto the tray.

'You want to eat?'

I shook my head. I could hardly breathe after so much crying, my eyes felt hot and swollen, and my stomach was aching from empty retching, the sharp taste of bile in my mouth.

Kristos poured a glass of water and pushed it at me.

'Drink.'

I gripped the glass tightly, staring back at him.

Then I needed the toilet. I don't remember asking him, but I must have because he showed me where the bathroom was. As I locked the door and sat on the loo, shaking, I realised I didn't have my panties on, I noticed my dress was inside out, so I wasn't hooked up properly. My silver ring had gone. Blood was drying on my leg from a large gouge on my knee. Over the basin was a small mirror. Peering in, I saw my face, smeared with mascara, hair wild, all the mermaid curls gone, purple bite marks all up my neck and on my breasts.

Forcing down the sob which was rising in my throat and threatening to escape, I scrambled out of my dress, and put it back on the right way round, swilling out my mouth with a handful of water and dabbing at my face with damp bits of toilet paper. Finally, I crept back out. Kristos was leaning on the kitchen table, looking at me with concern as I raised my eyes slowly to meet his, hugging my arms tightly around my chest.

'What has happened to you *moré*?' He was pouring out two small glasses of Tentura and offering one to me as he quickly necked his, but I shook my head.

'I'm okay.'

'You are not okay.' As he moved towards me, I leaped away in fear, fresh tears stinging, before finally howling as he pulled me in, my fists in tight balls, hammering at his chest, nails in my palms, a volcano of pain. Kristos just held me.

'You don't have to tell me, but I think I can guess,' he finally said. 'Did you see who it was, *moré*?'

I knew what he thought. He was so wrong, but I didn't correct him. I just shook my head over and over. All I could think was I still owed him for a bottle of water.

'Do you want the police? The hospital? Food? Maybe a drink? Can I do something, anything, please?' His voice was rising in desperation as I refused each suggestion with a vehement shake of the head.

'*Yamo to!*' He was clearly frustrated. '*Moré*, these men are out there somewhere. They are animals. You need to say something, or it could be another girl tomorrow.'

How could I even begin to explain? I shook my head again.

'At least think about it.' Kristos paced to the window. 'Look, I am in Aftonisi Town in the morning, but I am back later, so if you need me, need anything at all, you come and find me, okay?'

I nodded.

I was spent, my head was aching. Exhaustion took hold. Completely drained, I hardly trusted my legs to move a step further.

'Please can you take me home?' I asked, in a very small voice.

Creeping up the staircase, I pushed open the unlocked door, stepped out of my sandals and walked mechanically towards the bedroom. Operating on autopilot, my brain was totally refusing to process what had happened. Everything was dark, quiet. Everyone appeared to be out. I nearly opened

Sherri's door, but I didn't want questions, or to see Yiannis. I knew I wouldn't be able to sleep but I needed to be alone, in my own bed, in the darkness. I just wanted to curl into a tight little ball.

Unbelievably, I'd forgotten something.

Andreas.

I edged the door open, and stood there, unable to move another step. Everything was familiar but somehow alien to me as though the room belonged to someone else. The bed seemed a mile away.

Then I heard something.

I felt the swing of a hand as I spun under its blow.

I felt a fist as it connected with my jaw.

I felt a foot in my side again and again as I crumpled on the ground.

'*Putana*.'

Kick.

'Prostitute'.

Kick.

'*Skyla*.'

Kick.

34

Poison

I hadn't slept. I'd known the only way I'd survive the night would be to keep still, keep quiet, do nothing to else to anger him, so I'd curled on the floor in the dark, aching from the beating, listening to the rhythm of his breathing change until he was asleep. Terrified to make a sound or to move, I'd stayed that way, trying in vain to replay what had happened to me.

When the morning light had crept into our room, he'd made me get up and sit next to him on the bed, like nothing had happened, as he smoked his first cigarette, hunching over his knife, flicking the blade up and down, up and down.

'Get me coffee, *moré*.' Possessively, his strong arms circled my shoulders, while I sat rigidly, clamped under his arm. 'I have work to do but later, we will go out.'

This wasn't normal behaviour. Yesterday he'd punched and kicked me, today it was like nothing had happened. Last night he'd made me sleep on the floor. Like a dog, he'd said. I looked at him, helplessly, so he squeezed me in, lips on mine. Instantly, I winced, everything was bruised, tender, painful.

'Shh,' he breathed into my hair, 'Shh my baby, it's okay.'

I stiffened at his words.

My baby.

Sharp fragments of the night before briefly rattled through my brain like broken glass in a dustpan.

His finger softly swept the outline of my bruised lips.

I felt my eyes widen in alarm, sensing I was dealing with a madman. Your words *he's crazy* hit me full force, like boulders falling in a landslide. I couldn't overreact even though my instinct was to run screaming to safety. He drew the line of my clavicle with his fingertip, so gently, tracing the bruises as I held my breath. Kissing my hair, he cupped my face as I shrunk back.

'What's wrong, my baby?'

'Nothing,' I said, shaking my head over and over, aware I was shivering, my teeth beginning to chatter.

My baby.

He surveyed the blue and purple prints studding my arms and neck, his fingers running delicately, gently, like a feather stroke, across my jaw, down my throat until they rested on the bite-marks on my breasts. My breath drew in with a gasp.

'You know this is all your fault?' He kissed me again.

Unbelievably, I found myself nodding. Technically, it was. A fragmented part of me was noting how some of the bruises were ones you'd made. I couldn't see beyond how I'd caused all of this. I'd started the rack of dominoes falling, I'd lit the firework and watched it explode without a care where the glittering debris might fall. I'd played with fire and in return I now had third-degree burns, scars for life.

'So, you've learned your lesson now?'

I didn't answer. It wasn't a question. In that moment, I wondered what had really happened to the Cypriot girl.

He got up and walked to the balcony, knife still in his hand, and opened the shutters, peering outside as though it was just another day. It was anything but.

'Melanie?'

He was asking me again to answer. Climbing into his jeans and t-shirt, the buckle of his heavy belt clanged as he fastened it, drachma coins jangling in his pockets.

Fragments of last night.

He groped for his cigarettes and lighter.

'Yes, yes I have.'

He seemed pleased at that, smiling broadly, planting an unwanted kiss on my forehead before sitting down heavily at my side.

'And you're sorry for what you've done?' He turned, his eyes searching mine. I caught an echo of our last conversation.

I had no words. My brain was still trying in vain to process what you'd done to me, the humiliation, the pain, the heartbreak of the previous evening. It was still trying to recall all those missing slices of the night I couldn't claw back, no matter how hard I tried. I could never have imagined you would have ever been capable of doing of what you did. The beating from Andreas was nothing in comparison. Nothing at all.

'Do you need me to explain why I was angry?' He lit another cigarette, talking to me carefully, softly, deliberately, like I was a child as my brain tried to leapfrog ahead to what might come next. In the kitchen, I could hear someone moving around, mugs banging down on the counter, the kettle flicking on. I sensed a chance to get away from him into the protection of other people.

'I'll get us that coffee,' I said, far louder than necessary, trying to move away from the bed, but he wasn't listening.

'Why were you with Kristos?' He anchored me further to his side, hissing smoke through his teeth, eyes narrow. 'He brought you here, late, on his bike. I saw you both. You said you were selling crêpes but when I went to Wild West, they said you'd not been in, that you were out with a friend. Since when were you friends with him?'

His dark gaze seared my eyes as I rapidly tried to decide what best to say. Was it possible he didn't know about you? Had this violent reaction all been for his misinterpretation of events?

'Okay,' he said, nostrils flaring. I watched his ash fall to the floor as though in slow motion. 'I'll ask Kristos myself ...or you can tell me now?'

I hesitated, the full horror of what might happen beginning to unfold as he continued flicking the knife blade up and down. Up and down. I was impaled by his enquiring stare.

'He...he gave me a lift, that's all.'

'Why?'

'I... he just did. I wanted to get home and he was...there.'

I stood hesitating for a moment by the door.

'Coffee?' I tried to normalise this anything but normal situation.

He shook his head and, with a tight smile of disappointment, got up. I knew that look. Still shaking his head, he stamped the cigarette out on the floor and crossed over to me. Then, without warning, the back of his thick hand flew up, spinning me backwards into the wall, his skull ring catching my cheek.

'You don't lie to me, *skyla*, I am no fool, you understand?'

I gasped, slumped on the floor, my hand on my face.

'Mel, are you okay?' I could hear Sherri at the door, alarm in her voice, but before I could even cry out, Andreas had yanked it open.

Sherri's mouth was wide open in shock. I felt her arms close around me as I clung to her, tears spilling over, sobs shuddering through me.

'Your friend is a lying bitch, she's fucking that Athenian *malaka*, Kristos.'

'I am not.'

I yelled as loudly as I could through my sobs, feeling braver knowing I wasn't alone, my face contorting in absolute fury, for one moment forgetting what I was dealing with, only conscious of the need to defend my actions, my behaviour.

The next few minutes seemed like a dream sequence. Sakis appeared in the doorway and the rapid machine gunning of Greek began with Andreas waving his arms around, Sakis pointing at me, gesticulating at him. Elaine appeared behind him, clearly shocked, asking what was going on, pulling at his arm but Sakis told her in no uncertain terms to get back into the bedroom, giving her a vicious shove to ensure she complied. I had no idea what was going on, then Andreas pushed roughly past us all, his heavy footsteps ringing on the staircase.

Sakis turned to me, his lip curling disparagingly. Was there a trace of a smile, or something else, in his eyes? With a tutting sound, he scanned me up and down with a smirk.

'What have you done now, *moré?*'

I caught a glimpse of Elaine's worried face peering past him as he hunched his way back into her room, clicking the door shut behind him.

Sherri gently moved my head from side to side, checking my jaw, before going to get some ice and a tea-towel from the kitchen which I held to my cheek. She knelt next to me.

'Mel what on earth is going on?'

I tried to speak, but Sakis was in the next room. I didn't want him knowing. I looked at her helplessly.

'Okay, we are not staying here,' she said. 'You're coming with me right now; we're going to find somewhere quiet to talk and you are going to tell me everything, okay? No arguing.' Sherri was taking charge. At a time when I desperately needed someone to take care of me, she was stepping up.

'But I can't.'

What if someone saw me. Someone who'd seen me last night or had heard about what had happened. I felt like I was glued to the floor.

'Yes, you can. You've done nothing wrong and what's the alternative? You sit here meekly waiting for Andreas to come back and hit you again?'

She helped me to my feet, sat me down on the bed and gently cleaned the black streaks from my face with a baby wipe as I sat motionless, then she helped me into my shorts and a top like a child, before steering me by the shoulders through the doorway. I saw her grab my little lacy cardigan from a kitchen chair. With my sunglasses on, my hair loose around my neck, and the cardigan, she assured me I would look fine. No-one would notice the bruises.

We quietly sat on the shadiest part of the beach usually shunned by tourists. Splinters of light sliced through the pine trees as I explained everything I could remember, tears spilling over into sobs until I felt like I had no more tears left.

'I can't believe he'd deliberately plan to hurt and humiliate you like that,' she said. 'It's just horrific that Marios could plan something so awful.'

I wrapped the cardigan tightly around me. Despite the heat, I was shivering. I could smell the stench from the festering rubbish skips lining a nearby wall. All around us were little bits of windblown leaf, pine needles and fir cones in the sand giving it a greyish hue, relieved only by little spears of harsh seagrass. Behind me, the rolled umbrellas of the cypress trees scraped towards the dazzlingly blue sky, a harsh barricade of sentinels with staves, ready to defend their territory.

'I still can't get my head around any of it.'

'Where's he now?'

'I don't know.'

I blew my nose noisily on the tissues she offered me.

We sat in silence for a while, then I turned to her, an awful thought occurring to me.

'Sherri, I've got to find Kristos before Andreas does. He's got completely the wrong idea. He'll kill him.'

Kristos only came into the resort in the evenings to open his bar, so there was a good chance Andreas might not be able to find him and I remembered him saying he was going into town. I couldn't decide which might be worse, Andreas thinking I'd slept with Kristos, or Kristos telling Andreas where he'd found me and what he'd suspected had happened.

'I can't have Kristos telling Andreas that he thinks I've been raped.'

Sherri frowned.

'Isn't that exactly what happened, though?'

I stared at her, aghast.

'No, of course not.' I shook my head angrily. 'It wasn't like that at all. It was Marios. I thought we were making up. He didn't force me.'

Sherri paused, giving me a long, thoughtful look, before putting a hand on mine.

'Mel,' she said, 'Think about it. Rape's all about consent, isn't it. You wouldn't have consented if you'd known you were being deliberately led into a trap, would you?'

I closed my eyes, the evening taking on yet another perspective as I sat back, stunned at what she'd said. Images whirled in my head of you, me, us. I couldn't even begin to process things. I concentrated on drawing shapes in the sand with an old ice lolly stick I'd found as I let the tears flow again. You couldn't be a rapist. Surely that wasn't right? Rape was all about attacks, strangers in dark alleys, wasn't it? Not with someone you loved. I'd willingly gone there, but what Sherri said jolted through me like an electric shock. If I'd known what was being planned, of course I'd never have gone. I'd never consented to that. All those men, watching. Some of them, I knew, most of them, I didn't. Who was there, who wasn't? I couldn't be sure of anything any more.

Savagely, I stabbed at the sand, drawing concentric circles. The more I thought, the more the images evaded me. It was like trying to recall the confusing events of a dream that fades on awakening. Had an actual crime had been committed? Sherri seemed to think so. Faster and faster, I drew. Circle within circle within circle. Like waves lapping a shoreline, little swirls of consciousness were beginning to nudge their way towards me, yet I was unable to fully grasp them. The wooden stick split under the pressure of my fist.

'I need to work out what to do next.' Stabbing the shards of wood viciously under the soft, powdery sand, I tried to bite a small splinter out of my thumb. 'I hardly slept. I'm so tired, I can't think straight.'

I don't know how long we sat there, me still in a cardigan despite the sunlight burning down, trying to make sense of it all. Sherri was saying how she'd been ready to tell Yiannis she was going home in October, but the events of the previous night had made her acutely aware of different standards of behaviour. Now she was wary of telling him anything at all.

The beach was gradually filling up with holidaymakers, gaps in our conversation now punctuated by shrieks from swimmers and the laughter of children. In the distance, a cacophony of music from nearby bars vied with the whine of motorbikes. All around, the familiar sights and sounds of Lathos I'd loved had somehow distorted overnight into something I no longer recognised, a collage of disjointed images and clashing colours layered over an endless nightmare soundtrack.

As we continued, lost in disconnected conversation, I became aware of a man approaching up ahead. Looking into the sun, I followed his form as he got closer. It was Nikos. My mouth dried as my heart began racing. More forgotten images resurfaced.

I scrambled to my feet, scraping sand under my nails.

'He was there!'

Seeing him brought images rushing back, a crowded room, my discarded clothes, footsteps thudding across the marble floor. I couldn't remember seeing him after that, but I could clearly remember his expression as he'd bowed his head. I felt so ashamed he'd seen me naked, vulnerable, humiliated.

'Melanie,' he called, keeping a wary distance, as if approaching a wild animal. 'I…I have come looking for you.'

Anyone who didn't know the situation might have felt sorry for him, he looked so stricken as he tentatively moved closer, face etched with concern.

'Fuck off, Nikos,' I finally found my voice, the ferocity of my anger surprising me as I stemmed tears with the side of my hand. 'Just fuck off.'

I yelled so hard it made my throat vibrate.

'Go away, Nikos,' Sherri's voice was loud and forceful as she stood up, arms folded, a barrier between us, but he ignored her.

'Melanie, I am ashamed, I am sorry. I didn't want to be there. I want you to know that.'

His eyes met mine. What did he expect, forgiveness?

'Marios has gone, back to Kos now,' he said. 'Earlier, he left. I thought you should know.'

I shrugged, feeling hollow. What was I supposed to say to that?

More images played in my head, noises, the oppressive heat, the ticking clock, the balcony doors creaking, the black sky sprayed with tiny stars. You'd insisted I stayed on top to ensure everyone, including Nikos, could see as much as possible. I felt dirty, exposed, ashamed. I couldn't speak. It was hard to separate the awful realisation that everyone had seen my humiliation from the fact you had chosen to do that to me. How dark must your soul have been and how had I never realised before?

Nikos crouched in the sand, still keeping his distance.

'You have to understand, as soon as everyone came out, I...' My cardigan must have slid down over my shoulder exposing my bruises because his eyes bulged in shock. '*Yamo, moré*, did Marios do this?'

I couldn't speak but I managed to shake my head, over and over.

I found my voice.

'You know it wasn't Marios, you were there.'

'No, I left. Afterwards, I ran. I knew it was all wrong.'

'Not wrong enough to stop them though. Not wrong enough to warn me first. Not wrong enough to say something. What sort of man are you?'

He looked at the ground as I shrieked at him, venting as much anger as I could, screaming at him through ugly tears and great gulps of air.

'I wanted you to know I'm sorry. I didn't know how to say no to them, they are my friends. Marios was so hurt, so angry, he wanted to punish you, but I didn't agree with Sakis.'

I could hardly begin to process what I was hearing. What had Sakis got to do with this?

'Sakis, he said we should all take turns afterwards, but I didn't agree.'

Sakis? I searched my brain frantically. Take turns?

I really couldn't understand any of this.

'No, you're wrong.' I shook my head. 'Sakis wasn't there, I'd have remembered him.'

'No *moré*, he wasn't, but those apartments are his. He lent one to Marios. When he said he wanted to teach you a lesson, Sakis came up with a plan. It was all his idea.'

I could hardly believe what I was hearing.

'But why?'

'Because you interfere in his life. You've encouraged Elaine to go to school and made her argue with him. Marios told him how you said she could do better.'

Mosquitos whined nearby as Sherri flapped them away with a hand. The tops of her shoulders were turning pink now and she hugged her knees into her chest.

'It could so easily have been me,' she said. 'After Petros, I mean, when I got with Yiannis, then Kevin came out here. Why did all that happen to you, but not to me?'

I had no answer for her. Maybe Petros was more mature, less emotional or maybe you were just hardwired differently. You must have always been capable of something like this because no matter what we'd shared, this dark, insidious vengefulness must have always rippled beneath your surface. I just hadn't realised.

Even then, I still felt some responsibility. Maybe I'd hurt you, humiliated you more than I realised. Well, we were certainly even now. I thought you'd loved me. I thought I'd loved you, but if I'd really loved you, surely I'd have waited, so what did that say about me? How could that have been love?

In the year we'd shared, we'd hardly spent any real time together doing normal things, getting to know one another. At best, we were *in love*. We'd been totally infatuated with one another, both completely obsessed, but because I'd never felt that level of intensity before, I'd assumed it was love. But it wasn't. Strangely, amid all the chaos, it felt good to know real love wasn't like that, because, despite everything, I still believed in love. I still hoped for a future where I'd find it.

The only sound now was the crawl of the waves and the distant droning of Nikos's bike heading towards Alomenos. Sherri lifted her head, shading her eyes against the sun with her hand.

'Don't you think it's time to call it a day, Mel?'

'No. I'm not ready yet. Can't we just stay here a bit longer?' I didn't want to see Andreas just yet or know what to say to him, how I could even look at Sakis again after what Nikos had told me, and what the hell was I supposed to say to Elaine? Just when I thought I was over the worst shock, I had to face the fact her boyfriend had orchestrated the whole thing.

She fumbled in her pocket for her Marlboro and clicked her lighter.

'No,' she said, drawing the smoke deep into her throat. 'I mean, don't you think it's time we both went back home to England?

The next day

Sharp, morning sunlight had burned down on my arms as we'd leapt into the first taxi we'd found and we'd just disappeared, fading to white like old cine-camera footage, the sea behind us, a gritty mountain road ahead. Our footprints had already been erased from the sandy track by drifting breeze and tyre marks. It was like we'd never been there at all.

I'd burrowed back under the sheets earlier that morning, slowing my breathing, pretending to be nearly asleep again, yet listening with sharpened ears until the door had slammed behind Andreas. I'd counted his footsteps thudding down the outside stairs, waiting for his motorbike to splutter into life, hearing it roar up the beach track and onto the road.

As soon as its whine had receded, I'd sprung up, all my senses alight, ribs aching as I moved. Opening the wardrobe, I began dragging things out, ripping clothes off hangers, throwing everything into my suitcases and holdall.

'We have to be quick,' I'd called to Sherri, scrambling into my jeans and top. 'He'll be back soon.'

With so many people around dragging suitcases it had been easy to blend in and to flag down a taxi. My heart had been thrashing around so much when we'd jumped inside and demanded he drove quickly that I could feel blood pulsing in my ears. It was only later we discovered he wasn't a taxi driver at all. He was a commercial traveller selling backgammon sets. I still cringe when I think how forcefully I'd shouted *viasyni*. He'd given us a free backgammon set each.

I checked my watch. About now, Sakis would be showing Andreas the note I'd left for Elaine, and I knew he'd waste no time in racing to the airport. I pictured his fury after realising he'd been tricked. Even though I knew there was no way he'd catch up with us now, I found myself uneasy, continually glancing over my shoulder. Soon we were boarding the ferry to Kyllini as foot passengers, lugging our cases onto the sea deck, breathing in the sea air, filling our lungs with freedom, weak with a flood of emotions.

At Kyllini, we'd boarded a coach to Athens where we'd put our flights on my credit card. There'd been no direct flights that day, so we'd gone to Czechoslovakia first where we'd slept on the airport floor before our connecting flight to Heathrow the next day.

Neither of us had said very much on the ferry. We'd just slumped there, both lost in thought. Sherri had exhaled, relief clearly visible on her face as she'd sat back against the guard rail, her little diamond twinkling on her left hand. I'd just felt numb.

The early morning sun had stung my face as I'd watched the island, misted by the ferry's wash, slip out of view forever.

35

Back To Life

With the year nearly over, I've decided it's a time for endings and beginnings.

I've ended the quest to force Dad to be different. Instead of projecting unrealistic expectations onto him, I now understand he never deliberately withheld anything. He'd given me all he was capable of and although it wasn't much, I've come to accept it was all he had. He's never going to be the fairytale father I wanted, but he's the only one I have. So, finally, that's enough. *I'm* enough. I don't even mind his endless war stories now. I've never seen my troll since.

I've just written back to Elaine. She's started university and we're planning to meet up over Christmas. Once she learned what Sakis did, she left. I hadn't expected that, but Elaine has a strong moral compass, just one of the many things I didn't fully appreciate about her when we were in Aftonisi but I do now, given the benefit of distance.

I've also written another letter to Sherri. This will be my third, but if it remains unanswered like the others, it will be my last. It's up to her now. The phone number she gave me was unobtainable.

Yesterday I saw Rob for one last time because he'd fraudulently run up a catalogue debt in my name which I needed to sort out. Rob really is the gift that keeps on giving. I didn't get much at all for my share of the house sale after his dodgy deal backfired. I still don't know whether it was true or yet another of his lies. He's moving to Northampton soon. Angela's welcome to him.

I'm assistant manager at Alan's new estate agency, however I might not be staying for long, because today I have a big decision to make. I have something to do which might just change everything.

An unexpected letter with an Athens postmark was forwarded on from my old address. It took me a while to open it as I recognised the handwriting. Perhaps I should have just thrown it away, but not knowing what it said would have eaten me up.

'Melanie, my baby,

I know this letter will be a surprise for you, but I want to tell you I am now living in Athens with Tomas. He asks me to say hello.

After I left you, I was angry, but I felt bad later. I want you to know that, but I think you also know it was all your fault. You'd promised me I could trust you. I am a proud man. You must understand I could not let my friends see you disrespect me like that, but it's now in the past. I have forgiven you.

I've been sitting up at night, talking to Tomas, telling him about you, about how things once were with us, and he said if it really was like that, then you deserve another chance. So, I'm asking you now to come to Athens to be with me again. Tomas has a nice place here near Syntagma where we can stay, at least until Pascha. Anyway, I would like you to come out to be with me very much.

I want you to know you that Tomas said you will not need money for food or anything. Instead, you can repay his generosity by cleaning and cooking for us. It is also not necessary for you to sleep with me at first, but I hope we will soon be as we once were. I don't want us to go back to Lathos yet as too many people will remember your mistake, but soon they will forget. Then we can open our bar, and everything will be alright.

The number below is the telephone at the flat so you can call me and let me know about your flight.

Always yours, forever, Marios.'

Out of habit I count the row of kisses before I slip it under the elastic band that holds all his other airmail letters then, after thinking hard, I begin to write, reading and rereading until I'm happy with what I've put. I've made so many mistakes of late I just can't risk making another one, so I check and double check everything. I've got to be sure. This is one time in my life where words will really count, more than ever before. For the first time in months, I feel excited for my future and full of hope as I finally seal the envelope.

I'm now leaning out of my window. It's a perfect, golden autumn Saturday and I can see my elderly neighbour, Peter, tending his garden. He's just started raking up a pile of twigs and leaves in readiness for a bonfire. In a heartbeat, I have an idea.

Racing downstairs and into the garden I share with the other flats, I yell across the fence to him.

'You got a moment, Pete?'

'Sure,' he says, leaning on his garden rake, wiping the sweat from his forehead with the sleeve of his jumper.

Minutes later, I'm watching as he fans the flames, feeling curiously detached. The smoke from my bundle of blue airmail letters mingles with the dead wood and leaves, curling upwards, before disappearing forever over the rooftops.

In my hand is the envelope I've just written. I must listen to my heart, so, if I'm quick, my application for a trainee copywriting job in a London advertising agency will catch the lunchtime post.

36

Don't You Forget About Me

2021

I'm strolling barefoot at sunset along the beach at Lathos towards Dimitri's Place with my husband Mark. To my surprise, it's no longer a Taverna. It appears to be some sort of holiday villa now, a row of swimwear drying on a rope outside, a Lilo propped against the blue painted doorway, but just a little further up, not far from where Kristos held his full moon parties, is a row of bars I don't recognise. I can't face walking into Mayfair, so this suits me fine. I slip my sandals back on and together we walk into the nearest one and take a seat.

Mark orders us each a beer as I stare into the setting sun, watching the sky turn molten. Vibrant orange and blood red tips the waves. Aftonisi's sunsets are legendary and this one is spectacular. The evening air is heavy with oceanic saltiness, drifting with cigarette smoke and anticipation; alive with a magic all of its own that reminds me how much I love this country and its people. We've travelled all over Greece but this holiday in Ithaca is the closest I've ever come to the island since that summer.

'You okay?' Mark places his capable, warm hand reassuringly on mine as I nod back at him, winding his fingers in mine as the sun's rays embellish his skin. The day trip over on the ferry had been his idea. He'd said it might be healing, some sort of closure. Sometimes you must go backwards in order to go forwards. He knows what happened still haunts me, even though it was decades ago, even though I'm a different person now.

The last words I ever heard from Marios were his warning: 'Never come back to Aftonisi.'

Well, I have a long history of not doing as I'm told.

I'm still a little nervous though. Someone might recognise me, even though I know this is unlikely. I'm blonde now, and over thirty years older. It was all a lifetime ago. It happened to a different me.

As the waiter sets down our bottles of Mythos, I'm beginning to feel braver, in fact I'm now actually enjoying the idea I'm passing through Lathos invisibly, like a ghost, an undeveloped photograph, a mirage in the sand.

Something stops me tagging myself at the bar on Facebook. I prefer secrets. Instead, I take a quick selfie with 'our' beach in the background and send it on WhatsApp to Elaine. Who'd have thought back then that Elaine and I would now be so close, that she'd be Stella's godmother; that she'd be my best friend.

The beer's dry spitz prickles on my tongue. For a moment, there's a wash of sadness as I conjure up Sherri's carefree laughter, scarlet lips and blonde curls. I wonder where she is right now.

Tapping my French-manicured nails against my bottle to a Dua Lipa track playing in the background, I settle back against Mark's strong frame and glance around, watching the sunset rippling across waves the colour of Metaxa. It must be distorting my vision, because I find myself thinking how physically like Marios the young waiter is.

I watch him moving around the tables with animal grace, nodding, chatting, glass collecting, catching my breath as he stops for a moment to flirt with a girl at the bar. I'm guessing she's about mid-twenties, a little older than our Evie maybe, but probably younger than Stella.

For a moment, there's a sharp stab, something twists in the pit of my stomach at the thought of either of them hurting like I did, going through all that. But then again, they won't. They have so much confidence and self-worth it's astounding. Young women today are so very different to how I once was. My daughters are self-reliant, comfortable in their own skins. They have careers, lives, independence. To them, a relationship is a bonus, not a necessity. They don't *need* anyone. For a moment Mark's strong features distort as I smile at him, proud of our beautiful life, our beautiful girls.

'What?' he asks with a quizzical smile.

'Nothing,' I reply.

Even on holiday, he's impeccably groomed. In his white linen shirt, Armani deck shoes and navy Ralph Lauren shorts, he still looks every inch the handsome advertising agency director who interviewed me for my first copywriting job.

He always tells our girls how much they mean to him. I made sure the father of my children would. His demonstrativeness was one of the first things that drew me towards him. I briefly think of Dad and how I'd promised myself *this all stops with me* when I'd first held Stella in my arms. He'd been a better grandfather to her than the father he was to me. He never met Evie.

A local man has strolled into the bar. An older man in shorts, a vest top, and cheap plastic slides like the ones you get in the tourist shops, a cigarette clinging to his lip. He's clearly out of shape, his fleshy torso ripples as he moves, his greying hair is pulled into a ponytail. Probably a fisherman, I think, as my eyes follow him for no other reason than he's the only thing moving in my line of vision.

But then I look again.

He was handsome once, but time hasn't been kind to him. He looks tired, worn, unshaven, his forehead latticed with deep grooves. The young waiter calls him *papa* and I notice he's missing a few teeth as he grins back. They both chat for a moment then the man's mobile bursts into life.

'*Oristē,*' he bellows, slapping the phone to his ear.

All I can make out is *'ne, ne'* as he exuberantly nods, agreeing with his caller before striding back towards the beach. His voice has more than a touch of pomposity and there's a disproportionate amount of pride in the way he carries himself.

I watch the dying sunlight illuminate his slack jawline, noting a wrist full of leather and silver thongs as he waves his arm about for emphasis, flicks his cigarette stub to the path and continues shouting. He's right by our table now. A transient cloud of confusion crosses his features as our eyes briefly connect. I look away.

Mark drains his Mythos.

'Another?'

'I'm fine, thanks,' I reply, watching the man walk into the sun. 'But can we go now?'

Nodding, Mark throws a handful of euro onto the table.

'Thank you,' he calls, raising a hand to attract the boy's attention, giving him a thumbs-up. Mark's profile is so beautiful, from the noble bridge of his nose to the strong line of his jaw. In that moment, I have an overwhelming rush of love towards my husband of thirty years. Real love. Not obsessive infatuation, not destructive passion, not wounds, blood, bullets, or shards of glass embedded in the soul, but something I feel is deeply right on a cellular level, peaceful, connected, a knowingness of belonging. The real deal.

Together we wander back down the beach to the sea.

Then I spot the local man, a little further ahead.

He's staring incredulously at us now. His phone hangs limply in his hand, his mouth gapes open like a torn paper bag.

I pull on Marks arm.

'Hang on.'

Dad said I always had to have the last word.

I scoop up a pretty shell from the water's edge and gouge out I CAME BACK in the damp sand.

Then I draw a line under it.

THE END

37

Questions for Book Clubs about Poison Summer

1. What were your favourite and least favourite parts of the book?
2. Did the story keep you engaged and were you invested in the outcome?
3. Which scenes struck you as the most memorable and why?
4. What did you think of the quality of writing and the descriptions?
5. Did any sentence, passage or piece of dialogue make a specific impression on you?
6. Would you want to read another book by this author?
7. What surprised you most about the story?
8. Did your opinion of the characters and the story change as you read? Did you form any strong opinions about them?
9. Were there any loose ends or anything you'd like the author to clarify?
10. What genre would you place this book in? On what shelf would it sit in a bookshop?
11. Did this book remind you of any other books or the writing of other authors?
12. Who would you cast in a Netflix or TV adaptation of this story?
13. What did you think the themes and the messages of the story were?
14. How much was the outcome of this story influenced by the time in

which it was set?

15. What part of the book affected you the most?
16. Would you say this story was original?
17. The author chose a First Person Direct Address narration style. What was your opinion of this?
18. Would you recommend this book?

38

About the Author

Elle M Keating writes twisty, dark-edged, retro tales featuring emotionally complex, flawed characters, capturing the zeitgeist of each era with cultural, fashion and musical references.

She has an MA in Creative Writing from the University of Chichester and enjoys painting pictures with words, often digging deep into family history and genealogy for inspiration. She loves an unreliable narrator, and a protagonist with issues.

Happily throwing her unaware characters into situations which bring a tense 'It's behind you!' quality to the reader experience, Elle's writing has been described as 'leading you up a lovely garden path, then slamming you straight into a wall when you least expect it.'

Elle is also a trained yoga teacher and wellness coach. When she's not working, she can be found walking her dogs with her husband. Far from her West London roots, she now enjoys country life, living off the beaten track in a tiny hamlet that no one's ever heard of.

Subscribe to Elle's mailing list on www.ellemkeating.co.uk